THE FERRYMAN'S DAUGHTER

Juliet Greenwood

ORION

First published in Great Britain in 2020 by Orion Books,
an imprint of The Orion Publishing Group Ltd
Carmelite House, 50 Victoria Embankment,
London EC4Y 0DZ

An Hachette UK company

1 3 5 7 9 10 8 6 4 2

A CIP catalogue record for this book is
available from the British Library.

ISBN (Mass Market Paperback) 978 1 4091 9657 0
ISBN (eBook) 978 1 4091 9658 7

Typeset at The Spartan Press Ltd,
Lymington, Hants

Printed and bound in Great Britain by Clays Ltd,
Elcograf S.p.A.

MIX
Paper from
responsible sources
FSC® C104740

www.orionbooks.co.uk

For Janet Thomas.
Good friend – and mentor extraordinaire!

Chapter One

Cornwall
Autumn 1908

It was apple season, the best time of the year.

Eleven-year-old Hester Pearce held her basket tight, much-mended boots sodden with dew as she trudged towards the old manor house overlooking St Ives Bay.

'There you are, you see.' Her mother paused to catch her breath as they reached the high walls of Afalon's walled garden, from where branches of apple trees spilt over, laden with fruit. 'It's a good crop this year. We'll be able to make a good lot of my chutneys to sell in St Ives and plenty left over for apple cakes, too. This'll keep us busy for weeks.'

'Yes, Mum.' Hester felt warm inside at the relief on her mother's face. Apple season, with its richness and its scents, and its endless bounty, was also the harbinger of the cold and hungry months. Those were the seemingly endless days when wild weather left Dad with few passengers to row from one side of Hayle Estuary to the other and the vegetables from Mum's carefully tended garden were soon depleted.

For as long as Hester could remember, her mother's preserves had been in high demand in the hotels and restaurants in both Hayle and St Ives, easing the anxious look on Mum's face each week when Mr Bolsover arrived to collect the rent. Mum was a genius with small, sharp crab apples, as she was with blackberries and rosehips and the other riches to be had for free from the hedgerow. But crab apples were fiddly, needing endless straining before she achieved the required clarity of soft golden jelly. The apples escaping from the grounds of the big house, on the other hand, were plump and sweet, with exotic names like Cornish Gilliflower and Cornish Aromatic, along with Egremont Russet, Laxtons, Sturmers and Pearmains.

'You collect the windfalls, sweetheart, and I'll get the fruit from the higher branches,' said Mum, setting down her own basket. 'We need to work quickly.'

Hester nodded and dived on the windfalls, as her mother deftly twisted and removed the apples from the trees. They weren't exactly forbidden fruit, but that didn't mean the Elliots wouldn't view it that way. Rich people, as far as Hester could see, had more than anybody could possibly need, but weren't willing to share in their bounty, even when they couldn't possibly miss it.

The smells rising from the sun-warmed skins made her mouth water, sending an appreciative rumble into her belly. But she resisted the temptation to take a bite, concentrating on filling the basket as fast as possible.

Gran, who worked as Afalon's cook, said the walls of the walled garden had been built around an apple orchard once famed throughout Cornwall. A member of the family had been a passionate collector of different varieties in the old Queen's time, and no one had ever had the heart to grub them up when the Elliots had turned the modest Tudor manor into a grandiose mock-Gothic pile, complete with gargoyles and turrets, and the best walled garden this side of St Austell. Gran was always wrestling with ice cream and peaches to recreate M. Escoffier's peach Melba, as fine as if it had come straight from the Savoy Hotel in London. Not to mention the presenting of pineapples as a centrepiece, to rub the noses of the Elliots' neighbours firmly in their lack of such finely regulated pineapple pits.

Mum's face grew wistful at Gran's stories of the grand dinners the Elliots held at Afalon. It always made Hester feel a little uneasy, as if in her secret heart Mum wished that she didn't have to struggle with scrag end on their temperamental range, between cleaning at Mrs Leavan's guesthouse to supplement Dad's fares on the ferry. She had a feeling Mum might prefer to spend her days among gleaming copper pans, cooking up every delight a wealthy family could wish for.

Hester sighed and concentrated on searching out the best of the windfalls. She loved rare days like this, when she could escape the schoolroom and it was just her and Mum, without the need to keep an eye on Robbie, who at eight was growing adventurous, and five-year-old Alice, who was still forever falling over and scraping her knees, to howl loudly until comforted. These days, Mum was too busy, or too tired and ill, to sit and tell her stories of the days when she had worked as the only female head cook in one of the largest hotels in St Ives, or, even better, teach her some of the simpler recipes, the ones that didn't need exotic ingredients, like steak and caviar. It was only in apple season, when Mum needed all the help she could get, that Hester had her all to herself for a few precious hours.

Mum's basket was nearly full. She jumped up to catch a particularly heavy branch, pulling it down towards her, stripping it of its fruit. As she released the branch it shot back up, setting the remainder of the trees shaking, as if caught by an invisible wind. Russets scattered around, among the luscious red of Gilliflowers. Mum froze, waiting for the outraged shout from behind the wall, followed by the head gardener or one of his minions appearing, stick in hand, to avenge such outrage to Afalon's hallowed grounds. Nothing. Mum's face relaxed. They scurried to gather up the fallen apples and shot off back down the path towards the river.

'Oh, my goodness,' said Mum, laughing as they reached the riverbank. 'I thought we were done for then. I just couldn't resist the ones that had been in the sun.' She took out an apple, handing it to Hester as she retrieved one for herself.

They walked back towards their little hamlet at a more leisurely pace, silently munching on the perfumed flesh, sweet, with an edge of sharpness.

'It almost seems a pity to cook them,' said Mum, savouring the last of her russet. Her thin face lit up with mischief. 'But then I'd rather be toasty warm when winter comes.'

'And me,' said Hester, returning her conspiratorial smile. Dad, like most of the men in the row, placed his earnings on the kitchen table at the end of each day for Mum to sort out. But, however small the pile to satisfy the rent man, Dad always had enough to stop for a pint or two at the Fisherman's Arms, conveniently next to the small wooden jetty where the ferry was tethered. That's why Mum had her hiding places, deep underneath the eaves. Some of her wages from her cleaning job with Mrs Leavan went to paying Jenifry, from next door but one, to look after Alice while Hester was at school. The rest was stashed away, to fill the gap in the rent tin that could send them, without notice, out into the fields with no roof over their heads, and to make sure there was coal for the range and food on the table.

The money from the preserves was especially secret. Hester knew not to say anything when Mum made her regular journey to St Ives, joining Mr Rundle on his wagon as he took eggs from his farm to the nearby hotels and guest-houses, catering for the visitors that had flocked in since the railways had reached the little fishing town when Dad was a boy.

Mum always made sure she was back, dinner on the table, before Dad staggered home from the Fisherman's Arms. As long as Hester could remember, the profits from the chutneys had been hidden the deepest away as their only protection against the lean months.

She finished her apple slowly. Even in her short life, she could recall winters that seemed to stretch on forever, when Mum's carefully hidden store had to be kept solely for the rent man. She remembered the silent evenings, huddled up, when even the babies had been too cold to cry. The nights they all crawled under musty blankets, next to walls glistening with moisture, awaking to frost stretched in leafy patterns across every window that let through an eerie silver light.

Not all the most delicious Cornish Aromatics in the world were worth losing the warmth from the range that filled the whole cottage and meant Mum could cook rabbit stew or devilled herrings to fill their bellies. Hester saved the pips of her apple, stashing them in her pocket to plant in the garden. She had no idea how long it took to grow an apple tree, but she might as well start now. A whole orchard would surely mean they would be able to afford flour and butter and enough buckets of coal, right up to the spring.

'Come on.' Mum tucked her free arm into Hester's. 'If we're quick, we can get at least half of these ready before your dad comes home. Would you like that?'

Hester nodded. She was at her happiest helping Mum chopping and stirring, watching the magic as the fruit turned dark and delicious, coated in glossy juices that sent off scents of nutmeg and cinnamon, the smell, Mum said, of desert lands half a world away, where it never rained. Hester had never been outside the little hamlet where she had been born, while St Ives felt as far away as if it might be the moon. She always breathed in deep as Mum cooked, drawing the exotic perfumes inside her, firing her imagination.

'Hell and high water!' Mum came to an abrupt halt. Straight in front of them was a large carriage, drawn up at the side of the roadway, the horses chewing contentedly as they waited. More to the point, a woman encased in pale blue silk, trimmed at the cuffs and neckline with delicate lace, was sitting at an easel set right in the middle of the pathway, careless of any inconvenience she might cause. A disapproving maid watched over a boy and girl trawling the shallows with small nets fastened to sticks.

Hester swallowed. There was no mistaking Mrs Elliot of Afalon, with her flowing skirts and twist of lavender silk around her fair hair in place of a hat. None of the other ladies in Hayle dressed anything like Mrs Elliot, who, Gran said, preferred to look like the princesses in her pictures than a rich lady. Mrs Elliot's paintings were regularly displayed for everyone to see in the church hall just along from the Fisherman's Arms. It seemed to Hester that princesses spent their time just standing there, drooping, waiting to be eaten by dragons without even the sense to take to their heels and run.

'We'd better go this way.' Mum grabbed her hand, turning back towards a narrow side path disappearing behind scrubby trees and arches of brambles. But it was too late.

'Hester!' The girl on the beach was waving at them. 'Look, Mama!'

Mrs Elliot dismissed the interruption with her free hand. 'Isabella, my dear, what did I tell you about breaking the mood?'

'But Mama it's Hester. Don't you remember? She came

6

into the walled garden and you painted her as a flower girl. You said it was your best painting ever.'

Hester squirmed. It had been the last time Mum had been ill. It had been so sudden there had been no time for planning. The little ones were swept off by Jenifry, while Hester had been taken back with Gran to Afalon. She hadn't meant to disobey instructions to stay as quiet as she could among the steam and the rush and Gran's temper rising as the number of dinner guests for that evening's grand dinner increased by the hour. She'd only stepped outside to cool her cheeks with the breeze from the sea and hadn't been able to resist a tiny peek through the open door of the walled garden. But once there, she'd been unable to help herself, entranced by the rows of vegetable beds, not to mention the grapes and peaches she had only ever seen in a book at school and so luxurious she could barely believe they were real at all.

It had been an exasperated scullery maid sent to find her who had alerted Mrs Elliot to her presence. Hester had been thankful to escape being dragged back by the ear to the kitchens, until she'd found herself at the centre of the walled garden, wrapped in musty green chiffon that looked as if it had once formed part of a ball gown, and ordered to take one side of the basket of roses that Isabella, almost vanishing beneath the lace of an ancient wedding dress, was finding impossible to steady.

'We're supposed to be nymphs,' Isabella had whispered, as her mother disappeared out of earshot to fetch yet more roses. 'Don't look so horrified, Hester. No one will recognise you. They never do. Poor Mama. Her paintings are *so* very, very bad. Everyone knows it.' She bit her lip. 'Only we never tell her, that would be horribly unkind. And you mustn't say.'

'I won't,' Hester had promised solemnly. 'Not ever.'

7

'Then we'll always be friends,' Isabella replied, almost toppling over as she leant across the basket to kiss her.

'Ah, yes.' Mrs Elliot put down her brush. 'Sadie, isn't it? Cook's daughter?'

'Yes, Mrs Elliot.'

'Well, come along then. We shan't be in your way.'

Mum gave Hester's hand a reassuring squeeze, releasing it to pull her shawl from her shoulders, covering the contents of her basket. Hester hastily did the same, hoping the Elliots wouldn't spot the contraband being removed from beneath their noses. Mum's shoulders straightened. Her head went up, and she strode firmly towards the little party.

They were nearly safely past. Mum made a little bob of a curtsy as they approached, turning to make her way through the long grass and the potholes of the roadway, as if unwilling to disturb her superiors.

'Just stay there, will you.'

Hester's heart sank. Mrs Elliot was eyeing them with intent. Mum came slowly to a halt. 'Yes, Mrs Elliot?'

'Stay as you are. No, a little to the left. Your left,' she added impatiently, as Mum hesitated. 'Otherwise you will spoil the painting's composition.'

Hester saw her mother's shoulders tighten, the way they did when Dad came home after a particularly long evening at the Fisherman's Arms, with his cheeks flushed and full of himself, and treated her like a small child who knew nothing at all. She could practically hear her grit her teeth to keep the words back. 'Yes, Mrs Elliot.'

Mrs Elliot gazed thoughtfully at her canvas, then back towards them. 'But not the child.'

'Mama!' Isabella abandoned her net, face pink with embarrassment. 'You can't just send poor Hester away because she doesn't fit into your picture. Anything might happen to her.'

'My dear, I'm sure she won't come to any harm.'

'Well, she might. Come on, Hester, you can join me and Richard until Mama has finished.'

'Miss Isabella!' The maid was deeply disapproving. 'You can't invite village girls to join you, like that.'

'Why ever not? And Hester isn't just a village girl. She's Hester. She's my friend. And since Mama's making her mother stand still so she can put her in her picture, we have a duty to keep her safe. Don't we, Richard?'

The boy didn't look up from inspection of the contents of his net. 'I expect so.'

'Come on then, Hester. You can have my net. We're looking for specimens.'

Hester pushed her basket as far as she could beneath a bramble and went to join them. 'Specimens?'

'Sticklebacks and minnows and anything else we can find.' Isabella indicated a large glass jar at their feet, filled with river water and small wriggling creatures. 'Richard is studying everything we can catch. That's what he's going to do. Study things under a microscope, and make new discoveries and be famous, like Mr Darwin. When he's not running Afalon, of course.'

'Oh,' said Hester, feeling small and ignorant and knowing nothing of the world at all.

Richard looked round at her tone. Unlike his mother and sister, he was dark-haired, with eyes that were almost black in colour, fringed by thick eyelashes that gave him an appearance of great seriousness. He was watching her as if she was one of his specimens he was seeking to understand. Hester felt her limbs begin to tingle under his scrutiny.

'Aren't you interested in how everything works?' he demanded.

'Yes, of course.' She raised her chin. Just because they

9

didn't teach girls much, because they were only going to get married and have babies, didn't mean she wasn't curious.

'Hester's going to be a cook,' said Isabella, scowling at her brother. 'She told me.'

'I see.' He returned to his net, momentary interest in Hester gone.

'A proper cook,' said Hester fiercely. 'Like Mrs Rosa Lewis. She started off a scullery maid and now she's famous and she cooked for the Prince of Wales. One day, I'm going to run my own cafe, and I'm going to cook the best food ever, and no one is going to tell me what to do.'

Richard was back to inspecting her, head slightly on one side as if trying to determine if this was just bluff. 'Good for you.'

'Oh,' she said, the wind taken out of her sails. His smile lightened his face, softening the watchfulness of his eyes. A peculiar feeling stirred, deep inside, a kind of twisting in her belly. 'Did you find any sticklebacks?' she asked, bending over his net to hide her confusion.

But he wasn't listening. He was watching his mother, a faint crease between his brows. Hester followed his gaze. It was Mum he should be worried about, she thought indignantly, she was the one standing there still, the heavy basket weighing down her arm. All Mrs Elliot was doing was sitting splashing her paint over her canvas. But Mrs Elliot's brush had paused, her hand resting on her knee, as bright green paint slowly dripped, unheeded, onto her dress.

'Mama?' Richard ran towards her, catching the paintbrush as it fell. 'Mama, did you feel faint again?'

Isabella collapsed into tears, throwing her arms around the nursemaid, making it impossible for her to move. Hester was the nearest. She reached them in time to support Mrs Elliot as she began to slide from her chair, skirts billowing, face vacant, all life drained away.

'It's all right, Mama. We've got you. You're safe, we won't let you fall.' She could hear the shake in Richard's voice, the fear he was desperately trying to hide. She knew that fear all too well. The fear of losing love, of everything that made the world secure.

'It'll be all right,' she said, placing her hand on his, as they lowered Mrs Elliot gently onto the grass. His fingers closed around hers, returning the pressure, hanging on for dear life.

Then the maid reached them and he pulled away, resolutely blinking back tears, dignity back in charge, all sign of emotion gone. 'She'll be all right, Harris, she only fainted. There's no need to fuss so, Isabella, Mama's already coming round.'

The maid shook her head, disapprovingly. 'I told Mrs Elliot it was too much for her, especially after that last bout, and the sun still so strong. We need to get your mama home, Mr Richard. Dr Graham will be calling this afternoon, he'll have something to make her strong again. You had better go, Mrs Pearce. No point in staying.'

Hester grabbed her basket, catching up with Mum as the coachman helped Richard and the maid lift Mrs Elliot inside, followed by Isabella. The easel was left, abandoned on the pathway as the horses raced inland, in the direction of Afalon.

Chapter Two

'Will Mrs Elliot be all right?' asked Hester, as the carriage disappeared in a cloud of dust.

'Your gran says she has a weak heart,' replied Mum, stretching out her back. 'She's never been strong, not since she nearly died of fever after Miss Isabella was born.'

'Oh,' said Hester.

'But maybe she has just done too much, and she'll be as well as can be by tomorrow.'

'I hope so.' Hester put her arms around her mother, resting against the warmth of the stomach whose slight swelling was already becoming visible.

'What is it, sweetheart?' Mum's hands, large and roughened with work, but gentle to the touch, pushed back the tendrils of hair falling across Hester's face.

'Nothing.' She wasn't supposed to know about the babies that had come, almost every year for as long as she could remember. The babies who, unlike Robbie and Alice, had died before they were born, or lived for only a few hours, too weak to cry. She wasn't supposed to see the worry lines that appeared each time Mum suspected there might be another on the way. Most of all, no one knew she had slipped back from Jenifry's that time last year after Gran had been called, rushing down from Afalon the moment the serving of the Elliots' dinner for their important guests from London was done.

Hester had known that for Gran to defy her employers on such an occasion, risking her livelihood and the roof over her head, it had to be serious. Robbie and Alice had been asleep, curled up with Jenifry's ever-expanding brood, but Hester had been unable to wait, not knowing. She had pushed her way between the women in the row, gathered outside in the April dusk, many shaking their heads, muttering between them that this time had done for Sadie, good and proper, poor woman.

Hester had still been there, curled up tight in a corner, invisible in the darkened kitchen, when Gran finally insisted Dad called Dr Graham, who charged his rich clients an eye-watering sum and his poor as little as their pride would accept. Mum's agonised screams had ceased soon after his arrival, but there had been no answering cry from the little brother who had never drawn breath. There had only been a terrible silence, with Mum too weak to even grieve. The memory still made Hester's blood run cold.

'There's only one way you can repay me,' she'd heard Dr Graham say as he left, pushing away Dad's proffered handful of coins, almost a week's takings. 'And that's by putting her needs before your own.'

'I look after her.'

'That's not what I meant, man, and you know it. Come on, Robert. There are other ways if you need them. But for God's sake, put your wife first for once in your life. Isn't that what she does for you?'

In the dawn spilling through the small, deep-set windows, Hester had seen Dad turn white, the dangerous kind of white that sent the drinkers in the Fisherman's Arms hastily minding their own business. He hadn't dared argue with an important man like the doctor, but he'd had enough to say to Gran once Dr Graham was out of earshot. Mainly along the lines of who did he think he was to speak to a fellow like that, and in his own house, too? It was all very well for him, with half a dozen lonely spinsters in the neighbourhood, no doubt more than willing to satisfy him in any way he chose.

'He's equally blunt with the Elliots,' Gran had retorted, adding what sounded like a particularly pithy comment in her native Welsh. 'And they're his main livelihood. It's a brave man who tells truth equally to rich and poor.' Her round face had been lined with weariness, white hair straggling from her neatly corralled bun at the back of her head. A streak of blood lay across her forehead, another staining her usually pristine blouse. In her face, there had been a terrible kind of anger and grief that, even more than the screams and the silence, had sent a tight knot of fear into Hester's belly, the kind that never quite left.

'Well, the old fool's never to darken my door again. Or any other quack, come to that. They're only after a poor man's wages and to look down on him.'

Something had snapped in Gran's face. 'You and your bloody pride, Robert Pearce. One day, it will be the death of you. But not my child. Please, Robert. Please. Haven't you lost enough?'

Hester had curled up even tighter, bracing herself for Dad's temper to erupt. Instead, he was silent. When she looked up, she saw shame cross his face, like one of the boys at school caught out in a lie.

'I'll look after her, Mair, I swear.'

Gran put one hand on his arm. 'You're a good man, Robert, if you'd let yourself. Love is no weakness, whatever they might tell you. Haven't I lost a husband and five children of my own? What you've got is precious beyond all riches, *cariad*. Don't you risk losing it, my dear.'

Across the wide estuary, a cold wind began to blow.

'Hester? Are you all right, sweetheart?' Mum's voice was anxious. 'The Elliot children weren't unkind to you just now, were they?'

'No, Mum.' Hester smiled up into her mother's loving gaze.

'Good.' Mum tucked stray auburn curls back behind Hester's ears.

'Mum?'

'Yes, darling?'

'Is it wrong to want to do things? If you're a girl, that is.'

'No, of course not, sweetheart. When I was little, they told me no woman could ever be a head cook. But your gran thought otherwise. She made sure I went to the best hotels where I could learn and prove myself. Anything is possible.'

'Even having your own cafe?'

The hand on Hester's hair paused. 'Yes, of course, darling. It's not easy, but it's possible.' Mum turned to pick up her basket, balancing the weight on her hip as they set off back along the path again. 'Is that what you wish?'

'Yes. At least I think so. Isn't that what you and Gran were going to do?'

'Gran?' Mum stopped, busily adjusting the shawl still hiding the apples. 'Gran has always worked as cook at Afalon, at least after your grandad died when I was little. That's the only life she's ever wanted.'

'Oh.' Hester faltered slightly. Maybe she had misunderstood. 'But I thought Gran said you were once going to open a restaurant in St Ives, for the visitors and the artists.'

'Did she? That was a long time ago, Hester. Before I even met your dad, long before you were born.'

'But that's what you were going to do.' It mattered. For some reason, Hester could not have said why exactly, it mattered more than anything that Mum had once held such a dream.

'Yes. That's what I planned.' Mum set off again, her face hidden. 'All the time I was training, and then when I worked in the hotel in St Ives, that's what I planned to do. We even found a place, overlooking one of the beaches. Beautiful it was. It still is. Mr Carlton, who bought it in the end, made it a real success.'

'Like you would have done.'

'Maybe.'

There was something she couldn't quite work out. 'You and Dad,' she ventured.

There was a moment's silence. 'Dad would have hated St Ives,' said Mum at last. 'So perhaps it was as well, after all.' Her free arm came around Hester's shoulders. 'And I wouldn't have been without you and Robbie and Alice, for the world.'

'No, Mum.' But all the same, Hester couldn't quite shake off the feeling of something lost. It made her own determination to succeed stronger than ever.

Mum drew her closer. 'Listen to me, darling. You be careful when it comes to people like the Elliots. They may seem as nice as pie, and I'm sure they are, in their way. But they are not like us. They will never be like us. However much they may try not to, they see us as a convenience, the people who clean their houses and draw their baths and make their life comfortable. It doesn't really enter their heads that we are as real as they are, with dreams and ambitions and a desire to also walk in the sun. And that can make them cruel, even if they don't mean to be. You remember that and don't ever be distracted from the path you wish to take.'

It was a warning, from deep in Mum's heart and as serious as could be. Hester had a sense that it was something she didn't quite yet understand, but that it was Mum's way of keeping her safe. Rebellion shot through her. Why shouldn't she be friends with the Elliots, if she chose? She'd see with her own eyes that they weren't great or mighty, however much they pretended to be, and she could do as she pleased. But she didn't want to hurt Mum, or see the anxiety behind her eyes.

'I promise I'll remember.'

'Good girl. You make sure you always take your own way, no matter who tries to stop you. You are so like me, sweetheart, I know you will never be truly happy any other way. You make sure you get that cafe of yours, whatever it takes.'

'And you'll come and help me?'

Mum kissed her. 'Of course, my darling. Wild horses couldn't drag me away.'

Chapter Three

The ferryman's cottage stood at the end of a row of somewhat ramshackle dwellings set a little way back from the river. The tiled roofs sloped at odd angles, as if the builders had not made their minds up to create a row at all. The wood of the sash windows was rotting from the sea wind blowing in over Hayle Towans at the mouth of the estuary, where sands stretched for miles towards Godrevy beach, while the precarious chimneys were constantly blackened with smoke.

The cottages themselves were small, each crammed full to bursting with furniture and children. The main room, which acted as both kitchen and living room, was crowded around a range, carefully blackened into neatness, on which the family's meals were cooked and water heated for tea and the weekly bath. Most of the space was taken up by a kitchen table and a few easy chairs, leaving any children who could to spill out onto the cobbled street in all weathers, to chat in corners or play hopscotch and hide-and-seek, along with conkers when autumn came and football whenever a pig's bladder could be scrounged.

The row was generally a friendly, tightly knit community, the families skirting too close to disaster to set up any conflicts between themselves. Leave that to the sea and the vagaries of herring and pilchards, the women declared, nodding wisely on the doorsteps, between the endless scrubbing and cleaning. Most couldn't help but be thankful for sons who abandoned the fishing life to find work, up river, in the industrial workshops of Hayle.

The ferryman's cottage, while being part of the row, stood slightly apart. Mum, although born and bred in St Ives, was of foreign stock, from the slate quarries high up in the mountains of Wales, where the Celtic blood had taken an odd turn, breeding strange ways and even stranger ideas. Not, of course, as outlandish as the women with their safety bicycles and walking holidays, travelling down together from London on the railways, without a male companion in sight. The kind to chain themselves to the railings of Parliament, and blow up buildings to terrorise respectable citizens, all to be able to vote alongside the men, when so many men still weren't able to vote in the first place.

Gran, thank goodness, had never been suspected of chaining herself to anything, especially being employed as cook for the Elliots since anyone could remember. But she didn't quite have the ties that bound each member of the little community to each other, and, furthermore, had encouraged her daughter to have ambitions, even higher ambitions than being cook for a great house.

Hester was proud of Mum and her skills in preserving fruit and vegetables to tide her family over the lean months of winter, and being able to sell her preserves and chutneys wherever she chose. Mum had a genius for making a delicacy from nothing, from transforming the damsons growing wild among the hedgerows into chutney, to creating nettle syrup and violet jelly.

Over the next weeks, Hester and her mother worked hard, preparing the apples gleaned from Afalon on the scrubbed wooden table in front of the range. They cooked them up with onions and sultanas and a touch of ginger, while Dad was at work, setting the results to cool in Mum's carefully collected jars, which were stored at the very back of the tiny larder.

'Perhaps you would like to come with me to St Ives, this time?' said Mum, a few days later, as she returned from cleaning at Mrs Leavan's.

'Yes, please,' said Hester eagerly, removing a stray piece of coal from Alice's small fists.

'Good. Jenifry will look after these two, and it's not a school day, so we'll have the whole time to ourselves.'

The next morning, as soon as Dad left for the ferry and Jenifry had taken possession of a barely awake Robbie and Alice, they packed the baskets as tight as could be with the filled jars, and were on the roadside waiting when Mr Rundle's cart, pulled by a resigned-looking grey pony, came to a halt.

'You don't mind my daughter riding along too, do you, Mr Rundle? She's coming to help me.'

'Goodness me, no.' The old farmer grinned, revealing a lack of teeth to match the few remaining strands of hair peeping from beneath his cap. 'More the merrier, if you ask me, Mrs Pearce. Long way it is to St Ives, when it's just me and Flotsam, here, trotting along. He don't talk much, does Flotsam, at the best of times, and me, I like to chat. So there, you see, the more the merrier.'

He was right about the chat. Mum and Mr Rundle gossiped companionably over the goings-on in the farms and settlements along the estuary as the cart bumped its way along the narrow lanes, high on each side with hedgerows bursting with rosehips and the scarlet and orange of autumn leaves.

Hester sat in the back of the cart, surrounded by carefully packed eggs, and half a pig wedged into one corner, clutching the baskets on either side to keep them steady. She had never been this far from Hayle before. Between the hedgerows, she caught glimpses of Carbis Bay, with its long stretch of sand and a calm turquoise sea, flecked with green and swirls of deep indigo, stretching out towards the horizon, as if the world went on forever.

Before long, they were in the bustle of St Ives. With most of the summer visitors gone, it had returned to being a fishing town, with narrow-bottomed seine boats ranged on Porthminster beach, waiting for the glut of pilchards to be salted and packed in barrels for export.

Mr Rundle dropped them near the Queen's Hotel on the High Street, arranging to meet them there later for the journey home. As he set off on the business of the day, Hester followed Mum to a large hotel on the cliffs, at a discreet distance from the pervading smell of fish. The hotel looked down over the wide curve of Poethmeor beach, which, unlike the shelter of the harbour and Smeaton's Pier, caught the prevailing wind. Great waves swept in, to crash in flurries of spray, blown back on themselves into huge feathered arches.

They were ushered straight down to the kitchens, steaming with heat and cooking, where the chef greeted them warmly.

'Mrs Pearce, it's a pleasure as always. Now what have you got for us this time?'

The transaction was brief. Hester stared in amazement as every last one of Mum's jars were seized upon with delight and sent off in the hands of one of the under chefs, to be stored in the vast larder at one end of the kitchens.

'I shall have to lock them away,' remarked M. Alphonse, handing over payment without a quibble. He winked at Hester. 'They're my secret weapon, you know, missy. No one can make preserves quite like my Mrs Pearce. More than one hotelier would slit my throat for the secret, if I let them.'

'I hope not, M. Alphonse,' replied Mum, laughing. Her cheeks turned pink and there was a gleam of pleasure in her eyes.

'*En bien*, I let them believe I have them smuggled in across the Channel from Paris,' he replied. 'The English think a French chef can work miracles.' He ruffled Hester's hair. 'What they don't know is that I was trained by an English cook, the best in Cornwall.'

'The only female head cook in Cornwall,' said Mum.

'True. And also the best. Not even the great Escoffier could make an Apple Charlotte like your mother's,' he added, with a wistful sigh. 'And her Sauté of Chicken Lyonnaise was perfectly sublime.' He clapped his hands. 'Now, Madame and Mademoiselle Pearce, you are to be our guests for luncheon.' He sent another wink in Hester's direction. 'I still have hopes your mother will one day wish to return to the kitchens, so I must prove how badly we do without her.'

Badly or not, Hester had no way of telling. All she knew was that the meal was the most delicious she had ever tasted. She was terrified when they were first shown to a table next to the window, with a small bunch of hothouse flowers in the centre, quite sure she would use the wrong fork and spill her soup all over the pristine tablecloth. She glanced round nervously at table after table, set out all around the huge room, each with equally spotless coverings.

Imagine having to wash all those at the end of each week, maybe even each day! It took all of her and Mum's efforts to keep the family's clothes in a reasonable state of cleanliness, with all the boiling in the copper and the turning of the mangle to get as much water out as possible. Even then, there were frequently petticoats steaming in front of the fire when the drying wind was down, or it rained for days.

Hester smoothed down her shabby skirts, quite sure the rest of the diners were bound to insist such down and out creatures should not be allowed in civilised society and demand their instant removal. But, to her surprise, any disapproving glances in their direction were stopped in their tracks by M. Alphonse himself appearing at the end of each course to obtain Mum's opinion. Even the superior-looking waiters, who terrorised their clients into submission with an air of the deepest scorn, treated Mum with respect, as if she was a lady in an extravagantly feathered hat, rather than a woman in a patched and mended coat that could only ever have been in fashion in the old Queen's time.

'Is this where you used to work?' she ventured, in a whisper.

Mum nodded. 'I was head cook here for a while. They'd never have allowed a woman to rise any higher, and especially not into any position of authority. That's why I wanted to have my own restaurant, where I wouldn't have had to answer to anybody.' She dipped her spoon into the rich sweetness of her Waldorf Pudding, deep in thought. 'M. Alphonse is right, I was known for the clarity of my consommés. I should never have doubted myself. Perhaps we could have made it, after all.'

By the time they had finished all four courses – which Mum said was modest by the standards of the really grand hotels – Hester was so full she could barely move. She followed Mum back outside in a daze, wishing she could curl up in a corner and go to sleep.

Mum led them back to the more sheltered side of St Ives, where they sat for a while on Smeaton's Pier, watching the swell of waves and the coming and going of pleasure boats, until the chill wind blowing in from the sea revived them.

'How about we go to Porthgwidden beach,' said Mum, as they both began to shiver. 'It's much more sheltered. It's near that grassy bit sticking out into the sea they call the Island. We can wait there until it's time to meet up with Mr Rundle.'

'It's pretty,' said Hester, as they climbed over the Island, with its nets and washing spread out on the grass to dry, then clambered down into a much smaller cove, where the deep turquoise of the sea settled into calm against a golden beach.

'I always loved this view of Godrevy lighthouse,' said Mum wistfully, looking out to the column of white rising from a tiny rocky island far out into the bay. 'Sometimes you can see seals by the rocks just over there, and there are dolphins out in the deeper waters.' She turned to glance back towards the headland. Tucked into the shelter of the rocks there was a small whitewashed building, lined at the front with large windows. A wooden terrace ran along the front, where, despite the chill, men and women were sitting at tables, huddled into their coats, the women's scarves floating up now and again when a particularly strong breeze caught them, while eddies threatened to send men's hats high into the air.

She didn't have to ask. Hester could see from the expression on Mum's face that this was the cafe she had talked about, the one that might have been hers. She tucked her arm through her mother's.

Mum smiled down at her, blinking hard, as if the wind had flung sand in her eyes. 'The seals are still there,' she said, nodding towards the jagged line of rocks at one side of the beach. Sure enough, when she looked closely, Hester could make out a small head bobbing up and down in the waves, large dark eyes watching them with wary curiosity. 'They like to sun themselves on the rocks when the tide goes out. I could watch them for hours. Funny, it's always the little things you remember most.'

She sounded sad. So unbearably sad. Hester hung on tight, not sure what to say, but the old fear crept back into her belly. Mum was a fighter, Dr Graham had told Gran, that last time. That was what had saved her. Mum usually returned from her periodic trips to St Ives with colour in her cheeks and a renewed energy about her. It wasn't just, Hester suddenly saw, Mum's relief at having the resulting coins to stash away in her deepest hiding place, as insurance against disaster. Fear gripped her. Supposing one day she didn't come back at all?

'Mrs Pearce?' A woman's voice came from the terrace, drifting towards them on the wind. For a moment Hester had a horrible feeling they had stumbled across Mrs Elliot again, and Mum would be required to stand for hours as a picturesque figure caught within the renowned light of St Ives. To her relief, the woman making her way down from the terrace was dressed in a practical woollen walking dress and coat, without a hint of silk in sight, clutching a severe hat, with only the smallest of feathers and not the hint of a turban, to her head.

'Sadie. Mrs Pearce. I thought that must be you. How are you?'

'Very well, thank you,' replied Mum, a little stiffly, pulling her coat around her to obscure the curve of her belly.

'What a coincidence. Or perhaps not. I thought it might be your day to come with Mr Rundle.'

'We have to leave soon.'

'I can give you a lift back in the motor car.'

'I would rather go back with Mr Rundle, as arranged. I wouldn't want to offend him.'

'As you wish.' The woman glanced down at Hester. 'Is this your eldest? My goodness how she's grown. Lance and Clara are both almost as tall as me now. A few years, and they'll all be flying the nest.'

'Not quite yet,' said Mum firmly.

The woman held out her hand, opening it to reveal a shiny coin that looked as if it had never been used. 'Perhaps Hester would like to get herself an ice cream?'

Hester glanced at Mum. She knew bribery when she saw it. She knew when adults wanted her out of the way.

Mum hesitated for a moment. Then she nodded. 'Thank you, Mrs Trewarren. Go on, Hester, just mind you keep us in sight.'

Hester clutched the precious coin. She was still full from their meal, and she had a feeling a really virtuous older sister would find something to take back for Robbie and Alice, but the lure of something all to herself, and as exotically impossible as ice cream, was irresistible. She ran to the wheeled cart that had come to rest on the edge of the Island, in hope, rather than expectation, of a rush of customers, and walked back slowly, savouring the chilly sweetness. Mum and the woman were still at the water's edge, deep in conversation.

'It might yet be possible, Sadie,' Mrs Trewarren was saying as Hester hovered close by, not sure whether or not to join them, but dying to know what they could be discussing so earnestly.

'I'm not sure, Violet.'

'Why ever not? I'm not talking about now.' Mrs Trewarren nodded back towards the cafe. 'It looks as if the Carltons will carry on for a few more years yet, but they are both growing old, and neither of the sons is interested in taking it over.'

'Wasn't there a daughter?'

'She moved to Australia with her husband last year, to

start a new life. Do you think I didn't ask? A new life, Sadie. Isn't that what we both need?'

'It's not so simple. It was different before. Now we both have husbands and children. We can't just abandon them.'

'But in a few years' time, when our domestic responsibilities are lessened?'

Mum was silent for a while, as if choosing her words carefully. 'The past is the past, Violet. I don't think either of us can recapture it, however hard we try.'

'I let you down. That's what you mean. I was the one who lost courage and refused to defy convention and prove a woman could be as good at business as a man.'

'We both lost courage,' said Mum gently. 'I could still have made my own attempts, if I'd been brave enough. There is always a way, however hard the road. I lost faith in myself, too.'

'At least you had more sense than to tie yourself to a husband you despise,' retorted Violet. 'You, at least, married a man you loved, not for the financial security that was wafted so seductively in front of my nose. My family's financial security as much as my own,' she added bitterly. 'How could I have been such a fool to believe them when they told me it was my duty as a daughter, and my only role in life?'

'I'm sorry.'

'You think I'm suggesting this to simply escape my own unhappiness? For purely selfish reasons?' She grunted. 'No need to answer that. You'd be right. I never was much good at thinking of anyone but myself.'

'That's not entirely true,' replied Mum, with a smile.

'Thank you.' Violet's face cleared a little. 'Very well. I won't press you. I've no right. But I may go ahead on my own account, when the Carltons decide to sell. I have to do something, or I shall die of tedium. I should have known being waited on hand and foot would never suit me.'

'I'm sure,' said Mum, not quite keeping the dryness out of her voice. It had clearly escaped Violet Trewarren that Mum would have given heaven and earth to be waited on for just one day, while stopping long enough for boredom to set in was her idea of bliss.

'The offer will remain open, Sadie.'

In the distance, church bells began to toll the hour. 'We have to go,' said Mum, gathering up the empty baskets at her feet. 'Or Mr Rundle will be wondering where we are.'

'Yes, of course. You won't forget?'

The sadness was back in Mum's eyes. 'I won't forget, Violet,' she replied quietly. 'I won't ever forget.' She grasped Hester's hand, hurrying her back towards the town, to where Mr Rundle was waiting to take them home.

Chapter Four

Mum didn't return to St Ives again that autumn, selling her stocks of rosehip cordial, elderberry conserve and crab apple jelly to the Belleview Hotel in Hayle instead, even though the chef was less generous with his payments than the chef at the hotel in St Ives.

Maybe it was, as she said, the early setting in of cold weather that made the ride there unappealing. Although Hester suspected it was also that Mum's growing belly sapped her strength more and more each day. Hester found herself sitting in school unable to take in any lessons. Some days she didn't go at all, helping Mum, despite her protests, with the household chores instead. Her absence didn't go unnoticed, but no one attempted to stop her.

Even Miss Smith, the young idealistic teacher who had encouraged her over the past years, hadn't suggested she should be put in for a scholarship to continue her education. Only one or two were ever granted to such a small school, and those mostly went to boys, who might be able to make something of the privilege and escape from a life fishing or labouring on the neighbouring farms. Everyone knew girls would inevitably go into service before being married and having families of their own to take care of, and would have no time or energy to do more than take in washing, or cleaning for one of the large houses in the area, to supplement a husband's income.

Hester knew that with Dad earning so little, and two younger children at home, there was no point in even trying for a scholarship. She was lucky, at least she had Gran looking out for her at Afalon, to give her the chance, if she worked hard and was lucky, to train up to become cook in a neighbouring house one day, rather than becoming a general maid.

It took years, Gran said, to work up to becoming a cook, and even then you didn't earn a fortune, just enough to lay something aside for when you grew too old to work, and needed something to keep a roof over your head to keep yourself from the workhouse, or being a burden on your children, who were struggling to get by as it was.

As winter began to turn towards spring, and Mum appeared ever more tired with every day that passed, Hester could feel her childhood ending.

'One of the kitchen maids at Afalon will be getting married this April,' Gran said, the next time she came to visit them on her afternoon off, bringing with her a large Penzance Cake, bursting with mixed peel and crystallised ginger, along with fresh oatmeal scones and butter, and a mutton and potato pie to heat up for later. 'It could be a good opening for Hester, and you won't be able to clean much longer for Mrs Leavan, *cariad*, for a while, at least. You'll soon be needing the money.'

Mum busied herself with the teapot. 'I was thinking that maybe it might be better for Hester to be apprenticed.'

'Apprenticed?' Gran's mouth fell open, echoing Hester's own astonishment.

'I've written to M. Alphonse in St Ives. He's willing to take her on as soon as she leaves school and train her up to be a cook in a restaurant. That's if you wish, Hester.'

Hester put down the knife she was using to butter the

scones. 'Yes,' she said loudly, before she had a chance to think about it and get scared, or Gran could object. 'I'd like that. I'd like that very much.'

'Working in a restaurant.' Gran was frowning at Mum, as if she was a small child who had returned home with grubby knees and a torn skirt and no reasonable explanation. 'And what does Robert think of this?'

'Do I need a husband's permission to do what is best for my child?'

'No, of course not, *cariad*. It's just you are the one that has to live with him. Robert has very set ideas. You should know best of all that he's always been a man of convention.'

'Hester would have some wages, and the possibility of earning far more in the long run.' Mum handed Gran her tea. 'Isn't that what you wanted for me, Mam, all those years ago?'

'Yes, my darling. But you had flair and a passion. I might have been the one who encouraged you to be ambitious, but you were so determined nothing could have stopped you.'

'And you think Hester doesn't?'

'I just don't want to see either of you hurt. Hasn't there been enough of that already?' Gran leant across to help with the buttering of the scones. 'This was churned fresh this morning.' She grimaced. 'I'd thought I'd made enough clotted cream so there'd be some left over from last night, but the greedy devils polished off the lot.'

Mum laughed, her face easing as the conversation turned to general matters again. 'I can't say I blame them. Mind you, there's nothing like the butter you make in the dairy at Afalon.'

'Pity they sold the meadows and the cows,' said Gran, pulling Alice onto her knee, while Robbie perched on the chair next to her, chewing away contentedly. 'Makes no sense buying in the milk. There's talk they'll get rid of the dairy next.'

'And buy all their butter and cheese?'

Gran shrugged. 'Mr Elliot has new ideas. He's a London man at heart, not one for the countryside. He's used to milk being delivered to his door and an account at the grocer's, as well as the butcher. I've heard him say it's a waste of money keeping so many gardeners, especially now such a lot of young men are preferring to be clerks and shopkeepers rather than be out in all weathers until their backs are riddled with arthritis. He doesn't think of the families who rely on wages from Afalon.' She smiled reassuringly at Hester. 'Although they'll always need cooks and maids. You can't do without feeding and cleaning, however rich you might be.'

Gran left before Dad was due back from the ferry – or rather the Fisherman's Arms, since he tended to spend an additional hour or so there each Wednesday, Gran's after-noon off. Mum packed away the cake in a tin, wrapping up the scones and butter they had saved for him, placing them in the cool of the larder until he arrived.

'You can take the post with Gran at Afalon, if you prefer,' said Mum, as she began to prepare the knobbly turnips and the last of her cabbages to go with the mutton pie. 'I'm sorry, Hester, I should have asked you first. But I couldn't let Gran speak to Mrs Elliot, and risk her being seen as letting Mrs Elliot down.' She dug at a particularly tough corner of turnip. 'Nothing's ever certain in a big house like Afalon. They can take against you and get rid of you at a moment's notice. I've heard of some families who get their cook to train up a young kitchen maid, and then get rid of the cook as the maid is cheaper to employ, leaving the poor girl tearing her hair out, trying to do work she's not been properly prepared for.'

'Would they do that to Gran?'

'I'm sure they wouldn't. She's too good a cook. But then things change and you never quite know.' She chopped up the pieces of cleaned turnip, turning to help Hester tease out the most edible leaves from the sorry-looking remains of last year's kale and cabbage, the few greens available until Mum's carefully tended crop were ready to eat. 'I wanted you to have more control over your life and how you live, that is all.'

'You mean, being able to open my own cafe, like you wanted to do?'

'If that's what you wish. For that you need skills, even more than you need as a cook working for a rich family. You need to be able to delight people, like no other cook can do. You need to be able to stand out, so that people remember your food and want more of it. Rosa Lewis is known for her French cooking. That and her rich clientele. She's a wise woman. It's allowed her to rise from nothing to own the Cavendish Hotel.'

'I'm not sure I want to own a grand hotel!' exclaimed Hester, alarmed.

Mum paused, her hands resting on the greens. 'I'm not sure I'd want to, either. But you never know. I don't mind what you do, darling. All I want is for you to be free to make your own choices, and never have to live in fear of the rent man or growing too old or too ill. I'm sure you will marry and have children, but even that life is never certain. Your grandad was a strong, healthy man, but that didn't stop him from being lost at sea. That meant your gran lost her home. Everything. She had no choice but to spend her life working all hours for the Elliots. It's what she loves doing, but I'm not sure she would have chosen for it to take up every hour of her day, without any hope of ever having a comfortable home of her own. You take your time to think about it. There's no need to discuss it with your dad yet. You find out what you want first, then we'll tackle him.'

*

The next day, Hester could barely concentrate at all on her lessons, even when Miss Smith brought out her prized globe to show them where the spices came from for Easter hot cross buns. The idea of working in M. Alphonse's frenetic kitchen scared her more than she could say. Everyone there moved so fast and seemed to know what they were doing, and each plate of food she had seen served had looked like a work of art.

She knew nothing of flavours and sauces, or of the cooking of fish or meat beyond scrag end and bacon bits and the mackerel Dad got cheap from the fishermen landing their catch on the jetty. As for the baking of stiff, frothy meringue and the art of spun sugar – they both appeared nothing short of a miracle. Then she would be so far from home. That terrified her even more. Mum said she knew a very respectable lady Hester could lodge with in St Ives, but she was well aware she wouldn't have the time to come home to see them all for weeks on end. But then, even if she went to Afalon, her time would not be her own. She would be expected to work as long as Gran, maybe even longer, with only a few hours off every week.

For once, Hester didn't rush straight home when school ended, but sat on the banks of the estuary, carefully out of eyesight of Dad as he rowed the ferry, watching the tidal flow of fresh and salt water flow past. She knew what she wanted to do. The thing was to find the courage to take what would probably be the most momentous decision of her life.

'It isn't fair.' She looked up as Jimmy Harkness flopped down beside her and began tearing up the new grass in clumps.

Jimmy Harkness was one of the big boys, who kicked their heels around the playground, just waiting for the day they could leave school. Jimmy was tall and well built, with regular, fine-boned features that sent the older girls giggling in corners and elbowing each other out of the way for the privilege of being seen in his company.

She should have been flattered that she had attracted his attention, but today all she wanted was a few precious minutes to herself. On the other hand, she didn't want him to think she was too stuck up or self-absorbed to take an interest.

'What isn't fair?'

'Dad says I'm to start going out in the boats, first thing tomorrow.'

'Fishing, you mean?' Jimmy had always sworn he would never be a fisherman like his father and uncles. Jimmy had plans. Jimmy was the one, of all of them, who was going to leave the little hamlet, Cornwall itself, even, and make something of himself.

'What else?' he replied gloomily. 'I got the scholarship, of course.'

'That's good, isn't it?' She eyed him. There had been no talk of scholarships this year, even though usually the little school was buzzing when one of their own was given such a rare chance to break free. But maybe everyone was being kind. Jimmy had talked of nothing else for months than what he would do when he got his scholarship and how he'd come back a rich man and buy one of the villas overlooking St Ives, just for the summer months to escape the city heat.

'Dad says we need a wage coming in now.'

'I'm sorry.'

'Well, I'm not doing it.' He yanked up an entire patch of grass. 'There's a position open at Timson's. Just loading for now, but they'll teach me to drive their motorised vans. Then I can work my way up. You see, one day I'll be a manager of a motorised delivery company, taking goods to all the best houses and hotels in all of Cornwall.'

'Good for you.'

'And one day, I'll own my own company. Then you can come and work for me.'

'Driving a van?' The idea sounded rather exciting. Timpson's were one of the first delivery companies to start to replace their horse-drawn carts with motorised vans, which hurtled through the countryside at a breath-taking speed, terrorising cattle and sending dogs and young children howling with fright as they passed.

'No, silly. Girls can't drive vans. They're not strong enough. And they'd get scared. I shall need a clerk.' He waved his hands in a vague gesture of generosity. Hester suspected he had no more idea than her of what a clerk actually did. 'Girls are starting to become clerks now.'

'Oh,' said Hester. Over my dead body, she added silently to herself. Jimmy was just like the other boys. They all believed girls couldn't be clever or do things, however many times she beat them in tests, and could out-run most of them at the drop of a hat.

Jimmy was continuing to tell her his plans. Hester nodded and made sympathetic noises without really listening, her mind drifting back to her own dilemma.

Jimmy would never hesitate, she thought, as they walked back through the little hamlet. He was certain he could learn to drive motorised vans, despite never having even driven a cart in his life and being known, although he'd never admit it, to being somewhat short-sighted. He'd have no doubts about his ability to run his own cafe, if he set his mind to it. She glanced at him sideways. When Mum talked about her getting married, and her teachers declared her destiny was to be a wife, sooner or later, to be absorbed into her husband's existence, enabling him to work for as long hours as possible, she'd known it would be Jimmy, or one of the boys like him, to whom her fate would be sealed.

'I'm thinking I might become a cook,' she remarked, as an experiment, when he paused to take breath in outlining the number of vans and the drivers and mechanics he would have working for him by the time he was twenty.

'There's always work for cooks,' he said, without interest, before returning to the detail of his plans.

That settled it. Jimmy didn't listen to girls, any more than the other boys in her class. He liked her listening to him, but he'd only sought her out when there was no one else around. He wasn't interested in her, not really, not in the things that mattered.

Well, and bugger that, as Gran would say, when the Elliots demanded an ice sculpture at the height of summer to impress rich friends from London, with the Afalon ice house already depleted and not a bit of ice to be had for love nor money.

A vision came into her head of the cafe with the terrace overlooking the beach. She didn't know if she had Mum's skill, she hadn't had the chance to try. Watercress and potato soup and ginger fairings didn't exactly count, and she had a feeling the guests at M. Alphonse's hotel might turn their noses up at a dish of pilchards, or the pig's intestines of muggety pie. But she could learn. And if it turned out she wasn't good enough for M. Alphonse, she would just have to swallow her pride and find work as a maid at Afalon or one of the other big houses. She had to at least try.

'I might even buy Afalon, one day,' Jimmy was saying expansively, clearly under the impression she had been glued to his every word and her silence was down to the deepest of hero worship. 'If the Elliots choose to stay in London all year, that is. Having two houses like that, can you imagine?'

'I suppose they must be very rich.'

'And on speculation,' said Jimmy darkly. 'That's what my Uncle Harold says. Speculation and investments, so other people work hard so that they don't have to lift a finger.' He took a breath, clearly about to enlighten her further on the evils of this dubious subject.

'I have to go, Mum will be expecting me,' she said quickly. 'Good luck, I'm sure Timson's will take you on.'

She shot off before he had a chance to answer. From now on, she would take care to avoid Jimmy Harkness like the plague. Heaven help whichever wretched girl he might one day persuade to be his wife. She just knew as sure as eggs was eggs, it wasn't ever going to be her.

Chapter Five

'Mum!' Hester burst eagerly into the cottage, ready to tell her decision and work out a plan of how to persuade Dad. The moment she opened the door she knew something was wrong. Mum was crouched at the table, bent over a pile of half-cleaned potatoes for tonight's meal, not moving. Her eyes were shut, her face agonised and dripping with sweat. The range was nearly out, leaving the room cold and clammy. 'Mum?'

'She was like this when we got home,' said Robbie, who was attempting to entertain Alice with the contents of Mum's button box, a look of anxiety on his face. 'She wouldn't speak.'

'I'm hungry,' called Alice, the distraction of the buttons forgotten.

'I'll get you something in a minute.' Hester grasped her mother's hand. 'Mum, what is it?' The fear was back, a dark hole in her belly, larger than ever. She forced herself to remain calm. 'Is it the baby?'

Mum nodded. 'It's too early.' Her voice was a barely audible whisper, as if merely drawing breath was agony. 'I'm sorry, I'm so sorry.'

'It's not your fault, Mum. I'll get help.' She shot off down the row, to where Mrs Mitchell, who acted as the local midwife, was gathering in her washing.

'Hester!' Mrs Mitchell took one look at her face. 'Is it your mum?'

'Yes. The baby's coming, but it's too soon, and there's something wrong. I know there's something wrong.'

'It's all right. You get back to her, sweetheart, you stay with her. I'll be along in a minute.'

Hester ran back to the cottage. Mum had barely changed position. 'Mrs Mitchell is coming now, Mum.'

Mum's eyes were glazed, but her smile was as warm as ever. 'Thank you. You're a good girl, Hester. Don't you worry, it will be all right now.'

Mrs Mitchell was as good as her word, arriving with Jenifry and several of the other women in the row, just as Hester was feeding the range and putting the kettle on to boil.

'Robbie and Alice can come with me,' said Jenifry. 'I've potato scones on the go, my lovelies and you can see your mum when she's feeling better.'

'You go,' said Hester, to Robbie's anxious face, smiling as cheerfully as she could. She grabbed the remainder of Gran's fruitcake from the larder, thrusting it into Jenifry's hands. 'The best way to help Mum is to stop Alice from being frightened.'

Robbie nodded, taking Alice by the hand and leading her after Jenifry.

'Oh my lord,' muttered Mrs Mitchell, as she helped to lift Mum to her feet. Hester caught sight of the dark stain left on the chair and the floor beneath, and was spreading over the wool of Mum's skirts, as if it would never end. The sharp scent of iron filings filled the air. 'We'll get you up to bed, Sadie, you'll be more comfortable there, my dear. I'm afraid this is one for the doctor.'

'No, doctor,' whispered Mum, eyes shut, face concentrating with the effort of moving. 'Robert said...'

'I don't bloody care what Robert said,' retorted Mrs

Mitchell. 'I've not obeyed my husband in twenty years, and I'm not starting with yours now.' Her voice softened. 'If you love your children, Sadie, you'll let me send for Dr Graham. It's now, or later, and by that time it might be too late.' Slowly, almost imperceptibly, Mum nodded.

'I'll go,' said Hester. It was taking the strength of the women present to lift Mum up the few stairs to the bedroom, and she could run faster than any of them.

'Good girl,' said Mrs Mitchell. 'Don't you let him fob you off, now, and pray he's not been already called out.'

Hester ran until her legs shook and her lungs were bursting. She arrived at Dr Graham's house next to the Fisherman's Arms, just as he was stepping into his pony and trap.

'Hester, my dear girl. What is it? Is it your mother?'

'Yes,' she gasped. 'Mrs Mitchell said it wouldn't wait.'

'I see.' There was a flash of something that might have been anger in the doctor's face, then it was calm and impartial once more. 'Well, I rather suspect Mrs Elliot can wait, however much she might object to the idea, and she may even find she doesn't need my services after all. Peggy,' he called to the maid, who had appeared at the door at the sound of voices. 'Get one of your lads to run up to Afalon and tell Mrs Elliot I've been unavoidably detained and I'll be there as soon as I can. And they can call Dr Trenholm from Hayle, if they really feel it's that urgent.'

He lifted his medical bag down from the trap, leaving instructions to turn the pony out into the paddock, this being likely to prove a long night, and strode alongside Hester the short way to the ferryman's cottage.

The hours seemed endless. Hester boiled kettle after kettle, leaving only to fetch water from the standpipe at the bottom of the row. Above her, she could hear footsteps moving about, floorboards creaking under their weight, accompanied by the

41

reassuring tones of Dr Graham, and an occasional low moan of agony. Mrs Mitchell appeared periodically in the kitchen to fetch more hot water, which she took up without a word. Worse was when she came down to empty a covered pail, the contents of which Hester could only guess.

Someone alerted Dad, who arrived breathless, his face ashen.

'Ah, Mr Pearce,' said Dr Graham, appearing on the stairs, medical bag in hand.

Hester held her breath, waiting for Dad to shout at Dr Graham to get out of his house. But Dad's pride was nowhere to be seen.

'How is she? Is she...'

'Mrs Pearce is resting. You will be able to see her in a while.'

'Thank heavens,' whispered Dad, staggering, leaning against the doorframe for support.

'She's not out of the woods yet,' returned Dr Graham, sounding as severe as the minister on Sunday. 'I would prefer if your wife was taken to the hospital as soon as possible, but at the moment she is far too weak to be moved.'

'Hospital?' Any colour left in Dad's face drained away. Hospital was only for the most seriously sick, and a place from which many never returned.

'I'm afraid so. Your wife has suffered a catastrophic haemorrhage, Robert. If she doesn't improve within the next few hours, she may well need an operation.' He cleared his throat. 'Perhaps we could discuss this outside?'

'Yes, of course, doctor.'

As Dr Graham followed Dad towards the back door into the garden, he turned. 'You go up, Hester. Your mother is asking for you. Just a few minutes, mind. She needs all the rest she can get.'

Hester nodded and raced up the stairs.

'There you are, you see, Sadie. There's no need to distress yourself, Hester's here.' Mrs Mitchell was bent over the bed, tidying the blankets. She picked up a bundle of bloodied rags. 'I'll be back in a few minutes. Now, remember what the doctor said about rest.'

'Mum?' Hester took the pale hand held out to her. Her mother appeared to have shrunk in the last few hours, her face white and drawn, hair loose and damp with sweat. 'Mum, I'm sorry, I should have got back sooner.'

'It's not your fault, Hester dearest.' The pressure of her fingers was faint, but there. 'You brought Dr Graham. It's all right now.' She shut her eyes, as if even the effort of talking was too much for her. Hester was sure she had fallen asleep, but then her eyes opened again. For a moment they appeared dazed, then her gaze focused on Hester's face. 'You can fetch me something.'

'Yes, of course. Anything.'

'The piece of wood in the corner, under the eaves.' Mum's voice was a little stronger. 'It comes out.'

Hester found the wood, which looked as if it had been used to patch a hole in the wall. It came out of its position with a little manoeuvring, leaving a space behind.

'I can see a tin.'

'You'll need that. It's the money from M. Alphonse.'

'Mum ...' This was scaring her.

'If I go to hospital. You'll need to know where to find it. Leave it there and reach to one side.'

'There's a book.'

'That's the one. Shut it all up again and bring the book over here.'

Hester obeyed. When she looked closer, she saw that it was a leather-bound notebook, old and battered and stained

43

at the edges. She placed it into Mum's hands; she held it gently, as she would have done a child.

'What is it?'

'My recipe book. Every cook has her recipe book, where she writes down all the recipes she learns and collects over the years. It's the essential tool of her trade.' Mum opened it, allowing the well-thumbed pages, some with a streak of grease across the top, others with a hint of flour, to fall open. She smiled as she went through, page after page. 'This is the story of my life. Every one is a memory. A happy memory.' She paused at a much-stained page headed 'Apple Charlotte'. 'You are going to need it.'

Hester fought back tears. 'I can't, Mum.'

'Yes, of course you can, darling. This is yours now. There are still pages in the back for you to add your own recipes, or you can start your own book and use this to refer to. It's the only thing I have to give you, wherever you decide to go.'

'I was coming to tell you that I'd decided to take up M. Alphonse's offer.'

'I'm glad.' Mum's pale face gained a little colour. 'I know it's a risk, darling, but it will be worth it. I know you will be successful at anything you put your mind to. You stick to what you want to do, my dearest, whatever life throws at you. You'll get there in the end. I know you will. I'm proud of you, Hester, and I always will be.' Mum's face had turned pale once more, she barely seemed able to keep her eyes open. Below, there came the sound of men's voices as Dr Graham returned inside with Dad.

'You'd better sleep, Mum,' said Hester, kissing her. 'Or Dr Graham will never forgive me.'

Mum smiled. 'I'd like to look through this for a while. But don't forget, dearest, from now on it's yours. And don't worry about your father. We'll tackle him in the morning. He'll see sense in the end, you'll see.'

Hester made her way quietly out of the bedroom. At the door, she turned. In the fading light, Mum was lying, propped up on her pillows, slowly going through the recipe book, page by page. She was utterly absorbed, Hester could see, as if the world around her had vanished, and only the smells and tastes of a busy kitchen were left. Mum turned a page again. As Hester left, she could see she was smiling.

Chapter Six

Mum died that night, in the dark hours just before morning.

This time it was Dad who ran for Dr Graham, but it was already too late. Mrs Mitchell, who had stayed the night sitting next to Mum, while Hester looked after a restless Robbie and Alice downstairs, greeted them with a brief shake of the head. Then it was only left to Dr Graham to confirm what they already knew.

'Your dad's with her now,' said Mrs Mitchell, gathering up her belongings to return home as Dr Graham left. 'You leave him for a bit, my dear.' She held out the recipe book. 'This was in her hands. She said something before she went. I think she meant it was for you.'

Hester swallowed her tears. 'Thank you.'

'She was a good woman, my dear, and she loved you with all her heart. And she was as proud of you as she could be. Don't you ever forget that. Now, you know where I am if you need me.'

'Gran,' said Hester, her brain sluggish, but trying to stay on the practical.

'Don't you worry, my dear. Dr Graham is going up there first thing this morning to tend to Mrs Elliot. He'll break the news to your gran. There's nothing she can do now, it's best to leave her to rest while she can.' She patted Hester's hand. 'And you get as much rest as you can too, my dear. Heaven knows, you're going to need it.

There was no time to think, no time to grieve. Within hours, Dad was back rowing the ferry. With this being the family's only source of income, Dad was unwilling to keep a relief ferryman, there being little enough money in the business as it was and being afraid that, given half a chance, someone might steal his trade.

There was no question of Hester going back to school. From that first morning, she had the range to build up for Dad's cup of tea before he left, making his lunch from the remainder of the loaf of bread and a scraping of dripping. With no money to be seen, she was forced to brave the covered figure in the bed to raid Mum's tin to buy a loaf to feed Robbie and Alice on their way to school. Once left to herself again, she looked round the little kitchen, daunted by grief and responsibility.

Everything Mum had done every day of Hester's life was now up to her. There were the potatoes Mum had been pre-paring yesterday, a jar of dried beans and the last few heads of kale in the garden. It was Friday. Bereaved or not, Mr Bolsover would be there that evening. She climbed on a chair and fetched down the rent tin.

She knew the amount that needed to be there, she had seen Mum count it out often enough. Counting and recount-ing, putting the coins in piles to make sure, more often than not despairing at the inability of the coins to make up the necessary amount. To her relief, there was almost enough. If Dad came home with a few fares, they would be able to pay the rent. Then she would need to make sure he gave her money for coal and groceries, and to replace the bar of carbolic soap that was used to clean everything from hair to floors.

Already the house looked grubby at the edges. She couldn't

leave it that way, not when Mum had kept it so spick and span however ill or tired she might be. Hester sat at the table, fighting back the tears. The house without Mum's living presence was empty. She had no one to turn to, no one to ask. The women in the row were kind, but they had their own work to do and their families to care for, and not a moment to themselves as it was. Yesterday, she had been dreaming of M. Alphonse, running back eagerly to tell Mum. Now all that was gone.

'Hester?' She looked up to find Gran at the door, her hair a white halo behind her in the sunshine.

Hester jumped up and ran towards her, great sobs taking hold of her as she was gathered into her grandmother's arms.

Mum had left everything as ordered as she could. She had even scraped enough money together to cover the cost of her funeral, without having to mention the little tin hidden beneath the eaves.

Hester went through the burial in a daze, trying her best to comfort Robbie and Alice, who held on tight to either hand, as if afraid she might disappear without warning too.

As they slowly made their way back from the graveside, Hester found two figures on the edges of the little crowd of mourners. One was a woman, her face obscured by a veil, who stood under the shadow of the yew trees as if not wishing to be seen. She couldn't be certain, but she had a feeling it was Mrs Trewarren. Before she drew close enough to tell, the woman had vanished.

The other figure was M. Alphonse. As they passed, he stepped forward and took Hester's hand.

'My condolences, my dear. This is a great loss to us all, but to you and your family most of all.'

'Thank you, M. Alphonse.'

'It is too soon, you have much to arrange. But I want you to know that a place will be there for you with me, if that is your wish.'

'Thank you.' She swallowed. She should tell him it was out of the question, she had her mother's place to fill, and a family to care for. How could she think of herself and her ambitions at such a time? Then she remembered what Mum said about following her own path, whatever happened. 'It is my wish,' she said quickly, seeing Dad approaching out of the corner of her eye. 'I don't know how or when, but it will always remain my wish.'

M. Alphonse smiled. '*Bien*. I am glad. You look so like your mother when she was not much older than you are now. Very like.'

'She left me her recipe book.'

'Of course. I would have expected no less. It is an inheritance like no other, mademoiselle. Treasure it. This will be your guide and your companion, however long the road might be.' He tipped his hat as Dad arrived at her elbow. 'Again, my condolences.'

'Who was that?' demanded Dad, as M. Alphonse strode towards the entrance to the churchyard, through which the woman in the veil was already disappearing.

'Mum's employer,' replied Hester. Dad frowned. 'When she worked in a hotel in St Ives.'

'Why would he come so far, after all this time?'

'Possibly because he thought highly of her,' retorted Gran, joining them. 'M. Alphonse is a highly regarded chef, and not only in Cornwall. It's a great honour to Sadie that he took the time to come to pay his respects.'

Dad was chewing his lips, with no appearance of listening. 'I knew there was someone. Someone before.'

Gran snorted. 'If you think M. Alphonse came out of

49

some sentimental attachment, you are the biggest fool on earth, Robert Pearce. A man like that would never open himself up to gossip. It is one professional paying his respects to another. Sadie was a remarkable woman. It is her work, and that alone, he admired.'

Dad stuck his hands in his pockets. 'Whatever you might choose to believe, Mair, I won't have that man's name within my hearing again.'

Gran's lips tightened, but she let it go. As Dad strode on ahead, she fell back to join Hester. 'Give him time,' she said, quietly. 'Probably best not to mention M. Alphonse's offer for now. Don't listen to your dad's nonsense. What I said was true, and don't you ever think otherwise. M. Alphonse's only feelings towards your mother were simply those of the deepest respect for her skills. He will see you in the same way. Just wait a while. Let things settle down a bit.'

'But if I was in St Ives, how could I take care of Dad and the children?'

'We'll cross that bridge when we come to it. Don't think about that now. You've enough to deal with. You just do what you need to do, but keep that dream of yours alive.' She watched Dad striding out of the churchyard, determined to show no outward sign of emotion, keeping his pride intact. 'You have time and practicalities on your side.'

'I don't think Dad will ever change his mind.'

'Maybe. But I'm not sure your dad has ever understood how much your mum kept your family afloat. For all his pride, your dad is going to have to face the fact at some point that he will need you to earn to keep a roof over your heads. You might have to work with me at Afalon for a while, to get him used to the idea, but once you are able to earn, he can't stop you. Besides, you'll have me on your side.' She sighed, swinging Alice, who was growing tired, onto her hip.

'I should have fought more for your mother, when she had her dreams. I didn't, for reasons that seemed for the best at the time. I was certain she was heading for heartbreak and a life of isolation. It was only when it was too late that I understood I should have trusted her, and supported her in taking that chance. I promise I'll help you, *cariad*, in any way I can. Sadie was the last of my children. Now, my darlings, you are all I have left.'

Chapter Seven

Over the three years that followed, Hester did her best to fill her mother's place.

Even though she'd helped Mum before school and when she came home, she'd had no real idea of just how hard Mum had worked. And that was without making her conserves and cleaning for Mrs Leavan.

Every morning, Hester was up well before the rest of the family, to make sure they all had something to eat before leaving the house and Dad had his lunch ready to take with him as he set off for the ferry. Then there was the cleaning of every room, with mud from the street walked in with every step and soot from the range leaving a fine film of grime on every surface. Her arms permanently ached from fetching buckets of water from the standpipe at the end of the row, her fingers raw from water and carbolic, even before washing day came around each week. At first, she was afraid she would never be able to manage the boiling and scrubbing and wringing out of the family's clothes, followed by the attempt to dry them on damp winter afternoons, when there was not a breath to stir them, or the weeks when storms blew in bringing days of endless rain.

But worst of all, was the planning and the working out, trying to make the small pile of coins Dad left for her stretch to everything they needed. Rent was the first thing. Then coal for the range so that they had some warmth and means of cooking, or at least boiling a kettle. Finally, she had to ensure there was enough food to fill their bellies, while trying to put a little aside for when winter boots and coats would inevitably need replacing.

Mum had always been so cheerful and determined. However little Dad brought in, she'd always managed to keep them warm and their bellies full, with the touch of delicious treats of elderflower fritters or roasted chestnuts to supplement days of bread and jam. At least more passengers were using the ferry these days, on their way to visit family or take goods to sell to the rich houses on the other side.

To Hester's relief, there was generally enough in the rent tin each Friday and Dad put down a small pile of coins on the kitchen table for her each evening. But even then, she sometimes had to dip into Mum's little store. However careful she was, there never seemed enough, even though she tended the vegetables in the garden, with the help of Robbie, who set to each evening after school weeding and tying up the rows of peas and beans, and diligently removing slugs and snails at dawn and dusk. Each autumn, she dreaded to think how they would manage when winter returned.

It couldn't escape her notice that Dad was spending longer in the Fisherman's Arms after his day's final consignment of passengers. With it came an understanding that, for all he had treated Mum like a child at times, he hadn't dared keep too much of his earnings for himself and face her scorn. It wasn't the same when it came to a daughter, a slip of a girl he was convinced would never notice, and had no power to argue if she did. Within months, Dad had pushed out of his mind just how much they had relied on Mum's earnings, as well as her skill at managing to keep the little family afloat.

So much for raising the question of M. Alphonse and the offer of being trained as a professional cook. Through her exhaustion, Hester could feel the possibility drifting out of her grasp. The family needed money now, they didn't have the luxury of waiting for years when she might be able to earn enough to support them all with ease. As Mum's precious store of money began to become dangerously low, Hester could feel the inevitability of finding work that would supplement their income while allowing her to stay at home to look after the family. Whenever she broached the subject of the rent, Dad brushed her aside, or busied himself with mending the roof of the outhouse at the bottom of their little garden. Without Mum's steady hand, she could feel them drifting towards the day the rent would fall short, even if she put no food on the table or coal in the range.

She'd seen families turned out into the street for missing just a single week's rent. Poor Jenifry, with her six children and a husband who liked his drink even more than Dad, was always at her wits' end, especially now there was no money to pay for her to look after Alice and Robbie and fewer of those who could afford it wishing to trust their children to a house where there were sounds of violence every Friday night. Each week Hester watched Jenifry, with yet another bruise on her arms, or yet another black eye, waiting to be thrown out at any moment to join the tramps making shift in the fields, whatever the weather.

She couldn't bear the thought of Robbie and Alice being forced to sleep under the hedgerows, with their only other choice the workhouse, where the family would inevitably be separated. The workhouse was the ultimate disgrace, leaving a taint it would be almost impossible to escape for any of them. More than anything, she had to prevent them from ending up in the workhouse.

Already she could see that Robbie was quick at learning, and Alice had a way with sums she could only envy. Mum had been determined all three of them would finish their education and have a chance to escape the grinding poverty that, Hester could already see, would inevitably wear them down, so that life simply became a matter of survival.

She did her best to avoid Jimmy, who was as pleased as Punch at having quickly secured a job at Timson's, gleefully escaping spending the rest of his life as a fisherman. He had not forgotten her apparent interest in his extravagant dreams, and was just as eager for an audience.

'I got that promotion, you know,' he remarked as he passed her one morning, in his smart jacket and trousers, boots shining and squeaking with newness. 'Timson's is a grand place to work. The pay's not bad. Not what I'll get when I start driving the motorised vans, but better than anything I could earn out in the boats with Dad. It will do me for now.'

'I'm glad,' said Hester, wishing the water from the stand-pipe would fill up her bucket in an instant. She couldn't help, in her heart of hearts, being envious. Beside him, she felt grubby and dishevelled, already an old woman worn down with impossible responsibilities. So much for her own ambition. She had become one of the bystanders of this world, watching the rise of others, with only a hope of some kind of reflected glory and gratitude for being noticed at all.

'They're soon bound to be training me as a driver.'

'That will be good,' she murmured, glad to find Mrs Mitchell arriving next to her on the same mission, bucket in hand, and favouring Jimmy with a particularly hard glare, to which he was oblivious.

'So, you see. One day I really could buy Afalon. And then your gran wouldn't have to worry. She'd know she could stay on as cook forever. I wouldn't push your gran out in the cold, Hester. And I'd find work for you, too. I wouldn't forget you.'

'Jumped-up young idiot,' muttered Mrs Mitchell as Jimmy

strode off in the direction of the river. 'Don't you take no notice of him, Hester. It's the ones that are full of themselves like that that prove trouble, in the end.'

'What did he mean about Gran staying on as cook?'

'Just daydreaming. Trying to impress you. And himself, more like. There's been talk of the Elliots returning to London at the end of the summer. Permanent, like. But there's always talk, and besides, your gran could get a post as cook at the drop of a hat. Cooks, proper cooks, are hard to find, these days. What do they expect, when it takes so long to get anywhere and then you're at the beck and call of a family? I don't blame girls choosing to work as clerks or in factories instead. You wouldn't catch me sending my daughters into service. I've done it. Believe me, your life is never your own.'

Hester hauled her bucket back to the cottage to begin the weekly assault on the family's washing.

'Well, I'm not doing this for the rest of my life, not for anybody,' she growled to herself. Jimmy was making his way in life, and from his clothes, it was clear his mother hadn't demanded he hand over every penny of his earnings to support the family. She'd never had a new piece of clothing in her life, Mum always having carefully selected the best of the cast-offs from the second-hand clothing shop in Hayle. Hester wasn't bothered about new clothes, although something slightly less patched than her skirt wouldn't come amiss, and Alice was now growing fast. But she couldn't help feeling irritated at Jimmy's assumption that he had the right to spend his earnings on himself, even if it was for the purposes of getting on at work.

There had to be a way. M. Alphonse would understand that she couldn't take up his offer straight away, but the longer time went on, the more she feared he would think she had forgotten, or lost interest, or found a young man to apprentice instead.

Already she'd had enough of cooking and cleaning and never having a moment to herself to last a lifetime. If this was what running a home and family was like, she couldn't see much point in being married at all. She'd far rather earn her own money and be able to choose how she lived and not put everyone else in front of herself. It might be mean and selfish and not how a woman was supposed to be at all, but that was how she felt.

Once, the future had seemed to stretch on forever. Now, she was all too aware that life was precious and uncertain, and could be snatched away in a moment. She wanted to live. She didn't want fine clothes or jewels, or even to be wildly rich. She certainly didn't want to own a big house like Afalon and spend her life lording over everyone around her. All she wanted was not to have to spend her life in the shadows. It was such a simple wish. Was that really too much to ask? As she boiled up the copper and wielded the washing-dolly, thrashing the clothes into cleanliness, her mind was back working on her ambitions. She would find a way. Whatever it took, she would find a way.

Chapter Eight

'You're managing here very well, *cariad*,' said Gran later that week, as she arrived on her day off, a large fruitcake to hand. 'Your mum would be proud.'

'I hope so.'

'But not happy.'

'Gran?'

'Your mum would be proud of you for stepping in, but not happy that this is where it has left you.'

'It won't be forever.'

'Good for you.' Gran sounded thoughtful. 'Some people see it as a weakness not to put yourself first, especially those who don't understand what it is like to have no choice.'

'I can't just leave Robbie and Alice. Robbie's doing well, and the new headmistress is already talking about putting Alice in for a scholarship when she's old enough.'

'My goodness, she must think she's exceptional, in that case.'

'She is. They've already moved her up several classes and Miss Smith is giving her extra lessons in the sciences. Alice told me after Mum died that she wants to train to be a midwife, even a doctor. Her teachers think she can do it. "Academically gifted", that's what they called her. Even though she's still so young, she's one of the most academically gifted pupils the school has had for years. I'm not sure how, since there isn't a book in the house, apart from the Bible.'

'I'd say you were all pretty bright, and a lot of that is down to your mum encouraging you to be curious and think for yourselves.'

Hester handed her a cup of tea. 'I hope so.'

'Now then, you listen, *cariad*.' Gran placed a large slice of cake in front of Hester, nodding to her not to delay a minute longer. The cake was rich and sweet, filled with currants, with a scattering of sugar on top. Hester tried to savour every mouthful of deliciousness, but she was so ravenous that, once started, she couldn't stop. As soon as she finished, Gran cut her another slice. 'Don't worry, I've come prepared, I've another for the rest of them. This is for just you and me. I have a feeling you need the fuel to keep you going.' She crumbled her own small slice of cake in her hands. 'Now then, Hester. What do you say to me leaving Afalon?'

'Leaving?' Hester practically choked, hastily dispersing the crumbs with a gulp of tea. 'But you can't.'

'Well, my dear, I'm not sure it's a case of not being able to, but rather jumping before I am pushed.'

'They would never get rid of you!'

'If they know they won't return to Afalon after the winter season, they won't be keeping the expense of the staff.'

'Is Mrs Elliot worse, then?'

'It's not that. It seems Mr High and Mighty Elliot is not quite so clever as he thinks. Rumour is, his last investment crashed, and the one before it turned out to be a fraud. Not that I'm weeping for them. A taste of poverty might do them good.' She grinned. 'Don't look so shocked, Hester. People like the Elliots will never be truly poor. Richard will still get to go to Oxford and Isabella's gowns might be not quite as lavish this winter, but they'll be fine enough to attract a rich husband. And that's more silk than you or I will ever see in a lifetime. And even if you are accustomed to eleven courses each evening, the loss of one or two – even half – doesn't exactly mean starvation.'

'No,' said Hester. How different their lives had become since that day they had chatted together on the river's edge, so full of dreams of what the future held. Perhaps it was as well that they were unlikely ever to meet again.

'If things don't get better soon, they may even be forced to sell Afalon. That may be what Mr Elliot is already planning. As I said, better jump than be pushed. At least that way I keep my pride and cause them some inconvenience.'

'Would that mean you'd have to move away?'

'If I took up another post, it would. But I'm not sure I want to move far. There's a cottage just fallen empty near Afalon's walls. It's a bit rough and ready, but there's a garden for growing vegetables and the range is a good one. I've my savings, and I could eke it out with making preserves. They might not be as good as your mum's but at least I know there's an opening that no one else has thought to try and fill yet.' A stubborn look came over her face. 'And it has come to me that I'd like to spend more time with my grandchildren.'

'Gran—'

'This is not self-sacrifice. I don't approve of self-sacrifice, especially not in members of my own sex. I would like to spend more time with Robbie and Alice. And with you, of course, my dear. All these years of you growing up, I've only seen you for a few hours for one day a week. That wasn't my choice, that was the only way I could keep food in my belly and a roof over my head. But I'm growing old, my dear. I've no intention of fading away, but I've a hankering after a quieter life. Besides, if I take care of Robbie and Alice, that will free you to train with M. Alphonse.' A touch of mischief appeared in her eyes. 'Which means when you are rich and have a cafe of your own, I will have someone who can provide a roof over my head in my old age.'

'I'd always look after you, Gran!'

'I know you would, sweetheart. I'm only joking. Or nearly only joking.' Her face became serious again. 'Let me do this for you, Hester. It would soothe my heart as much as help you. I should have encouraged your mother to rise as far as she could go, instead of wanting to keep her safe. Things could have been so different. I can't help thinking that, if only I'd kept faith, I wouldn't have lost her.'

'It's not your fault, Gran.'

'I know. But sometimes I can't sleep for wondering.' She shook herself. 'So will you let me help you?'

'Dad won't like it.'

'I bet he bloody won't. Your mother was so convinced if she loved him enough, she could weed the selfishness out of him. That's the trouble with being older, as you'll find one day. The young always think they know best, never imagining you've been through the same thing and seen more than they can ever imagine. Anyhow, you leave your dad to me.'

Hester took a deep breath. 'Yes. Yes, a thousand yeses. I won't let you down, Gran. I'll work until I drop.'

'I rather think you are doing that already.'

'But this time it'll be for the future. I will start my own cafe, and I promise you'll always have a place and a roof over your head, Gran. Forever and ever.'

'I'm not sure about the forever, but while I'm still above ground will do.'

Hester laughed. It was the first time she had laughed, properly laughed, since Mum died. The sound echoed around them, strange, yet warm and comforting.

'For as long as you wish, Gran. I want to be able to help

Robbie if he needs it, and make sure Alice is able to train as a doctor when she grows up, if that's what she wants.'

'And you, my dear? You are quite the young woman now and fast growing up yourself.'

'I want to be the best cook I can be, and have my own business that's mine, all mine, so I never, ever have to hide from the rent man again. I want to see people having pleasure from what I cook, not just filling them with as much as I can for as little as I can, just to keep them alive. That time I went to St Ives with Mum, she showed me the cafe, the one she wanted to run as her own.'

'The one on Porthgwidden beach, with the view towards Godrevy lighthouse?'

'Yes. That's the one that's going to be mine, I can feel it in my bones. And I'm going to do my best to make it the best cafe in St Ives, the best in Cornwall. Just as Mum wanted to do.'

'That sounds a good ambition,' said Gran, a little wistfully. She finished her tea, straightened her shoulders and cleared her throat loudly. 'Hester, I think there is something you really ought to know—' She came to an abrupt halt as the door was flung open and Robbie stumbled inside.

'Hester!'

'Robbie, what is it?' She could see the concern in his face. 'Is it Dad?'

He nodded. 'There was an accident. He slipped while he was tying up the ferry. Right between the wall and the boat.'

'Is he bad?' demanded Gran.

'Dr Graham took him to the hospital in Hayle.' Robbie burst into tears. 'They said Dad's arm is badly crushed. He isn't going to be able to row the ferry for weeks, maybe months, and Dr Graham said he might even lose it altogether. What are we going to do?'

'It's all right.' Hester hugged him tight. 'We'll work something out. The main thing now is to try and see Dad and make sure he's all right, and he knows he's not been abandoned.'

'It's too far,' said Gran. 'You can't walk to Hayle from here, it will take ages. Is there anyone who can row you over the estuary? At least that will take you closer to the hospital. What about that relief ferryman who worked with your dad over Easter?'

Robbie shook his head. 'Dad said there wasn't enough passengers to support two families. Peter left to work on the Fowey ferry last week.'

'I could row,' said Hester. 'I've been over with Dad often enough.'

'That's not the same as rowing the thing!'

'I know about the tides,' put in Robbie. 'And Dad has been showing me what to do. I can help.'

'I'm sure Jenifry will look after Alice, if I ask.'

'I'll go and talk to her,' said Gran. 'Don't you worry about paying her, either, that's the least I can do. You'll need money for rent.'

'There's enough,' said Hester quickly, seeing her grandmother reaching in her pocket for her purse. 'It's all there in the rent tin ready. Thank you for offering to pay for Jenifry so we can see Dad, but I won't take your savings, Gran. Even if Dad can't row the ferry for a while, we'll find a way.'

'*Duw*, child, you're as stubborn as your mother, and just as proud. Go on with you. You get what you need for your dad, I'll go and see Jenifry.'

Hester collected Dad's spare shirt and trousers, placing them in a bag with his best jacket, the one he usually kept for church. She had to hope his boots had survived as, like the rest of them, he had no second pair.

Gran accompanied Hester and Robbie as far as the schoolyard, to take Alice to Jenifry, who was more than happy at the thought of an extra few coins in her pocket.

'Go on, then. And let's hope you can bring your dad back with you, or he'll be well enough to come home soon.'

Hester took the little alleyway to one side of the Fisherman's Arms leading to the wooden jetty where the ferry was moored. She clambered down into the large rowing boat, settling herself onto Dad's seat, thankful that someone had had the sense to stash the oars in their usual position on the bottom of the boat. She fitted each onto its support. The handles felt large and heavy and she could barely fit her hands around each one. She pulled them experimentally through the water, feeling the flow. Looking over her shoulder, the estuary looked wider than ever. She took a deep breath. At least the tide was nearly in. It was calm, and there was no rush of seawater to drag them down towards the sand dunes of Hayle Towans and the open ocean beyond.

'Ready,' she called to Robbie, who began to unwind the rope holding the boat to its moorings.

'You going across?' A middle-aged woman appeared on the jetty, a basket of protesting chickens in one hand.

She couldn't take passengers! She hadn't thought of that. She'd been so focused on seeing Dad, on making sure he didn't think he'd been abandoned, she hadn't considered that side of things. She didn't know what she was doing, she'd probably turn the ferry round and round and not get anywhere. Before she could reply several young men spilt out of the Fisherman's Arms, making their way towards her.

'That looks like an improvement,' called one, who, by his slightly unsteady gait, had been drowning any sorrows he could think of for some time.

'Well, well,' said his companion, with an unmistakable leer, sent vaguely in her direction.

Robbie went bright red. By the looks of him, he was deciding which one to floor first.

Hester braced herself. 'So, d'you want to get across?' she demanded loudly.

'No harm meant,' muttered the first drinker, who at least had the grace to look a little shamefaced. His friend closed one eye, all effort focused on keeping himself upright.

Several more men and women, attracted by the commotion, were appearing on the jetty, relief in their voices and the chink of coins in their hands.

Hester met Robbie's eyes. The coins represented precious coal for a kettle of hot water, and something more substantial than peas and beans from the garden to fill their bellies that night. Robbie looped the rope back around the mooring, pulling it tight to allow the passengers to take their places, making sure to safely pocket the proffered fares.

With the boat almost full, it felt impossibly heavy. Hester steadied it with her oars as Robbie freed them from the moorings and jumped into the final space. Dad had been proud to show her when she was little how to pull the oars deep so they didn't break the surface and waste their force. Pull evenly. Slowly and evenly, that was the trick. Carefully, she manoeuvred away from the bank, doing her best not to swerve from one side to the other, or even worse pull more on one side and go round in circles. With a boat full of passengers, whose lives were entirely in her hands, she had no time for doubts, or for failure. She concentrated, getting the feel of the oars.

For a short while, it was more of a zigzag than a smooth ride across, but gradually she began to even up her strokes. At least she knew where she was heading. When she turned her head, she could make out the quay next to the smart houses on the outskirts of Hayle. Her arms were burning and she had no breath left in her body, but she was making her way across. It was too late to turn back now, and she was not about to relinquish the coins they had taken. She pushed the discomfort to one side and set out determinedly for the opposite shore. As she did, she was aware of the stench of stale beer drifting across her face. It was the more inebriated of the drinkers, who had managed to edge close to her and was staring pointedly at the neckline of her dress.

'I like to see sweat on a woman,' he slurred. 'And her putting her back into it.'

Right, that did it. No one spoke to her like that, drink or no drink. Hester steadied the boat, slowing it down without quite bringing it to a halt.

'Good at swimming, are you?'

'You wouldn't dare, you little bitch.'

'Try me.'

The drunk wavered. He seemed to at least come to his senses enough to notice the rock of the waves and the distance between the boat and the shore, but his expression said he wasn't about to be told, and especially not by some mouthy female.

An elderly farmer, with an equally grizzled sheepdog at his feet, tapped the drunk on one shoulder.

'Just you show a bit of respect, you young fool, or I'll be landing you among the fishes myself.'

'Quite right,' piped up the woman with the chickens. 'Any more out of you, Bert Carpenter, and I'll be telling your mother the way you carry on. Not to mention that nice young girl of yours, too.'

At the farmer's feet, the sheepdog bared its teeth with a warning growl in the direction of the offender's ankles.

'All right, all right.' Bert subsided a little, doing his best to vanish out of sight behind an elderly woman of generous proportions, who fixed him with a baleful glare. 'It was just a joke. Can't any of you take a joke?'

The boat fell silent. Even the sheepdog and the chickens didn't favour that one with a response. Hester grinned. The rest from pulling the oars had eased the tightness of her arms, giving her renewed strength as she set the ferry back in motion.

To her relief, they reached the other side without any further trouble. Confident now, she brought the ferry alongside, while Robbie leapt up onto the quay to secure the boat. The passengers disembarked, with Bert Carpenter slithering out, shoulders up, head down, not quite avoiding a quick nip from the sheepdog as he passed. With a muffled yelp, he set off in the direction of Hayle.

'Good girl, Jess,' said the farmer, with a wink in Hester's direction. 'Always was able to sort the sheep from the goats, this one.'

With the passengers disembarked, Hester found the hospital without difficulty. Dad was on the ward, one among seemingly endless rows of patients. He was as white as the sheets that covered him, but clearly pleased to see them. Dad had never been one to do well on his own, without his family or his drinking companions at the Fisherman's Arms around him. Since Mum died, he had been more than a little lost. Hester bent over, careful not to jar his heavily bandaged right arm, to kiss him gently on the forehead.

'You shouldn't have bothered, coming all this way,' he muttered.

'We were worried about you, Dad. We had to see how you were. We've brought you some things.'

'I'll be out of here, in a day or two,' he replied, patting

Robbie on the head with his good hand. 'Right as rain. Just you see. Right as rain. They can't keep me in here. I'll be back on the ferry in no time.'

A few minutes was more than enough for Dad. It didn't take the pointed cough from the nurse who came to check on him to show that already he was exhausted and sinking into sleep.

As they left, they passed Dr Graham, making his way towards the ward. 'Ah, Hester. I was just on the way to see your father. He's a lucky man, you know. That was a nasty crush, between the wall and the ferry. If it had caught him full on, it could have killed him. As it is . . .' He hesitated. 'Have any of the doctors here spoken to you?'

Hester shook her head. 'They all seemed so busy, and the nurses too, we didn't like to trouble them.'

'Yes, of course.' Dr Graham cleared his throat. 'You are going to have to prepare yourself, my dear. Your father's arm was almost completely crushed. I'm afraid it's quite beyond saving. The surgeons are planning to operate later tonight.'

'An operation? Is it that serious?' Hester felt sick.

'Your father's a fit and healthy man, Hester. No promises, but I'd say he'll have every chance of pulling through. They are going to try and save what they can, but I'm afraid it looks as if your father could lose his arm below the elbow. I'm sorry, my dear. You get yourself home, there's nothing either of you can do. I'll make sure you know how he gets on, as soon as I can.'

'Thank you,' whispered Hester, as Dr Graham was swept away by an anxious-looking matron to inspect a patient.

'Come on,' she said to Robbie. 'At least we've seen Dad, and he's in the best place and is being looked after. We need to get back. Poor Alice will be worried.'

As they reached the quay, they found passengers waiting

for them, ready to be rowed back over the estuary. Hester didn't hesitate to take her place while Robbie collected the fares. Her arms were tired and her back ached, but this time she felt more sure of herself, making the journey easier. Her passengers were all of the sober variety this time, happily gossiping among themselves. One or two had heard of Dad's accident, which seemed to answer any questions about the novelty of a ferrywoman taking his place.

By the time they reached the Fisherman's Arms, Hester was so hungry it hurt. The very thought of cooking anything was quite beyond her. Instead, she bought the largest remaining loaf from the bakery, and a small hunk of cheese from Mrs Dowrick, the widow who ran a small shop from her front room, and was prepared to sell things cheap, much to the annoyance of Mr Treves the grocer.

That night, the three of them crouched around the range, gratefully drinking hot tea and wolfing down the loaf. Their small amount of cheese was soon gone, so Hester brought out the one remaining jar of Mum's blackcurrant jam. It was the last thing Mum had made, and she had been saving it for Christmas. But she knew Mum would understand. They toasted the remainder of the loaf in front of the fire, savouring the deliciousness of the jam, and the memories it held, in silence.

As Robbie and Alice curled up either side of her in the warmth, Hester held them tight. Heaven knew what they were going to do with no income coming in. She blinked back the threatening tears. At least tonight she had proved she could row the ferry. She hadn't depended on Dad for the small pile of coins waiting on the table to be portioned out into the bits towards next week's rent, and the bits left over for coal and other necessities. Without that, they would be heading for the workhouse within weeks. She had found a way for them to keep going until Dad returned.

And M. Alphonse? Even if Dad's arm couldn't be saved, one day Robbie would be old enough to take over the ferry. At least if she kept it going, they could survive and the family had a future. She would not forget M. Alphonse. One day, she would find a way to take up his offer. Tonight, the cafe on the beach seemed further away than ever. But she'd get there one day. Even if it was too late, or M. Alphonse grew impatient, she would find a way to fulfil her dreams.

She squared her shoulders. At least if she continued to row the ferry she had a chance of keeping them with a roof over their heads and the family together. She hadn't let Mum down, that was the most important part. The rest would have to wait.

Chapter Nine

Autumn 1913

The wind was getting up. Hester hauled at the oars with all her might, steadying her course as the tide began to turn, threatening to drag the ferry downstream and out into St Ives Bay.

She had been ferrying the flow of passengers across the estuary since dawn. With evening beginning to fall and the boat nearly empty, her arms ached and hunger had settled tight in her belly. But today had been a busy one and the small bag safely stowed under her seat was fuller than usual. She had already pawned Dad's best coat to make sure Mr Bolsover would be paid. It meant the gently chinking coins would mostly be stashed away to get the coat out again before being needed for church on Sunday, but at least they could eat tonight.

Over the two years since the surgeon at the hospital had removed Dad's right arm below the elbow, she had fought with all her might to keep the family together. It had been a struggle, with the fares from her passengers as their only income. But even through last year's bitter winter, when few people had ventured across the estuary, she had managed. After the first weeks, she had felt her body grow stronger and healthier with the exercise and being outdoors in all weather, breathing in the sea air. Her arms had strengthened and her back rarely ached.

At least dealing with her passengers, especially the most troublesome, had ensured she'd become more forceful and quick-witted and better at heading off problems before they began. These were all things that would come in useful when she was finally able to run her own cafe.

'What a beautiful old house.' Her sole passenger, a middle-aged woman in boots and an ankle-length walking dress, was gazing back towards the little hamlet. The spire of the church was barely visible behind the trees, but a line of low, white-washed cottages could be clearly seen snaking up the hillside, chimneys sending the smoke of cooking fires dancing crazily into the breeze.

Hester followed the woman's gaze to the turrets and mock-Gothic windows just beyond the cottages.

'It's called Afalon.'

'So *that's* Afalon.' The woman gave a low chuckle. 'I'm afraid Mrs Elliot's paintings did it less than justice, poor woman. But then, having seen her other work, I should have known.'

'Yes, ma'am,' replied Hester. Her passengers, particularly when there were only a few, tended to like to pass the time of day. She had learnt the art of humouring them, without expending too much precious energy on conversation. On the other hand, this was Afalon and her curiosity was aroused. 'The family haven't lived there for some time.'

'I'm not surprised. I thought it had been sold off a couple of years ago, like the house in Kensington. I can't say I had much in common with Mrs Elliot, but she seemed a pleasant enough woman whenever our paths crossed. Perhaps it was a blessing she didn't live to see her husband's fortunes fall quite so low. I'm not sure she would have survived the shock.'

'No, ma'am.' Hester had heard that Mrs Elliot's heart had

failed, only a year after the family had left Afalon for the final time.

'But surely a place like that can't have just been left to rot?' Hester's passenger was still gazing up at the house. 'There must be a solicitor dealing with it. I expect the hotel will be able to direct me.' The woman's face lit up with an unexpectedly youthful glow. 'I should have known. I never was one to resist lost causes.'

'Yes, indeed, ma'am.' Hester barely heard her, concentrating on manoeuvring the ferry over the centre of the estuary, into increasingly choppy waters, and directing it safely alongside the quay on the other side. She had seen the clouds racing towards them from the sea. The sooner she made the return journey the better.

For once, she was thankful there was no sign of passengers waiting for passage back over. Not all the money in the world could tempt her to stay here any longer than was strictly necessary, let alone tackle baskets of squawking geese and the odd pig or so. Not to mention Fred Crowther, rolling back from market day drunk as a lord, ready to pick a fight with anyone he imagined might be looking at him askance.

As she pulled the boat alongside the quay, a shower of spray hurled in her face, almost blinding her. Hester shook her head vigorously, blinking away the water as she concentrated on securing the rope, bracing the boat as tight against the wall as she could to allow her passenger to step onto dry land.

The moment the woman was safely on the quay, swinging her canvas knapsack over one shoulder and striding purposefully towards the splendour of the Carbis View Hotel, Hester released the boat, setting out once more across the darkening river with an increasing sense of urgency.

As she cleared the quay, a squall of rain enveloped her,

creeping under the collar of her coat, to trickle its cold way down the back of her neck.

'Hell and high water!' That would teach her to be tempted by one last fare. Any woman wealthy enough to engage in a walking tour of Cornwall and stay in the Carbis View Hotel, just beyond the row of smart town houses enjoying the peace of the riverfront, had the means to pay for accommodation. Mrs Leavan's guesthouse might be small, but it was clean and so late in the season was bound to have at least one room available.

Hester steadied the boat, trying to regain her rhythm, speeding through the waves as fast as she dared. The light was beginning to fade, and the tug on her craft was harder to fight with every stroke.

A small knot of fear replaced the hunger in her belly. If she didn't get to shore before the tide race became too strong, she would be swept out into the great rolling waves of the Atlantic. If the ferry was dragged out into that wildness, it would be lost, and with it the family's only hope of keeping a roof over their heads.

Hester pulled faster, glancing briefly over her shoulder towards the rough wooden jetty next to the Fisherman's Arms. She had already been swept a little way downstream. She was never going to be able to fight the tide to make her way back up to the ferry's mooring.

Don't think of what might happen. Don't give in to panic. That wasn't going to help anyone. Hester forced her breathing to remain steady, and her mind clear. Go through all the possibilities, Dad had taught her, when he'd finally accepted he had no choice but to see his eldest child support the family. At least he had overcome his humiliation enough to teach her everything he knew, as soon as he'd sufficiently recovered to be able to join her on the boat.

She was thankful that, for all his impotent anger, Dad loved her enough to teach her how to survive. There is always a solution, he had told her. However impossible it seems, there is always a way out. Unless it was a great whale, the size of a small island, that some of the fishermen spoke about, its size increasing with every pint they downed. And great whales didn't make their way up rivers in Cornwall, at least not for as long as anyone could remember.

Fear shuts the mind down, he'd taught her, turning on itself into a circle of terror. Hester breathed deep, picturing the opposite shore below the jetty. There was a sandy inlet a little further down. If she was lucky, she would be able to avoid any rocks and reach the relative safety of calmer waters until the tide turned. Hester settled herself back to row, concentrating on keeping the boat steady and not being swept too far down towards the sea as she steered her craft towards the centre of the estuary.

With a final scattering of rain, the clouds hurried on inland, allowing low rays of sun to streak across, lighting up the quay she had just left.

'What the—?' Her gaze was caught by something flapping, spotlighted in the deep orange glow. It was an unmistakably female figure, white dress billowing around her as she unwound the rope holding a small rowing boat in place. 'Doesn't she know she'll get herself killed?' Obviously not. The woman leapt down into the boat, setting off towards Hester, unmistakably heading for the broad centre of the estuary.

Hester gripped her oars hard. She had enough to do without being responsible for some rich man's wife or daughter, who clearly hadn't the sense she was born with. Or was desperate. Hester bit her lip. The rower was strong, holding her own against the swirling waves, but there was recklessness in the way she was ploughing towards the centre of the estuary, as if careless of the consequences. The rowing boat, being lighter than the ferry, was already being swept past, heading towards the eddies and whirlpools of the tidal race, and the breakers waiting out in the stormy bay.

'Idiot!' When it came to it, she couldn't just leave. She couldn't moor herself safely on the far side and watch a fellow human being, however foolish, being swept to her death in front of her.

Hester reached the boat before it was caught in the fastest part of the outward flow, but it was already being violently bounced around, twisting uncontrollably. The girl struggling with the oars looked about her own age, seventeen at most. Her hair had been torn from its ribbon, half obscuring her face. She was soaked to the skin and pale as a ghost in the encroaching darkness.

Hester grabbed the rope at her feet. 'Catch this. I'll tow you back to shore.'

'Go away.'

'That thing's never going to survive. You could be dragged under at any minute.'

'I don't need your help. Leave me alone.'

'Well, you might have a death wish, but I don't. Grab the rope. It's your only chance.'

The rowing boat lurched again. Spray broke over one side as it was caught in the edges of a more powerful eddy, snatching the nearest oar from the girl's hands.

'It's all right.' Hester remained as calm as she could. The girl made no sound, but Hester could see from the widening of her eyes that the terror of her predicament had finally sunk in. 'I can still pull you free. Grab the rope.'

'I can't. I just can't.' This time there was panic in the girl's voice. She was tugging desperately at the remaining oar, trying in vain to steady herself. But she was now being pulled helplessly, this way and that, the side of the boat dipping closer to the water with each turn.

'Yes, you bloody can. All you need to do is catch.' Hester flung the rope. The end hit the side, sliding into the water. She stowed one oar and retrieved the slimy rope with her free hand. This time it landed next to the girl, who scrabbled for it, just as her boat was bounced round again, tearing the rope back into the water, taking with it the rowing boat's remaining oar, leaving the tiny craft helpless in the water.

Hester tried again. The rope was now waterlogged and felt almost impossibly heavy as she dragged it back towards her. She manoeuvred one-handedly as close to the smaller vessel as she dared. 'Ready?'

'Ready.'

This time it fell close enough for the girl to grasp with both hands and attempt to secure it. But they had strayed too near the tidal race. The rowing boat was spun round again, this time with no escape. With a sickening crunch, it upended, flinging the girl headlong into the waves.

'Hang on to the boat, to anything you can!' yelled Hester, trying to make out any sign of struggling in the water. The girl could be unconscious, or trapped beneath the surface. She could already have been swept hopelessly downstream. From the corner of her eye, Hester glimpsed something white. Instinctively she reached out, grasping the heaviness of sodden material. It tore, but there was enough for Hester to grasp an arm, then a shoulder.

She tugged with all her strength, the side of the ferry dipping dangerously near the waves. 'You'll have to help me,' she shouted above the roar of the water. 'Grab the side.' To her relief, she saw hands tighten on the rim of the boat. Hester hauled again, until the girl slithered over into a heap at the bottom of the boat. 'Stay still.' As fast as she could, Hester replaced her oar and pulled with all her might. They were caught fast. From the corner of her eye she could see the upturned rowing boat spiralling through the waves, disappearing from view.

Then the eddy shifted, sending them shooting out into calmer waters. Hester steadied the ferry, bringing it back under control. When she dared look up again, she found they were still on the Hayle side of the river, close to the shore. The quay was already too far upstream to even consider. Even drifting with the current, she no longer had the energy to fight the water.

At least the shore next to them was a sandy beach, with a promenade and the last of the row of houses. If she hesitated, the beach would be gone, leaving them to be swept out to sea. With the last of her strength, Hester impelled the ferry forwards as fast as she could, beaching it firmly onto the sand.

Chapter Ten

'Are you all right?' The distant voices were reassuring, at least their escape had not gone unnoticed and help was at hand. As she hauled the girl to her feet, Hester could make out figures on the promenade, silhouetted against the lights of the large houses fronting onto the river, frozen by the drama of life or death unfolding in front of their eyes. Several were already racing across the sand.

The first man to reach them lifted the girl out of the ferry without ceremony. 'You idiot! What on earth were you thinking of?'

'I'm all right.'

'No you're not. You could have killed yourself.'

'Well, I didn't.' The girl was defiant, but could barely get the words out for the chattering of her teeth. 'I had to get across to try and see him. He thinks I don't care.'

'Don't be such goose. He knows it's just Papa. You don't think Ralph is going to give up that easily, do you?'

'But Papa said such horrid things. You should have seen Ralph's face. He's never going to speak to me again.'

'Don't worry, Clara, we can sort this out. I'll talk to Ralph. You need to get warm before you catch your death.' He turned to Hester. 'Thank you, Miss—'

'Pearce.'

'Thank you, Miss Pearce. What you did was very brave. It

all happened so fast, I'd no chance to get out to her in time. I've no doubt you saved my sister's life.'

'I'm just glad I was there.' Now the danger was over, Hester couldn't afford to think of Clara, or her brother. From their speech, they belonged to one of the smart houses where the lawyers and the businessmen idled away the summer months, where their problems could be settled with a hot bath in front of the fire and a change of clothes. Personally, she had more pressing matters to deal with.

'What will you do now, Miss Pearce?'

'Wait for the tide.'

'But that's hours away! You must be nearly as wet through as Clara. Don't you need to get back to your family?'

'Yes.'

'I'll drive you.'

'What?'

'In the Ford. The motor car, that is. It won't take long, the road through Hayle only goes a few miles inland, it won't take more than an hour.'

'But I still have to get back for the ferry.'

'I can fetch you early in the morning. It's no trouble.'

'No! Thank you. It's very kind of you, but I'd rather not, if you don't mind.'

'Don't trust my driving, eh?'

'I didn't mean that. Well, a bit.' She'd seen them, over the past few years, the young men from the town, driving their motorised vehicles at an impossible speed, twenty miles an hour or so, the dust churning up behind them, sending dogs barking and small children shrieking with alarm, for all the world as if a dragon had come to terrorise the neighbourhood.

'Lance, don't be such a clot.' Clara's teeth were chattering.

She flapped her arms against her body in an attempt to get the blood flowing.

'Oh!' Hester could almost hear his blush. 'I see. I do beg your pardon, Miss Pearce. That was thoughtless of me. I hadn't considered how that might, ah, look, you turning up unaccompanied. Not my best idea. Well, there's nothing for it. You'll have to come home with us. At least Clara can act as some kind of chaperone.'

'I don't need a chaperone,' said Hester, irritated. His sister might need guarding, but personally, she'd never needed looking after in her life. Besides, she was the daughter of Pearce the ferryman, and, one-armed or not, everyone this side of St Ives knew not to mess with Dad, especially with a few pints inside him and a wrong to right. While Gran was not above boxing the ears of one twice her size, in broad daylight, and in such a way as could make a grown man weep.

That, Gran had informed her when she first took over the ferry, was the best protection a girl could have, along with keeping your wits about you and not falling for any flim-flammery from the boys who were after whatever they could get, and not too fussed how they went about it or that the mess they left you with afterwards was forever and a day.

'You could help me with Clara, Miss Pearce, if you wouldn't mind,' said Lance, slightly more tentatively. 'She's more solid than she looks.'

'I am not fat!'

'I didn't say you were. It's supposed to be a compliment, you goose. It's just your brain that's like gossamer.'

Hester swallowed a sudden urge to giggle. Rich or poor, families were all the same. 'Of course. She should get warm as soon as possible.'

'Excellent. The least we can do is offer you a chance to get dried off too, Miss Pearce. The house is only a few minutes' walk. Mama will know what's best to do.'

Hester grabbed the bag with the precious day's takings from the bottom of the ferry, tying it firmly around her waist, and pulled her shawl – which was almost as damp as her dress – across her shoulders. She could only trust that no one was in the market for stealing a battered old ferry boat, and that she had not hit a rock on the way in so it would sink the moment she tried to float it again next morning.

As she rejoined them, she could hear Clara's teeth chattering more violently than ever, while Lance was struggling to keep her on her feet. There were still a few passers-by on the promenade, but the drama, now there was no death or danger to be seen, appeared to have lost its interest, while Lance was keeping his voice down to avoid attracting attention. Hester took Clara's free arm, and between them they supported her along the beach towards the steps leading up to the houses. Not a moment too soon. Clara was moving increasing stiffly, as if her limbs refused to obey her, and as they reached the steps she grew ominously quiet.

'We need to be as quick as we can,' said Hester, as Clara slumped, her face a white blur in the light from the houses, eyes shut.

'Clara?' Lance's voice shook. 'Clara, stay awake. It's only a few more minutes, we need you to stay awake.' There was no answer. 'That's not good.' Lance swept his sister into his arms and hurried up the remainder of the steps. Hester followed close behind, as he rushed across the roadway, pausing only for a wagon to rumble past, lantern swinging, sending out strange shadows into the dark. Then he shot along the pavement and through a small gate to a path leading along the side of one of the tall houses facing the sea.

'I'll open it,' said Hester, as he came to a halt in front

of a small door. It swung back into light and heat and the overwhelming smells of cooking.

'Watch it, my girl!' roared a voice at the far end, accompanied by the sound of metal clattering to the floor. 'Do that with Mrs Trewarren's best plates and I'll have your guts for garters, make no mistake.'

'Yes, Mrs Tims. Sorry, Mrs Tims.' A girl of no more than fifteen, face reddened with the heat, hands raw from washing soda, abandoned the stone sink at one side of the kitchen to retrieve the fallen pans.

'And get a move on. If we're late by a minute according to that pocket watch of his, Mr Trewarren will make sure there's all hell to pay and I— good grief!' A short, wiry little woman emerged from the steam. 'Mr Lance. What on earth has happened?'

The cacophony of plates and spoons fell silent around them. The hapless maid shrieked, the copper milk pan clattering onto the stone slabs in the silence. 'Oh my lord, she's dead.'

'Nonsense. If you haven't anything better to offer, Daisy, make sure those pans are clean. And the rest of you, back to your work.'

'I'm sorry, Cook,' said Lance. 'I didn't know what else to do. She needs warmth, and quickly.'

'She's soaked through!'

'There was an accident. She fell into the river. If it hadn't been for Miss Pearce here, heaven knows what would have happened.'

'Of course.' Mrs Tims beckoned to Daisy, who looked as if she was still convinced it was a corpse resting in Lance's arms and was rapidly going green round the gills. 'Get as much water as you can on to boil.' Daisy's eyes widened further. 'Oh, for goodness sake, you silly child, of course Miss Clara's not having a baby. This is a respectable household. She's just so cold her blood is in danger of freezing. We need to get her warm.'

'Yes, Mrs Tims.' Reassured, Daisy set to with surprising speed and efficiency, as if boiling pans of water was an occupation she knew all too well. Cook pushed a chair next to the range as close as it would go, and Lance set Clara down. She roused slightly in the warmth, shivering violently.

'She needs dry clothes Mr Lance,' said Mrs Tims, in a no-nonsense manner.

'Yes, of course. I ought to fetch Mama.'

'I rather think you should. I'll make sure no one here says anything, so you can keep it from Mr Trewarren, but your mother needs to know.'

'Yes, of course.' He glanced uncertainly towards Hester. He was a little older than his sister, with the same regular features and startlingly blue eyes. Hester hardened her heart. He might have the appearance of kindness while he was still worried how close his sister had come to death, but there was no point in relying on it. Flim-flammery, as Gran always said, only ever led to trouble, and these days, Hester had quite enough trouble keeping the increasingly insistent attentions of Jimmy Harkness, which at least included marriage in its rather dubious mix, at bay.

'Don't worry about Miss Pearce, Mr Lance, we'll look after her here. She can stay in the warmth. Although I suspect she might be in need of dry clothing as well.'

'I'm drier already,' said Hester quickly. 'I didn't get very wet.' She had an uneasy feeling that Mrs Tims, who was not the kind of woman you could easily disobey, was about to insist she strip to her underclothes there and then, to expose the shamefully patched and shabby state of her petticoats to the stares of the maids, not to mention the holes in her boots.

'Well, you look wet through to me, dear. I'm sure Mrs Trewarren wouldn't want to hear that the saviour of her daughter had been repaid by catching her death. I'm sure we can find something for you.'

'I'll find Mama,' muttered Lance, scarlet-cheeked at this sudden feminine turn of conversation, fleeing hastily through an inner door.

As Daisy filled a bowl with steaming water, Hester undid Clara's sodden boots.

'Ow,' muttered Clara, as they eased her feet into the warmth. Her eyes opened.

'Is it too hot?'

'It's lovely. I thought it was the sea.'

A faintly worried frown appeared on Mrs Tims's face. 'You're in the kitchens, miss. At home.'

'I'll be late for dinner. That always makes Papa cross. I hate dinners.'

'I think you'll be safe from that this evening, Miss Clara. Now, you keep talking to Miss Pearce, and we'll have a hot cup of tea with you in a minute. Just don't let her wander in her mind,' she added under her breath, as she vanished back into the steam of cooking, roaring orders as she went.

'You'll be warm in a bit.' Hester smiled and rubbed the chilled hands. Steam was rising from Clara's wet skirts, mingling with the almost equal amounts from her own. She was beginning to feel the deep cold of the river settling in her stomach, reaching tendrils into the very core of her being. Heaven knows what it must be doing to Clara, who had been totally immersed in the freezing waters and was not accustomed to being out in all weathers, hardened to the wind and the rain. Living so close to the shore, she'd seen grown men, who had worked the river all their lives, pulled alive from the water only to succumb to the cold that had chilled every part of them, stopping their hearts despite every warmth that could be applied.

'Hester, isn't it? Pearce the ferryman's daughter?' She looked up to find Mrs Tims had returned from restoring order to her domain, with a couple of blankets in her arms.

'Yes.' Hester pulled the proffered blanket around her, pride attempting to keep her teeth from chattering as she continued to rub Clara's hands.

'I thought it must be. I knew your mother. We worked together for a while in a hotel in St Ives. We were the only two women there. Most of the men didn't like it, but your mother was the best there was, and M. Alphonse knew it, so there was nothing they could do. There were plenty of visitors who tried to persuade her to work for them. One family offered her a post as cook in one of the finest houses in London. If she'd taken it up, she might have been cooking for royalty.'

'Mum didn't tell us that!'

'That would be to save your father's pride, my dear. Men, you'll find, don't like it when their wives are cleverer than they are.'

'Oh,' said Hester. A vision of Jimmy Harkness's narrow face, with the sentimental gaze that declared he would wrap her up and cosset her, and keep her from worry until the end of time, floated in front of her.

Mrs Tims sighed. 'Your mother truly had a magic touch. I'd have given my eye teeth for her recipes for preserves and chutneys. I can never quite get them the same, and then with it being so hard to get staff nowadays, there isn't the time. Mr Trewarren insists we buy in all this newfangled canned and pre-made things in jars. He likes to show them off. Some of them come all the way from America, you know. They might be fancy, but they are not the same.'

'Mum could make anything taste delicious at home,' said Hester wistfully. She felt guilty at the thought of Dad sitting alone in the cottage with Robbie and Alice, who would have returned from school to find no stew on the stove, and no ferry boat returned to the jetty. She hated the thought of them all cold and hungry and fearing the worst. She dreaded even more the thought of Dad searching high and low and finally finding her hiding place for the rent money, not to be touched even if there was nothing but a half-rotten cabbage and a bit of stale bread to still their hunger.

But there was nothing she could do about that now. She had to hope someone had seen what had happened and let them know that she and the ferry boat were safe. As for the rent money – at least she had yesterday's earnings safe, and she'd just have to face that problem when she came to it.

Hester touched the precious coins in her pocket. She had seen the humiliation in Dad's eyes when he had first returned from hospital to find that he was no longer the one in charge of the family's finances. She knew it still grated that, instead of choosing how much money to put on the table each evening, he was now the one waiting for, of all things, a daughter, to hand over the price of a pint, stretching only to two on a Friday if all the essential bills could be paid.

Personally, Hester would rather have put the amount towards a visit to the second-hand clothes shops in Hayle, to find a warm winter coat for Alice and serviceable boots for Robbie. But Dad without his regular visits to the Fisherman's Arms was like a bear with a sore head, and impossible to live with. She understood why Mum had never begged him not to go, even when they had been desperate. It wasn't worth the trouble. Besides, with Dad being in control of the family's finances, he'd had the power to punish Mum, if he chose, by handing over even less.

Dad wanted that control back. It hadn't been so bad when he first came home, but over the last six months it had become increasingly obvious. It was now an uneasy niggle at the back of her head. He'd developed that same way of talking to her he'd used with Mum, as if she were a slightly foolish child who needed protecting, a fragile creature, who knew little of the world and was certainly incapable of understanding its devious ways.

It was always worse when he rolled back from the Fisherman's Arms, with more than one pint inside him, however few coins he'd had in his pocket earlier that evening. He was never violent, just full of himself and his opinions. That was the lure of the Fisherman's Arms, even more than the beer; it was an exclusively masculine space to hold forth and be listened to, the other men nodding away in agreement. There were few who would openly argue with Robert Pearce. Grumble behind their hands when he wasn't looking, maybe even laugh. But, these days, their neighbours' natural urge to stay out of trouble was tinged with pity.

There was no doubt about it, however much she tried to push it out of her mind. Dad wanted the control of his household back, and over the last few months he'd convinced himself he'd found a way. He hadn't said anything, least of all to her, about who was to be the agent of his restored pride. At first she hoped she'd imagined it, and in the relentless busyness of her life she had been able to put the thought to one side. But not tonight, not from the distance of the Trewarrens' house across the river, when life itself had so nearly been taken from her, and the preciousness of simply breathing was tingling with the warming blood flowing through her veins.

Dad saw reliance on a daughter as humiliating, a lessening of his manhood. Reliance on a son-in-law, particularly one who would, in turn, be reliant on his instruction and his expertise, would restore the natural order of things. Her feelings on the matter were irrelevant. Dad and Jimmy Harkness were going to organise the world as it suited them and nothing she could say would make any difference.

Well, if either of them thought she was just going to roll over for their convenience, they had another think coming.

'Mrs Tims—' A slightly built woman with mousy hair greying at the temples swept through the kitchen, resplendent in an emerald-green evening gown, careless of the dangers of flour to her satin hem. 'Good grief!'

Hester jumped to her feet. The woman was staring at her as if she had seen a ghost.

'This is Miss Pearce, ma'am,' said Mrs Tims. 'The young woman who saved Miss Clara's life.'

'Yes. Yes of course.' Mrs Trewarren had turned as white as a sheet. 'I didn't make the connection when Lance told me. You are the image of your mother when she was young.'

'Yes, ma'am.' It didn't take much to recognise Mrs Trewarren as the woman on Porthgwidden beach.

Mrs Trewarren turned away, gathering up Clara in her arms. 'Clara, my dearest. What's this Lance has been telling me? What on earth have you been doing?'

'Nothing, Mama,' said Clara, in a small, but determined voice. Then her face crumpled and she held on tight to her mother as she knelt down beside her, green satin billowing over the tiles. 'I'm so sorry, Mama. I didn't mean to. I really didn't. I just couldn't bear Ralph to think I didn't care for him, I didn't think. Is Papa very cross?'

'There's no need to bother your father with this. We shall tell him you have one of your sick headaches and have gone to bed. Tilly is building a fire up in your room. We'll have you warm in no time.'

'Hester,' muttered Clara, trying to push herself up from the chair.

'It's all right, my dear. Lance explained. The maids are preparing a guest room for Miss Pearce, and we've found some dry clothes. Now, if you feel you can walk...' However hard she tried, Clara was still too weak to rise from the chair. Hester took her free arm, raising her to her feet.

'I'll help you take her upstairs, if you wish, Mrs Trewarren.'

'There really is no need, Miss Pearce.'

Mrs Tims snorted. 'I rather think there is, Mrs Trewarren. I don't know how else you are going to get Miss Clara upstairs before Mr Trewarren has finished dressing for dinner.'

'I— Very well. If you wouldn't mind, Miss Pearce. Mr Trewarren is very punctual about meal times, and I'm afraid the remainder of the staff are rather preoccupied.'

'Not at all,' said Hester. Mrs Trewarren could think what she liked. This was not her idea, and she had no intention of ever coming back to trouble them. So Violet Trewarren could think she was a spy for a gang of ruffians, or was trying to worm her way into Lance's heart (or rather his pockets), all she liked. That's how rich people always thought about the poor, she told herself with a sniff, and there was no point in trying to change their minds. Once dawn came, she would never have to see any of them again.

'Lance is speaking to Mrs Leavan,' said Mrs Trewarren. 'By telephone,' she added, to Hester's startled look. 'Mrs Leavan has had a telephone installed for the convenience of her guests. I'm sure she'll send one of her boys to explain things to your father, Miss Pearce, and take some food over, so none of them has to go hungry tonight.'

'Thank you,' murmured Hester.

'It's the least I could do,' returned Mrs Trewarren, with chilly severity. 'Under the circumstances.'

Charming. At least Mrs Trewarren ignored her as they supported Clara between them, allowing Hester to focus on her immediate problems. She could only hope that the local grapevine meant that Mr Bolsover had also heard enough of the nature of her temporary disappearance not to trouble Dad.

She tried not to think that Dad, even if he didn't find her hiding place, was quite likely to seek solace for the near-loss of his daughter within the Fisherman's Arms, promising her earnings when she returned in lieu of payment and taking any pint offered in sympathy. There were occasions when Dad's troublesome pride could become mysteriously absent.

Hester suppressed a sigh. What with that, and the need to repay Mrs Leavan (who, as a woman on her own, couldn't be expected to offer boundless charity) for any food she sent to the family for tonight, the few additional coins she had earned that day, which, only hours ago, she had so proudly marked as a buffer against a bad week, were already promised away. It was always the same, every time she thought she had got ahead. However long she worked, however hard she tried, she could never win. Maybe Dad was right after all, and her natural optimism was simply the product of inexperience, and good things didn't happen to people like them.

She had to hang on to some hope, however small. Besides, she'd rather die an old maid than walk down the aisle with the narrow-faced, self-absorbed solution Dad had selected to restore his own standing in their little hamlet. She had an uneasy feeling that particular solution was currently providing Dad with all the pints and shows of deference he desired, in the cause of hurrying on his ambition to sneak himself into the ferry business.

'Well bugger that,' she muttered under her breath, as she helped Clara up the last few stairs towards the bedrooms.

Chapter Eleven

Once they reached the landing, two maids appeared to help Clara to her room, while a third, referred to as 'Sanders' by Mrs Trewarren, swept Hester away to a small bedroom on the floor above. As the door opened, the warmth hit her like a delicious wall. She did her best not to stare in amazement at the fire roaring away in the grate as if coal was rapidly going out of fashion.

'Oh, my lord.' Her eyes rested on the large bath set in front of the fire. One of the girls she had seen scrubbing dishes in the kitchens with Daisy was pouring a pitcher of hot water into the tub, before being instantly shooed off to fetch more. 'It's really not necessary. I'm not cold, not any more.'

'Mrs Trewarren's orders,' said Sanders, her eyes resting pointedly on Hester's patched and less than pristine skirt.

'But they've got so much to do already.' Inside, she was curling up with embarrassment. She'd recognised several of the kitchen maids from school. The one with the pitcher had even been in the same class until she'd left to go into service. Local gossip had a tendency to be liberal with the truth, and she'd never live it down if it got back to their families that she had demanded they wait on her hand and foot, as if she was Queen Mary herself. Not to mention the humiliating rags, mostly beyond patching, that passed for her drawers.

Sanders shrugged. 'As you please. I don't have time to wait on you. Put your clothes on the chair for washing. There's a nightdress of Miss Clara's on the bed. I take it you know how to use soap?'

'Of course I bloody know how to use soap,' snapped Hester indignantly. The kitchen maid appearing with the next pitcher of water collapsed into hiccups, almost sending the container flying.

'Indeed.' Sanders had refined contempt to its highest art form. 'Don't take too long. Mr and Mrs Trewarren have guests this evening. The staff have quite enough to do, without being expected to undertake additional duties.'

Hester bit her lip and allowed Sanders to sweep out in triumph.

'D'you need any help?' It was the kitchen maid, passing with the empty water pitcher dangling from one hand.

'No, thank you. I can manage. Really.'

'Don't worry about Sanders. She's only put out because she thinks she should be promoted to Miss Clara's personal maid and she ain't having it. I don't blame her, neither, even though we're the ones who catch it.' She gave a conspiratorial wink. 'And I'll make sure me and Daisy is in charge of washing your things. Most of them here don't know what it's like. I've seen you row the ferry. There's not one of them could do that, and cook and clean and everything else, too. Certainly not Mr Trewarren, mean-tempered old bugger that he is.'

'Thanks.'

'Put them just inside the door once you've undressed, then I can grab them. They don't care how we see them, but I'm not flaunting my bits and pieces in front of no one. And they think us village girls have no pride.'

Hester hastily stifled a laugh. As the maid's footsteps faded into the distance, her body relaxed. The luxury of a hot bath, with the water freshly drawn, just for her and only her, was irresistible. At home, baths meant a weekly splash in a small tin bath, with the water grubby, and at best lukewarm, by the time it had been used by Dad, followed by her brother and sister, with the remaining water used for soaking clothes ready for washday.

The feeling of hot water on her skin as she stepped in a little gingerly and sank down so it surrounded her was wonderful. It almost felt as if she was floating. She scrubbed every bit of skin and hair, trying not to notice the grime.

When the water finally began to cool, she regretfully climbed out, drying herself with a towel that looked as if it had barely ever been used. The nightdress also looked barely worn. It was soft, with delicate lace at the collar and at the end of each sleeve. She breathed in deep. It smelt of soap and washing lines. Not even when Mum was alive had she ever smelt anything quite so clean. A woollen shawl had been left draped over one of the bedposts. She pulled it around her and explored the open door at the far side, which led into a small sitting room, where a fire had also been set, with a table laid out with a plate of meat and vegetables.

Hester forgot to feel guilty at being waited on, even by an invisible hand, and made short work of the dinner, followed by the generous dish of steamed pudding and custard.

By the time she had finished her meal, the bath had been cleared away and her clothes had vanished.

'You all right?' whispered Daisy, putting her head round the door.

'Thank you. I've never felt so clean, or so full.'

'Mrs Trewarren has left orders for you to be left to sleep and not be disturbed.' She pointed upwards. 'Me and Katy and Tilly are right above you, at the top of the stairs. Come and ask if you need anything.'

'I can't imagine needing anything, ever again.'

Daisy grinned and vanished.

A moment before, Hester had barely been able to keep her eyes open, but now, despite the bone weariness of her body, her mind would not let her think of sleep. She curled herself up on the window seat, wrapping the shawl around her bare feet. Her hair was nearly dry, the salt that never left it these days gone, so that it was soft to the touch.

It felt strange, slightly unnerving even, to be here on her own, in an entire suite of rooms that, even if it was for only one night, were for her sole use. There was no one at her elbow, no calls for her to do this, that, and the other. There was no need to step in to break up an argument between Robbie and Alice, or keep an eye out for when Dad might be getting tired and crotchety and it was time to bundle them off to bed.

Now she knew Mrs Leavan was sending over food for Dad and the children, and so no longer needed to worry that they were going cold and hungry, she could luxuriate in having no dinner to cook, no dishes to be washed. No fire to be carefully built up to save coal, and no clothes to be mended, however exhausted she was after a day taking the ferry to and fro across the estuary.

So this was what it meant to be rich. Her belly felt pleasantly round and full, rather than its usual half-emptiness, always craving more, but knowing that the others needed to be fed. She was clean and warm, and, most of all, she had nothing she had to do. Nothing. Her body was for once free, as was her mind.

She hardly remembered a day since Mum died when she hadn't been rushing about, working out how to get the money together for the rent, whether she could afford bacon bits to add taste to the stew, whether it would be possible to get Robbie some second-hand boots to replace the ones he was rapidly growing out of, so he could continue to go to school.

Her eyes closed, savouring the stillness. 'This is what I want,' she said aloud. She had no hankering to be waited on like a queen, as she had been this evening. She just didn't want to spend her life as a drudge, the one who got up first, who went to bed last. The invisible hand who did the cleaning and the cooking and the mending, along with the juggling of a meagre budget, the conjuring up of meals out of the barest of essentials.

Most of all, she didn't want to wake up in the middle of the night in a blind panic of the impossibility of finding enough to get through the next week, and what would happen if no one used the ferry, and the abyss of no money coming in at all opening up under her feet.

Hester hugged her knees tight. People like the Trewarrens thought the poor were lazy or stupid, or lacked skills, courage and ingenuity. They had no idea that working all hours just to make ends meet left no time or energy to better yourself, and how could anyone with a conscience dare to risk investing in a business that might fail, when they barely had enough money to survive from week to week and it was their families who would be cast out on the streets. And it wasn't just that. It was being told again and again that such things were beyond you. Not for people like you. It was almost impossible to defy the world when it felt ranged against you.

Ever since Dad's accident, her mind, like the rest of the women she knew, had been so busy on just the matter of surviving that day, she didn't have time to think of that dream of learning the skills to start her own cafe, to become skilled and respected and mistress of her fate. And to have this tranquillity even if it was only for a few hours each day.

She would never push away the memory of this evening,

she determined, with its simple pleasures and its freedom of peace and quiet. She didn't care about satin dresses, or the finest necklaces and earrings. Not unless they were hers to sell, that is.

In her mind, she could see clearly the cafe on Porthgwidden beach, where Mum had once dreamt of creating her own independence. She wasn't going to lose sight of it again. She didn't know how she was going to do it, she didn't even care, but one day, however long it took, she was going to find a way to buy that cafe and make it her own. She would own it, not rent it, so she would never have to dread the knock of the rent man, ever again. It would be a place where she could sit in peace and quiet of an evening and just be her. A place where she had food enough to be satisfied, a comfortable bed, and coal to stay warm even when the frost froze every grass in the hedgerow and ice reached out over the shallows of the river.

There was only one way to achieve all that. It would take money. More money than she could earn with the ferry. However hard she tried, that was barely enough to keep them fed and a roof over their heads, and left them just a sprained wrist, or bad fever, away from disaster. If she was going to fulfil her dream, she would have to find another way.

She wasn't going to marry into money. She didn't know how, and she could never look delicate, or even particularly clean. Besides, as far as she could see, Mrs Trewarren had to kowtow to her husband as much as Mum had had to keep Dad happy, because they were the ones bringing in the money. Mrs Trewarren even seemed to be a little afraid of her husband.

No, the only way was to be able to make her fortune herself. There had to be a way. Wasn't it what Mum had been telling her all along? That she needed to learn a skill, one that people wanted and not many could do, or not to such a high standard, and so people with money would pay. She didn't know if M. Alphonse would still be prepared to train her after all this time. She didn't even know if he was still alive or not.

'Rosa Lewis,' she whispered, her breath forming like mist on the windowpane. Mum had kept a cutting from the newspaper, about the woman who had risen from nothing to be a cook to royalty, and had made a fortune. Hester had found the faded page tucked into the back of Mum's recipe book, like a talisman, keeping faith with a dream she had never quite let go. As exhaustion finally enveloped her, Hester found the old fire back in her belly.

She crawled between the sheets of the comfortable bed and was asleep within minutes.

Chapter Twelve

Early the following morning, Hester crept downstairs into the kitchen, where bleary-eyed maids were already stoking up the range, ready to cook breakfast.

Her own clothes had been returned to her before she woke, clean and dry and with even the gap where the material had given way as she pulled Clara over the side so neatly mended you would not have thought it there at all. Her boots were still a little stiff, but they had also been cleaned and a skilled hand had sewn up the parting seams and polished them until they shone.

'You going then?' said Daisy, bringing a basketful of eggs from the larder.

'I need to get to the ferry as soon as I can.'

'There'll be no one around yet. We won't hear the last of it if Mrs Trewarren finds you've left without being given breakfast.'

Hester opened her mouth to say she wasn't hungry. She wanted above all things to avoid meeting the family again. Last night they had been grateful, but she wasn't quite sure how they might react to their unexpected guest this morning, and she'd no desire to bump into Mr Trewarren. If he'd been kept in the dark about his daughter's escapade, heaven knows what he would think she was doing in the house. Of course, he might assume she was just another maid, but if he didn't, she had no wish to guess the right answers to awkward questions.

On the other hand, despite having eaten a substantial meal last night, she was ravenous, and the smell of bacon sizzling at her elbow was enough to send any woman weak at the knees. As she hesitated, she was gestured to the nearest chair, a cup of tea appearing in front of her, as Katy and Tilly continued the rush of preparations for the family's breakfast.

A little while later, she said her thanks and slipped out of the kitchen door, to make good her escape along the little side path and the anonymity of the river front.

'Miss Pearce!' She had only taken a few steps when Lance appeared.

'Good morning, Mr Trewarren.'

'Are you leaving so soon?'

'My passengers will expect me to be on the other side at this hour of the morning. I need to get the ferry back as soon as possible.'

'I see. Only I thought you might join us. I'm sure Clara would love to thank you properly before you go.'

'Is she well enough to get out of bed?' She must be of a stronger constitution than she looked.

'Dr Graham advised against her getting up, but Clara is perfectly determined.' He gave a wry grimace. 'I'm afraid my sister is as stubborn as they come. And headstrong. But I'm sure she'll take care not to risk her own life, and that of others, in future.'

'Good. She scared me good and proper.'

'But you still went after her.'

'Yes, well, I wasn't thinking. I'm sorry, Mr Trewarren, but I need to get back to my boat.'

'I'll walk with you, if I may? You may need help. It's the least I can do.'

She hesitated, torn between offending him and the embarrassment of the gossip that would race around the hamlet and the market in Hayle for weeks, if not months. She'd be the deluded creature who had dared set her cap at a Trewarren, and we all know where that would end. She'd no wish to have her neighbours sniggering behind her back. She was grateful that any necessity of a reply was prevented by the appearance of Mrs Trewarren, making her way down the front steps in a grey walking dress and coat, walking cane at the ready.

'This is most fortunate, Miss Pearce. Cook told me you were eager to return to your boat. I'm on my way to take my morning stroll. Perhaps you would be so good as to let me accompany you?'

'Yes, of course, Mrs Trewarren.'

'Lance, your father is asking for you. I would be grateful if you could keep him company until breakfast.'

Lance opened his mouth to demur, but his mother sent him a forbidding look very difficult to disobey. Hester tactfully suppressed a grin. Mrs Trewarren clearly had worries of her own about the possibilities of gossip.

'Yes, of course, Mama. Thank you again, Miss Pearce, for your help yesterday, and I hope your boat is unharmed.'

'Thank you, Mr Trewarren. It's survived worse.'

Lance disappeared back inside, leaving Mrs Trewarren to fall into step beside Hester. The two walked in silence along the promenade until they reached the steps down to the beach. To her relief, Hester could see that the ferry was still there, surrounded by several fishermen, deep in inspection of the strange craft that had appeared overnight. At least one of them drank with Dad in the Fisherman's Arms on occasion, which meant she had a chance of persuading them to help her push it out into deeper water, even if it did cost her a large part of yesterday's earnings in beer.

'That seems very cumbersome for a young girl to row,' remarked Mrs Trewarren as they came to a halt.

'It's no trouble. Not once you get used to it.'

'Hmm.' Mrs Trewarren appeared lost in thought.

'I must go. I need to get down to the ferry before it begins to float.'

'Just one moment.' Mrs Trewarren removed a small velvet bag from her pocket, thrusting it hastily into Hester's hands, as if she could barely endure its touch. 'For you.'

The bag was heavy. Even a quick glimpse revealed more money inside than Hester had ever seen in her life. 'I don't need to be paid.'

'None the less, I trust you will accept.'

Hester glanced at the set face. Mrs Trewarren appeared to have shrunk since the day she had met her and Mum on Porthgwidden beach. There were hollows beneath her eyes and tight lines indented the flesh either side of her mouth. Not even the finely woven wool of her coat could disguise the rounding of the thin shoulders, as if, in the intervening years, she had turned in on herself.

Was this really just to stop the story of Clara's unlady-like recklessness from getting out? Mrs Trewarren abruptly turned her head away, the feathers of her hat obscuring her expression.

That day on Porthgwidden beach, Mrs Trewarren had been so very insistent on bribing her with ice cream to get her out of earshot. Hester searched her memory for the snippets of conversation she had overheard. The words hadn't made much sense at the time, but she remembered the tone of their voices. Something about the cafe and a new chance, a new life. Mrs Trewarren persuading, Mum refusing. Mrs

Trewarren sounding so very bitter, Mum digging her heels in, despite the expression of longing on her face.

Hester knew in her bones that Mum would have jumped at an opportunity to work in a professional kitchen again, instead of the drudgery of cleaning for Mrs Leavan, even if it had meant waiting until the baby was old enough and only for a few hours a week. But her refusal had been so very final.

That meant Mum hadn't trusted Mrs Trewarren. Hester felt sure Mum would tell her to hand back the purse and walk away. But she wasn't Mum. And how else was she ever going to be able to gather enough money together to follow her dreams?

'Thank you,' she muttered, shoving the purse deep inside her pocket. Mrs Trewarren nodded and strode back towards the house, walking cane beating out a rapid staccato on the pavement.

Hester watched her for a moment, with a faint sense of unease. Then she hurried as fast as she could towards the ferry, calling loudly to the fishermen, as the far end of the boat began to rock in the encroaching tide.

Chapter Thirteen

Clara watched from the bedroom as her mother and Hester made their way along the promenade towards the ferry.

'She's already left,' she said to Lance, as he joined her. 'I didn't have a chance to thank her.'

'I'm sure Miss Pearce will understand.' Lance, for some reason, was looking slightly out of sorts, his usual good humour ruffled. 'She had to leave early to get to the ferry before the tide rose.'

'Oh.' Clara bit her lip. 'But I can't not thank her. Hester saved my life. I don't want her to think I don't care.'

'Then I'll take you in the Ford, if you like, when you are feeling better.'

'I'm feeling well enough now.'

'Clara—'

'I'm not in the least fragile, you know. When I stayed in France with cousin Térèse we climbed the Pyrenees. It was wonderful. And I didn't get tired or feel faint once.'

'I can well imagine. I've played tennis with you, remember? I've seen you chase down every ball, however hopeless. You never give up, and you are always determined to win.'

'Is that so very bad of me?'

'Of course not.'

'But you're my brother. No one else thinks like that. Except for Ralph. The young men Papa invites to meet me don't approve at all. They expect me to watch from the sidelines and just applaud, not beat them.'

'I'm afraid Papa doesn't have a young woman's taste in men.'

'But don't you see? That's why I fell in love with Ralph. He didn't mind me beating him at tennis, and he didn't feel sorry for me when he won. We were made for each other. Papa only looks down on him because his father's in trade and Ralph is being trained up to run the family hotels. Ralph has so many ideas, he doesn't just want to take over the Belleview Hotel when his father retires, he wants to expand and set up hotels in Europe. He loves the idea of setting one up in Switzerland, to cater especially for English guests. So many people, men and women, go walking there nowadays. It's such a good idea. And he doesn't mind me helping him. I need to be busy, Lance. I can't just sit around trying to look pretty. I'd love to help manage a hotel.'

'Are you sure he was serious?'

'Of course. Why wouldn't he be?'

'Dearest, young men will say all kinds of things when they are in love. Take it from me, I've promised the most reckless things. Fortunately, so far no young lady has been foolish enough to test whether I would make them good after we were married.'

'Of course you would. Dear Lance, you are so horribly honourable. You'd always do exactly what you promised. Anyhow, you're a hopeless liar.'

'Don't remind me. Papa won't take it that I'll never make a good diplomat.' He gave a wry grin. 'And he certainly won't ever accept I'd rather be a professor of classics or a poet.'

Clara kissed his cheek affectionately. 'Well then, my dear, you'll just have to find a girl who's rich enough to support you both, and then you won't need your allowance and you won't have to do what Papa says. I'm sure you'll make a splendid poet.'

'Thank you, but easier said than done. And I'm not sure there are many young ladies who would agree with your plan.'

'Only the ones worthy of you.'

'I'll remind you of that when the time comes,' he replied, colouring slightly. Clara glanced at him curiously, remembering the tones of admiration when he described Hester's actions last night. An idea was forming in her head. 'Lance—'

'Come on,' he said hastily. 'I'll take you for a drive before Mama comes back. We can always say you needed a bit of fresh air.'

'And Ralph?'

'I'm not promising anything, he may refuse to see us.'

'I don't care. At least he'll know that I tried, and that I wasn't just a milksop who gave him up, simply because Papa told him he was never, ever, to come near me again.'

'I'm sure Ralph is sensible enough to know that already.'

'But I have to make sure. I couldn't bear the thought he'd forgotten me, because he thought I was weak and foolish.'

'Make sure you wear your warmest coat,' said Lance, 'or we'll never hear the last of it.'

Clara sat back against the leather of the Ford, watching the fields fly by as Lance followed the path of the estuary inland towards Hayle.

Her anxiety had eased a little, now she was going to be able to speak to Ralph. He did love her, she knew it, but she had to see it in his eyes, especially after Papa had been so high-handed, and so pointedly remarked that Clive St John (who might be a third son, but was still the son of a lord) had been most attentive, implying he'd practically fallen on his knees the last time he had been invited for dinner.

Clara had been so angry, it was only Lance treading hard on her foot that had stopped her from yelling that it was a lie and Clive had done no such thing, and never would, especially if someone prettier and richer came along.

She wasn't an idiot. She knew she wasn't naturally pretty, and wrestling her hair into curls and her waist into the impossible eighteen inches of Mama's girlhood, seemed utterly pointless. Besides, anyone who lived in the same house as her, let alone shared the same bed, was bound to notice she had neither, so why pretend? However hard she tried, she fidgeted with boredom during Papa's interminable dinners, longing to escape before even half the obligatory eleven courses (of which she was supposed to take only a mouthful of each) had been set down in front of her.

Worse still, she would sometimes follow the men's conversation too closely, putting in a remark without thinking. Whatever she said was always ignored, as if she hadn't spoken at all, but she knew it had given her a reputation as a bluestocking and a wife a man might not find the most comforting of angels of the hearth to return to after a long day keeping the Empire from running riot and being overrun by heathens and cannibals.

The bald truth was, if it wasn't for Papa's money, none of the young men obediently following their mamas' instructions to sit next to her would have looked at her twice. Which was where Ralph had been so splendid, appearing with Lance one afternoon to make up the numbers for tennis. He had turned out not to be stuffy at all, but had listened and laughed and hadn't minded when her hair flew wildly round her head as she ran, and she'd argued that the French weren't all weak-willed and cowards, and she'd met plenty who were quite as brave as any Englishman when she'd stayed with her cousins in Paris. He'd even spoken

French with her, candidly admitting her fluency left him far behind. She'd never met anyone quite like him, and she was convinced she never would again. This was her one chance of happiness, and no one, not even Papa, was going to stop her.

It was only once they had crossed the bridge at Hayle, and drew up in front of a modest town house on the other side of the estuary, that her courage began to fail. Perhaps Ralph would refuse to see her. Perhaps he had already heard of her escapade last evening and decided that she was a hysteric and not the kind of wife he wanted at his side, after all. Why, oh why was she always so impetuous? Perhaps she ought to make an effort to be more ladylike, after all.

But, after waiting a short while in the Ford while Lance went inside, relief flooded through her as Ralph appeared.

'Come on,' said Lance, as Ralph slipped into the rear seat and they shot off again, heading for a small park. There, Lance discreetly retrieved a picnic blanket and folding chair from the boot, and settled down with book, leaving Clara and Ralph to walk down the footpath to the lake.

'You're not cross?' said Clara, as they emerged out of earshot.

'With you, my darling? How could I be?'

'But Papa was perfectly horrid to you. I was so worried you might never want to see me again.'

'Of course I want to see you again.' He squeezed her hand. 'I know you are not your father, my love. He's only trying to protect you. With such a difference between us, I can understand him suspecting me of being a money-digger.'

'Then you are much nicer than me,' said Clara gloomily, 'especially as he doesn't mind the ones who really are only after me for my money.'

'But perhaps in those cases there is also something in it for him?'

'Ouch. Yes, you are quite right. An introduction to King George and the hope of a peerage. For him, not me. Is that a very mean thing to say?'

'Not if it's true.'

Clara laughed, her body relaxing. 'I wish everyone was as honest as you, instead of being so polite and keeping on pretending.'

'Possibly not.' He risked tucking her arm into his. 'The world might be a bit uncomfortable if there was no pretence at all.'

'Maybe.' She tightened her arm, aware that this time was so precious and just wanting to be with him, breathing him in, rather than discussing anything at all. 'I'll wait for you.'

'Clara, dear Clara, I don't want you to waste your life away, and I can see the pressure you're under at home. The last thing I want is to cause you pain.'

'But I want to wait until you are in a position to set up your own hotel in Switzerland for walking parties and sight-seers, just as you always planned. Then we can escape and earn enough between us to live on and it won't matter what our families, or anyone else, might think.' She glanced at him, uncertainty back again. 'If you don't mind Papa cutting me off and not giving me anything at all, that is.'

'Of course not. All I want is a reasonably comfortable life and a sense of purpose. I'm not ambitious for riches. But I want you to be happy, too.' He walked in silence for a while. 'I only worry that you are accustomed to having so much – I don't want to be a disappointment.'

'You could never be a disappointment!' The fear came sweeping back. Maybe he had changed his mind after that bruising encounter with Papa. Perhaps Lance had told him of her recklessness and he thought her too unhinged to be his wife and this was his way of saying goodbye. Terror shot through her, with a terrible sense of isolation.

'What I mean is, Clara, that you are used to having your house here, and one in London, and visits to your family in Paris. Life with me wouldn't be at all like that. Not that we are poor,' he added hastily. 'We're nothing like it. But we have to work hard and guard our money. If you and I set up our own hotel in Switzerland, it would be the same for us. It wouldn't be possible for us to spend months travelling around France and Italy, the things you are accustomed to doing.'

'That doesn't matter! I love spending time with Térèse, and I adored boating and swimming on Lake Geneva and walking in the Alps and the Pyrenees. They were the best things I've ever done. But don't you see, darling, that's because they meant I was free, and away from Papa and trying to fit in with his idea of what a lady should be? I do love him, but he is so unbearably stuffy, and he thinks things should be just as they were when the old Queen was alive and women shouldn't have ideas. He only lets me stay with Térèse because he thinks we spend all the time in Paris and I might become more sophisticated, and if I stay too long in London I might join the suffragettes and start burning down buildings.'

'You wouldn't do that, would you?'

'Of course not.' She gave him a mischievous grin. 'At least only your rival hotels.'

He laughed. 'Oh well, in that case...'

'Seriously, though.' She held him as tight as she dared without stopping the blood flow to his arm. 'You will let me wait for you? I don't want you to throw over your plans just so we can be together sooner, and get a tedious job as a clerk in an office, or anything like that. Something you'd really hate. I'll find a way of putting off Papa.'

'If you are sure.'

'Can you doubt me?'

Lance was deep in his book, face hidden despite technically still keeping them in view. Clara shivered in delicious anticipation as Ralph's arms came around her, his lips meeting hers, tongue flicking inside her mouth, sending a tingling sensation through her limbs, desire flooding through her.

'Never,' he whispered as he released her. 'Darling Clara, I can't imagine life without you.'

They stepped regretfully apart as a party of nannies, complete with monstrous black perambulators, emerged from the path between the trees and began to make their way towards the benches set alongside the lake. The sun was beginning to slant, signalling the encroaching of the afternoon. Their stolen time was over. Clara dragged herself unwillingly back to practicalities.

'I'll ask Térèse to invite me to stay with her in Paris. I'll tell Papa I want to finish my studies of French and German literature and music. I'll even enrol on a course in deportment. He won't say no if he thinks I'm acquiring accomplishments that will make me much more marriageable, and Térèse's family is well connected. He'll think I'm meeting all sorts of famous artists and French intellectuals and return very finished. And very quiet. By the time you have saved enough to start your hotel, I'm bound to be of age, and then no one can stop us. And if I'm not, we can always run away.' They began to make their way slowly back towards Lance, who was busying himself packing away the chair and blanket in the boot of the Ford with his back to them. 'It will mean we might not see each other for a year, or even more. You won't mind that, will you?'

'Of course not. At least, I'll mind. I'll miss you every hour

112

of the day, but it will be worth it to be with you for the rest of our lives.'

'And we can write.'

'Every day.'

'And when I'm in France, we're bound to visit my uncle's house in Geneva. I can find out all I can about guesthouses and hotels, and we can work out a way of having all the best people from England flocking to stay with us.'

'And meanwhile I'll learn everything I can from the Belleview, and helping with my father's other hotels, so our own is certain to be a success.'

'It will be wonderfully exciting, I know it will.' She held his hands, despite the nannies, now sitting on the bench and in full view. 'It will be worth being apart for a while. It's better than never, ever seeing you again.'

'Nothing will ever make me feel any different than I do now,' he replied, daring to brush his lips against hers. 'I swear it. I'll love you, dearest Clara, for as long as I live.'

All three of them were quiet as Lance drove them back, stopping only for Ralph to alight at a discreet distance from his home.

Clara fought back a sensation of intense loneliness, deep inside, feeling the chill of yesterday's plunge into the river, making her a little sick and dizzy. She wasn't ready to return home and the pretence of being quiet and cheerful and not at all hurt about never being able to see Ralph again, as far as her father was concerned.

She would write tonight to ask cousin Térèse to find her a convenient course on deportment and household management, and tell Papa she intended to stay only a few weeks. Once there, she would find a way to stay safely away from Papa's choice of suitors for as long as she needed. Térèse would understand. She was even more rebellious than Clara, throwing aside tight corsets and adopting the rational dress style as soon as they escaped to the open air and beauty of Geneva. Térèse had even been known to throw off her skirts to climb in her brother Pierre's cut-down trousers, although careful to hide them under a convenient rock so as not to cause too much outrage to the villagers once the walking party returned down to the quiet lushness of alpine meadows.

Clara roused herself. 'Can we see Hester? It isn't so far, is it? I want to thank her and this way no one at home need ever know.'

'With pleasure. If you are not too tired?'

'I'll have plenty of time to rest when we get home. Don't worry, I'll take to my bed for a week.'

'I'll believe that when I see it.' Lance took the next turning at speed, rushing along the winding lane, slowing only to allow a herd of cows being moved from one field to another to pass, followed by a farmer failing to hide his disapproval of these young people of today, and a slinking collie that appeared unsure of whether the Ford was also to be rounded up and kept from pausing to nibble the juiciest flowers lingering in the hedgerow.

Lance pulled into a convenient space near the Fisherman's Arms and they made their way towards the jetty.

'There, you see,' said Clara. 'Perfect timing. The ferry is making its way back.'

They waited among the small crowd gathering on the jetty, while Hester expertly manoeuvred the ferry alongside, one of the fishermen mending nets on the neighbouring wall stepping forward to help her with the rope, followed by the unloading of the human passengers and a somewhat reluctant goat.

'Thanks, Mick,' Hester called up to the fisherman, who

nodded in reply. She was, Clara noted guiltily, moving a little stiffly, flexing one arm as she followed her passengers onto dry land. She was smaller than Clara had thought, short and compact, face and arms browned with wind and weather, the low sun sending a gleam of copper through her auburn curls. She was younger than she'd imagined, too. She hadn't thought of the woman who had shown such bravery and skill, let alone sheer physical strength, being about her own age. It made Clara feel even more foolish, and very small.

'She's very pretty,' she said, having been too dazed and chilled to take a close look at her rescuer's face once they had arrived in Mrs Tim's kitchen. She only remembered it in the dusk, surrounded by the roar of the river, contorted with fear and effort.

'So she is,' replied Lance, sounding thoughtful.

Clara pushed through the crowd as Hester arrived on shore, hands on hips, breathing heavily. She looked, thought Clara, guilt rising again, pale beneath the brown of her skin and completely exhausted, rubbing her arm as if to dispel an ache.

'Hester!'

For a moment Hester's gaze was blank, then her face eased into a smile. 'Miss Trewarren. I'm sorry, I didn't recognise you.'

Clara blushed. 'I'm not surprised.' To her relief, Hester followed her, stepping away from the crowd of now curious onlookers.

'Mr Trewarren.'

'Miss Pearce. Good to meet you again.'

'I'm afraid I'll need to get back to the ferry in a minute.'

'I don't want to keep you, Hester,' said Clara quickly. 'I just wanted to thank you. I didn't have a chance last night, and you'd gone this morning, so I got Lance to bring me over.'

'There's no need to thank me.'

'Yes there is.' Clara grasped her hands. 'You saved my life. I was so stupid. I'm used to rowing boats, but on a lake, not a river. I should have known I wouldn't be strong enough to row across the estuary to see Ralph. I'm an utter fool.'

'It really doesn't matter, Miss Trewarren.'

'But it does. It always will. Every breath I breathe from now on is down to you. I'll never forget that. I'll be forever in your debt.'

'Clara,' said Lance gently. 'I think you are embarrassing Miss Pearce.'

'I don't mean to. I wish I could do things right. It's just, when I woke up this morning, I realised that I could have killed you, too. You risked your life to save mine. No one's ever done that for me before. It's the most splendid thing. It made me feel I need to do something special with my life, because every moment from now on is a gift.'

'I'm sure you will,' said Hester, with a smile.

'Now you think I'm an idiot.'

'Not at all. I'm just glad I was there. Although it might be better to use the ferry next time?'

'I will. I promise.' There was so much more she wanted to say, but didn't know how. Hester might be the same age, but she seemed infinitely older in strength and experience. Beside her, Clara felt like an untried child, cosseted and kept from the harsher realities of life. From Hester's clothes, she could see she must be very poor, and although she was strong, there wasn't an ounce of flesh on her. Clara thought of her own boredom and picking at the abundance of food each evening, let alone the extravagance of Papa's dinners, when so much must be thrown away. Her impatience with her life turned into something like disgust. Shame, even.

'I'm afraid I need to get back to the ferry.'

'Yes of course, Miss Pearce,' said Lance. 'We won't keep you. If there is anything we can do ...'

'There's no need.'

Lance was embarrassing Hester even more, Clara realised, with his open look of admiration, and even his wish to offer help. Something shifted inside. She could have kicked herself for bringing him here. What else were they but Lord and Lady Bountiful, displaying their fine clothes, and their motor vehicle that none of those around them could probably ever hope to have a ride in, let alone own? Lord and Lady Bountiful being gracious to a woman they would never normally have known existed, and so opening up Hester to gossip and questioning.

'Thank you,' she said. 'I won't forget.'

She watched as Hester wearily made her way back towards the ferry and the swelling crowd waiting to board. She'd had an impulse to persuade Lance to leave her to return home on the ferry, but now she was glad she hadn't even tried. She would only have embarrassed Hester further, and caused more gossip, and in the loud chatter and the banter flying between those boarding, there would have been no opportunity to continue a conversation.

'Come on,' said Lance gently, as if sensing her sadness. 'You look worn out. I'll take you home.'

'Yes,' she replied, scarcely hearing him. As they reached the Ford, Hester cast off again, wielding the oars as if they were nothing, sending the ferry back over the wide expanse of river.

'My life is so easy,' said Clara thoughtfully. 'I don't do anything useful.'

'You are a comfort to Mama.'

'But that's not useful. In the big wide world and the great scheme of things, that's not great deeds.'

'Is that what you want to do? Great deeds?'

'Yes. No. I don't know. I don't know what I want. I just know that I was born with enormous privilege. We're not like those people down there, just having to survive. And that means I ought to do something with all the time and the money I've been given. I swear, even if Ralph ever throws me over, I'm never going to be the wife of a rich man and host dinner parties.'

'Ralph won't throw you over. And anyhow, many women spend their time volunteering for charitable work, like Mama.'

'But that's not the same. That's just knitting and collecting money and proving how virtuous you are. I want to do something real.'

'Then, knowing you, I expect you'll find something,' said Lance, setting them off on the journey back.

'I know I will,' she replied firmly.

Chapter Fourteen

Evening was closing in around her later that day, as Hester finally tied up the ferry, and wearily made her way towards home.

She was aware of the curiosity that had been aroused by the unexpected appearance of a well-dressed couple in a motor vehicle addressing her as if they were on equal terms. She hadn't attempted to enlighten anybody for fear the story would soon find itself being embellished in every shop and at every street corner for miles around, turning rapidly into high drama of virtue lost (hers or Clara's, depending on the teller), and of those Pearces, who were a mouthy lot, letting the side down and getting ideas above their station.

Besides, the last thing she needed was for Dad to get wind of such a thing, especially when one of her visitors had been a more than personable young man, who could make the heart of a less level-headed girl flutter. Hester pushed the thought aside. She was too weary and bruised, and worried that the strained muscles in her shoulder might be even worse tomorrow, to consider a handsome face and a pair of understanding blue eyes. In any case, Gran would say, it was only flim-flammery, and best left well alone. Although not so easy once such understanding eyes have entered your mind.

As she reached the little hamlet, Hester paused to buy bread and the luxury of a few ounces of meat from Mrs Dowrick.

'You were missed.' She might have known he'd be waiting. As she set out again, she found Jimmy Harkness falling into step beside her.

'Missed?'

'You didn't come home last night. Your dad was worried.'

'I got a message to him as soon as I could. I was too late, that was all. I was caught on the other side. I was lucky to be given shelter for the night.'

'Oh?'

'I'll take care not to do that again,' she said, side-stepping the unspoken question.

'I'd have fetched you, Hester. I'd have found a way.'

'I was quite safe.'

'If you get stuck again, you only have to ask, you know. I'm great friends with the manager at Timson's, he lets me use any van whenever I need it.'

'Thank you,' murmured Hester, quickening her pace a little. She'd heard enough of Jimmy's boasting to recognise his promise as an empty one. For all his triumph when he had been taught to drive, Jimmy hadn't lasted long at Timson's. It was the lads whose families were in with old Mr Timson who were the only ones promoted to full-time drivers, he'd declared to anyone who'd listen. He wasn't going to stand for that, he had better fish to fry.

Whatever those particular fish might be, they hadn't made their appearance yet. Jimmy had moved from one position to the next, first with loud plans of rising to be an overseer at the National Explosive Works in Hayle, then as chief signalman for all the railways throughout Cornwall. The factory post had fallen foul of the trickery of his fellow workers within the year, while his career with the railways had become unbearable as a result of the incompetence of his fellow signalman. How there wasn't a violent crash each week, with hundreds of lives lost, Jimmy declared, he didn't know, and it was beyond his conscience to remain any part of it.

Mrs Mitchell, who in her capacity as unofficial midwife knew every family for miles around and collected every morsel of gossip worth knowing, was one of the few to lack sympathy for Jimmy's misfortunes.

'You can't pull the wool over people's eyes all of the time,' she'd muttered darkly, when Jimmy returned from St Ives, full of indignity at his mistreatment and the evils of the ruling classes who would never give a working man a chance.

That had been last year. Since when, Jimmy had been employed in a succession of menial jobs in and around the Fisherman's Arms, none of which had lasted for more than a week or so. It was during those months that Hester had found Jimmy spending more time with Dad and had become increasingly aware of him watching her as she rowed the ferry.

'You've got an admirer there,' had sniffed Mary-Anne, the landlord's youngest daughter, who'd acted so superior when Jimmy had stepped out with her, just before he was given the position of barman in the Fisherman's Arms.

Mary-Anne wasn't the only unmarried girl to send Hester green-eyed looks at having attracted the attention of the handsomest unmarried man still remaining in the little hamlet. One who, by his own admission, possessed so many skills that attracted the envy of each of his employers, threatening their position, resulting in their plots to get rid of him, using any underhand method they could find. The kind of young man who only needed the care of a good woman to rise far higher than any mere fisherman could do in a month of Sundays.

Hester quickened her pace yet again, hoping that Dad or at least one of the others would be waiting for her at home.

Jimmy, however, was not about to let this go. 'So, Hester, where did you stay then?'

'In one of the big houses. Mum knew one of the cooks there. The staff were kind to me for her sake.'

'Which house?' There was a proprietorial edge to his voice that made her itch to tell him to mind his own business. But to be openly rude and offend Jimmy would only cause a row with Dad. She hadn't the energy to yet again lay out to Dad that she felt no attraction to Jimmy. And that no, it wasn't maidenly modesty or a fear of the opposite sex, just a matter of knowing her own mind. And she certainly wasn't going to marry a man just because her father found him good company, even one who'd taken to buying pints and mending the roof and window frames where the rain came in, along with other small tasks requiring two hands to complete.

These days, she seemed to spend her life keeping the peace. It was even more exhausting than rowing the ferry.

'On the front somewhere, just before the dunes. It was dark, I couldn't properly see. I was just glad to have a place to shelter. I must get home, I haven't had a chance to get back all day.'

'Have I offended you?'

'No, Jimmy, of course not.'

'Because I wouldn't wish to offend you, Hester, you know that, don't you?'

'I'm sure you wouldn't wish to offend me. I'm tired, I need to get back home, the children won't have eaten today and Dad'll be wondering where I am.'

'You know you break my heart when you are like this.'

'Oh, for heaven's sake.' She squashed her exasperation. 'Please, Jimmy. We've been through this. I've never led you on. I've never given you any encouragement. I'm sure you'll soon find a girl who'll make you a perfect wife. I'm just not that girl, believe me.'

'But I love you.' He grabbed her hand. 'You can't choose who you fall in love with.'

'Can't you?'

She saw the flick in the back of his eyes and instantly regretted her flash of temper. The glance between them was probably the most honest communication they had ever shared. It was of the soul laid bare kind, from which there was no going back.

Had he really thought she was so easily flattered she hadn't known what he'd been up to? That she hadn't understood all that feeding of Dad's fragile pride, along with the extra pints her father always felt he deserved?

She had managed to avoid him as much as possible until his mother died last spring and his dad had vanished, saying he'd been offered more regular employment in Plymouth. For all his boasting, Jimmy hadn't managed to keep on the rent of the neat little cottage that had been his mother's pride and joy, moving instead into one of the ramshackle dwellings jumbled together around the Fisherman's Arms, where Mrs Gowlais, whose husband had been lost at sea some twenty years ago, eked out a living cramming in as many single men as was humanly possibly between her damp and cheerless walls, along with a full complement of lice and bedbugs.

Compared to Mrs Gowlais who, as a fervent follower of the Temperance movement, was known to forbid even the hint of alcohol on the breath of her lodgers on pain of spending the night under the nearest hedge, the ferry-man's cottage was a palace. It might not be as spotless as his mother's cottage, and there was only just enough space for them all around the kitchen table, but there was a fire in

123

the range each evening, with a stew bubbling away and the kettle boiling, and easy chairs on either side, battered but comfortable. Just the kind of place a man might like to find himself head of the household, with a disabled father-in-law to depend on him and a brother-in-law too young to oppose his wishes.

Hester shuddered at the very thought. She hurried away, as fast as she could. Jimmy had never yet taken 'no' as her final answer, just as a prelude to the inevitable 'yes'. He wasn't the only one to see an unmarried girl as a challenge, but Jimmy couldn't be sent packing with a no-holds-barred piece of her mind or a smartly placed knee. Jimmy had already won with Dad, and that was where it counted.

Well, she wasn't going to be walked over, as if she didn't matter. She shoved the velvet purse deeper out of sight. That settled it. She was hiding Mrs Trewarren's money safely away. What Dad didn't know, he couldn't object to and she wasn't giving up that easily.

Hester pushed open the door to the cottage to the sound of squabbling. It didn't take much to see that the range hadn't been lit, the table was strewn with dirty bowls, and a pan that had held last night's stew, the generous gift from Mrs Leavan, stood in the corner, the burnt remains of its contents ingrained around the rim.

'Hester!' Alice rushed towards her, tears pouring down her grubby face. 'I thought you'd never come home.'

'Now, I wouldn't leave you like that sweetheart. You know that. I came back as soon as I could.'

'There's no coal,' said Robbie, a worried look on his face. 'Mrs Mitchell gave us some bread and dripping this morning, but it's all gone.'

'That was kind of her. Did the rent man come?'

'We hid,' whispered Alice.

'Good girl.' She followed Robbie's eyes towards the rent tin. 'Where's Dad?' It didn't take Robbie's blush to know the answer. She smiled reassuringly. 'Don't worry, I didn't put all the rent money in there.' She winked. 'I must have forgot.'

Her brother's face collapsed. 'I tried to stop him, Hester. He said he wouldn't take much. Just enough for a pint.'

'That's all right. We've got enough. I had a good day yesterday. We won't have to hide when Mr Bolsover comes again.'

She removed her shawl and set to. Dad would expect the place to be warm and tidy by the time he came back, and he might have taken only enough for one pint, but he would have his drink quietly filled up all evening. Probably even more so than usual, if the expression on Jimmy's face had been anything to go by. She braced herself for the inevitable battle to come.

Even when Dad was stone-cold sober, there was no point in arguing with him. She'd tried. It was a waste of energy. He had an ability to give every sign of listening while remaining deaf to the meaning of anything that might threaten his own comfort. When she'd been little, she'd wondered why Mum hadn't fought him more. She'd even, she admitted to herself, seen her mother as weak for not standing up to him. Well, she was paid back now, good and proper, now she was the one spending her time working around him, keeping him happy so he wouldn't interfere and she could do things her own way.

She sent Robbie to buy a bucketful of coal and Alice to fetch water from the standpipe at the end of the row. At least there was still a little kindling and a few of the logs drying out in a corner. She cleaned out the range, lit the fire, and collected the dirty cups and bowls together. Once Robbie returned, they built up the flames with coal, until there was enough boiling water for the fresh tea carefully hidden away out of sight, only to be used when the tea leaves which had been dried and dried again gave up no semblance of a taste. As the children chopped vegetables to make a quick and easy soup, Hester hurried upstairs, reaching into the tiny space in the roof where each week she hid most of the rent money out of temptation's way.

She breathed a sigh of relief. It was still there. Dad wasn't stupid, he must know it was only part of the rent money she kept, for form's sake, in the tin in the kitchen, and she had her squirreling places, just like Mum had done, to keep some control over the family's finances.

Hester often felt she wasn't good enough at managing, that she would never have Mum's skills of eking out the little there was, and her gift of finding food in the woods and the hedgerows, even in the depths of winter. She leant her head against the coolness of the wall, grief gripping her, as strong as it had been the day Mum died. It still felt that a silence had settled in the little cottage, as if its heart had been torn away.

'Hester?' Alice's voice was small and frightened as a peremptory banging started up on the door.

'It's all right, sweetheart, let Mr Bolsover in. Tell him I'll be down in a minute.' She quickly hid enough of her takings to make sure the next week's rent was covered, and clambered back downstairs.

'Evening, Miss Pearce.'

'Good evening, Mr Bolsover.' She smiled at the stocky little man who had the unenviable task of wresting the weekly rent from each and every family in the row, often in the face of hungry children and no fire in the grate. Then there were the pleas that it would be ready for him next week, or the silence as the inhabitants he knew very well were hidden out of sight barely dared draw breath.

He wasn't a bad man, Mum used to say. He had children himself, and it was no good blaming him. It was just shooting the messenger. If he didn't go back to the office with the correct amount, he'd be the one out on the street, watching his children starve. You could hardly blame him for putting the interests of his own family first. After all, wasn't that what they were all doing? They helped each other as much as they could, but never to the point where their own children suffered.

'Not bad weather we're having,' he remarked, as she reached for the tin. 'For the time of year.'

'Not at all.' She counted out the coins on the table, inwardly cursing as she found just how much Dad had taken. That was more than enough for one pint. A small flicker of fear went through her. If Dad was going to do this every week, they would soon be in trouble. She felt the coins Violet Trewarren had given her weighing heavy in her pocket, their promise of freedom again slipping away. If she hid all the rent money, Dad would be bound to tear the walls down to find it, until she had no hiding place left to keep any of it safe. Her only other sensible choice would be to use her little secret store to support the family, until it was all gone. She pushed the thought aside, and handed the rent man the correct amount.

'Thank you, Miss Pearce.' Mr Bolsover tucked the money away, scribbling in his notebook. 'I'll be on my way then.' He gave a slight cough. 'I hear there was trouble last night on the river.'

'Nothing much.'

'I heard there was a boat got caught in the tide.' His

usually severe face eased a little. 'I also heard our ferrywoman was quite the heroine.'

'I just happened to be there, Mr Bolsover.' She might have known the story would get out and spread like wildfire. Nothing ever remained a secret for long in the little communities along the river. The last thing she needed was for Dad to hear of the danger she had been in, and how near they had come to losing the ferry boat. 'You know how things are exaggerated.'

'Still a brave thing for a girl to do. Shows enterprise. We could do with a little more of that round here.' The rent man sighed, shook his head and crammed his hat back onto his thinning hair, pursing his lips with the air of one about to engage in a battle he would rather avoid, more than likely with Jenifry, who had missed last week's payment.

Hester felt a shot of guilt that she never had enough spare these days to pay Jenifry to look after Alice after school, relying on Robbie instead. Not that poor Jenifry had many children entrusted to her care these days, what with the bruises that appeared ever more frequently on her face and arms. It was no secret that with a child sick, and her husband drinking away any money he earned, Jenifry was either holding out for a midnight flit, or would be on the streets by next week.

Hester shut the door behind Mr Bolsover, and placed just enough of the remainder of the day's earnings in the tin to make it look as if she had put in as much as she could to start the whole process again of making sure it was full enough for next week. She felt horrible, not rushing to Jenifry with her hands full of coins. But they all knew both Jenifry's sisters had put their own households in jeopardy by trying to help her. All it did was give her husband even less sense of any consequences for his actions and more permission to get himself blind drunk. That didn't help Jenifry, who over the past week had been nursing yet another black eye and walking hunched over, as if holding an unbearable pain in her belly.

Better to be out on the streets than dead, Mrs Mitchell had been heard to mutter to the women gossiping as they waited for their buckets to fill at the standpipe. At least that way she might finally get rid of the snivelling little bastard, even if she had to beg for a roof over her head.

Wearily, Hester turned back to the fire, where Alice was watching the soup, stirring it every now and again to make sure it didn't stick to the bottom, just as she had taught her.

'There you are,' she said, ruffling her hair. 'All safe until next week.'

It was growing late. She tidied the kitchen as much as she could and finished washing up the dirty bowls. In the distance, church bells chimed the hour. Dad wasn't usually this late home, even when every man in the Fisherman's Arms had bought him a drink, and he came rolling back, singing sentimental songs and feeling profoundly sorry for himself.

Well, they weren't going to wait. She fed Robbie and Alice, who fell on the hot soup, having had nothing more since this morning than Mrs Mitchell's bread and dripping. She was so ravenous, she couldn't resist putting some in her own bowl, saving plenty for Dad, with enough for her to make a show of eating with him.

With everything cleared away again, ready for Dad's return, she sat by the warmth of the fire, while Robbie pored over his schoolbooks, brushing Alice's hair, which even after a few hours without attention was growing tangled.

She wanted to hug them both tight and keep them safe forever. She had never spent a night away from the cottage, but already she could see the chaos that would take over if she was not there. That was what had always distressed Mum, that there would be no one to look after them all and that Dad would assume Hester would take over her role. Mum had been so insistent that all her children would learn as much as they could, and for as long as they were able, despite Dad's mutterings that Robbie would succeed him on the ferry, and what did a ferryman need with book learning? It was the tides and the weather a ferryman needed, not the words of some dead man.

Was this all her life was ever to be? There were women who did escape. Mrs Leavan had been left a widow with three small children when she had started up her guesthouse. She had struggled for years, but her reputation for comfort and the best of home cooking had grown.

Hester shut her eyes, remembering the silence of the room in the Trewarrens' house, until the determination was back. Mum had risen by hard work and skill to become a head cook in a smart hotel, cooking for visitors coming in by steam train to St Ives. Mum had wanted to give her the chance to do the same, to have a better life, maybe even open her own cafe one day. Mum would want her to at least try.

The trouble was, Hester had an uneasy feeling she hadn't much time left to do anything at all.

Chapter Fifteen

As the evening wore on, still with no sign of Dad, Hester sent the children off to bed and sat by the cooling range, mending the hem of Alice's skirt ready for school, trying not to give in to sleep. Her head was nodding in earnest by the time there was a scrabbling at the front door, followed by a rumble of male laughter. Dad was home, and, by the sounds of things, having to be supported on the way back.

She rose wearily to her feet. The ache in her shoulder from pulling Clara over the side of the boat had stiffened up, protesting each time she moved. She rubbed the muscles to ease them as she pushed the kettle back onto the range to boil.

'You're back, then.' Dad stumbled through the door, straight to his customary seat at the head of the table.

'I came as soon as I could, Dad. There were plenty of passengers today. I'm sorry I couldn't get back at lunchtime. The rent has been paid and your dinner is on the stove ...' She was talking fast to distract him. If she avoided questions now, he was more likely to forget about them as they fell back into the routine of their lives and he returned to his usual concerns. 'I managed to get mutton, I know it's your favourite. It seemed a pity to wait until Sunday ...' She came to a halt. A second figure was leaning on the doorpost, blinking in the lamplight after the complete darkness outside. From the way Jimmy was standing, he was inviting himself in, and there was not enough left in the pot to feed two hungry men, while the bread was all she had saved to give Robbie and Alice something to fill their bellies before they set off on the walk to school.

'Take a seat,' said Dad, in his best lord of the manor tones. 'We've enough to share.'

That was another time she'd seen Mum as weak, when she'd not protested at Dad's habit, after one too many, of bringing back his companions from the Fisherman's Arms expecting them to be fed, as if the food on the table appeared like magic. Then, it had been Mum's share that had been eaten. To be fair to the men, most had been far too polite to accept and swayed home unsteadily to face the wrath of their own wives or mothers, or to one of the tiny dwellings on the edge of the hamlet inhabited by those who had no family. Jimmy took his seat, at Dad's right hand, instantly making himself at home.

Hester gritted her teeth, her already growling belly making her wish she hadn't tried to keep the peace by leaving so much of her dinner to eat with Dad. She had been doing hard physical work all day, followed by cleaning and cooking that evening. But she knew Dad when he was in one of his expansive moods. Any argument only meant trouble, and she hadn't the energy. Besides, she'd no wish to disturb Robbie and Alice, who must have been so afraid when she didn't return home last night, that she might be like Mum, and never return again.

'It will just be a minute,' she said, pushing the pan back on the stove, stirring vigorously while trying not to breathe in its heady smell. She filled two clean bowls, placing a hunk of bread by each one, keeping back as much as she dared, so that Robbie and Alice wouldn't have entirely empty bellies next morning, and poured water onto the precious tea leaves in the pot.

'Come on then, you join us,' said Dad, as she placed the food in front of them.

'If you don't mind, I'm tired.' She wasn't going to sit there, audience to them filling their bellies, or to their conversation, with neither of them talking directly to her or expecting her to contribute an opinion, just be an observer, her presence there an audience to confirm their wisdom.

'Join us. You'll want to hear this.'

'Can't it wait until tomorrow, Dad? It's getting late.'

'Join us.'

'Very well, but just for a few minutes. Then I need to sleep, I've an early start.' She took her cup of tea and sat on the opposite side of the table to Jimmy and as far out of his eye-line as possible.

'So, you'll be glad to be free of that, then.'

'Dad?'

'Jimmy is taking over the ferry. From next week.'

'Monday,' put in Jimmy. His face was turned so that his expression was hidden from Dad, but not from her. The faint air of triumph sent any thought of hunger flying.

'But I thought Robbie—'

'He's too young, he won't be ready for a few years yet. Besides, aren't you always saying he needs to finish his education?'

'Well, yes.'

'There you are then.'

'But, Dad—' What was he thinking of? She'd always been confident that nothing would happen until they could actually persuade her to marry Jimmy, and that was never going to happen. Even for a beer-addled brain this made no sense. The family could barely make ends meet as it was, and with a wage to pay, they would surely never survive. There were only so many who crossed the river each day, and that wasn't going to change, especially not with the rich increasingly taking to motor vehicles that could go round through Hayle, with no need of the ferry.

'You're needed here. Besides, it's not right, a girl doing heavy work like that, open to all kinds of insult.'

'I've only ever been treated with respect.' Which might not be true, but since word had got around that she was no pushover, most of those braving the odd cow and the ever-present baskets of chickens understood where their immediate self-interest lay.

'Then there was that accident, last night,' said Jimmy. 'I'm sure you want to make light of it so as not to worry your dad, Hester, but the word is that you might have got yourself killed.'

'It wasn't anything, Dad. I wasn't in any danger, and I brought the ferry back safely.'

'After having to beach it on the other side, where you've no friends or family to look after you,' added Jimmy, with a sly glance towards Dad. 'You were lucky this time. Who knows what might happen if you were to be caught in the tide again? Even a grown man would struggle, what chance does a girl have against the might of the sea? There are plenty of strangers in Hayle, visitors from London among them, who don't understand Cornish ways and are quite prepared to lure an innocent young girl into dangers she can hardly understand.'

'I'm not a child, and I'm not about to be lured anywhere.'

'Not even by Lance Trewarren? I saw the way he was looking at you. He'd love you to be deceived by his gentlemanly ways.'

'I've plenty of men looking at me,' she retorted angrily. 'I'm well aware that doesn't mean a thing, and I soon put them straight if they try anything.' She'd made a mistake.

She knew it the moment the words left her mouth. She saw it in her father's frown and the faint curl of Jimmy's lips. Talk about being lured in! Jimmy had just hauled her in good and proper, like mackerel caught writhing in the net. He'd managed to touch Dad where it hurt, in his fear of being a laughing stock as a man unable to keep his females under control. 'Dad, you know I'm not a fool and I can look after myself, and there are plenty at the jetty who will help me.'

'You're needed here, girl, and that's an end of it. I'll be showing Jimmy on Monday all there is to know. There'll be no need to trouble you.'

'It'll be no trouble,' remarked Jimmy, still smiling at her. This time there was no mistaking the triumph in his eyes.

Hester glanced towards Dad. He looked happier than he had done since before he'd lost his arm. He would enjoy instructing Jimmy on how to run the ferry, and discuss the day afterwards, man to man. It would be the nearest thing to having a son taking over his work, the way things were meant to be. Dad had never been patient and this way he wouldn't have to wait until Robbie was old enough. His dignity would be restored. Dad was already seeing himself resuming his position as head of the household, while she would return to her mother's role of looking after her younger siblings, supplementing the family's income with jobs he didn't need to acknowledge existed, or that had any bearing at all on the household finances. Perhaps that was how he thought they would pay Jimmy.

There was a bitter taste in her mouth. She watched under her lashes as the two men returned to their meal, subject settled, the world organised according to their convenience. She could see they were both already assuming there would be no need to pay Jimmy a wage any longer than a week or two, just so he could keep on renting his place with Mrs

Gowlais, for form's sake. They had already decided the future. It would start with Jimmy joining the family for meals, until she could be persuaded, or threatened, or simply worn down by the inevitability of it all.

Dad might be blind to the fact now, but by the time Robbie was old enough to take over, it would be too late. Jimmy would be established as the ferryman, his own sons already being raised to eventually take his place. Barring accident, the natural course of things would leave him as the head of the household, with the power of keeping the rent paid and food on the table, leaving the rest of them subject to his every whim, lord of all he surveyed.

Over her dead body. Rising, Hester filled the kettle from the water in the pitcher and pushed it back onto the stove. Hurt flooded through her. Dad was supposed to be the one who protected her, who made sure she never came to harm and that her life would be a good one. She had learnt to live with his pride, and that his first consideration was always for himself. But this was a betrayal of the worst kind. Trapped between the two of them, she would have no escape. They would know that, in the end, she would have no choice. They both must have calculated, deep down, and for their own separate reasons, that her sense of responsibility would allow them to trap her into doing exactly what suited them.

She couldn't fight them. Not in the way she'd shoved her elbow smartly into the delicate place John Corrington was attempting to rub against her thigh, or the look she'd given the farmer's boys making comments on the movement of her breasts as she rowed. On the ferry, she had power. Here, she had none. The only influence she could bring to bear would be Dad's love, but that love was not as strong as his need to regain his position. She had no doubt he loved her in his way, as he did all of them, but his needs would always come first.

Excusing herself, she went to the little privy at the end of the garden, breathing in deep the clarity of the night air. Around her, candles flickered in windows, as families prepared for bed, with the deeper glow of firelight in the more prosperous homes. There was a hint of frost, hanging under cold, clear stars, and the whiter arch of the Milky Way.

If she married, she would lose her last morsel of freedom to be herself. For all that her days were taken up with working to support the family and looking after them when she came home, her soul was still her own. She did not have a husband in her bed, or a child in a cradle at one side, another already swelling in her belly. She'd seen how it had worn Mum out, the babies who, one by one had died at birth, or after a few days of clinging on to life. It had worn out her body, and her spirit, until there was nothing left.

Hester hugged herself. She didn't want the life of drudgery she saw around her, the women taking in washing, ruining their eyes with mending, in between looking after children and the endless cleaning of their own houses, until they were old and bent, hands twisted with arthritis, dependent on the gratitude of their children to support them in their old age, praying they would not be left to fend for themselves.

All right, so she couldn't fight them head-on. In that case, she would just have to use her wits, as she had seen the other women in the row use cunning and persuasion to make sure they and their children were fed and had a roof over their heads. The men talked as if their wives were always demanding money to spend on themselves. From what Hester could see, a woman was the last in consideration in the household, forever going hungry to make sure others were fed.

She only had a few days before Jimmy took over the ferry, and Dad would once again be in control of the money placed on the table to pay the rent and keep the family fed and warm. She still had the coins hidden in their velvet purse. It was a sin to be selfish. At least, it was for a girl. Well, she had done man's work and she was as strong and resourceful as any man. This time, she was going to put herself first, she was going to find a way to escape spending her life serving Jimmy, a man she despised, body and soul, until she was a worn shadow of who she was now, let alone of who she might have been. And she would find a way to support Robbie and Alice, so they could finish their education, and find their own paths to freedom.

Alice was still getting the highest marks of the whole school, and, young as she was, still just as determined to train as a doctor one day. From what Hester had heard, good doctors like Dr Graham were few and far between, and even Mrs Mitchell, who'd seen enough babies born than anyone she knew, was shy about consulting any man about 'women's problems', so heaven knew what the rest might be hiding. Even Dr Graham had encouraged Alice, telling her there were female doctors in London who ran their own practices, and his own niece was working as a doctor for a charitable hospital in Spitalfields. Jimmy wasn't about to stop that, either.

Slowly, clearing her face of any tell-tale expression, she made her way back inside.

Chapter Sixteen

The next evening, Hester fed her family early, leaving Robbie in charge as Dad slipped off to the Fisherman's Arms, and made her way to the tiny, higgledy-piggledy cottage where Gran had lived since her retirement.

She found her grandmother digging in an ancient pair of Grandad's trousers, held in at the waist with a belt. Gran, being elderly, and strange in her ways in the first place, could get away with such eccentricities within the privacy of her own garden, with a skirt to hand to regain her respectability, should anyone call.

'Why, Hester, now this is a pleasure.'

Hester kissed her. 'I'll put the kettle on, Gran. I'm sure you could do with a rest.'

'That sounds the best idea I've heard all day.'

'Mint?'

'Spearmint, I think,' said Gran, nodding towards the dark spikes pushing through the walls and the grass, on a bid to take over the place. Like Hester, Gran could rarely afford to buy tea leaves these days, but took fresh leaves from the garden when they were available, drying as much as she could to last her through the winter.

Hester nodded and took handfuls of the spearmint, breathing in its richness as she stepped into the tiny single room that formed the cottage, apart from the cramped attic, reached only by a rickety ladder, where Gran slept.

Once the water had boiled, she poured it over the leaves, taking the steaming cups out into the garden.

'Well, now,' said Gran, as they settled into the last warmth of the sun. 'There's lovely to see you, my dear. We barely have any time together, these days.'

'I'm sorry, Gran. I should come and see you more often.'

'Nonsense. Don't you think I know you work until you drop? I'm the one who should be making the time to see you. After all, that was the idea of my leaving Afalon in the first place.'

Hester concentrated on her tea. Since Mum died, Dad had made it clearer than ever that Gran had no place in his domain, even to take care of Alice and Robbie and cook an evening meal now and again, to help out. 'Interfering old busybody', he'd called her more than once, not caring whether or not she was within hearing. It had even become difficult for Gran to meet her grandchildren from school and take them back to her cottage. Robbie knew not to say anything to Dad, but Alice was still too young to understand. These days, Dad was even more irascible than ever if he believed his authority was being in any way questioned, or his dignity sullied.

Dad enjoyed the flattering attention of pretty girls, however meaningless, but could never bear to be seen in the company of an older woman, let alone speak to her. He clearly felt it was beneath him to even notice such creatures, as if being in the company of a young woman made him young, while even acknowledging he was on speaking terms an older woman might taint him with age. Or rather, Hester had come to understand, he was terrified by any woman free with her opinions, who'd seen too much of the world to give a fig for his masculine approval. The recognition still mortified her.

'Well now, Hester, my dear, what is it that's troubling you?'

'Do I have to have trouble to come and see you?'

'No, *cariad*, but I can see it in your face. It wouldn't have something to do with young Harkness, would it?'

Hester started. 'How did you know?'

'Nothing is secret round here, you should know that. Especially when a young man with few means of his own starts buying a young woman's father all the beer he can drink.'

'Well, it's worked. He's persuaded Dad to let him take over the ferry.'

'I see.'

'You don't sound surprised.'

'Should I be?'

Hester sighed. 'No, of course not.'

'Your father always was a self-centred creature. And I don't need to give him a piece of my mind for him to know that's what I think.' Gran gave her a sharp look. 'So, have you come to ask my blessing?'

'Never!'

'Well, and thank goodness for that. *Duw*, child, you had me worried for a moment there. I thought all your mother's training of you to watch your back had gone for nothing.'

'Is that what she was doing?'

'Of course. She loved you. She wanted to make sure you followed your heart and made a good life for yourself. I just wish I'd been more insistent myself when Sadie was your age. But then the young never listen to the old. It seems human beings have to make the same mistakes over and over again. All you can do is hope that something will stick.' She grimaced. 'And besides, I was too worried about respectability in them days. Your grandad was the one who really encouraged Sadie to dream of more than the fishing life. He said he'd seen too many good men lost at sea and too many women and children left with nothing to support them. He always wanted better for Sadie. He'd want better for you, too.'

'Jimmy is taking over the ferry straight away. I shall need to find a new way of earning some money of my own, or I'll be dependent on him and Dad for every penny.'

'I see.' Gran was silent for a while. 'Well, my dear, I can put in a word with Mrs Leavan, if that's what you are thinking? She's desperate for someone reliable to make sure her rooms are clean for guests from London and she knows you are a hard worker.'

'Thank you, Gran. I know it's the sensible thing to do, and it's a way of having money coming in each week. I know Mrs Leavan was good to Mum, but I don't want a job that means I'll never be able to completely support myself, however hard I work, but takes all my time and energy so I can't try for something else.' She crushed the fading heads of lavender sprawling alongside the bench, releasing their scent. 'That will still lead to the same thing in the end.'

'I can't say I blame you, *cariad*. If you wish to take up M. Alphonse's offer to train you, I am more than happy to look after the children. I'll even look after your father, if the stubborn old fool will let me.'

'I can't ask you to do that, Gran. You work hard enough as it is. Besides, now I know what Jimmy is up to, I can't leave Dad. At least not until Robbie is old enough to take over the ferry and Alice leaves school and is safely away from here.' She took a deep breath. 'But I thought maybe you could teach me. Proper cooking. The things you used to make at Afalon. Things like soufflés, consommés and mousseline. Then one day, when Robbie and Alice don't need me any more, I could find work as a cook in a big house, like you did at Afalon. Or be like Mum and be a cook in a restaurant or a hotel, and work my way up, like Rosa Lewis. Maybe even start a cafe of my own one day.'

'Hester, Mrs Lewis worked her way up from the bottom, from being just a kitchen maid to being able to buy the Cavendish Hotel. It took her years, and the most extraordinary skill and willpower, and a touch of luck. And, if you read the papers, one of two other things I'd rather you didn't engage in, particularly when it comes to rich men. Always a dangerous game, my dear.'

'Oh.' Hester had read the rumours of Mrs Lewis's affair with Edward VII when he was Prince of Wales, and she couldn't help going slightly pink round the ears. 'But I don't have any ambition to cook for lords and ladies or fancy hotels in London. Mrs Leavan told Mum the guesthouse was doing so well because more and more visitors have been coming to Cornwall since the railways and there are more artists in St Ives. That means hotels and guesthouses are bound to be in need of cooks.'

'It's still a difficult profession for a woman to enter, or at least to be taken seriously if she tries. More women might be working these days, but it's still hard. And, to be honest with you, Robert won't ever approve, especially if he's set on you marrying.'

'I've thought of that. The thing is, he can't stop me from earning a bit of money, like Mum used to do, and especially if he needs to pay Jimmy until they can persuade me to marry him. I thought maybe I could start helping you with making preserves and taking them to sell in Hayle and St Ives. Didn't you say you didn't have time to fill all the new orders you are getting?'

'That's true. People still want country fare now there's all these new tins and jars you see in the grocer's. Your mum's reputation is still as strong as ever. I could easily expand. The trouble is, my dear, finding the money to pay for ingredients and fuel. I'm afraid neither of us is in a position to take such a risk, when we might never be able to get such an investment back. I know how tight money is for you these days.'

'I've got money. Money Dad doesn't know anything about. It would be enough to buy what we need.'

'Do you indeed? And where did you get that kind of money from?'

'Mrs Trewarren.'

Gran put down her tea so hard it spilt over one side. 'What were you doing talking to Violet Trewarren? What lies did she tell you?'

Hester blinked at her grandmother's fierceness. 'Nothing, Gran. I helped her daughter, that's all.' Gran's expression of suspicion deepened. 'To tell the truth, I saved her life.'

'I heard there was an accident on the estuary, some young woman nearly getting herself drowned for an affair of the heart.' Gran sniffed. 'I suppose I should have known it would be Clara Trewarren. Like mother, like daughter.'

This wasn't exactly a promising start. It had been on the tip of Hester's tongue to tell Gran about Mum and Mrs Trewarren meeting on the beach all those years ago. At Gran's tone, she thought better of it.

'I didn't want to take the money at first, Gran, but she was insistent.'

'I bet she was.'

Hester lifted her chin. 'I'm glad I did. Without it, I'd have nothing, and I wouldn't have dared ask you and I'd have no chance of escape.'

Gran appeared to barely hear her. 'Violet Trewarren has a son, doesn't she? Grown up into a pleasant young man, so I hear.'

'Gran!'

'I'm not accusing you of anything, *cariad*. Just cautioning you to stay well away.'

'You know you can trust me better than that. I've no intention of falling in love with anyone. Not until I know I'll never have to depend on any man. Even if that takes forever.'

'That's the trouble with love. That's what your mother found, all those years ago. It has a tendency to sneak up and get you when you least expect it.'

'No one's doing any sneaking up on me.'

Gran chuckled. 'You're your mother's daughter, all right. Stubborn as they come and just as passionate, and so sure you know your own mind.' She picked a stray sprig of mint next to her, crushing it in her hand, releasing its aromatic oils. 'Very well, the truth is, my dear, I could easily expand my little business, and could do with the help. Your mum is still missed and there's others out there ready to take advantage if they hear I can't supply everyone who wants old country preserves.'

'Good. And maybe you could teach me the other things in between?'

'I don't see why not.' Gran was thoughtful. 'Most of the big houses are finding cooks hard to come by these days, and so many girls don't want to be servants when they can have more freedom working in factories or as clerks. If I knew I could produce them regularly, there's more than one cook who might be happy to buy in things like cakes that take time and are fiddly. I've so many tried and tested recipes, and I'm sure your mum had too. It's worth a try, I suppose.'

'Then one day we might be able to open a cafe.'

'Hold your horses, girl. Never wise to run before you can walk. You leave it with me. I can sound out one or two of the young women I trained up in my time at Afalon, the ones who've become cooks themselves. I don't want to take your money, Hester. You keep it to put towards that cafe of yours. I'll settle for your youthful energy instead. We can start with rosehips and blackberries, things that won't cost us. There are several crab apple trees no one bothers with any more, and next year, if you help me, we could grow more in my vegetable patch and make use of all my gooseberries once they ripen.'

'Yes, Gran. Anything.'

'Now, the place we could really make the most of would be the old gardens at Afalon. My kitchen used to be filled to the brim with apples and redcurrants, let alone the vegetables. I used to spend half the summer making preserves. It's all been going to waste since the Elliots left. Whoever buys the house isn't likely to make use of the walled garden. They never do, nowadays. Besides, so few of the young men want to be gardeners, when there's an easier life to be had as shop assistants in Hayle, out of the wind and weather.' Gran sent the sprig of mint flying into the borders of fading cranesbills. 'But then none of us ever know what's around the corner, do we?'

When she left Gran's, Hester didn't return through the hamlet, but followed the path below the high garden walls of Afalon. She hadn't been this way since Mum died, the memories were too painful. It had been another good year for fruit. The apples were there, just as they had been that day with Mum, spilling over the wall, the windfalls scattered on the ground.

She itched to pick them all now, before anyone else thought to look, but they would most probably spoil before she and Gran were ready to use them. Her foot crunched on a windfall. There were plenty more scattered around on the grass. She had flour and a little butter left. Tomorrow, she could pick up lard and sugar and make an apple pie with thick pastry on top. If Mrs Dowrick's chickens were still laying, she could even make custard. The very thought made her mouth water and her stomach rumble appreciatively. However much she cooked, she always seemed hungry these days, and soon there would be even less of each meal to go around.

Between the trees, she could make out Afalon, set slightly higher than the garden. Tall sash windows looked out, glinting blankly between ivy creeping over the walls. Moss had begun to settle on the roof, and a sapling clung precariously to one of the chimneys. Even from a distance it had an air of neglect.

There was no one in sight. Hester took her shopping bag from her pocket, filling it with the best of the windfalls. She then gathered as many blackberries as she could find, making a container out of leaves and placing the little parcel carefully among the apples. As she gathered the bag up to set off towards home, she hesitated. The lower branches of the nearest tree appeared strong enough to take her weight. She could take a look. Just one little look to see what was left of the Elliots' walled garden. After all, who would miss a few peaches and melons? And surely anything made from grapes would be exotic enough to command a higher price than hedgerow fare? Mum's recipe book had instructions for grape marmalade, collected from a woman who had come all the way from America to paint in the renowned light of this part of Cornwall. That was something she was just itching to try.

The wall was rough, giving her footholds as she braced the weight of her body against its solidness, pulling herself up into the higher branches. Hester reached the top of the wall easily, hanging onto the largest branch she could find as she balanced herself on the coping stones. There were no traps or sharp obstacles to deter intruders, but it was higher than she had imagined.

Hester glanced back over her shoulder. From up here, she could see over the scrubland to the hamlet clustered in the dips in the rolling patchwork of farmland, and the gleaming turquoise of the sea. She turned her attention to the garden laid out beneath her. Mostly it was obscured by branches, but she could make out the paths, overgrown with weeds, criss-crossing the carefully laid out beds and fruit trees.

Even from up here, it had a forlorn appearance. A tangle of climbing roses still clung to a half-collapsed trellis among the lavender of the herb garden, where she had once been commandeered as a flower girl for Mrs Elliot's painting. Then it had been rich with life, humming with bees and the distant chatter of men weeding or tending to the pineapple pits; now it was silent, already choked with bindweed and brambles.

Gran said the Elliots had left quickly and put the place up for sale without even bothering to remove the furniture. There had certainly been no sign of anyone grubbing up the walled garden, which meant there might be the remains of self-seeded vegetables, as well as fruit, that were simply going to waste. Who would notice if some of it quietly disappeared?

Hester stepped gingerly onto the nearest branch, as close to the trunk as she could go, and climbed down. She reached the ground safely, taking care to note the position of the tree and make sure she could find it again as her only certain way of escape. Apples surrounded her, rich globes of green and red, some the paper-bag brown of russets. There were sufficient here for all the apple chutney she and Gran could ever wish to make. All they would need were enough jars and they could stash it away, selling it bit by bit over the winter months, maybe trying big hotels further along the coast. They could even take the train as far as Penzance. Pushing her way between the branches of the little orchard, she stepped out into the garden.

As she emerged, she gasped at the sheer size. As a child it had seemed vast. Even as an adult she had never imagined such a huge space could be given over entirely to the growing of fruit and vegetables. It was a true walled garden, completely enclosed to keep out the worst of the sea winds, holding in its richness and its warmth. She had never been among such a promise of abundance.

If she and Gran could use just a fraction of the self-seeded leeks and potatoes she could see pushing through the weeds, or the abundance of pears and peaches espaliered against the walls, they would have all the ingredients they would ever need. Then next year there would be the redcurrants and blackcurrants and the rows of gooseberry bushes she could make out next to the apple orchard.

It might take years for Afalon to acquire a new owner. If she and Gran used what remained, they would surely soon have enough money put by to afford even the most exotic of ingredients, or have a greenhouse constructed to grow their own grapes and melons.

In fact, she considered, ambition getting the better of her, would anyone notice if one or two of the fruit bushes were dug up that winter? They could easily find a new home in Gran's garden, where they would be loved and cared for as if they had a whole complement of gardeners attending to their needs.

The clicking of a latch broke into her plans, followed by the unwilling creak of rusty hinges. Hester shot back into the shelter of the orchard, pulling herself up into the tree as a small wooden door in the far side of the garden was pushed open. She kept still, afraid of betraying herself by any creaking or shaking, or, even worse, a branch cracking and sending her to the floor.

A man with dark hair stepped through the doorway and made his way along the overgrown pathways with the familiarity of one who had walked them all his life. He had changed over the years, just as she had, but she would have known Richard Elliot anywhere. As he came closer, she could see that he had the unguarded look of one who did not expect to be observed and would never have willingly made himself so vulnerable. There was memory in his face, and the unbearable rawness of grief.

She kept very still. As children they had once shared their unspoken fears of what they might lose. She had a feeling it wasn't the same now they were both adults. Besides, she didn't like the idea of him finding her as an intruder and a would-be thief.

'Richard? Richard, are you in here?' A woman's voice echoed around the walls. 'Miss Chesterfield would like us to show her the gardens.'

'It's all right, Isabella, I'm over here,' he replied, all emotion instantly removed from view.

'Do come in, Miss Chesterfield. Take all the time you like. I'll try to answer any questions you may have, but I'm afraid I'm not very knowledgeable about gardens.'

'Well, I have to confess, Miss Elliot, neither am I. Not a walled garden like this one. That's what makes it so intriguing.'

Hester almost lost her grip, hands slipping, threatening to send her tumbling down to the ground. She steadied herself at the last moment, holding her breath as the leaves around her rustled in the stillness. Not only could she make out Isabella making her way along the central path, but her companion was easily recognisable as the middle-aged woman she had ferried over the evening she had rescued Clara.

It might not be more than a few days ago, but it felt like a lifetime. It sounded as if Miss Chesterfield was planning on renting, or even buying, Afalon. She cursed silently. That would scupper any idea of using any remaining fruit.

For now, however, that appeared to be the least of her worries. When she dared open her eyes again, Hester could see that Richard had turned his head, his attention caught by the movement in the apple trees. It felt as if he was looking straight at her. Hester held her breath and kept as still as she could.

'I'm glad it was you out here, Richard. I told Miss Chesterfield it must be you.'

'I beg your pardon?'

'When I was showing Miss Chesterfield the bedrooms just now, I happened to glance out of the window. I thought I saw someone, standing just here, where you are now, looking up at the house. It was odd, I thought you were still downstairs sorting out the papers for Papa. I was so certain I could hear you putting things into boxes. But it must have been you.'

'Or a trick of the light.'

'It could have been that, I suppose.'

'Well, I'm afraid I didn't see a thing,' said Miss Chesterfield. 'And besides, I never had much belief in the supernatural, so apparitions of any kind are unlikely to worry me. I would like to walk around and see what's what, if that's all right with you?'

'Yes, of course,' said Isabella quickly. 'Take all the time you need.'

Hester's legs were beginning to shake, and even the

muscles in her arms were screaming with the effort of keeping motionless. She was sure she couldn't hold on any longer, and if Miss Chesterfield came into the little orchard, she couldn't miss her.

'It's very beautiful here,' Miss Chesterfield was saying, as the three began to move in her direction. 'Is your father sure about this? I can't imagine being able to let a place like this go.'

'The house has been shut up since our mother died, several years ago,' said Richard. 'Neither Isabella nor I have done more than visit briefly when our father wished to reassure himself it wasn't about to fall down. And now with increasing talk of war in Europe—'

'Which is only talk,' put in Isabella hastily.

'Ah. You mean it's the sort of house that might be requisitioned by the army, if British forces should become involved in such a conflict?'

'It's a possibility,' said Richard. 'Particularly if it's not in use. France is not that far away. If there is to be war with Germany, casualties could well be evacuated to anywhere in the south of England, or it could be used for training purposes.'

'I see.'

'But hopefully it won't come to that,' said Isabella.

'I wouldn't be too sure,' replied Miss Chesterfield. 'I volunteered as a nurse for the war in Africa when I was young. I saw enough then to learn that war is total madness, whatever the rights and wrongs of how it might have begun, and it's the ordinary soldiers and the civilians, who have no say and nothing to gain, who suffer the most.' She coughed. 'But you are right, Miss Elliot. We have to hope our heads of state see sense and it doesn't come to that. The view of the house from here is particularly fine, don't you think? Although I'm not entirely sure about the state of the roof on that side ...'

As the three turned to focus their attention on Afalon, deep in questions of maintenance and the possibility of rot in the window frames, Hester took her chance. She pulled herself up and over the wall, and slithered recklessly down the other side, landing on the grass in a heap. Grabbing her bag of apples and blackberries, she took to her heels, fleeing through the undergrowth towards home.

Once she was at a safe distance from Afalon she stopped to catch her breath and ease the stitch that had become agony in her side. As her breathing slowed, she removed the sticks from her hair and clothes, cooling her cheeks in water from a small stream.

There was no sign of anyone following her from Afalon. Hopefully, Richard would believe Isabella had been mistaken. If he remained suspicious that there had been an intruder and looked carefully, he would be bound to find the evidence of broken branches. But he might take it to be simply the mischief of small boys in search of adventure and idle amusement, whose only interest was not being caught.

She smoothed her hair as best she could and set off at a more sedate pace towards the hamlet. As she emerged into the fields, she gazed down at the cluster of homes, with the grocer's shop, the smithy and bakery all settled tightly around the church. Beyond, fishing boats lay secured alongside the jetty, the outlying cottages of farm labourers weaving their way between meadows.

On the far side, cattle were being urged down from the higher fields towards the nearest farm, dogs nipping at the heels of any who stopped too long to nibble at delicacies in the hedgerow. In the gardens of the nearest cottages, women were unpinning washing from their lines, deep in conversation, their laughter drifting up towards her in the still air. On the estuary, a small pleasure boat was making its way home from the sea, heading upstream towards Hayle, white sails glowing a soft peach in the sinking sun. Along the water's edge, children were playing, the younger ones dashing in and out, shrieking at the cold, while the older children skimmed pebbles and floated homemade boats of bits of wood and reed.

Despite her need to get home, Hester could not tear her eyes away. It was a scene that had surrounded her all her life, something she had always taken for granted. Like the fact that hay would be brought in each year and ploughing would signal the beginning of spring. That the world would turn endlessly in the same way, punctuated by births and by deaths, but essentially unchanged, the future opening out for her, with all its promises.

There had been talk of war, of course, over the past year, but it had remained on the edges of her existence, like the change of governments and taxes. It had been something so far away it could not possibly touch her. Several men from Hayle had been killed in the war in the Transvaal, an un-imaginable place, in a country that was just a distant blob on the globe in the schoolroom, where there were said to be sav-ages and elephants who didn't seem to want to be absorbed into the vast pink sections of the world that denoted the British Empire.

But there were no savages, or elephants, in France. Miss Smith was accustomed to travel there with her sister during the summer holidays, on their way to visit friends in Florence. She'd brought back postcards showing wheat fields and church spires and said it wasn't really very different from Cornwall. Compared to the Transvaal, France was hardly any distance away. Hester clearly remembered the line on the papier mâché globe in Miss Smith's classroom that represented the English Channel, a barely visible strip of blue water that could be crossed in a few hours. Miss Smith had described whole families travelling over on steamers, to take steam trains that ran on iron tracks stretching throughout the continent. They were not in search of distant deserts, but warmer seas and ancient monuments, only a few days' journey away, with some even climbing up into mountains too high for the snow to ever melt, where great rivers of ice stood forever, frozen in time.

Hester shivered. She'd seen the old soldier who came on the tramp each summer, sleeping under hedges, doing a little work here and there where he could find it, never stepping indoors, even when it rained the heaviest. She'd watched him start at the slightest noise, body rigid. Once, when there had been an earthquake that shook the ground, sending a low rumble under their feet, he had flung himself into the nearest ditch, barely seeming to notice, when he finally emerged, that he was covered entirely in mud. Mum had always found something to spare when he passed, from slices of bread and jam to Dad's cast-off old trousers, shaking her head as the old man went on his endless, restless way.

Could there really be fighting so close? But whether it happened was being decided by men in places far away, who knew nothing of the little communities tucked into the countryside around Hayle and the lives lived there. She had never felt so small and insignificant, like a fly to be brushed away into oblivion if convenient. She wished there was something she could do to stop such a thing, or at least sweep all she loved away somewhere safe. But where would they go? And they'd still have to live, and she couldn't possibly take away all her neighbours and her friends, and she'd hate to think of them being left behind when she was safe from danger.

Like Isabella Elliot, she just had to hope that it would be sorted out sensibly and go away, like frost once the sun appeared. All the same, she couldn't quite free herself from a lingering sensation of unease.

Chapter Seventeen

There was no point in brooding over something she couldn't control, Hester told herself over the next few days. If she was to get anywhere, she had to carry on as if there was no prospect of any kind of war and that life would continue just as it had always done.

Through the rest of that autumn of 1913, Hester joined Gran each morning once Dad left to join Jimmy on the ferry, Robbie and Alice were on their way to school and her own chores were done.

At first, it was a relief to have the house to herself for an hour or so, to pour her energies into cleaning and mending and making what preparations she could for the evening meal. It felt like freedom to be able to slip out to collect the ingredients to take to Gran, then making preserves and chutneys to sell in Hayle and beginning to learn the skills she would need to earn her living as a cook.

Despite her fear of being caught, she could not resist returning to Afalon's gardens to collect as much as she could. There was no sign of anyone, or any rumours of the place being sold. Which probably meant Miss Chesterfield had changed her mind. All the same, she hadn't quite dared strip the trees of all their apples, taking as many as might not be missed by a casual observer. For this year at least, they had an abundance of ingredients.

While the little business might be growing in success, her

lack of independence at home soon began to grate. With Jimmy to pay, and more often than not joining them for an evening meal, there was now even less money to make sure the family was fed with enough left over to pay the rent. Even worse, she never knew from day to day how many coins Dad would place on the kitchen table, and, however hard she tried, with no say over how the income from the ferry was spent.

More than once over those first months, while any money she and Gran made needed to be put straight back into ingredients and fuel and improving their equipment, she nearly gave in to fear of the coins dwindling to nothing, just as they had done with poor Jenifry once her husband had developed a serious taste for the drink.

The temptation to take up Mrs Leavan's offer of a position cleaning for her several hours each day, which would at least mean steady money she could count on each week, wore away at her. If it hadn't been for Mrs Trewarren's coins, carefully stashed away deep inside the walls of Gran's cottage where Dad would never find them, she would have given up by the time December came. The first of the cold weather brought a need for additional buckets of coal to keep some semblance of warmth, as the storms roared in up the estuary from the sea, and not even Jimmy could persuade passengers to risk the journey across.

As it was, she and Gran continued to make their preserves, following the carefully noted recipes in Mum's notebook, along with one or two of Gran's favourites.

Gran's cottage might be tiny, but one of its attractions had been the outbuilding at the bottom of the garden, which a previous tenant had used for taking in washing. Along with the copper, there was a sturdy range, containing its own small oven.

'Well, now,' said Gran, after a particularly successful visit to St Ives in the first week of December, placing a satisfying pile of coins on the table. With Hester not quite daring to alert Dad by being seen at such a distance, Gran had used the last of their carefully stored apples to bake up several large apple pies to be used as bribery for Mr Rundle and his grandson, to help with the delivery of as many jars as they could carry. 'What do you say to us taking a chance and investing our earnings again?'

Hester gazed at the coins, the result of several months of hard work collecting and washing, preparing and boiling. Not to mention the terror of being hauled up in front of the magistrates as an apple thief, and the vicious rips from the most fiercely guarded of brambles still scabbing on her arms. There was at least two weeks' rent in her share, not to mention tea leaves and a few bacon bits to liven up the beans and cabbage that, along with a few potatoes, had become the monotonous mainstay of each night's stew. They represented weeks of not having to dip into Mrs Trewarren's money.

But, nothing ventured, nothing gained. They already had orders for next year for the preserves. They hadn't let Mum's memory down, and there was still a market for their wares. They had risked this and it had paid off. Surely they could risk again? Hester took a deep breath.

'What were you thinking, Gran?'

'Christmas puddings and cakes.'

'But isn't it too late? Won't most cooks have made theirs already?'

'Not as far as I can see. Or at least enough haven't got around to it yet, so it would be worth our while. It was Mrs Leavan who gave me the idea. She said she was sick of making them, they take so long, and with reliable kitchen maids so hard to find. I told her I'd think about it. I've been talking to several of the cooks I've trained over the years who are now working in hotels in Hayle and St Ives, and I've written to a few in Penzance. I've several orders already.' She grinned. 'I was always known for my plum puddings. I'm not surprised at more than one cook wanting to pass them off as her own.'

'Don't you mind?'

'*Duw*, child, so long as they pay handsomely, they can say it was made by the hands of the Queen herself. There won't be much we can collect to make preserves over the winter, and I'm thinking that if places discover the convenience of buying in Christmas cakes, why not other cakes as well? Your mum was more one for savoury dishes, but she has some fine recipes, and I've plenty in my own book. Mr Elliot always did have a sweet tooth, and Miss Isabella loved my saffron cake. Besides, if it works, it will start to get your name known.'

'Our name, Gran.'

Gran laughed. 'I haven't forgotten your offer of employing me once you get your cafe, Hester Pearce. I think we need to come up with a good name. One you can take with you and give you a head start once you get that cafe up and going. Reputation is everything, worth more than all the fancy decoration in the world.'

Gran knew she couldn't resist. It was hard to have faith in the future, especially with uncertainty in the wider world as well as at home. But, in the end, that was the only thing they had. Besides, the longer Jimmy worked his influence over Dad, the less time she would have for any choices at all.

Hester nodded. 'I think we should take the chance.'

'Good girl. I'll tell Mrs Leavan and get as many orders as I can.' She gave a wry smile. 'And if any change their minds at the last minute, at least we'll know we'll have full bellies at Christmas, and I doubt Robbie and Alice will ever tire of cake.'

Hester enjoyed learning to beat sugar and butter to the right consistency, adding eggs slowly so as to prevent curdling, before finely judging the addition of dried fruit along with spices and flour. The plum puddings they boiled up in the copper, baking the Christmas cakes in the oven, relying on Gran's expertise to know when they were cooked through without becoming dry and tasteless.

Gran was right. They may only have had a small number of orders for Christmas, but as winter turned into the spring of 1914, orders for seed cakes and rich plum cakes came through the kitchen maids Gran had trained up to be cooks during her time at Afalon. Word was clearly spreading of this simple and reliable way to impress visitors and wedding guests with the skills of a pastry chef without the trouble and expense of employing one.

'Well now,' said Gran, as they fulfilled an order for a hotel in Hayle in early July, with a delivery van sent out to collect the goods. 'I think that's a good start. It'll soon be apple season again, and we've more orders than we can manage for raspberry jam. If we carry on like this, you'll soon be having your cafe, just you see.'

Hester breathed a sigh of relief. Since Christmas, they had finally begun to turn a profit. She still had a little of Mrs Trewarren's money left, and she now had enough in her pocket each week to add a little to her store, even after she had made sure there was enough coal for the range and food at home so that no one went hungry.

She didn't dare ask about the cafe on Porthgwidden beach, or what the Carltons had decided to do with the place. She was still a long way off being able to pay rent on a cafe, but at least she was making a start. She was beginning to put money aside to add to what was left from Mrs Trewarren and she was learning all the skills she would need. Jimmy and Dad could plan all they like. By the time they realised what she was up to, it would be too late. For the first time in months, she felt herself beginning to relax.

At last she was confident she had found a way of escaping being tied to Jimmy for the rest of her life. She could choose who she wanted to marry, or even never marry at all, like Miss Smith, who declared she was happier being a school-teacher. Robbie and Alice were growing older, and she could feel the dream of running her own cafe almost in her grasp.

Finally, she was on her way.

Chapter Eighteen

'She took the place after all, my dear,' remarked Albert Trewarren one morning in mid-July, looking up from his gloomy perusal of the paper.

Clara prodded her lamb collops without listening, waiting for the moment she could escape upstairs to her own room. For months now, the papers had seemed permanently full of the inevitability of war, with Papa shaking his head each morning over the breakfast table.

She hated it. It had nothing to do with her, but Papa had forbidden her to go to Paris, which, he declared, would be the first place to feel the wrath of the Prussian army, should war break out. He had also refused to allow her to spend the summer with Aunt June in Twickenham, or even return with him to Mayfair. In times like these, he had informed her, heavily, her duty was at her mother's side.

'Who did?' replied Mrs Trewarren, sounding more than usually disinterested in Papa's love of tittle-tattle, which, when coming from her own mouth was described as gossip but from his was a discussion of the deep workings of this world.

'The Chesterfield woman. She purchased Afalon outright.'

Mrs Trewarren paused in her needlework. 'I didn't know the Elliots had sold the place.'

'I've told you often enough, Violet, my dear, the family are in a shocking state. The London house has had to go too, and not even that will cover the entire debt. I warned Elliot years ago he was getting in too deep in his investments, but he never was one to listen.'

'I thought they'd keep it, however bad things got. Laura loved the house and the grounds. She would have wanted Afalon to go to Richard.'

Clara looked up from her book at her mother's tone. 'I didn't know you knew the Elliots, Mama.'

'It was a long time ago. Before you and Lance were born. I met Richard and Isabella's mother when we trained in first aid with the Red Cross. I used to visit her after she was married. She always preferred Afalon to their house in London. I remember it as being very beautiful. I can't believe it's gone. I would have liked to have seen the place for one last time.'

'Perhaps we should pay a visit to Miss Chesterfield, once she has settled, Mama? I'm sure all the other families will. It's ages since anyone new came to live here.'

Mr Trewarren snorted. 'Flock to see some fusty old spinster? Anyhow, she's probably an embittered suffragette, who can't bear to see the happiness of others and takes out her frustrations on planting bombs and burning down houses.'

'Only a man could assume a woman who has never married is bound to be bitter,' retorted Mrs Trewarren. 'Especially one with enough wealth to buy Afalon.'

Mr Trewarren gave the paper a quick shake, to signal he was too engrossed in the importance of world affairs to hear this trivial remark.

'It would be exciting if she was a suffragette,' put in Clara, to irritate him further.

The paper was rustled even more vigorously, and Mrs Trewarren returned to her stitching, lips set in a tight line. Clara sighed. It was so tedious, so very mundane. She and Ralph would never be like that. They would always discuss things as equals, like they did now, and never resort to running battles over who was the wisest and the best informed. And she would never, ever, have to sneak out, pretending she didn't have a life of her own. Ralph laughed at such stupidity. He never saw himself as the centre of the universe, with everything naturally bending to his greatness. She loved him more than ever.

Clara turned on the window seat to gaze out over the river. Upstream, the ferry was halfway across, making its way towards the opposite shore. Even from here, she could see it was not Hester bending over the oars, but the man who had taken over from her. Guilt nagged at her belly. The new ferryman had appeared only days after Hester had saved her life. Clara had tried to convince herself the change was a coincidence, but she couldn't help thinking it had been down to her own recklessness, which had forced Hester to beach the ferry and stay a night away from her family. Maybe it had made them think a woman couldn't handle the boat, after all.

With Lance at Oxford, she couldn't find a way of visiting Hester to ask. Clara itched with frustration at not being allowed through the front door without a chaperone. Even Ralph had gone, sent by his father to manage the family's hotel in Scotland, an impossible distance away.

She was glad Mama had no wish to go to London and Papa had long ago declared London would not be a safe place for women in the event of war, and they should both stay here when he was urgently recalled to advise the War Office, an event he seemed to think would happen at any moment.

She had dreaded being dragged, yet again, to every social gathering with the slightest hint of eligible young men. He could do what he liked. She could be just as stubborn as Mama, and nothing would induce her to ever again go through the boredom and mortification of a London season. Besides, Mama hated London and would do anything not to have to go back there. Clara didn't blame her. It was open knowledge that Papa kept a mistress in an apartment near Hyde Park. Clara had overheard one of the maids whispering that the latest was reputed to be half his age, more shame on him, and she'd not let any old goat lay a hand on her, thank you very much, not for all the fancy new gowns from Worth and a box at the opera.

Clara was even more determined to dig in her heels, due to a lurking suspicion that her father had been the one to point out the advantages of Ralph taking over the hotel in Scotland. Some days she was so angry she could hardly bear to look at him, even more than when she had first heard rumours of him taking a mistress. He was clearly convinced he was going to win, and she would eventually give in and marry some gout-ridden duke as old as the hills and become lady-in-waiting to Queen Mary at the drop of a hat.

She'd elope with Ralph to the gold mines of Australia first, and live in a tent and crush rocks until they had enough to open a hotel where even Papa could never reach them.

Chapter Nineteen

In the end, Mrs Trewarren didn't have to waste any time in finding a way to visit Afalon. After the customary exchange of cards and pleasantries in the tearooms at the Belleview Hotel, an invitation arrived from Miss Chesterfield for Mrs and Miss Trewarren to join her for afternoon tea.

Clara took the opportunity to put her recent driving lessons from Lance into practice, sitting proud, but slightly nervous, in the driver's seat, as the Ford bumped over the potholes all the way round the estuary. She tried desperately to control the urge to swerve whenever they passed a horse and cart or a motorised van, while anyone on a bicycle sent her into an agony of indecision. Her mother maintained a stoic silence throughout, although Clara could have sworn she only began breathing again once they swept up the driveway at Afalon, pulling alongside a serviceable Austin and a smart Daimler coupé already parked in gleaming splendour.

'You must excuse the house,' said Miss Chesterfield, leading them through corridors with empty rooms opening up on either side, each of which appeared to be in the middle of having its dark and heavily patterned wallpaper stripped away. 'The workmen aren't here today, so we shall at least have the afternoon in peace.' She took them to a large sunroom, overlooking the walled garden, with a glimpse of the wide stretch of estuary, opening up to the dunes leading to the sea.

'This looks lovely,' said Mrs Trewarren, as they took their

seats around a table already set with cups and saucers and small plates decorated with stylised irises, in the art nouveau fashion. She glanced round at the variety of exotic palms and ferns, accompanied by a scented creeper climbing up the back wall. 'I'm glad the plants survived.'

'You said you'd visited here,' said Miss Chesterfield. 'I'd hoped you'd be able to tell me something more about the house.'

'It was a long time ago. This was where we sat, whenever I came. I assumed it must have been completely changed over the years.'

'It's very much as I found it, apart from the furniture. The house is generally in better repair than I at first expected. It's strange, I'd made so many plans when I first saw the place, but, once I came here, I felt reluctant to change anything, apart from the décor. I may be a Victorian by birth, but not by outlook. I'm not sure houses can hang on to the past, but it felt as if this one was attempting to.' She smiled. 'Unless that was just me, daunted by what I'd taken on.'

'It's possible,' murmured Mrs Trewarren, looking uncomfortable.

'I'm not sure I believe in ghosts, but I do believe in atmosphere, as if the emotions a house has witnessed can be absorbed into its very wall. I felt from the moment I saw it that this one is intriguing.'

'What kind of atmosphere?'

Miss Chesterfield waited while an elderly maid brought in a tray with a teapot and a Madeira cake.

'I can't decide,' Miss Chesterfield said, as she poured the tea, to be handed round by the maid. 'When I first came in, I decided it was unbearably mournful. To be honest, I very nearly turned and walked straight out again. But then the more I went through the rooms, the more I felt something else.'

'Happiness?'

'I think I'd rather have called it love.'

'Oh.' Mrs Trewarren turned to gaze back into her teacup. There was a moment's silence. 'You must compliment your cook, Miss Chesterfield. This cake is delicious.'

'I would, with pleasure, Mrs Trewarren, but I'm afraid I haven't yet found one. Lottie has been with me for years, but I've not yet hired any other members of staff. There doesn't seem much point until the work has been done. And besides, given all this talk of conflict in Europe, I may need to change my original plans a little. As may we all, before very long.'

'Then you must be very accomplished,' said Mrs Trewarren hastily, as if to head off any prospect of the conversation turning towards unpleasant matters.

'Oh, good lord no. Lottie manages for just the two of us, but I wouldn't dare ask her to try something so time-consuming. I ordered this from a local woman, who has recently begun to provide cakes to local hotels and guest-houses as well as an excellent line in preserves. Your visit seemed an excellent excuse to see if her cakes taste as good as her apple compote. It's a pity she's retired, and suffers from arthritis, or I'd have offered her a post the moment I saw her handiwork.'

'But she managed this.'

'Ah, now that was mostly done by her granddaughter, who I believe she's training up. Miss Pearce. Maybe you know of her?'

'You mean Hester?' Clara, who had been sinking with boredom, shot upright. 'Hester made this?'

'Hester Pearce. Yes, that sounds right. You know her, then?'

'She's wonderful. She's brave and strong, and she never

gives up, and she can do anything—' Clara came to a halt at the look of mortification on her mother's face. 'I once saw her do something amazingly brave,' she mumbled. 'She risked her life to help a stranger when she rowed the ferry.'

'So *that's* Hester Pearce. Well, well. She rowed me over the river when I first saw Afalon, you know. I'd never seen a ferrywoman before, I was wondering what had happened to her. I can't say I was impressed by the young man who has taken over. Far too full of himself. I'm not surprised she's proved such an enterprising young woman, and I've no doubt, if circumstances were different, she could make a success of her business.' She sighed. 'My brother's an army man, he's already talking of the possibility of shortages and panic buying. One of the items he was advising me to stockpile was sugar. He's certain that would be the first to disappear from the shelves, should war be declared, as well as becoming prohibitive in price. If the worst happens, I'm not sure even the finest houses will be having the luxury of such cakes, let alone jams and preserves. Such a pity.'

'Perhaps,' put in Mrs Trewarren, with the air of wishing to change the subject. 'If you don't mind, Miss Chesterfield, Clara and I might have a glimpse of the gardens?'

'Of course, with the greatest of pleasure. They are in a sorry state, I'm afraid to say, far worse than the house. I've barely had time to look at them. I believe they were once very productive?'

'One of the best in Cornwall.'

'So I was told. Then perhaps you can advise me. The gardens were what settled it for me, despite the work needed on the house. So many of these old walled gardens have been destroyed. My intention was always to make Afalon fairly self-sufficient again, with the addition of a few luxuries from overseas, of course. I'm not completely in thrall to the past.' She frowned. 'Although, perhaps with things as they are, it might be as well to make any ground as productive as it can be.'

Mrs Trewarren quickly turned the conversation again towards safer waters, as they finished their tea and made their way down to the gardens. Miss Chesterfield unlocked a small wooden door, its bright blue paint faded and peeling. It opened, a little stiffly, onto an expanse of glasshouses, with the rest an overgrown wilderness of wildflowers and fading yellow rattle.

'The gardeners I've engaged have uncovered a whole network of vegetable beds,' said Miss Chesterfield, as they made their way a little gingerly along a path that had been roughly cleared to reach the fountain set just beyond the sheds and glasshouses. 'At least we have been able to do some planting this year, although far later than I'd like. We've found numerous fruit bushes and a small orchard at the far end and there are pots in the sheds that I presume were used to force rhubarb. I understand the old head gardener died last year, and I can find little information as to how the garden was organised. I'm afraid we are going to have to make it up as we go along. The fountain was completely covered in creepers. It must have a source of water somewhere, which I presume was the same supply used to keep the garden irrigated in the summer months. Although I expect any system is blocked, and the pipes could be completely corroded.'

'I believe it was fed from a spring on the hillside,' said Mrs Trewarren, peering up at the figure of a Greek nymph, her flowing robes covered in green slime, one hand reaching up towards the sky. She gently disentangled a coil of morning glory making its way among the marble branches and flowers at the nymph's feet. 'There must be someone nearby who worked on the pipeline. I seem to remember it was quite a business to keep it cleared of leaves. Several local families had men who were employed as gardeners here, but they were all dismissed when the family left, about three years ago. Most will have moved away to find work, but there should be someone who remembers. Hester Pearce's grandmother would be the one to ask, and about the planting, too. She was cook at Afalon, when the family were here.'

'Was she now? Most interesting. Thank you, I'll make sure I do. To be honest with you, Mrs Trewarren, it looks as if my plans will have to change a little. I was looking for a place to set up a charitable institution to treat men and women who have suffered industrial injuries. As one who has made her fortune from manufacturing, I've seen too many such injuries in my time, and how long it can take to restore the mind, as well as the body, after the loss of a limb or severe burns and scalding. That's still my intention, but, now that war seems almost inevitable, I feel it is my duty to offer Afalon as a private recuperation hospital for soldiers. It's the least I can do for any war effort.'

'Very commendable,' murmured Mrs Trewarren.

'In which case, I shall hope the men as they recover will work in here too, alongside the gardeners I've employed. From what I have seen, working with the soil is a good healer of the mind, as well as being beneficial when it comes to strengthening the body.'

Clara, who had barely been able to conceal her sense of tedium, stopped in her tracks. In front of her, a frog, disturbed by their intrusion, dived across the path, heading for some hidden source of water. Despite the heat, there was ice in her blood, travelling round every last part of her, sending a strange prickling feeling around her scalp.

Why, for all Papa's wealth, had she been brought up with so little education and told the world outside of politicians and trade policies, of lands grabbed and people enslaved, was nothing to do with her? That was her father's domain, she had been informed, until a husband appeared to take his place. She was to be protected from anything unpleasant, her female mind quite unable to grasp such complexities, her female weakness quite likely to result in any effort to understand sending her into a swoon, or even madness.

It was men who dealt with the world, women who remained, queen of the domestic sphere, the angel of the hearth, ready to sooth the fevered brow of those returning from offices where they conducted the arduous matter of keeping the Empire – and thus the entire world – in a state of Christian civilisation. Even with Ralph, their discussions had been of literature and history and ideals of how men and women should live, nothing of political machinations and armed conflict.

The stifling heat of the garden, with its scent of recently turned earth and the distant perfume of wild honeysuckle, settled back around her. She'd been a fool. A blind, ignorant, self-absorbed fool. This war, if it came, had everything to do with her. Just as it would with Hester, who had even less to do with heads of state and arguments over territories, but was simply doing her best to make a better life for herself and her family. Hester's business must mean everything to her, but the world saw it as irrelevant, just as her own hopes and dreams, even her life, didn't matter at all.

Slowly, she turned to follow Mama and Miss Chesterfield, who were making their way towards the greenhouses, deep in conversation. Serious conversation, the kind of which Papa declared women to be incapable. Clara listened intently to the discussion of logistics and potential casualties and how this could be a very different kind of conflict to the Boer War, being so close to home, particularly with so much of the country's supply of food and materials now being shipped in from all over the world. Not to mention reports of the German army having developed a kind of underwater vessel that could not be spotted from the surface, but rumoured to have enough firepower to sink even the largest of merchant shipping. The regular army, according to Miss Chesterfield, was most probably already being called up in preparation. But that would not be enough, not nearly enough.

'I fear you are right,' Mama was saying, almost too low for Clara to hear. 'And who is to stop them? The last time my son was home from university he was full of idealism about keeping his sister from invasion and brutality. I thought I could make sure he was safe if he was at Oxford, being so young and so passionate about his studies. But I'm not sure even that will keep him from volunteering if he sees it as his duty. He seemed to think it would be some kind of medieval tournament, as if it was something out of *Ivanhoe*.'

'Sir Walter Scott has a lot to answer for,' replied Miss Chesterfield drily. 'Along with all those *Boy's Own* stories of heroics and preserving female virtue from rampaging natives. Most of the indigenous populations I've seen in my time have been more rampaged upon than rampaging, if you ask me. While how the women and children, who always suffer the most in the end, are supposed to rampage, heaven only knows. And men tell us they are rational and the only ones to have a firm grasp on reality. I have to say, the longer I live the more thankful I am that I have my own means and don't have to look to a husband to survive. At least I'm not told what I should think within the walls of my own home.'

Their voices sank even further. But Clara didn't need to hear any more. She couldn't escape. If it came, this war would have everything to do with her. Lance was a romantic, full of high ideals. She knew as well as Mama that he would be one of the first to volunteer if he thought it was to protect his family, and the land of Shakespeare and Keats, and everything he held dear.

And Ralph? Utter terror shot through her. She couldn't fool herself and believe that Ralph wouldn't volunteer as well. The few letters she'd had from him, collected when she had managed to escape Mama, from the Post Office in Hayle, where they had been directed to avoid scrutiny, had been cheerful for her sake, but she could feel his unhappiness and frustration at the monotony – the uselessness – of his life. He wanted to do something to prove himself, he had said in his last letter, to show his true worth and gain her father's respect, so they wouldn't need any more of this cloak and dagger stuff.

She hadn't dared keep any of the letters, burning them before they might be discovered and her only contact with Ralph removed, but the words came back with a horrible clarity. What better than a war hero, who had proved his worth fighting for King and country, to impress Papa and remove any objections to their marriage?

She didn't care about impressing Papa. She didn't want his, or anyone else's approval. Every last part of her longed to run to Ralph and sweep him away to somewhere safe, where there would just be the two of them and the world need never intrude.

But the world was intruding. It was already keeping them apart, and now there was something far more terrifying appearing on the horizon. Clara looked back at the peace of the garden, vibrant with life and the humming of insects. It suddenly seemed to her that she had never seen anything so beautiful. She swore she would never take the fragile delights of any season for granted, ever again.

She wondered how many other women were standing in the heat of that perfect summer's day, holding a vague dread close to their hearts. How many were even now trying not to think what might happen, and how decisions taken far away, by men who didn't even know of their existence, let alone cared, might change their lives forever.

'I won't be so self-centred, or so thoughtless,' she determined. 'Not ever again. And I'm not just going to sit and let things happen.'

In the wider scheme of things, she had no idea what she could do, but at least Miss Chesterfield had given her a kernel of an idea of where she might start.

Chapter Twenty

'Well,' said Gran regretfully. 'That's the last of it. Heaven knows what we do from now on.'

Hester stared down at the small pile of sugar, thankfully just enough to finish their existing commissions, but they had already been unable to accept any more. There were ways of making preserves without sugar, which Mum had taught her when they'd been able to afford such a thing, but they didn't last as long, and weren't quite as satisfying to those with a really sweet tooth.

After all the months of war being talked of as inevitable, it had still been a jolt when the declaration had finally been made on the fourth of August. Since then, there were no visible signs of anything having been changed, but within days there had been panic buying and stockpiling, with flour and sugar being the first in short supply, with any that was still available far too expensive for a small enterprise that could not afford to take any losses.

It was all supposed to be a short, sharp shock, to put the Germans in their place and to be over by Christmas, at the latest. That was all very well, but they needed to start making their preserves now, while summer lasted. If sugar was still so expensive and in short supply that autumn, their main source of income would be gone, as well as the cakes that had kept them afloat last winter, when there were few fruits and vegetables to be had.

'I expect things will settle down,' said Gran, not quite able to sound totally convincing. Yesterday, the delivery boy collecting from the hotel in St Ives had been full of the government declaring it was a patriotic duty to have fewer courses, and that the talk was that petrol and the railways would soon be preserved for the movement of troops and essential supplies, and at this rate they'd be back to horse and cart, if there were any horses left, that is, so many were being earmarked to be shipped out to France.

Hester tried to feel patriotic and ready to sacrifice anything. But her life was her life, and all she could think was that she had reached so close to her dream only to see it vanish, yet again. With things so uncertain, she was going to have to be practical. To prevent all her hard-fought savings from vanishing, she would need to take the first cleaning job she could find, wearing out her energies for very little pay between cooking and cleaning at home. That also meant keeping Jimmy at bay was going to be so much more difficult.

'Come on in, Bob, the cakes are all waiting for you,' called Gran, at the hesitant knock on the door. The delivery boy for the hotel was new, his predecessor having already volunteered for the army, and painfully shy, being far too scared of Gran to try and enter before asked.

'Excuse me, I'm looking for Hester? Hester Pearce?'

Hester paused in reaching for the cake tins at the sight of the head peering round the door. 'Miss Trewarren!'

'Oh, it is here. Thank goodness. The lane is far too narrow, so I had to leave the Ford by the church and walk. People were terribly helpful, but I thought I was never going to find you.'

'Good morning, Miss Trewarren,' said Gran. 'What can we

do for you? I'm afraid we're not able to take any more orders at present.'

'Yes, I heard. I mean, at least I heard there were shortages and the price of sugar is beyond everything, and even Papa says we need to cut down on sugar in our tea for the war effort.' She was speaking rapidly as if nervous. 'But I expect you don't need me to tell you that.'

'No, indeed,' said Gran, hands on hips.

Clara blushed. 'Oh, I'm not going to offer you charity, Mrs Evans, I wouldn't dare. That is, I wouldn't want to insult you. But I would like to help.' She took a deep breath. 'Miss Chesterfield, who took over Afalon, is looking to employ a cook. A proper cook. Mama wondered if you would consider returning to your old post?'

Gran shook her head. 'Never return to the past. Besides, I'm not sure my arthritis would allow me to work at that kind of pace again. Especially if the rumours are right and the new owner is turning the place into some kind of recuperation hospital.'

'Yes, she is.'

'That's a whole different style of cooking, in that case. I'm beyond the age of learning anything new.'

'Oh,' said Clara. 'Mama did wonder. She was talking this morning of contacting other retired cooks and some who might be losing their posts in the hotels, if fewer visitors are going to be able to come to Cornwall because of the trains and the lack of petrol.' She twisted her hands in her skirt. 'But I wondered if Hester might consider applying.'

'Me?' Hester stared at her. 'I don't have any experience.'

'Miss Chesterfield says she's willing to interview you.'

'Indeed.' Gran was disapproving.

'I'm not trying to play lady of the manor, really I'm not, Mrs Evans. It's just that, well, Papa has been called back to

London and Mama is at one of her voluntary ladies' meetings this morning, something about rolling bandages. I just thought it might be the only chance. So I telephoned Miss Chesterfield. I promised I'd go with you, Hester, so you don't have to be on your own. I know it doesn't give you any time to prepare, but Lance is home for a few days with a friend, and they said they'd chaperone me, and Papa's given strict instructions I'm not allowed to take the Ford out without someone with me. Don't worry, they've gone off walking, they won't trouble us. I should have given you more warning, but I don't expect I'll ever be allowed out again, and at least you'll have a chance for her to like you before Mama tries to find someone else. I'm afraid Mama can be quite fearsome when she puts her mind to something.' Her eyes filled with tears. 'I haven't forgotten that you risked your life to save mine, Hester. I'm not trying to patronise you or tell you what to do. It's just, when I heard about the shortages, I wanted to try and repay you, just a little.'

Gran untied Hester's apron. 'Right, my girl. No time to lose. Wash your hands and brush your hair.' She clucked at the sight of Hester's dress. 'Pity it's too hot for a coat, I've barely worn the one Mrs Elliot gave me when they left. Well, at least you're reasonably clean and if Miss Chesterfield is an employer worth her salt she'll want to see you in uniform. Go on, hurry up. You'd better not keep Miss Chesterfield waiting.'

Hester obeyed. As Gran cleaned the evidence of flour from her patched skirts, while Clara skilfully tucked her unruly hair into a neat bun at the back of her head, panic set in.

'But I can't cook for a big house like Afalon, I don't know how.'

'You cook for your family,' retorted Gran. 'You know how to make a tasty meal from few ingredients, which may be the most useful thing you know if this war drags on beyond Christmas. Besides, I've taught you as much as I can of the fancier things without a fully equipped kitchen. You know the basics and you can follow a recipe. You have Sadie's recipe book. That's all you'll ever need. The rest you can learn as you go along. I'll always be here to help you if you need it.'

'But what about you, Gran? I don't want to let you down.'

'Don't you worry about that, *cariad*. I'll go back to my garden and making what preserves I can without sugar until this all dies down again. Listen, darling, Miss Clara here is giving you a chance. This war might have closed one door for now, but it's opened up another. This might be the only chance you have for now to pursue your ambition. Besides, working as a cook in a big house, especially at such a young age, will give you invaluable experience. This could lead to work in a hotel once this is over and the visitors return, even if M. Alphonse is no longer able to offer you training in the skills of fine dining. Our little business can wait for now. This could still give you a chance to open your own cafe one day, after all.'

'But Dad—'

'And when did your dad ever put your interests above his? We'll sort something out.'

'It would be a full-time post,' said Clara. 'But I don't think Miss Chesterfield will expect you to work for a pittance, Hester.'

'There you go,' said Gran. 'You may find you can pay a woman to go in a couple of times a week to cook and clean for your dad. And if Jimmy wants to eat, he'll just have to learn to shift for himself, rather than you waiting on him hand and foot. With any luck, it might make him start looking elsewhere for a comfortable existence.'

'That's true.'

'Won't that be worth it, just to be free of doing it yourself for the rest of your life? And don't worry about the children, we can do as we planned. It will be a pleasure to look after them. Besides, Robbie will be leaving school soon, he's a reliable lad who'll easily find work and Alice is no trouble and usually has her nose in a book or in investigating bones. I'm not having mouse skeletons in the house, for love nor money, but she's welcome to come here and do her book studying. There, you see, you needn't worry about her getting stuck with the household chores.'

'Your grandmother is talking sense,' said Clara anxiously.

Hester swallowed. 'I'm not sure...'

'Rubbish.' Gran sniffed loudly. 'Look here, *cariad*. Choices are never easy, and every woman I've ever met has had it drilled into her from birth that she doesn't count, and not all the flim-flammery in the world can make up for that. Now, I'm not saying your grandfather was of that opinion, or he'd have had nothing more than a boxed ear when he asked me to marry him. There are good men out there, you just have to be very sure of them.' She sighed. 'And never marry in haste, my dear, and hope for the best. Your mother loved you with all her heart, she would never have wanted that for you. And most decidedly not the likes of that self-serving young creature your father is so determined to foist on you.'

Hester shut her eyes. The very thought of not having to see Jimmy and be an audience to his boastful conversation with Dad each evening, while trying to resist any need to venture to the privy, to avoid his increasingly unsubtle attempts to meet her on the way back, wandering hands at the ready, was a prospect of bliss she could not resist. She threw any lingering doubts to the wind.

'Yes, Gran.'

Clara grabbed her hand. 'I knew you would. Come on, if we hurry, you'll see Miss Chesterfield before anyone else has a chance.'

Chapter Twenty-One

Hester followed Clara along the path under the garden walls, joining the lane just as it opened up to the main gates of Afalon. They were greeted by a maid, who led the way through corridors, all newly whitewashed, with large, strangely empty-looking rooms on either side. The maid stopped in front of a small office, knocked on the door, ushering Hester and Clara inside.

'This is Miss Pearce, Miss Chesterfield,' said Clara. 'The young woman who makes such wonderful cakes.'

'Of course.' Miss Chesterfield climbed down the small wooden ladder she was using to place files on the highest shelves and motioned Hester to take a seat. 'Pleased to meet you, Miss Pearce, I'll be with you now.'

Clara mouthed good luck, followed by an encouraging grin and disappeared, shutting the door behind her, leaving Hester to sit rigidly in her chair, watching every move of the rather imperious-looking lady, in a practical-looking skirt and blouse, who had most probably organised an entire palace of servants in her time and terrorised the lot of them. On her own territory, Miss Chesterfield looked a lot fiercer than she had in her walking skirt and boots when Hester had rowed her across on the ferry.

'Good morning, Miss Pearce. Now then, first things first. I understand from Miss Trewarren that you wish to be considered for the post of cook.'

'Yes, Miss Chesterfield.' The clear brown eyes were watching her closely from the other side of the desk. For an unnerving moment, Hester was convinced Miss Chesterfield had spotted her trying to hide in the apple tree that day in the walled garden and was about to call the local constabulary. She met the direct gaze. Whatever happened, she wasn't going to be treated like a thief, or the lookout for a band of robbers, depending on the fruitfulness of Miss Chesterfield's imagination and her preferences when it came to the more sensational variety of detective fiction.

'And yet you have no experience.'

Hester blinked. But she wasn't giving up that easily. Her chin shot up. 'Not in a big kitchen, but my mother died when I was eleven, so I've cooked for my family much of my life, and my grandmother has been training me in how to be a proper cook.'

'Hence the cakes.'

'Yes, Miss Chesterfield.'

'I'm not looking for fancy sugar work, or dishes to pander to the jaded appetites of those who have never known hunger and view the tasting of food as a form of sport. Good, plain, nutritious food is what I'm after, Miss Pearce, and plenty of it.'

'I'm used to that. Not in large quantities, but my grandmother will be able to tell me anything I'm not sure about.'

'I understand you have two younger siblings, still at home?'

'A brother and a sister, both at school.'

'You do understand, Miss Pearce, that this post would require you to live in?'

'Yes, Miss Chesterfield.'

Miss Chesterfield unbent a little. 'I won't change my mind on that, Hester. It's always been my policy.' She gave a faint smile. 'I wasn't born with money, I've had to earn every penny I've ever owned. Believe me, my dear, I know what it's like, being expected to go home after a day's work to start all over again cooking and cleaning and getting the family washing done. Here, it will be all or nothing, especially when recuperating soldiers arrive. I need someone who can think on their feet and not faint at the sight of missing limbs and skin burnt to the bone.'

'Yes, Miss Chesterfield.'

'So I hope you understand there would be no opportunities for showing off, as you might expect in such a large house. Like I said, good, plain cooking, using as much as possible of fresh produce from the walled garden as it comes into season. I will offer a practitioner in physical massage to those who need it, but I'm a great believer in the benefits of fresh air and gainful exercise. Once the gardens have been prepared and laid out, I hope as many of the men as possible will be encouraged to undertake some of the lighter work, maybe even have small allotments of their own. Sometimes, in my experience, it is as hard for the mind to heal and adjust to injury, as for the body. I believe you may have experience of such things.'

'My dad lost his arm in an accident several years ago.'

'So Clara told me.'

Miss Chesterfield was not quite as fearsome as she had first seemed. More to the point, she appeared prepared to listen.

'I don't think Dad's ever got used to it. He's always trying to make things as they were before. I think it tears him apart, and that can make him rather unkind at times, even though he doesn't mean to be.'

'And it's not easy being an eldest daughter.'

Hester swallowed back sudden tears. 'He doesn't mean it. But that doesn't make any difference.'

'It never does.' Miss Chesterfield became brisk and practical again. 'It also makes me think that perhaps you might not be afraid of such injuries, or treat men who have suffered them any differently from those who are whole.'

'I hope not.'

'Good. Now, if you follow me, I'll show you the kitchens.' She stood up. 'If you are prepared to comply with the conditions, Miss Pearce, I'm willing to give you a month's trial. If that is successful, the post is yours.'

'But the other applicants...'

'Who said there were any other applicants?' Miss Chesterfield placed her hands on her hips, more in the manner of a fishwife than a fine lady. She must, Hester decided, have been a mildly terrifying figure for any employees on the factory floor. 'I like you, Miss Pearce. I like your honesty. And I like a woman who can row a ferry when her father is incapacitated and, when things change, pick herself up and try her hand at something different and make a success of it. Besides, I've tasted your work. I may not be one with much time for fine dining, but I can recognise a cook who knows her flavours. You have initiative and ambition and a capacity for hard work. Everything else can be learnt. Don't worry, I know this has come out of the blue for you, I don't want an answer now. I understand that this would be a big step, and that you will therefore need to be sure in your own mind. I will give you three days to think it over and discuss it with your family. Then I will need an answer, one way or another, as I will require a cook in earnest before long.'

'Thank you, Miss Chesterfield.'

'Oh, and Miss Pearce—'

'Yes, Miss Chesterfield?'

'I'm fully aware there are rumours flying round as to the source of my wealth. Well, you can reassure your father that

I've never run a string of houses of ill repute, and I certainly have never been in the habit of entertaining the Prince of Wales when the moon is full.'

Hester found her mouth had dropped open, and quickly shut it again. 'I'll make sure he knows.'

'The truth is, I invented a manufacturing process in my youth. Officially, it's in my brother's name, of course, or it would never have been accepted. But he's an army man, with no interest in the manufacture of domestic conveniences, and he's happy to be the patent holder in name only. But knowing that women are still assumed to lack the brainpower to do anything more than embroider cushions, I find it simpler to let it be generally assumed I inherited a manufacturing empire.'

'Yes, Miss Chesterfield,' said Hester, feeling she'd rather shout such an achievement from the rooftops.

'Excellent. I'm glad we understand each other. Now, if you'll follow me, I will show you the kitchens.'

Hester emerged into daylight, nerves strung to bits and feeling more than a little dazed.

She'd expected to be grilled within an inch of her life on the intricacies of filleting a gurnard or megrim sole, or ensuring a soufflé didn't sink before it got to the table. In the end, she wasn't sure that she'd been asked anything much about cooking at all. Miss Chesterfield was certainly an eccentric, but, oddly, she felt more at home in her presence than that of many of the more respected women of Hayle.

She had arrived at Afalon uncertain and full of doubt, for all Gran's reassurance, the complexities of finding an alternative arrangement for Dad and the children niggling at her mind. But she came out knowing deep in her bones that this was what she wanted. This was more than being cook in a grand house, catering to the rich, this was something that would have a sense of purpose.

'Hester!' She found Clara waiting for her. 'Well? Did Miss Chesterfield offer you the post? I'm dying to know. Only, you don't have to tell me, of course.'

'She offered me a month's trial.'

'That's wonderful! I knew she would. You are perfect for the post, Hester.'

'I might not pass the trial.'

'Yes you will, you know you will. She's only doing that for form's sake, otherwise she wouldn't have bothered.'

'Thank you for dragging me here. I'd never have dared to apply if I'd just seen the post advertised in the newspapers.'

Clara tucked her arm into hers as they made their way down the driveway. 'Yes you would, Hester. You are brave and determined and I know you'd have seen it and tried, even if you didn't think you had a chance. Miss Chesterfield is a businesswoman, she wouldn't have let you near her kitchens if she wasn't sure of you. So really, you've nothing to thank me for at all.' She turned to wave to the Ford pulling to a halt just outside the gates. 'Lance said they'd meet me here. We'll give you a lift.'

'There's no need, I can walk.'

'It's starting to rain, and I'm sure you've got enough to do when you get there, I know how hard you must work. Besides, there's plenty of room, it would be churlish not to offer you a place. Lance, we can take Hester back home, can't we? It's not too far out of our way.'

'Not in the least. It will be a pleasure, Miss Pearce.'

'Thank you,' said Hester, resisting an unexpected urge to blush. She wasn't accustomed to young men smiling at her in open admiration. At least not since she'd taken up the oars of the ferry, so gaining the reputation of a Cornish Amazon, unlikely to submit meekly to a husband's directions, a rather uncomfortable prospect for any suitor in search of an angel to return to at the end of the working day.

Lance turned to his companion. 'This is Miss Pearce, Elliot. Mrs Evans's granddaughter. It seems rather appropriate that Hester may soon be taking her place here as cook.'

'I believe we met as children.' Close to, he had changed, and yet at the same time remained the same. His face had lost the roundness of childhood, but his eyes were still as dark as ever. Deep grey rather than a true black, she could see now, with a flick of green near the iris. The watchfulness was still there, even sharper than before, as if, over the intervening years, he had honed his skills of observing sticklebacks and any other creatures that came to his attention. She had an uncomfortable feeling of being at the magnified end of a microscope. She did her best not to wriggle.

'I think we did, Mr Elliot,' she replied.

'I'm sorry your mother was kept standing that day. I'm sure if Mama had any idea ...'

'She wasn't to know. None of us could know what would happen.'

'All the same.' He grimaced. 'My mother always meant well, but she could be a little thoughtless when it came to her painting.'

'I'm sure Mum understood.'

'I hope so.' His expression lightened a little. 'And now I can see that Isabella was bound to win the bet she made with me that it wasn't Clara in the walled garden, after all.'

'I didn't know you were a betting man, Elliot,' said Lance good-humouredly. 'And you a scientist. I understood students of botany were entirely rational.'

Clara laughed. 'It's the painting, you dolt. The one Mama swore was of me. She liked the idea of me being a flower girl, however many times Isabella said it was really a friend from the village. I didn't know you'd been to Afalon, Hester.'

'Only that once,' she replied, blushing furiously despite herself. 'Gran was looking after me. Does the painting still exist, then?'

'Isabella insisted on taking it with her when we left,' said Richard. 'She loves that picture. She says it brings happy memories.' He was back to inspecting Hester again. 'I think she is right, Mama actually caught a likeness, for once. Although the one of my sister doesn't resemble her at all.'

'So, I'm afraid we're not long-lost sisters, Hester,' said Clara. 'Much as I'd like us to be. Mama just assumed the flower girl had to be me.' She sent an apologetic look in Richard's direction. 'I'm afraid she didn't expect it to be recognisable.'

'I can see my poor mother's artistic reputation went before her,' said Richard drily.

'Dear Richard, I know how fond you were of her, and it really doesn't matter in the least.'

'I suppose not.' He turned to Hester. 'I remember you said you were going to be a cook, Miss Pearce.'

'Hester isn't going to stay at Afalon,' said Clara. 'When things have settled down a bit she's going to make her wonderful cakes and open a cafe.'

'So I remember.'

'And you needn't worry about the gardens, Richard, not with Hester employed as cook. Her grandmother is bound to remember the old planting schemes. I'm sure the gardeners will consult her, rather than just tearing the place up.'

'I hope so. Perhaps it won't be completely destroyed after all,' he winced. 'Not that I have any say in it any more, of course. Perhaps I was wrong to come back, they say the past should never be revisited.'

'Not all pasts,' exclaimed Hester, without thinking. 'I'd hate to lose my memories.'

'Even the most painful?'

'Especially those. They made me think and question and see every moment as precious. And things like grief and loss are what everybody shares. They made me more human. I wouldn't want to stay a child all my life. Children can be horribly cruel.'

'That's true.' This time she could not read his expression. 'Although I seem to remember at least one who once showed me kindness when I needed it most.'

'I hope anyone would, Mr Elliot.' Hester's stomach gave an unexpected twist. She squashed it firmly. Lance's admiration was one thing. It was flattering, but she knew deep down that he wasn't the kind to defy his family's expectation of marrying a girl of his own social standing, with a fortune to her name.

Richard Elliot was quite another matter. They might have been children that first time they met, but they had shared a moment of intense emotion, the fear of a loss too terrible to bear. It felt like a breaking down of the usual barriers between strangers, especially ones social convention dictated would never meet on equal terms.

It was probably different for a man, but for her it felt like suddenly being on uncertain ground. That inner determination about setting up her cafe wavered slightly, like a boat sent off course by an unexpected riptide. What was she doing, putting all her energies into an impossible task? Did she really want to end up an elderly spinster who might have a comfortable living, but having seen the possibility of love passing her by?

Miss Chesterfield claimed to be happy in her single state. It struck Hester for the first time that she was not so sure she could be equally contented without a family around her, however absorbing her work. She pulled herself together. She was being stupid. What was Richard Elliot to her, to bring up such thoughts? There were plenty of young men this side of Truro eager for a wife. Just because she was spending her time fighting off Jimmy didn't mean she wouldn't one day find someone she could love and who would love her in return. All the same, the unsettled feeling wouldn't quite leave.

Hester had never been so glad the journey from Afalon was brief. Even the novelty of sitting next to Clara in the back seat of a motor car, watching the hedgerows rush towards her at the most terrifying speed, couldn't ease her desire to escape and get as far away from Richard Elliot as she possibly could.

'Good luck, and I'll come and see you as soon as I'm back, I promise,' called Clara, as Lance courteously handed Hester down next to the shop declaring itself 'Treves and Sons, Grocers', to the sudden appearance of shopkeepers at every door and windows being flung open as far as the eye could see. Hester dusted herself down as the motor car roared off into the distance.

'Bugger off,' she growled to the delivery boy, who had stopped his bicycle to stare and was now sending a mocking wolf whistle in her direction. Ignoring the curious glances from all sides, she took the nearest side street, and strode purposefully towards her grandmother's cottage.

Chapter Twenty-Two

Dad, as she had expected, was furious.

'What about Robbie and Alice? You can't just abandon them.'

'I'll be earning money, Dad. Miss Chesterfield's offering me more than I would get in a shop or as a housemaid. Robbie will be leaving school soon, he'll be earning too. I'm not that far away, I can pop in to make sure things are running smoothly.'

'You have your responsibilities here.'

'But isn't it better to have me earning? Gran has said she'll help with Robbie and Alice, and I can help you pay for a girl to come in to cook and clean.'

'I'm not having anyone being paid to look after me.'

'You pay Jimmy,' she retorted.

He bristled. 'What's that got to do with it?'

'Dad, don't you see? This is not just for me. This is a chance for us to have good money. I've been given an opportunity to have a real skill. A profession. Most girls like me are never offered such a thing.'

'What do you need with a "profession"? You cook well enough for here. You should be settling down and cooking for a husband, not spending your time cooking for strangers.' He shuffled himself into his coat. 'I'll speak to this Miss Chesterfield first thing tomorrow and tell her you've changed your mind, and that your place is here, with us.'

Before Hester could open her mouth to argue he had gone, stomping in the direction of the Fisherman's Arms.

Hester pushed away the potatoes she was peeling. At least Gran was looking after Robbie and Alice for a few hours, to give her time to talk to Dad alone. If Dad thought she was going to give up so easily, he had another think coming. She reached inside Dad's hiding place, for the bottle of brandy, bought cheap and kept for medicinal purposes. She poured herself as much as she dared into a cup, carefully replacing the bottle in the same place, and escaped into the garden, to the bench where Mum had used to sit of an evening, beneath an arch of musky climbing roses.

Hester swallowed a large gulp. The unaccustomed alcohol burnt her throat, sending her coughing, but it warmed her empty stomach and went straight to her head. She finished the remainder slowly. Her mind was clearer than ever. She had to take this chance and go to Afalon. Gran was right. With the uncertainty of war making their little business impossible to continue, let alone expand, this had become her only chance to escape the unpaid drudgery of her life and keep her dream of independence and the cafe on the beach alive.

She jumped to her feet. Supposing Dad was already making his way to see Miss Chesterfield? Heaven knew what he would say in his temper, especially if he called in to the Fisherman's Arms first. She doubted Miss Chesterfield would be intimidated by Dad, however much he swore and threatened her, and she probably wouldn't believe him when he said she'd changed her mind. But Miss Chesterfield might find it too much trouble, employing a Pearce, especially when the head of the family was likely to turn up at any time to march her off home.

She couldn't just wait for him to return, calmly cooking

his tea, without knowing. If he was going to try and see Miss Chesterfield this evening, she at least had to try and stop him or be there to fight her corner. The rest of the vegetables would have to wait. She returned to the cottage, carefully washing out the cup to remove any evidence that she had taken, however briefly, to hard liquor, and ran down into the hamlet, heavy with the smoke of fires as evening fell.

There was no sign of Dad, even when desperation made her brave the stares in the Fisherman's Arms at the sight of a respectable female daring to cross its threshold. Mr Pearce had not been near the place, the landlord assured her, practically shooing her out before he could be accused of running a house of ill repute, and having half the matrons arriving with their brooms and their washing dollies to restore order and hauling their menfolk away from petticoat temptation, with orders never to set foot inside its unhallowed walls again.

That meant Dad might have gone rushing up to Afalon. The only other place would be the ferry. It must be making its final run of the day, which meant he could have gone to recruit Jimmy to settle the matter once and for all. Well, she'd soon put a stop to that. She wasn't having both of them going at her for the rest of the evening, while expecting her to feed them as they ranged up against her.

Temper rising, Hester strode down the narrow alleyway at the back of the Fisherman's Arms leading to the ferry. There was no sign of Dad. The ferry had recently moored and had been secured for the night, while the last of the passengers finished putting the world to rights and made their way wearily back towards home, with several of the men slipping into the Fisherman's Arms for a swift one their wives and mothers just might not notice.

Across the wide expanse of estuary, she could make out the lights of the houses and the glow of gaslights lighting the streets that served the grand houses on the riverfront. The headlights of a motor car streaked along the roadway, heading in the direction of Hayle. It was a world that seemed a lifetime away.

She looked back at the little hamlet, encased in its swirl of smoke, the cottages almost in complete darkness apart from the glow of the occasional candle and the warm reflection of a fire. Doubt set in. Maybe Dad was right, maybe she was fooling herself. Most who were born in the hamlet died there, never having travelled more than a mile or two in their whole lives, marrying someone they'd known from their schooldays. Sometimes the men brought back a girl from the next village, who was eyed slightly askance until she showed she understood their ways and didn't try to bring any foreign influences to disturb the peace and the way things had always been.

Dad must have headed off straight to Afalon, after all. He was probably hectoring Miss Chesterfield already. Hester stood in the encroaching darkness, the black ripple of water at her feet. He wasn't going to win. He couldn't. As much as the dreams disturbed her, she could feel the promise of freedom telling her how much she ached for independence. If she stayed, it would kill her.

'I thought you might be here.' She started. She'd been so deep in thought she hadn't noticed Jimmy joining her. She suddenly felt how quiet it was, the fishermen, and even the courting couples stealing precious moments, had disappeared. She cursed herself for letting him find her in such a secluded place, after successfully avoiding him for so long.

'I was looking for Dad,' she replied, turning to make her way up among the houses.

'I sent him back home.'

Relief made her dizzy. 'You saw him?'

'He came down to the ferry. He told me what happened. He was on his way to the Fisherman's Arms, but I suggested he should go back and make peace with you first.'

'Thank you. That was thoughtful of you.'

'I was only thinking of you. I wouldn't wish you to be unhappy, Hester. You wouldn't really abandon us, would you?'

'Abandon?'

He grasped her arm. 'Hester, you know how I feel about you. I couldn't bear to let you go. You know your father's wishes. I can already support you, and your dad and brother and sister. You don't need to find work for some old woman and a house full of men, who could offer you all kinds of insults. Who could protect you there? Besides, you know no one will employ you once you are married. How else are you to look after the children?' His voice lowered as if offering her a priceless gift. 'Our children, Hester.'

Well, what else could she possibly want in life but the honour of bearing his offspring and tending to his every need?

'And if I don't want to marry? At least not yet.'

'Don't be ridiculous.' His grip tightened. 'Don't you know everyone is talking of how you arrived in Lance Trewarren's motor car, bold as brass, for all to see? They're saying he's already ruined you and abandoned you to your shame. No one else will ever go near you now.'

She pulled herself free. 'Anyone who was there would have seen it was Clara Trewarren who had kindly given me a lift. You don't expect she'd be visiting this side of the river without her brother acting as chaperone, would you? And you can't think much of me, if you think I'm that stupid.'

'I'm only trying to protect you, Hester. You know so little of the world.'

'And you do?'

'Don't you dare.' He grabbed her arm again, harder this time, pulling her around to face him. 'Think you're better than me, Miss Hoity-toity? Think you know more than me because you've got rich friends? You know nothing.'

'I didn't say that. And I don't have rich friends. I think we both know very little of the world. I just want to know a little more.'

'I can teach you.' He pulled her towards him, mouth trying to find hers in the dark, his hands pawing clumsily at her breasts. How he thought that might arouse her to irresistible heights of passion she couldn't imagine.

She knocked his hands away. 'Let me go.'

'You know how I feel about you.'

'So that means I have to feel the same?' She shook him off, walking as smartly as she could towards the nearest cottage with the light of a fire in the window. Hal Solver was a respectable family man, a fisherman she had known all her life. One knock on his door and he and his wife would sweep her inside and make sure she was accompanied the rest of the way home.

'You little—' Jimmy instantly caught up with her, pulling her against him, his breathing uneven. Fear settled cold and hard in her belly. He was angry at her resistance, but she could also feel the excitement in his ragged breathing, not so much for love, but anticipation at subjecting her will to his. Conquest, he would no doubt call it. 'Time to bring you down a peg or two, looking down your nose at me.'

'I don't look down my nose. I just don't like you. Now bugger off.'

This time he was in earnest. He flung her roughly against the wall. It caught the side of her face, dazing her. She felt the trickle of warmth down her cheek, as he pulled her to face him, hands pulling at her clothes.

She would only have one chance. She stilled the panic, as she had done when the tide threatened to take the boat, keeping her body rigid, not fighting him. He had not noticed, intent on raising her skirts until her legs were free. His hand found the inside of her thigh, pulling at her underclothes.

'Hester,' he whispered, leaning in to her. Her one chance. Her knee jerked up with all the force fear and anger could lend her. As he collapsed with an agonised yelp, she fled, the yell of 'bitch!' ringing in her ear.

Hester raced through the narrow streets, not daring to stop until she reached the ferryman's cottage. Dad looked up from the fireplace as she shot through, slamming the door behind her.

'Hester!' Her head was spinning. She put her hand to her temple and it came away covered in blood. 'What on earth happened to you?'

'It was an accident.' Jimmy was right behind her, red-faced, mouth a thin line of temper. 'Hester slipped and hit her head against a wall. She was lucky I was with her. Anything could have happened.'

She saw Dad's gaze waver. It was her word against Jimmy's. A silly girl with an overheated imagination against a rational man whose only wish was to protect her. Dad was already convinced she had taken a frigid maidenly dislike to Jimmy. He hadn't believed her before, why should he now? He'd think she was simply overreacting to a clumsy attempt to kiss her.

'I'm all right,' she muttered. She found a rag and poured some of the still-warm water from the kettle into a bowl. Her head was pounding.

'Let me see?' Dad pushed the hair from her temple with a surprisingly gentle hand. 'That's a nasty graze.'

'I've had worse.'

'Are you hurt in any other way?'

'No,' she replied firmly, meeting his eyes. She pulled away as Robbie appeared at the door, followed by Alice, keeping her head bent as she finished chopping the vegetables, until she was certain the bleeding had stopped.

It was an unnaturally quiet evening, without the usual flow of conversation around the table. Jimmy didn't move from his place next to Dad, regaling him with the activities of the day, pretending he didn't notice Dad replying in monosyllables, his eyes travelling from the scratches reddening on Jimmy's cheek and Hester stirring their stew, as if not watching them at all. Even Robbie was quiet, not joining in the day's events, as if sensing something was not as it should be, and that a storm was about to break.

After their meal, Dad didn't go with Jimmy to the Fisherman's Arms, muttering something about it being too late. Jimmy waited as long as he could, until after Robbie and Alice had gone to bed and he had no choice but to head back before Mrs Gowlais locked her door against the world, leaving him to face a night under the stars.

There was silence in the little cottage as Jimmy's footsteps vanished into the next street. Hester finished wiping the table and putting away the clean bowls on the shelves. Dad didn't say a thing, not even when she handed him a cup of tea, drinking her own as she continued to make the kitchen as clean and orderly as she could, ready for tomorrow.

As she finally turned towards the small bedroom she shared with Alice, he put a hand on her arm.

'Hester—'

'I'm tired, Dad.' She felt tears welling up, threatening to disarm her. It would take only a little kindness and a few promises from him, for her to rush up to Afalon tomorrow to tell Miss Chesterfield that she couldn't take the post. It wouldn't take much for her to stop fighting him and do as he wished, putting the interests of the rest of the family before her own, just as all women should.

But, deep in her heart, she knew that, for all he might listen to her this evening, while he was still shaken out of his self-absorption by the signs of violence on her face, tomorrow Dad might find it convenient to change his mind. She knew him too well, she thought sadly, to trust him with her life. Whatever happened now, this was a parting of the ways. She had never felt more alone.

'I'll see you in the morning, Dad. Goodnight.'

Alice was already fast asleep when Hester reached the tiny back bedroom. Her stomach clenched as she pulled the covers closer over her sister. She couldn't leave Alice here, for Jimmy to turn his attention towards in a few years' time. She would have to make sure her little sister stayed permanently with Gran from now on, at least until she was old enough to leave school and begin training as a doctor.

She looked round the little room in the flicker of her candle. It was only just large enough to fit the bedstead, with a broken chair to hold their skirts from creasing while they slept and a wooden box beside it for their meagre underclothes. The pane of the tiny window was cracked and a sheen of damp glistened on one wall. All the same, it was where she had slept for as long as she could remember. Like the rest of the shabby little cottage, it was home, holding memories of Mum kissing her good night, and Mum singing in the kitchen as she prepared vegetables for the day's meal, before heading off to work with Gran or clean for Mrs Leavan.

Carefully, so as not to wake Alice, she placed her spare skirt and blouse over the bedpost, wrapping her torn and muddied clothing into a tight ball, out of sight. She could not bear to even look at them. Pulling her much-mended nightdress over her head, she crept into the lumpy part of the mattress that formed her side of the bed and that had, over the years, moulded itself to her shape.

Hester shivered. Her feet were cold. Her head throbbed violently, and she could feel the bruising taking hold of her body. Whenever she shut her eyes, she could see Jimmy's face next to hers, monstrous in the light reflected from the river. She could feel the clawing at her clothes, like a wild animal, that had nothing to do with passion, but a desire for mastery of her, body and soul. She curled up tight, trying to sleep, her mind racing with all the practicalities of the next few days and, most of all, how she was to avoid being alone anywhere Jimmy could find her, ever again.

All her life, the protective world of the little hamlet had given her the freedom to walk where she pleased, within reason, and to never think twice about taking the secluded path to Gran's cottage, or to collect apples from Afalon. She wasn't a fool. She'd known not to take risks. But she'd always had the security that her own reputation for not being a flirt or a pushover would keep her as safe as anyone could be, supported by fear of Robert Pearce's rage at her back. But Jimmy was different. He was the enemy in the camp, the thief with a carefully nurtured reputation for helpfulness and reliability, for being not the kind of man who would do such a thing.

She would always hate him for attempting to obliterate her sense of herself, and for taking away her freedom, and for making it impossible for her to remain, even if she had wanted to. For making her afraid.

Dad was back to his old self the next morning, although he showed no signs of rushing to confront Miss Chesterfield. He didn't mention any possibility of change to the household, as if he had already pushed the idea from his mind, convinced that things would carry on as they had always done.

Hester waited until she could make out both Dad and Jimmy safely on the ferry and rowing over towards Hayle, before she took the short walk to Gran's.

'Good grief!' Gran looked up in horror as Hester appeared at the door. 'What on earth happened to you?'

'It's all right.'

'No, it's not all right. That's a nasty cut, and your arms are black and blue. That had better not be your dad.'

'No.' Hester shook her head, fighting back tears.

'I see. So that's how it is. Did he—'

'No. But he'll try again. I know he will.'

'Well, in that case, my darling, you can't stay under that roof a moment longer.'

'I'm on my way to tell Miss Chesterfield I can take up the post straight away.'

'Good girl. Now, you sit still while I sort out that cut, and we can arrange your hair so it's not that obvious.'

'Gran—'

'Now, don't you worry, *cariad*. There's no need to ask. I'd already made up my mind to suggest Robbie and Alice should stay with me. I'll take care to meet Alice from school and I won't let her out of my sight. Alice's a good girl. Neither she nor Robbie will be of any trouble at all. They can stay with me for as long as they need.'

'Thank you, Gran. That means more than I can ever say. I couldn't leave them there, not once I've gone. I'll find someone to cook and clean for Dad, and I'll be able to pay for the children's food out of my wages, and anything else they need.'

'Don't worry about that.' Gran finished adjusting Hester's

curls. 'That will do for now. You go and see Miss Chesterfield while young Jimmy's occupied.'

Hester hurried to Afalon as fast as she could. Miss Chesterfield gave her a sharp glance, but made no comment on the state of her face.

'I suggest you start tomorrow morning,' she remarked. 'Unless that is too soon for you to make arrangements?'

'Not at all. Tomorrow will be perfect.'

'Excellent,' said Miss Chesterfield, pulling the bell pull beside her. 'Your room will be ready for you. Lottie will show you where it is and take your measurements for your uniform. I'll see you tomorrow morning, then, Miss Pearce.'

Lottie arrived within minutes, brushing flour from her arms with distaste, as if she'd be perfectly contented never to have to come in contact with such a thing again. She was not quite able to repress a broad grin at the news that the new cook was starting so soon.

Hester followed the elderly maid up to the very top of the house. 'Is this all for me?' she exclaimed, as Lottie opened the door to a room that, while small compared to the rest of the house, was as large as the entire living space at home. It contained a single bed and a chest of drawers, with an old, but comfortable-looking armchair set next to a window with a view over the walled garden. There was a rug on the floor and sheets and blankets sitting in a neat pile on a mattress that looked as if it had never been used.

'I'm just next door,' said Lottie. 'And there's a small sitting room at the end of the corridor. Miss Chesterfield's strict, but fair, and she looks after us all right. She's got some very new-fangled ideas on nutrition, mind. She doesn't believe in too much meat, especially now we're all supposed to be eating so much less for the war effort, which doesn't half make it awkward cooking. Some days I've scratched my head, especially now there's the gardeners to be fed, and then there'll be nurses and doctors before long, if this war lasts, and that's before any patients. Am I glad it's not my responsibility any more.'

'I'm glad to be able to take over, in that case,' said Hester, squashing the sudden terror running through her. Talk about being thrown in at the deep end! She hadn't thought that there would be so many people to be fed from the very start. She was going to have to get this right straight away, or she would be back where she began, and worse, having to go home with her tail between her legs, with Dad and Jimmy knowing she wouldn't even get a good reference to enable her to find another post, and so with no choice left.

Hester squared her shoulders. This was one step closer to her dream. One day, when this war was over, she was going to move to St Ives, or even Truro or London, if that's what it took to be free of Jimmy Harkness and his schemes.

She wasn't going to spend her life looking over her shoulder, afraid to leave the cottage, knowing Jimmy might be waiting, this time determined not to let her escape.

Whatever it took, and whatever lay ahead, she wasn't about to fail. Not at any price.

Chapter Twenty-Three

The next morning, Hester tidied up the cottage once Robbie and Alice were safely in school and Dad and Jimmy were on the ferry, and placed her few spare pieces of underclothing in a bag, along with Mum's recipe book. There was soup ready to be heated up that evening and enough rent money in the tin.

She took a last look around. The cottage had been the centre of her world for as long as she could remember. It was the place where all her most passionate memories were held, the place to run to, where she had belonged and where she felt secure. But no longer, she reminded herself, as tears sent the table and the range dancing in front of her eyes. Thanks to Jimmy and his schemes, this was no longer a place of safety. From now on, she would only ever be a visitor. This would never be home again.

Closing the door behind her, she made her way along the row, thankful that it was quiet this morning leaving little time to chat, or for questions about the fading bruises on her face. Once she reached the path to Afalon, she looked back towards the estuary. The ferry was just setting out towards Hayle. She waited until she was sure she could make out Dad, with Jimmy at the oars. With a sigh of relief, she hurried along the secluded path under the garden walls, jumping, despite herself, at every crack of a twig or the scurry of a rabbit across her path. It wasn't until she was within shouting distance of the house that she could breathe freely again. At least here, within Afalon, she could feel safe.

The kitchen felt vast, with two ranges installed along the walls on either side, both looking as if they had been there since before the Elliots arrived at Afalon. Between them stood a long wooden table, and, proudly in view, a new cooker, the very latest kind, powered by the electricity Miss Chesterfield had installed, run by a generator in one of the outbuildings.

'I wouldn't touch it, me,' muttered Lottie, who volunteered to help her with breakfast for the first day, but was unable to hide her relief at the prospect of being finally able to escape from kitchen duties. 'They say if you put a finger on it when it's lit, the electricity goes straight through you and you die like that, as you stand, and anyone else who is touching you, too.'

'Well, I ain't touching it either, then,' said Molly, the kitchen maid, who, at just fourteen, looked as scrawny and undernourished as if a gust of wind might blow her away. She had arrived that morning and looked overwhelmed at the size of the kitchen, let alone the appearance of all the new-fanged equipment. 'That is, unless you want me to, Cook. Then I will, I promise. I don't want to cause no trouble.'

'I'm sure Miss Chesterfield has made certain it's safe,' Hester reassured her. 'She's a businesswoman, she knows it's not good business to kill your staff on a daily basis.'

'Oh.' Molly caught her lower lip in her teeth, as if not sure how to take this.

'It's all right, Molly. There's a book of instructions on the shelves. That'll tell us what to do. We can use the range for now and work it out bit by bit. If we've any doubts, there has to be someone in Hayle who can explain.'

'Yes, Cook.' A look of relief went over Molly's face. 'I wouldn't mind, being electrificated to bits, that is, only Mum's relying on my wages, see.'

Hester hadn't considered being in charge of staff, especially not familiar faces. She'd instantly recognised Molly as Jenifry's eldest daughter, who had played with Alice in the street outside, until the morning the family had been evicted. The prospect of organising anyone else, when she didn't know what she was doing herself, was almost as daunting as getting the kitchen up and running.

She'd kept a family together, she reminded herself. And in a much smaller space than this, where they were constantly falling over each other. Besides, she always had Gran, who might not know anything about electric cookers, but would surely know about everything else, and had worked for years in these very same kitchens.

At least breakfast was a reasonably simple matter. Miss Chesterfield, she had been relieved to discover when they had briefly discussed menus, had no great taste for the vast amounts Hester had heard were still served up at the local hotels, despite the number of courses having been reduced as a contribution for the war effort. Whatever might be expected in the future, for now the household settled for omelettes rather than mutton kidneys and bacon, or sirloin steak and mutton chops, delicacies Hester had only heard of. She had a feeling that, war or no war, the bacon bits she'd been proud to afford to add tastiness to a stew when she was rowing the ferry wouldn't cut the mustard here. Thank heaven for knowing she could rely on Gran's experience and being a quick learner.

With everyone fed, and Lottie disappearing upstairs with

the air of a woman who wished never to experience the inner workings of a kitchen again, Hester turned her attention to making her new surroundings her own.

The walls had been freshly whitewashed, but the wooden surface of the central table was ingrained with grime from the builders putting up new shelving and the new lights and cooker. Miss Chesterfield had confessed that she and Lottie had lived in a style more suited to camping under canvas while the work had been finished, with a prevalence of toast and butter, along with greens from the garden to supplement pies delivered on a daily basis from the bakers to be heated up in the oven.

Lottie had quite enough to do in the rest of the house, and both the vast larder and the long arrays of shelves on each wall were deep in dust. At home, it was almost impossible to boil enough water to keep the pans and the surfaces spotless, but the ferryman's cottage was lit only by the glow of daylight creeping in through the windows during the day, and the fire at night, supplemented by candles and a lamp at most. Here, there were large windows that allowed sunlight to flood in, while the electric lights, bristling with newness, revealed each scratch and smudge on every single surface.

The first thing Gran had drilled into Hester had been the importance of cleanliness. She was certain it would be even more important here once patients arrived to convalesce, with their systems weakened by illness. Hester rolled up her sleeves. This, at least, was something she knew how to organise. The rest she could work out later.

'Right, Molly. We are going to need to boil plenty of hot water and find the brooms and the scrubbing brushes. This all needs to be spotless before we really start.'

'Yes, Cook.'

Molly was a hard worker, and, despite her size, surprisingly strong. She moved sacks of flour and jars of dried beans, before scrubbing the larder from top to bottom, while Hester kneaded bread and turned the vegetables brought in by Tom, the youngest of the gardeners, into the tastiest soup she could manage. As the bread proved, and the soup simmered away gently on the range, she helped Molly brush away the worst of the grime and the dust, and set to with mops and scrubbing brushes. Before long, the kitchen was gleaming, each pan bright as could be, hung up and ready for action, shelves and table scrubbed within an inch of their lives.

'There,' said Hester, as she and Molly sat down at last for their own bread and soup, before starting on preparations for the evening meal. 'That's more like it. Now I feel I can rustle up anything, at a moment's notice.'

'Yes, Cook,' said Molly, tucking into the fresh bread and butter as if she had never seen such plenty before and was fearful it might be snatched away by a stronger hand at any moment. Which, come to think of it, was probably her experience of life so far. Heaven knows what had happened to them all after Jenifry had been evicted. It was the talk of the row that Jenifry's husband had abandoned them, slipping out of the back door, while Mr Bolsover was in the process of evicting the family at the front.

Molly's father was now rumoured to be living in a terraced house in Hayle, with a woman young enough to be his daughter, who already had a baby on the way and had been seen with more than one black eye for her pains. Jenifry had stayed with one of her sisters for a while, a few streets away, and then her mother, but it was common knowledge that she and the children had ended up in the workhouse, in the end.

Hester silently cut another thick slice for Molly and a thinner one for herself to keep her company. Mum had always made sure, whatever happened, they never went hungry. There was a sudden unbearable ache to be able to see her mother again, this time with her adult understanding of how hard that must have been. For all she had been worn down by her life, Mum had kept the fire inside her, and done her best to pass it on to her children. They had been lucky. Hester felt her anger at Dad ease a little. For all his selfishness, Dad had always loved Mum in his own way, and while he might never have put much care into his offspring, he had never laid a finger on any of them. She shuddered to think what Molly had seen, or what blows, or worse, she had known in her short life.

Hester had a sudden urge to run down and hug Dad, while he was still there, while she could, in some kind of acknowledgement of the side of him that was so often hidden from view by his self-absorption. Except, of course, she recognised sadly, he would most probably take it as a sign she had recovered her sense of duty and agreed to marry Jimmy, after all.

'Slow down, Molly,' she exclaimed, alarmed at the sight of the kitchen maid trying to cram as much of both slices of bread into her mouth as she could. 'We've been working hard all morning, and there's nothing fancy to cook for tonight. We've plenty of time.'

With a mouth too full to speak, Molly chewed and swallowed hastily, practically choking herself. Hester poured her a second cup of tea, which Molly downed in one, finally able to breathe again.

'Yes, Cook.' Molly couldn't quite help herself from making the most of the plenty in front of her, but at least finished her meal rather more slowly, and sat back, colour already lighting up her face.

'Now, Molly, how about we finish what's in the teapot before we start again. Have you ever made a fruitcake?'

'No, miss – I mean, Cook.'

'Well, I saw some dried fruit left in the larder that needs using, Miss Chesterfield said there's honey to take the place of sugar and we've eggs and butter. I happen to know Miss Chesterfield is partial to a bit of cake, so how about you help me with that?' Molly looked wary, as if this was a trap of some kind. 'I'll need help with cooking, especially once the patients arrive, not just with scrubbing vegetables and washing up. And anyone who learns cooking skills can always find work. Besides, I think with all this cleaning we're doing, you and me could do with cake with our afternoon tea, to help us along.'

'Yes, Cook,' said Molly, the faintest of gleams in her eye.

Later that afternoon, with a large fruitcake in the oven and the pastry made for the meat pie for the evening meal, Hester left Molly in charge of cleaning cake tins and ornate jelly moulds, and made her way down into the garden. She had no need of the key in her pocket, the door was slightly ajar and there was a murmur of voices in the distance, echoing hollowly within the walls. For a moment she hesitated, feeling an intruder.

'Idiot.' Unlike her reckless climb of the apple trees, she now had every right to be here. This was going to be her larder, the basis of everything she would ever make as cook at Afalon, and no one would question her wishing to inspect her ingredients, least of all the gardeners Miss Chesterfield had hired to make the space productive again.

'Afternoon, miss.' A small, elderly man, bent from years of heavy work, appeared, followed by a young man of twenty or so, pushing a wheelbarrow filled with spades and an alarming array of saws.

'Good afternoon. Mr Hicks, isn't it?'

'That it is, Miss Pearce. Pleased to meet you.' The young man with the wheelbarrow grinned broadly, his pleasant face lit up with the novelty of so young a cook. He had clearly been expecting some ancient termagant, with set ideas and a habit of working gardeners to the bone.

'I won't keep you,' she said. 'I just wanted to get a look at the gardens.'

'Yes, of course, miss,' said Mr Hicks. 'Anything I can get you? I can send Gareth here, or Ben or young Tom up to the house with anything you need.'

'That's quite all right, Mr Hicks, Tom brought us plenty of greens this morning, thank you. Everything looks delicious. I just came to have a look around, if that's all right. I don't want to disturb you.'

'Not at all, miss. You carry on. It's a bit of a mess you'll find. None of the old gardeners would come back, the ones who were here when the Elliots owned the place.' He grinned, his weather-beaten face almost disappearing into wrinkles. 'Not so hardy the young, these days. Not easy to get gardeners, they're all off serving in department stores or working in factories. It could do with more here, to get the place back to the way it was, but we'll make do with what we've got. They might not know much, but they'll learn.'

'I'm sure they will, Mr Hicks.'

Mr Hicks had retired from one of the large houses down the coast several years ago and had been hired for his expertise rather than his physical prowess. He nodded and indicated to Gareth to continue pushing the wheelbarrow towards the orchard. A lanky young man of Gareth's age, and a boy who looked as if he should be still in the schoolroom, stopped their digging of a patch of soil. They followed the wheelbarrow as it bounced along over the rough paths towards the next task of the day.

As the men vanished into the wilderness at the far end, followed by the sounds of energetic cutting back to start preparing the ground for next year, Hester turned to explore the buildings around her. She had only glimpsed the glass-houses before, here they loomed above her, even larger than she remembered. With the lack of available manpower, these had clearly been left for now, in the more urgent clearing of ground while the weather held.

She gingerly opened the door of the first. Several of the panes were cracked or missing, and the wood of the frame had rotted in places. But inside was surprisingly intact, given the general air of neglect. The grapevine stretched under the glass, ripening black grapes hanging in tightly packed bunches, with tendrils escaping through any crack they could find. The heat and the damp was oppressive in the August sun. She was glad to get back out into the fresh air, to inspect a slightly smaller glasshouse.

'Melons,' said Hester aloud. She pushed the door, which was swollen and distorted with damp and creaked unwill-ingly to let her pass. Inside, there was a musty smell, with the faintest hint of mushrooms. Beds had been built up on either side, which must once have been home to the exotic fruit, leaving only a narrow path in between, for the gardeners to tend to their every need.

'Well, and we won't be growing melons. Or pineapples,' she added. 'Nothing so fancy.' She could just imagine the gardeners' reaction if barrowing tons of manure to the pineapple pit was added to what she suspected was already an unending list of duties. She'd read in the newspaper the reports of young men all over the country rushing to volunteer for the army. Miss Chesterfield was probably lucky to have found any gardeners at all.

Past the greenhouses, she found several sheds, all of them in less than good repair, encased in brambles and buddleia, with one sporting the tip of a willow from its roof. She peered in through small-paned windows frosted with grime and the webs of spiders. In one, she could see spades and rakes hanging from wooden hooks, waiting for the gardeners to return. The furthest shed appeared to be a storeroom, with an office set off on one side. The large chair had been pushed back at an angle from the desk in the office, as if the head gardener had just stepped out to harangue one of the boys brought in on trial. Rusting shears and a large metal syringe contraption with a pump of some kind lay on the seat of a less official chair, with the look of being misplaced as their owner joined the fray.

There was something eerie about the sense of abrupt abandonment, as if the inhabitants had stepped out for a moment, expecting to return and resume their daily duties before sundown, but then been forced to abandon ship.

Beyond the office, the garden opened out into vast stretches of partially cleared vegetable beds, interspersed with herbs and flowers. Several of the smaller patches had been roughly dug over, as if more in haste and out of necessity than any expertise. She could make out earth piled up in rows where potatoes had been planted and the half-finished structure of twigs ready to support peas and beans. Behind them lay the green of kale, along with cabbage, and a vast swathe of what looked like spinach.

Beyond that lay the overgrown beds now being tackled by the gardeners, set either side of a path that was lined with pear and apple trees, espaliered into an arch to offer some protection from the weather.

It all seemed normal. Peaceful. As if war could not touch such a quiet, out of the way place as Afalon. She glanced back towards the abandoned office with its carelessly discarded equipment and pushed away a lurking sense of unease.

Chapter Twenty-Four

'So you're not too grand to come and visit us,' said Dad, as Hester joined him on the jetty a few weeks later, having carefully waited until she'd seen the ferry set off across the estuary towards Hayle.

'I'll never be too grand, Dad. You know me better than that.'

'But you won't come back to the cottage,' he grumbled. 'There's nothing like your cooking, Hester. That Jenifry isn't nearly as good, and not a word to say for herself.'

'Jenifry's a good cook, Dad. She's just shy, that's all. Don't you remember, her husband wasn't always kind to her? She'll be better once she gets a bit more used to you.'

'But it's not the same. I miss your cheerful face, and your company.'

'I'm sorry, Dad. It's hard for me to get away from Afalon for now, even on my afternoon off. There's so much to do, before it can be ready as a convalescent home for soldiers, and so few people to help. I don't like to leave them for long.'

'The war won't come here. You mark my words. It won't be long and it'll all be over. And then that Miss Chesterfield will look a fool for her busybodying.'

'It's not just at Afalon,' replied Hester. 'Miss Chesterfield says there are large houses up and down the country being prepared, as well as the hospitals, just in case they are needed.'

'Over by Christmas.' One of the elderly fishermen mending

nets on the jetty nodded. 'That's what they're saying. Over by Christmas.'

'Bound to be,' added Hal Solver, who was easing his arthritis in the sun while putting the world to rights with Dad and the steady stream of passengers waiting for the ferry. 'Them young lads as joined up on the first day, they'll be back afore they've finished their training, just you see, and not a shot fired.'

'Stands to reason,' remarked the fisherman, looking up from his net. 'An Englishman is worth twenty of them Germans.'

'And a Cornishman twenty,' added Hal Solver triumphantly, to comfortable nods all round.

'But still too late for the farmers,' opined Mr Blewett, the landlord of the Fisherman's Arms, stepping out to join them on the jetty to finish his pipe, bringing with him the lingering aroma of cheap tobacco mixed with stale beer. 'They're all complaining there's whole crops rotting in the ground for the lack of anyone to harvest. That'll be even less cash around this winter, that's the long and short of it.'

A sense of gloom descended on the jetty, followed by conversation quickly turning to last night's catch and the terrible price of things, these days, what with profiteers making the most of things, as they always did.

Hester shivered slightly in the sun. Out here, with the familiar routine of life carrying on as it had always done, it was still hard to imagine there was a war on at all. Even in Afalon, among the rush of preparations, it didn't seem quite real. Over the past weeks, every time she emerged from the kitchens something had changed. From the drawing room to the library, the bedrooms to Mrs Elliot's old sitting room, every available space had been cleared of the cumbersome old furniture, much of it from the old Queen's time, before being whitewashed and fresh new curtains hung to replace the old moth-eaten velvet that shut out the light even on the brightest day.

Next, beds had been lined up in each one, with the old library being set up as a room where the expected patients would meet and socialise, with the best of the old sofas and armchairs being kept to provide some home comforts.

Over the last few days, with the sense of urgency fading, a stillness had settled over Afalon. It had become a matter of waiting, which Hester had found even more unnerving than preparations to receive casualties being readied to return to the front line. It was the silence that could set the imagination working.

On the far side of the estuary, the ferry was returning. 'I'd better go, Dad,' said Hester, kissing him. 'I'm walking back to Afalon with Jenifry's Molly and Miss Chesterfield will be expecting us.'

'She works you too hard,' grumbled Dad. 'That's the trouble with fine folk, don't think their servants should have a family, or time to themselves.'

Hester ignored this and shot off to find Molly before Jimmy reached the shore. She felt sorry for dragging Molly away, especially now Jenifry had managed to earn enough through cleaning Dr Graham's surgery, with the cooking for Dad thrown in, to rent a tiny cottage set next to the church hall. She kicked herself for still not having the courage to make the short walk back to Afalon on her own. But even when she could clearly see Jimmy on the ferry, she could still feel his hands tearing at her clothes, his breath on her face, smothering hers. The only way she could make the journey to see Dad was when she could arrange for Molly to see her mother at the same time, and even then, she hated staying too long.

Molly however, was out of the door before she had a chance to knock, pulling her coat on as she reached the street with hands red and swollen from being immersed in hot water, face pink with exertion.

'Mum's started to take in washing, on top of all the rest,' she explained gloomily as the two set off towards Afalon. 'She's got my sisters at it, day and night. She'd have me back there, if it wasn't for Miss Chesterfield being a good payer and Mum needing the wages coming in regular.'

'Would you like to go home?'

'Bloody hell, no! Share a bed with five wrigglers? I'd never get a wink's sleep. And I don't know what washing soda Mum's using, but it strips the skin off you. Then who'll marry me? There's precious few lads to step out with as it is.'

'They'll be back, just you see,' replied Hester, with a smile. She glanced back over the estuary. Jimmy had set out again. She breathed a sigh of relief. 'We don't have to hurry. How about we gather blackberries on the way? Miss Chesterfield still has plenty of honey. I think apple and blackberry pie sounds every tempting.'

The two spent a happy half-hour gleaning the fruit that had ripened since their last excursion, fat and luscious and warmed by the sun, which they placed in Molly's basket, along with the bright red of the first rosehips, ready for making cordial to sooth coughs and keep colds at bay. Black bunches of shiny black elderberries were added to the mix, while they noted where the best of this year's sloes were already beginning to darken towards their winter gloss.

Hester couldn't help feel a tug of regret at the abrupt rise in the price of sugar, as with so many things, that meant she and Gran could no longer make use of such bounty. But still, she was luckier than most, having a post with a woman commanding enough wealth to be able to afford sugar at all.

At least it meant she could take some of their rosehip cordial to Gran, who suffered with her chest each winter.

They reached the grounds of Afalon, chatting away cheerfully, hands purple with blackberries.

'Oh, my lord,' said Molly, as they approached the house. 'I promised I'd be back before she arrived for tea. Lottie's going to skin me alive.'

'It's only tea,' Hester reassured her, glancing up at the severe figure sitting on the terrace with Miss Chesterfield in the slanting warmth of the afternoon sun. 'And I left a whole Madeira cake for them. Lottie won't have had much to do.'

'Ah, Hester.' Miss Chesterfield spotted them before they could make good their escape. 'Do come and join us.'

'Of course, Miss Chesterfield.'

'D'you think they expect me, too?' hissed Molly, eyeing Mrs Trewarren nervously. 'That old dragon scares the living daylights out of me, that she does.'

'It's all right, Molly. I need you to put these in separate bowls in the coolest place in the larder so we can start working on them tomorrow. Then you can prepare the blackberries for tonight.'

'Yes, Cook, thank you, Cook.' Molly bobbed a curtsy in relief, half towards Molly and half towards their fearsome visitor, before scurrying out of sight, the contents of her basket bobbing perilously at her side.

'Mrs Trewarren is volunteering her services in obtaining volunteer nurses to help us,' announced Miss Chesterfield.

'Yes, miss,' said Hester, hoping the sinking feeling in her belly wasn't betrayed in her voice.

'For which I'm truly grateful, still being a relative stranger in these parts and so having very few useful contacts.'

'As I told you, Maud, I need to do my bit for the war effort. I've volunteered with the Red Cross for years. I've taught hundreds of local girls first aid, and I've already been contacted by at least a dozen who are eager to volunteer their services as VADs. It seemed the sensible thing to do, to direct them here.'

'Excellent,' said Miss Chesterfield, sipping tea. 'I'm grateful for the sacrifice of your time.'

'I had to do something.' Mrs Trewarren put down her tea next to her untouched slice of Madeira cake. 'I can't just sit at home now Lance has volunteered. He and Richard Elliot went to sign up together last week.'

'They're going to fight?' exclaimed Hester, stomach lurching.

'They've already left for training. Young men are volunteering in droves for King and country. And now Mr Trewarren tells me he will be required to stay in London for the duration of hostilities. So, you see, I have to do something. The very least I can do is to volunteer the use of the motor car and to find some reliable VADs. I am hoping to persuade Clara to join me. It turns out her young man joined up the day war was declared. He could be out in France before any of them. The poor child is distraught, she's quite convinced herself she'll never see him again.'

'I'm sorry,' said Hester. She couldn't bear to remain a moment longer. The golden afternoon of laughter and summer richness had turned unbearably cold, as if warmth would never touch her body, ever again. 'I'll make you another pot, that one must have stewed by now.' She collected the teapot and fled towards the safety of the kitchens.

Hester came down to make preparations for breakfast the following morning after a restless night. Her head was fuzzy with lack of sleep as she waited for the kettle to come back to the boil. The range had been lit and the floor swept, but there was no sign of Molly, who could usually be guaranteed not to move far from her side until they had served Miss Chesterfield her breakfast and settled down to their own.

She was just about to set off to look for her, when the kitchen door was flung open, followed by Molly shooting inside, a basket of potatoes on her arm, her hair wild, cheeks red from running.

'They've gone!'

'Who's gone, Molly?'

'Ben and Gareth. And Tom, too. They've gone to be soldiers.'

'Soldiers?' Hester stared at her. 'But Tom's only sixteen!'

'But they have. When I opened the door just now, there was no basket of vegetables outside. So I went to look. Old Mr Hicks dug up these, but I had to help him, his back's so bad. He said they'd gone. They'd been telling me they'd go for days, but I never thought they would. Not really. I thought it was just boys showing off, like they do. Gareth kept on saying it was a chance at adventure and seeing places and maybe getting a position far better than gardening at the end of it. Oh, but, Cook, I never thought they'd really leave. What are we going to do now?'

'It's all right, Molly. You carry on here and I'll speak to Mr Hicks. I'm sure this can be sorted out.'

Hester poured a cup of tea into one of the tin mugs favoured by the gardeners, sweetening it with spoonfuls of precious sugar, and hurried down to the walled garden. As she pushed through the door she could feel the stillness and the silence. No sound of digging or pruning, or of young men's laughter as they bantered with each other while they cleared the ground.

'Mr Hicks?' She found the elderly gardener bent over his

spade in the potato patch, cheeks red with effort, beads of sweat covering his forehead.

'It won't take me long, Cook,' he said, setting to again with a start. 'Like I told young Molly, I'll bring the rest of the potatoes along in a bit.'

'Thank you, Mr Hicks, but we've enough to go on with. That can wait.' She held out the tea. 'Drink this while it's fresh.'

'Thank you, miss.' He took the cup without protest and sat down, breathing hard. 'Molly told you the lads have gone, then?'

'So it's true.'

'I should have known. I thought there was something up, the moment they arrived this morning. Gareth was telling them there's a recruiting officer at Hayle town hall today. I had a hunch Gareth and Ben might well volunteer sooner or later. Especially after them women and their white feathers shamed Ben's cousin, right outside church for all to see, and him in a reserved occupation too.' He shook his head. 'I wouldn't want to stop them doing their duty, they're both over nineteen. But they were telling Tom to say he was nineteen too, so they can all go over together to France once they have finished their training. Tom's far too young, even if they never get near a battlefield.' He looked round despairingly at the garden, with, despite their late start, so much ready for harvesting. 'And heaven knows what we're going to do here.'

'It's all right, Mr Hicks, there's bound to be a way round it.' Fear had begun niggling at the back of Hester's mind. She pushed it away, concentrating on the matter at hand. 'Take time and finish your tea, Mr Hicks, then I think you'd better come up to the house. I'll explain things to Miss Chesterfield, I'm sure we can find a solution between us. There are plenty of people who want to volunteer to do their best for the war effort.'

Hester hurried back, catching Miss Chesterfield as she settled down for breakfast on the terrace with Mrs Trewarren, who had driven over early to make the most of the cool of the morning to sort out Afalon's supplies of sheets and bandages.

'Breakfast will be a little delayed, I'm afraid,' she explained breathlessly. 'I'm very sorry, Miss Chesterfield, but the young gardeners have all left to sign up.'

Miss Chesterfield set down her teacup. 'Damn them, the young idiots. It's hard enough to recruit gardeners as it is. It's very commendable, but it doesn't stop there being work here to be done and precious few to do it.' She frowned. 'Isn't young Tom only sixteen?'

'That's what Mr Hicks said.'

'I understood they had to be at least eighteen to sign up?' said Mrs Trewarren. 'And nineteen to be sent abroad once they've finished their training. Surely they'll just send him back.'

'Not if he's got enough between the ears to lie,' said Miss Chesterfield. 'Which I rather suspect he has. Friends near London have told me the army's taking any lad who claims to be over eighteen and is strong enough. Tom's tall for his age, and a lot more muscular than much older men who've been working as clerks or shopkeepers.'

'Dear me,' said Mrs Trewarren, shaking her head.

Hester found Miss Chesterfield watching her closely. 'What is it, my dear?'

'Mr Hicks said the recruiting officer was at Hayle town hall. I know I only had my afternoon off yesterday, but could I please go there after breakfast, Miss Chesterfield? I'll make sure Molly knows what to do to prepare for luncheon.'

'You've a younger brother, haven't you?'

Hester nodded. 'He turned fourteen last week. But he's almost as tall as Tom and he's strong for his age. He's just started working with Harbottle's the bootmakers in Hayle.' She swallowed. 'I've just got this feeling…I promise I won't be long, and I'll try to find Tom as well.'

'Of course.' Miss Chesterfield reached out and squeezed her hand reassuringly. 'You go now, Hester. Don't worry about breakfast. I'll go and terrorise Molly by making bacon and eggs for us all and we can join her and Lottie in the kitchen to eat. This is more important. You go.'

'Thank you, Miss Chesterfield.'

'I'll drive you, Hester,' said Mrs Trewarren, abruptly. 'It'll take hours to get there otherwise.'

Hester looked at her in dismay. The last thing she wanted was to be cooped up in a motor car, most probably needing to answer questions as to whether she'd frittered away the money she'd been given on boots and dresses and ribbons for her hair. 'But you've plenty to do here, Mrs Trewarren.'

'That can wait. You need to make sure your brother isn't doing anything stupid. Besides, I can find Tom and return him home. His mother is the best seamstress in Hayle. She must be frantic.'

'Thank you,' said Hester, glancing towards Miss Chesterfield, who nodded. Mrs Trewarren was already on her feet.

'Come on then, Hester, the sooner we get to Hayle town hall the better.'

The drive was as wild as could be. At least Mrs Trewarren was too occupied to grill Hester on any subject, as she hurtled round potholes at full speed, pushing Lance's Ford to its limit, sounding her horn loudly at carts and delivery boys as she sailed past them, enveloping them in clouds of dust.

They arrived in Hayle to find the streets crowded, even more so than on market day. As they passed the town hall, they saw that it was surrounded by a large crowd of men, patiently queuing in snaking lines to go inside.

'There are hundreds of them!' exclaimed Hester. 'I'll never find Tom and Robbie if they're among that lot.'

'We'll find them,' said Mrs Trewarren, bringing the Ford to a screeching halt. Hester jumped out the moment the wheels stopped turning, running as fast as she could towards Harbottle's. The shop was strangely quiet, with just a few older men working away in the back room. There was no sign of Robbie.

'Robbie's sister, isn't it?' said Mr Harbottle, a wizened little man, who appeared permanently bent over, as he abandoned his last to meet her at the counter. 'Hester Pearce?'

'Yes,' she said, gasping for air, ignoring the stitch in her side.

'Well, he ain't here. Turned up this morning, bright and early. Then off he goes with two of me apprentices and half a dozen youngsters from Vernon's the draper's and the hardware shop down the road. Boasting they were getting out of here and seeing the world they did. And never mind my boots. How am I supposed to get them done now? I've orders due.'

'I'll find him,' she said firmly. 'Robbie's far too young to join up and he needs a trade. I'll bring him back within the hour, I promise, and I'll make sure he doesn't try anything like this ever again.'

'I'll give you an hour,' said Mr Harbottle, returning to his work. 'And that's only because there's no chance of the others coming back, and after all the hours I put into training them,' he snorted. 'My only hope is if they fail to pass the medical, and they're saying there's plenty of them out there. Shocking the state of some of them, and them two always were a weedy pair, the both of them. Gone soft have young men, nowadays. Need a bit of backbone, the lot of them.'

'Yes, Mr Harbottle,' said Hester meekly, taking to her heels once more. She raced to the town hall, ignoring the disapproving looks at a young woman dodging through the crowds like a wild thing, hat streaming from its ribbons behind her.

Once she reached the crowd of waiting men, which had grown even larger, Hester moved from line to line, seeking out Robbie's face, or any sign of the gardeners from Afalon. It was a boisterous, cheerful crowd, one that seemed to be setting out on an adventure, rather than on their way to war.

'You joining up too, miss?' called the grocer's lad who had never quite forgotten the sight of her stepping down from that posh motor car, like a lady and all. He was no more than seventeen himself, grin as cheeky as ever.

'I'm looking for Robbie. Have you seen him?'

'Not here, Miss Pearce, but then we've only just arrived ourselves.'

'You don't mean Pearce's son, do you?' called a voice from the next line.

'Yes, Robbie Pearce. I was told he'd come here.'

'Oh, it's you Hester.' To her relief, she recognised one of the younger fishermen from the jetty outside the Fisherman's Arms, who'd known Robbie all his life. 'He's a bit young, isn't he?'

'I'm worried he's going to lie about his age.'

'Wouldn't be the first,' said a man from further down the line. 'They're telling the lads who say they're less than nineteen to go out and come straight back a few years older.'

'Then I've got to find him.' Hester pushed through the line, but there was no Robbie or Tom, and she could find no sign of Mrs Trewarren. After a while, she didn't dare call out, terrified that Robbie would hide from her behind the other men, or, if he had already signed up, make sure he was out of sight until it was time to be moved out for training, and heaven knows how they'd find him.

By the time she'd pushed to the front of the queue, she was desperate. Among the noise and the confusion and the good-humoured jostling, she dodged under the arm of the men on the door and into the town hall.

'Robbie!' She spotted him immediately, just leaving the nearest table.

A man in uniform grasped her arm. 'Miss, you can't come in here.'

'Yes, I can.' She shook him off. 'I've come to fetch my brother.'

'My dear lady, we understand your natural sisterly anxiety, but the young man bravely wishes to serve his country.'

'He's fourteen,' she retorted. 'Are you recruiting children?'

The recruiting officer at the table looked up. 'And what do you have to say about this, young man? Do you still say you are over nineteen?'

'I—' Robbie hesitated. Hester's heart twisted. He had looked so proud standing there, ready to head out to France to do a man's job, to get away from them all. He was as tall as the men around him, and looked a good deal healthier than many in the queue, more than one of whom were stunted, with barely an ounce of muscle on them, having never tasted a square meal in their lives. Thanks to Mum's care, and then her own, it was no wonder he passed as older than his years.

'I think you should go with your sister, don't you, son?' said one of those waiting to sign up. 'I'm a teacher at a local school. I can confirm Robbie Pearce was with us until a very short while ago. A matter of days, in fact. The lad's only just fourteen, let alone anything older.'

Robbie's face collapsed in humiliation, tears springing to his eyes.

'Well, in that case ...' Already the recruiting officer had lost interest. The line moved on, another man taking Robbie's place.

'Thank you, Mr Allison,' said Hester, grabbing Robbie's hand, pulling him out of the hall.

They emerged to find Mrs Trewarren conducting her own search of the lines. 'Well, at least that's one.'

'No sign of Tom?'

'None. There has to be someone who saw the three of them.'

'They could have crossed by the ferry and walked the rest of the way. Dad would know.'

'That's true. I'll fetch the Ford.'

Hester held Robbie's hand tight until Mrs Trewarren returned, bundling him into the back seat without releasing him, before they were bumped along more potholes to the quay on the outskirts of town.

The ferry was just coming in. Hester did her best to ignore Jimmy, who, as if by some sixth sense, spotted her immediately. She was surrounded by people, she reminded herself, there was nothing he could do. But still the sight of him brought back the weight of him pinning her to the wall, intent on bending her to his will. To her shame, the memory still had the power to send her stomach clenching and her legs beginning to shake. At least they didn't have to go any closer. Dad leapt from the boat to meet them.

'Hester? What is it? Is anything wrong?'

Hester let Mrs Trewarren do the talking. Yes, Dad had

seen the three young gardeners making their way over, but that was several hours ago. They'd all been in high spirits.

Mrs Trewarren's lips tightened. 'They must have been at the front of the queue. I'll see if I can get any information from the soldiers at the town hall. They can't just cart them off like that for training, surely? You wait here, Hester, until I return.'

'It's all right Mrs Trewarren, I'll go over on the ferry with Dad. I don't like leaving Molly on her own.'

Mrs Trewarren hesitated, then nodded. 'Very well. Inform Miss Chesterfield I'll be back as soon as I can. Drat young Tom. Those arrangements about volunteer nurses really can't wait. Who knows when they might be needed.'

They watched in silence as the Ford raced back towards the centre of Hayle.

'Hester?' Dad was pale under the weathering of his face. 'What happened? Why aren't you at work?' He frowned at Robbie. 'You weren't fired were you?'

'No, of course not, Dad.' Robbie pulled his hand free from Hester's grasp, blinking away tears. For all his height, he was clearly no more than a child. If they hadn't found him...

'It was nothing like that,' said Hester. 'Nothing of the sort.'

'I'd better get back to Harbottle's,' muttered Robbie. 'If they'll have me.'

Relief turned to fear. She could insist he went back over on the ferry with her for today, but his employer might have lost patience by then and she couldn't keep Robbie locked up forever.

'Mr Harbottle promised me he would, Robbie. But you need to get back in the next few minutes. You don't have to stay there, dearest, not if you hate it. Only until we can find something else. Promise me you won't do anything like that again?'

'Promise,' he whispered, eyes earnest on hers, as she straightened his jacket and smoothed his hair before replacing his cap as neatly as she could. Then all she could do was watch as he made his way back to the bootmakers, hands in his pockets, shoulders hunched, a very picture of defeat.

'Hester?'

'We nearly lost him, Dad.' Fear was replaced by anger. 'Don't you see? You've driven him away. He'd joined up. He'd do anything to leave here. We can't keep him prisoner and if he tries again, he might succeed.'

'But he's a child.'

'He lied about his age. Don't you see what you've done, Dad? Can't you see that you've shut him out of the ferry, that he's nothing to keep him here? A few more years, and he'll leave, and who knows where he'll end up. I may be able to find him work in the gardens at Afalon to try and keep an eye on him, but that won't stop him, not if he's got no reason to stay. It's up to you, Dad, if you want him to remain here. You're the only one who can give him a reason not to go.'

For once, Dad didn't say a word. When they took their places on the ferry, he didn't take the seat next to Jimmy, with the air of directing operations, but sat next to Hester among the rest of the passengers.

Hester looked down into the dark water, the memory of Clara being swept past the ferry clear in her mind. She shuddered. How fragile life was. Lost in a moment. If she had looked the other way, or her hand had slipped on Clara's dress, she would have been powerless to do anything but watch her drowning figure being swept down the estuary to the impossible vastness of the sea, to be lost forever.

She hoped Mrs Trewarren had found Tom. She had seen the anxiety in the older woman's eyes, which wasn't entirely for the young gardener, but rather for Lance, who would soon be heading into war.

She became aware of being watched. Jimmy's eyes were fixed on her face. That wasn't love, or even passion, in his gaze. It was a cold, hard stare, one that told her his humiliation had not been forgotten and now she was succeeding in turning Dad against him, he would never let the matter rest. One way or another, he would make sure she would pay. His very look was enough to send chills up her spine. There was something obsessive about it she had never met before, something she sensed went beyond normal hurt pride. She felt like a fly, the obliterating thumb slowly descending.

For the rest of the journey, she could feel his gaze, never moving. She was glad to reach the other side. For all her haste to get back to Afalon, she made sure she waited until the ferry was ready to set off again and she could see clearly that it was Jimmy at the oars. Dad was sitting where she had left him, in among the new complement of passengers, but ignoring everyone around him, as if lost in thought.

As soon as the ferry cleared the jetty, Hester headed towards Afalon. She had done what she could. She had found Robbie. She had stopped him from leaving. It was up to Dad now.

She called in briefly to tell Gran what had happened, and that Robbie was safe, for now at least. But she did not dare linger. Miss Chesterfield might be understanding about how long it had taken her to find her brother, but from now on, the only time she would ever feel safe walking the secluded path beneath the walls was when she could clearly see that Jimmy was on the boat and could not possibly reach her. From the look in his eyes just now, not even Molly's presence would prevent him from paying her back for putting his carefully laid plans in jeopardy. She had a feeling Jimmy was not the kind to leave a witness to any revenge he might take on her. In which case, she was putting Molly in danger as well.

At the garden walls, she suddenly stopped. She was a fool! Why had she not seen? If Dad came to his senses and began to train up Robbie to take over the ferry, she wouldn't even have that time when she knew Jimmy was fully occupied. She might have saved Robbie, but in doing so, she had put herself in even more danger.

Hester hurried on back towards Afalon, cursing Jimmy, as her world closed in, ever tighter, around her.

Chapter Twenty-Five

It was a frosty morning in October when Clara returned from a fruitless visit to the Post Office in Hayle, where Ralph's letters were still being delivered, safe from her mother's eagle eyes, to find an envelope addressed to her among the rest of the family's post on the hallway table. The moment she saw Lance's handwriting, she knew.

There had been rumours over the past weeks of fierce fighting in France, near a place called Ypres. Several families in Hayle had already received the dreaded telegram to tell of a son missing or dead. Ralph's letters had become briefer and more sporadic, still filled with longing to see her, while telling her very little of his life in France. She had dragged Daisy to the Post Office this morning in desperation, in the hope that there would be a letter waiting for her after all, to say Ralph was on his way home, or had been wounded and was one of those being evacuated. But there had been nothing.

"'Scuse me, miss.' Daisy, who was in too much of a rush to notice Clara's stillness, disappeared to assist Mrs Tims. As the only maid left for the household, she had enough to do without playing chaperone, particularly with Mr Trewarren due to arrive this evening on one of his rare visits, and some semblance of the former plenty to be created.

Clara tore the letter open. Any last hope that her fears were nothing vanished at the very first words. She crumpled the paper into her fist, longing with every ache in her body that she could obliterate Lance's kindness, his attempts to comfort her with the thought that the end had been peaceful, and the last words on Ralph's lips had been her own name.

Ralph was gone.

She would never see him again. She could see his eyes, feel his kiss, and the clean smell of him, tinged with the dark smokiness of the cigarellos he favoured, surrounding her. How could he be so alive in every part of her, yet gone forever?

She could not stay in the house a moment longer. She shot out of the door, racing blindly along the promenade, heedless of curious glances, the woman's voice calling to see if she needed help.

Finally she came to a halt, breath gone. Grief went through her like a knife. She gripped the railings until her palms bled. Ralph was dead. She would never hold him, never laugh or share a loving glance. She would never bear his children, watching them grow, seeing the mix of her features and his in their faces, knowing there was a part of them that would live on beyond them both. In all eternity, she would never hear his voice again.

The mist lying over the estuary was clearing to a perfect autumn day, sending the frost shimmering into water droplets gleaming against the fragile blue of the sky. It was too cruel that Ralph, who loved the crystal light of winter days, and knew the name of every bird singing among summer meadows, would never see or hear them ever again.

It wasn't just Ralph. How self-absorbed she had been all her life! How blind, how selfish, to only think of those she loved, and to believe that they alone were invincible. It was like a wave of agonised understanding breaking inside her. It wasn't just Ralph. It wasn't even just Lance and Richard. It was every soldier, every civilian. Every small child whose life was snuffed out even before it was begun.

She glanced towards the house. She couldn't go back, not yet. She couldn't help her mother get ready for Papa's return, trying to pretend nothing had happened. To hell with convention. Nothing mattered any more. She no longer cared if she lived or died. All she knew was that she had to get away from here. Somewhere safe. Somewhere she didn't have to pretend.

A shout sent her eyes focusing. Without realising it, she had reached the quay. Just a few paces away, the ferry was loading the last of its passengers, ready to set off.

'Wait! Please, wait!' She ran as fast as she could, leaping into the boat, careless of her skirts flying. She was caught and guided to a corner, where she huddled, shrinking from curious glances towards a well-dressed young woman making her way over unaccompanied. The ferryman was on his own, for once without Hester's father sitting next to him. She slowly became aware of his eyes following her every move. Clara turned her face away, as if watching the river, blocking out his insistent stare.

She was glad no one attempted to engage her in conversation as the ferry made its way across the wide stretch of water, or instruct her to return home. She couldn't have answered. As it was, she could barely keep the tears from falling. She sat there, numb, barely feeling the chill wind blowing through the fine wool of her coat.

At the jetty, the ferry was tied up and the passengers disembarked.

'You look as if you need help, miss.' The ferryman was at her elbow. 'Miss Trewarren, isn't it? You know Hester Pearce, I believe. Visiting her, are you? I'm a friend of hers. It's a secluded path to Afalon, miss. Far too secluded, for a respectable young woman to attempt on her own. I can accompany you. Make sure you are safe.'

Clara shook her head.

'The passengers can wait. I'd like to see Hester again, have an idea of the place where she works. We miss her, she's so busy we hardly see her these days. I hear her employer is an interesting woman. I'd like to meet her.' He took her arm. 'I'd thought of offering my services as a volunteer at the big house in my spare time. The gardens, I hear, need plenty of helpers, and will need even more in the spring. I wouldn't want to let anyone on the ferry down, but I'd still like to do something for the war effort, and an old woman like Miss Chesterfield must need any help she can get.'

'Leave Miss Trewarren alone, Jimmy.' A middle-aged woman, sturdily built, with an even sturdier basket on her arm, brushed him aside. 'No more of your scheming.'

'Just trying to be helpful, Mrs Mitchell. A friend of Hester's is a friend of mine.'

Mrs Mitchell sniffed. 'I can't see Hester looking at it that way. Besides, you've got work to do. I'll show you the way, Miss Trewarren.'

Clara shot her a grateful glance. Even in the midst of her anguish, the ferryman was sending shivers of alarm shooting up her back. It felt as if his words were bludgeoning her into submission. 'Thank you.'

Mrs Mitchell beckoned to one of the delivery lads leaning their bicycles to watch the ferry. 'Here, take this to the Fisherman's Arms, will you, Joe. Ask them to look after it until I'm back. And no one' – she gave a pointed glare in the ferryman's direction – 'is to collect it but me.' She waited until an unwilling Jimmy returned to his boat, which was already half-full, then led the way up towards Afalon. 'You get one of Miss Chesterfield's maids to accompany you when you're ready to return, miss, and don't you listen to a word that young man has to say. Them that are as sharp as young Harkness will cut themselves good and proper one day, but not before they've done damage to others first.'

'Thank you. I'll remember.'

Mrs Mitchell paused as the path began to wind steeply towards Afalon's walls. 'You are quite well, Miss Trewarren? You look very pale.'

Her kindness nearly undid Clara. She swallowed back tears. 'I need to see Hester. I don't know what I'm going to do, but I need to see Hester.'

'Yes, of course, my dear. I'm not one for prying where it's not needed, especially not these days. But I'm a midwife by profession, I see women at their most joyous and their most despairing. What I've learnt over the years is that we women are the great survivors. We take whatever is thrown at us, picking ourselves up and carrying on. How else do you think the human race has lasted this long?'

'But I can't.' Clara could feel herself breaking apart, until she no longer knew where she was or who to cling to. 'I can't. I don't want to. How can I live with this emptiness? There's nothing any more. Nothing.'

Mrs Mitchell's muscular arms came around her, holding her tight as Clara sobbed uncontrollably against her solid frame. 'There, there, my lovely. You give in to it, now. You will find a way. When my Jamie was lost to the sea, long ago, when you was nought but a little girl, I thought my life had ended. But I made a new one. It might not be the life I'd thought of, but it's still a life.' She handed Clara a much-washed handkerchief. 'Come on, let's get you to Afalon.'

*

The smell of baking bread swept out as Mrs Mitchell pulled open the kitchen door.

'Someone to see you, Hester,' she called, as Clara hung back, unable to face the cheerful voices inside.

'Come on in.' Hester put down the bowl of scones she was bringing together, wiping floured hands on her apron. 'Is anything the matter, Mrs Mitchell?'

'Nothing to worry you at home, love. Your dad's fine. Your gran's had one of her chesty coughs the last few days, but she won't thank me for telling you, and she's on the mend. And young Harkness is still in one piece, more's the pity, and trying to throw his weight around with Jenifry, as if he owns the place.'

'Poor Mum,' said the kitchen maid, pausing in washing up the breakfast dishes.

'Don't you worry, love, she's had to put up with worse than that in her time, and at least she can leave once her work is done.'

Hester frowned. 'Dad shouldn't let Jimmy speak to her like that.'

'Don't you worry, Hester. Your dad's not slow in the head, for all he's ruled by his pride. He knows if Jenifry walks they'll find no one willing to replace her, not at any money. He'll make sure Jimmy keeps a civil tongue in his head. Don't even think about it. It's Miss Trewarren who's needing to see you.'

'Clara!' Hester pushed the mixing bowl towards the kitchen maid, who was staring open-mouthed. 'Finish the scones, for me, would you, please, Molly. You can leave the washing up for now. And then there are vegetables to prepare for the soup, if I'm not back by the time you're done.'

'Yes, Cook.'

'Good girl, I won't be long.' Hester pulled off her apron

and joined them at the door. 'Clara, what is it? You're as white as a ghost.'

'I'd best go,' said Mrs Mitchell. 'I've two ladies due any minute, and one looks like twins.'

'Yes, of course,' said Hester, as the midwife hurried away.

'I'm sorry, Hester. I didn't mean to disturb your work. I forgot. How could I be so selfish? I forgot.'

'Don't be silly. It will do Molly good to be in charge for a bit. Would you like Miss Chesterfield to telephone your mother?'

Clara shook her head, a new wave of grief threatening to overwhelm her. 'No! I can't bear to speak to her again. Her or Papa. They looked down their noses at him because he wasn't one of their wealthy friends from London. They thought he wasn't good enough to be seen with me. They thought he wasn't rich enough to make me happy. We weren't going to let them stop us, but now I'm never going to see him again.'

'You mean Ralph? The young man you were trying to reach when you took the boat out on the estuary that day?'

'He's dead.' It was so bleak, so final, hearing the words from her own mouth. 'I didn't even know until I got Lance's letter, just now. Oh, Hester, I've lived for days and been happy and sometimes I've even forgotten about him. And all that time he was dead. How can I live when he's not here, when I'll never see him again?'

'You'll find a way, Clara.'

'I don't want to. And I'm not going home. Not ever. I couldn't bear to. I couldn't bear to see either of them again. All those months we could have had together when they kept us apart. I'll never have those. I'll never have those memories.'

Hester held Clara tight until the sobs died into an exhausted silence. 'Come on,' she said gently. 'I'll take you up to my room. You can stay there for now. For as long as you like. You will have to let Miss Chesterfield tell your mother that you are safe, though. She'll be out of her wits otherwise.'

'Yes,' mumbled Clara, too weary and empty to fight.

'Miss Chesterfield will understand. She won't force you to do anything you don't want to do. For now, you need to rest. We'll work out what comes next whenever you are ready.'

'Thank you.' Clara hugged her tight. 'I knew you were the right person to come to. You were the only one I knew would understand. You saved my life, Hester. You'll always save my life.'

Clara followed Hester up to the little room under the eaves at the top of Afalon, legs shaking until she was no longer sure if she could place one foot in front of the other. By the time they reached it, she only had the strength left to collapse on the bed. She was vaguely aware of Hester placing a cover over her, of the warmth surrounding her body, comforting, despite nothing being able to change the deep cold inside her. Nothing would ever take away the chill again, she thought, before she sank into welcome oblivion.

Chapter Twenty-Six

Once she was sure Clara was safely asleep, Hester returned to the kitchens.

There was an unaccustomed lack of conversation as they continued finishing the luncheon and made preparations for that night's evening meal. Molly, whose two older brothers were serving in France, absorbed herself in her work, lost in thought. Lottie, too, had little to say for herself when she arrived to collect the soup and bread that constituted Miss Chesterfield's midday meal. Lottie's grandson, being a Quaker, had refused to be a combatant, but was working as a stretcher-bearer on the front line. The lack of any detailed information of what might be happening had clearly sent both their imaginations to an unknown battle, raging somewhere across the Channel.

Hester was glad to escape to the walled gardens, to salvage the last of the parsley from the greenhouses. As she went through the partially opened door into the garden she could hear the distant sound of spades, wearily attempting to clear the ground against hopeless odds. The preparing of the new beds for next year's planting had slowed to almost nothing since the loss of the young gardeners. Despite Mrs Trewarren's best efforts, Tom had never been traced, slipping away to training before he was found. Heaven knew where he was now. Meanwhile, they were relying on Molly's younger brother, who had arrived as a skinny, woefully underfed specimen, with no knowledge of plants and very little in the way of the brute strength Mr Hicks desperately required.

Miss Chesterfield had recently been trying to persuade a deeply scandalised Mr Hicks that the only solution lay in recruiting local young women, who were all eager to do their bit for the war effort in any way they could.

Many young ladies who were too young, or whose family had refused permission for them to go abroad, had volunteered as VADs. After the first flush of enthusiasm, they were now growing bored of the lack of any recuperating soldiers arriving at Afalon in need of their tender care. Several had joined the groups of women meeting in Hayle town hall to knit socks and mufflers for the troops, along with rolling bandages, collect together food parcels, and help those who could not write with letters to loved ones at the front. But there were still plenty who had expressed a longing to be more active in filling the gaps left by the men.

Mr Hicks, being, like the captain of a ship, superstitious about allowing any human female near his crops for fear of instant destruction, was taking some time to be persuaded that women had the strength to pick up a spade and were unlikely to faint in droves if engaged in physical work.

As she reached the glasshouse, Hester found Mrs Trewarren inside, pacing restlessly between the beds on either side.

'Hester! I came as soon as Maud telephoned, but now Lottie's telling me that Clara is refusing to see me. I'm hoping she'll change her mind once she's calmed down a little. I can't possibly leave her here. She should be coming home with me.'

'She was very distressed when she arrived, Mrs Trewarren. She was completely exhausted.'

'But she should feel she could come to me. Not run away like that, to find solace with strangers.' There was a moment's silence. 'How did she seem?'

There was no point in mincing words. 'Heartbroken.'

'You say that as if you think it's my responsibility.' Hester stepped back out of reach, bruising her heel against the upturned tiles marking where the now-empty tomato beds began.

Instantly, Mrs Trewarren's fury collapsed. She covered her face with her hands. 'I thought I was trying to protect her. I know young love doesn't always last, but maybe I should have trusted her to know her own heart. At least given them a chance. They could have had a few months of happiness, and my poor Clara might have had a child to console her in her grief.'

'I'm sure you did what you thought was for the best, Mrs Trewarren,' murmured Hester, hastily slicing through the surviving parsley.

'I suppose this is my punishment for causing others such pain.' Mrs Trewarren took a pruning knife hanging on the wall and began viciously detaching the few remaining bunches on the vine above their heads. The grapes hung like shrivelled raisins, completely overcome with a hair-like froth of grey mould. 'Heaven knows, I'd have given anything to spare Clara. But it's too late for that now.'

Clara did not return home, for all her mother's attempts at persuasion.

'She's welcome to stay here,' said Miss Chesterfield, as Mrs Trewarren finally accepted the inevitable and left Afalon before her husband could arrive from London to find an empty house and his womenfolk totally ungovernable in his absence. 'At least you'll know she is safe, Violet. We'll all keep an eye on her. In such cases, I've found it's often best to be away from the familiar, and to find an occupation that wears out the body and so calms the mind.'

'It's your room,' said Clara, when Hester took her a cup of tea, sweetened with honey from the bees Mr Hicks had persuaded to settle in the hives among the apple trees last summer.

'Don't worry about that. I've made up a bed in the room next door. It'll be a change.'

'You won't sleep a wink, you mean. I should take it.' She bit her lip. 'Do you mind? I like being here among your things, Hester. It feels friendly.'

'Of course not.'

Clara curled up in the armchair set at the window over-looking the walled garden, pulling an eiderdown over her, shivering as if she would never grow warm again. 'I know I should see Papa. He'll only blame Mama if I don't. But I can't. I just can't. I can't sit at dinner and pretend that nothing's wrong and that Ralph didn't matter. I can't bear it.'

It was grief speaking. Hester recognised it all too well and that there was no point in arguing. Clara would have to find her own way through her anger, as she would with her grief. All she could do was listen and keep her safe.

Early next morning, Hester emerged from her new room to find the door to her bedroom ajar. The bed had been slept in, but there was no sign of Clara. Alarm stirring, she hurried downstairs. The front door was still bolted and the shutters were in place. Which meant Clara could only have left the house through the kitchen. There she found a yawning Molly, who looked as if she had just fallen out of bed, stoking up the range, with the kettle already set to boil.

'Molly—'

'Oh, miss. I mean Cook.' Molly jumped guiltily. 'I tried to stop her, honest I did. Miss Clara, that is.'

'It's too early for the ferry. She didn't mean to walk home?'

'Oh no, Cook. She asked for the key to the walled garden. I couldn't stop her.' She bit her lip. 'Well, I didn't. She was so fierce, see.'

'It's all right, Molly, it's not your fault. I didn't mean to sleep so deeply. I should have heard her get up. I'll be back in a minute.'

She raced down to the walled garden. The door was wide open. Heart in mouth, she stood in the frosted silence, the first light glistening on grasses and spiders' webs. The absence of any sign of life was terrifying. Then, in the distance, there came the sound of a spade. It was too early for Mr Hicks, who took a while to get going, and Molly would have said if her brother had already arrived and collected a key.

'Clara?'

The digging stopped. 'I'm over here.' Clara emerged from a tangle of saplings overgrown with brambles, wearing yesterday's dress, her elegant boots caked in mud. 'This is half cleared, I could see them working on it yesterday from the window. I'm not doing any harm. It seemed a pity not to finish it. Please don't stop me.'

'Of course not. Mr Hicks needs all the help he can get, and don't let him tell you otherwise. I'll have a word with Miss Chesterfield, she'll set him straight if he has any objections.'

'I have to do something, Hester. I feel I shall go insane if

I'm still. I want to do something useful. I can't bear to roll bandages, or anything like that. This is something I can do.'

'Yes, of course. It's the most helpful thing you can do for Afalon, Clara. No one will stop you. But come back with me and have some breakfast first. You didn't eat a thing yesterday.'

'I'm not hungry.'

'That won't stop you from fainting, then Mr Hicks will say women are too feeble to work the land. I'm sure we can find you more suitable clothes and there are wellingtons to save your boots. If you are going to do this, it needs to be done properly.'

'Thank you.'

Hester kissed her. 'The most practical thing would be to find a pair of men's trousers, like my gran wears for gardening. Although that might send Mr Hicks fainting away in shock, so we might have to work on that.'

Clara giggled. Face flushed with effort, her hair wild and unbrushed, she looked more like the girl who had boldly taken out a rowing boat, determined not to be beaten. Immediately, her face fell. 'I forgot. For that minute I forgot and thought everything was all right. How could I forget?'

'You didn't forget,' said Hester gently. 'You'll never forget. I'm certain Ralph will be with you for the rest of your days, there will be something that will remind you of him every day of your life. He'll always live inside you.'

Clara reached for her fallen spade, propping it up against the trunk of an apple tree. 'It doesn't feel like it. But I'll try. For your sake and Mama's, I'll try.' She straightened. 'You're right. I suddenly feel I could eat a horse. Is that very wicked?'

'No, it's just exertion. But I think you might have to make do with porridge and toast.'

Clara tucked Hester's arm into hers. 'I'm glad you're

here, Hester. You are a true friend. I don't know what I'd do without you. This is the second time you're saved my life. One day, I'm going to have to save yours.'

'I sincerely hope you won't ever need to,' said Hester with a smile, as they made their way back to the house.

Chapter Twenty-Seven

Clara proved herself a hard worker. Despite much shaking of the head and predictions of disaster, even Mr Hicks grudgingly accepted that she wasn't one to give up, not even in the face of blisters and rain. After a few days, he listened with slightly more patience to Miss Chesterfield's suggestion that perhaps using young women volunteers in the gardens might not be such a bad thing, after all.

Then, abruptly, all thought of the work in the gardens halted. The news from France had grown even more terrible, with an unimaginable number of men killed or injured at Ypres. The most badly wounded were being evacuated to hospitals in London, but there was talk of even those being overwhelmed and men being evacuated to whatever makeshift hospital could be pressed into service all along the south coast.

Early one morning, just as Hester and Molly were starting to prepare breakfast, the telephone rang in the hall.

'They're sending men here,' said Miss Chesterfield, appearing in the kitchen. 'Dr Graham will join us as soon as he can, and I need to round up as many of our VADs as I can find. Heaven knows how many we'll need to cater for, and I dread to think what state those men will be in. I was told the hospitals just can't cope with the numbers so some will come straight here. They're bringing them in by train and by truck, whatever they can lay their hands on. I'm sure we can all show what we are made of.'

Breakfast was a hurried affair, with Miss Chesterfield taking hers in the hallway, as she telephoned all the volunteers she could muster between mouthfuls of toast. By the time it grew light, VADs had begun arriving on foot or peddling bicycles. Several young women from the large houses in Hayle had commandeered their brothers' motor cars, which needed to be parked on the grass at the side of the house, leaving the front free for the vehicles bringing in the wounded men.

The house was filled with an air of nervousness, combined with excitement.

'This is what we trained for,' said one of the VADs, as Hester left Molly in charge of the kitchen and helped make up the beds that had remained empty for so long, while medicines and bandages were laid out neatly on the side in preparation. 'I thought we'd never be given the chance to practise our skills.'

'I never expected to see a man come straight from a battlefield,' said Phyllida, the youngest of the volunteers. 'I so hope I don't faint.'

'Don't worry, Phyl, you'll be fine,' replied one of the others, giving her shoulder an encouraging squeeze as she passed. 'Anyhow, the nurses who trained us said that you're generally so busy you don't have time to think.'

'Do you think they will really be horribly injured?' asked Clara, who had been pressed into the rush of preparations, the haunted look back in her eyes.

'There are plenty here to help,' said Hester. 'Everyone will understand if you return to the garden once the beds are made up. We'll need someone to collect as many vegetables as they can.'

'Mr Hicks can do that, I'll be all right here,' she replied. 'I'd like to stay. I may not know much about nursing, but I can clean and carry and free up the VADs.'

When the men finally arrived, it was in an overwhelming rush. Hester was aware of wheels on the ground outside, followed by doors being flung open and urgent shouts echoing around the misty air.

'Oh, miss,' exclaimed Molly, who had been collecting potatoes from the store in the walled garden. She dropped the basket at Hester's feet and burst into tears. 'You've never seen such a sight. They're covered in mud and all kinds of filth, and the smell...'

'It's horrible,' said Clara, appearing behind her with freshly cut kale and a cabbage. 'I've never known anything like it.'

'Putrefaction,' pronounced Miss Chesterfield, arriving in the kitchen. 'I'd know that smell anywhere. Heaven help us, it looks as if there's been no opportunity for their wounds to be cleaned or treated since they left the battlefield, and many of them are lying in their own filth. If gangrene sets in...' She washed her hands and changed her grubby apron to one of the pristine, all-enveloping variety hanging up ready in the corridor outside. 'As much water as you can boil, Hester. Dr Graham is on his way, he's bringing the new young doctor with him. I've told Dr Graham they should come through this door. They are still bringing in ambulances, so the front of the house is impossible. I'm not even sure we have enough beds. It also appears they haven't had a hot meal in days, and those who are awake are desperate for a cup of tea.' She tied the apron and took a deep breath. 'In the meantime, I just hope I can remember my training.'

The next hour or so passed in a whirl of boiling as much water as possible and preparing cups of tea between chopping vegetables for huge pans of soup. Despite the sense of urgency, Hester could not resist joining Clara, who had slipped outside as she waited for the next lot of water to boil, to see the scene for herself. The next consignment of men were being brought from Hayle station, some in ambulances, others in the backs of trucks. It looked as if as many of Timson's motorised vans as could be spared had also been pressed into service.

'These look even worse than the ones before. I never imagined it would be like that. What must it be like out there?'

'It's all right, Clara. They're safe now they're here. It's the nurses they need for now.' She turned back to her work, not sure she would ever get the sight out of her mind, thinking of all the men out there on the front line.

She wished with all her heart that she had been in time to stop Tom as well as Robbie signing up. It had been a shock when Gareth had been killed, but, as far as she knew, Ben and Tom were still out there somewhere, living this horror. She hoped Tom's mother, who had never recovered from learning her only son had headed off for the battlefield, despite being only just sixteen, would not hear the worst of the details of this sudden invasion of desperately wounded men.

She was relieved to find Dr Graham weaving his motor car between trucks and ambulances, driving the last part of the way on the grass to avoid them, pulling up outside the kitchens.

'Good grief,' he exclaimed, as he jumped out. 'When I was told it was entire trainloads that were arriving, I assumed it was an exaggeration.' He turned to his passenger, who was standing, one hand still on the open door, as if she couldn't quite believe her eyes. 'Juno, are you quite sure...'

'Absolutely. I saw far worse than this out in France.'

'Very well. This is my niece, Dr Villiers, who has

volunteered to assist me. This is Miss Pearce, Juno, who is a very level-headed young woman, as well as an excellent cook, and this is Miss Trewarren, who has turned out to be redoubtable with a spade.'

'Pleased to meet you both,' said Dr Villiers. She was tall, with fair hair tied firmly back from her face, cheeks pale and slightly drawn, as if in pain. Hester took in a raw scar running down one side of her face, and hastily averted her eyes.

'Mortars don't respect the nursing staff either,' said Dr Villiers, by way of gruff explanation. She fished a wooden walking stick from under her seat. 'I lost three experienced nurses in France, and they won't allow me back until my leg has healed. At least I can make myself useful here.' She stomped off towards the VADs helping those who could walk down from the back of a truck.

'What she didn't say is that she's lucky to be alive herself,' said Dr Graham. 'My niece is one headstrong young woman, but even she knows she'd be a liability out in the field until she is fully recovered. I'm supposed to be keeping her out of trouble. I should have known.'

'Are all the hospitals like this?' demanded Clara, still watching the new arrivals with undisguised horror.

'I'm afraid so. I've never heard of anything approaching this before. I dread to think what it's like out in France. And some of those injuries – this is a new kind of warfare. The human body wasn't built to withstand such mechanised slaughter. No one expected this, the system has been overwhelmed, that's why they've been sent here, despite it not being set up as a front-line hospital. Let's pray there's not another train on its way. I've no idea where we're going to put all these, let alone any more. The beds here must be overflowing already. Thank goodness Miss Chesterfield is a resourceful woman.'

One of the men being helped towards the front door stumbled as he reached the first step, bringing down Phyllida, whose slight frame was doing its best to support him.

'It's all right,' called Clara. 'I'll help you.' She took a deep breath as if steeling herself. 'At least I've become physically strong, if nothing else.'

As Clara raced to help the fallen patient, Hester returned to the kitchen. She did her best to shut away the memory of all she had seen for now, to allow her to concentrate all her energies on what needed to be done.

For the first few hours, she and Molly were run off their feet taking hot water in any spare containers they could find, for men who had not been washed or out of their uniforms since they had been wounded, and who first needed to be cleaned of the mud and grime that stuck to every part of them.

The beds were soon full, supplemented by patients laid out on camp beds and mattresses wherever they could be placed. Miss Chesterfield made full use of the telephone in the hall to harangue the local volunteer ladies and the mayor into putting out a call for donations of all the beds and bedding they could find.

Between supervising Molly in the kitchen, Hester helped as much as she could, feeding and cleaning men mortified by being attended to by young women, for even the most intimate of tasks, and no less nervous of a female doctor inspecting their wounds.

Dr Villiers limped between patients, stubbornly refusing to use the chair Miss Chesterfield had found for her, a look of grim determination on her face. Nothing seemed to shock her, which Hester found strangely the most disturbing part of the scene, as she paused in delivering trays of tea, to hold the hand of a young man who appeared no more than twenty, clearly unlikely to last the night, while Dr Villiers administered morphine.

'A curse on both your houses,' muttered Dr Villiers, accepting a cup of tea before limping off to do what she could to ease the suffering of the next man. 'We had German soldiers more than once in my field hospital. Most of them were no more than children, too. All they wanted was their mothers, whichever side they were on. God help us.'

On the other side of the bed, Hester caught sight of Clara's face, pale and large-eyed. For a moment she looked as if she was about to collapse into tears, but she straightened, and continued to collect the empty bowls and teacups to take down to the kitchen to wash, freeing Molly to make as many loaves as she could, until their small stores of flour ran out and potato bread was the only option.

The onslaught went on all that day. At least Dr Graham's prayers were answered and no more trains of wounded men arrived. Late in the afternoon, it eased a little, enough for some of the VADs to arrive wearily in the kitchen for hot soup and freshly made bread, more than one falling asleep over her teacup, before they stirred themselves, finished their tea in one and set off back to the main part of the house.

'You'd never think most of them are polite young ladies from the best drawing rooms in the county,' said Miss Chesterfield, finally appearing for her share of soup. 'Well, I take my hats off to them, I never thought half of them would stick it, even if it had been half as bad as this. And they did it for the most part on empty bellies and not even a sip of water between them. They're clearly made of sterner stuff than their respectable mamas and papas might choose to believe.'

She had just finished her meal and was rising stiffly to her feet, as if afraid she too might doze off if she rested for more than a few minutes, when Clara appeared, supporting a tearful Phyllida.

'I didn't know what else to do,' said Clara. 'She nearly fainted just now.'

'I'm all right,' muttered the young VAD, although the extreme pallor of her face and the way she was clinging on tightly to Clara's arm told another story. 'I can't let down the others.'

'When did you last eat?' demanded Miss Chesterfield.

'I'm not sure. There was a telephone message at home before the servants were up.' She hiccupped, swallowing down a sob. 'I'm sorry, I didn't think it was going to be like this.'

'Don't worry about it, Phyllida,' said Miss Chesterfield. 'This has come as a shock to all of us. I'm sure you've not stopped since you got here. You need something to drink and eat, and to sit quietly for a few minutes.'

'You're all right staying here, miss,' said Hester, seeing the distress on the girl's face. 'How about you sit and help us peel vegetables for a bit, once you've had something to eat? We need help down here as well.'

Phyllida nodded slowly, wan face easing a little. 'Only, I'm afraid you'll have to show me how. I've never done anything like that in my life. I didn't even know how to light a fire to make a cup of tea this morning. Sally always does it before any of us get up. I've never thought about it. I didn't ever imagine I was so helpless.'

'I didn't, either,' said Clara, helping her to a seat. 'But I'm learning.'

'Molly will show you, miss,' said Hester, as Clara returned to washing up, while the kettle boiled for the next round of tea. 'But we'll get you something to eat first. You'll feel better after that. My head always goes woozy and I feel I want to cry if I keep on going without anything to eat.'

Phyllida obediently ate her soup and drank her tea, demolishing the last of her bread with enthusiasm, abandoning the ladylike pretence of having no untoward appetites to her name.

'I feel so ashamed,' she said, as she settled down to help Molly chop carrots, wielding the knife in an alarmingly cavalier manner, until she caught the horrified look on Molly's face and followed her lead. 'I was so longing to go to France with my sister, but I'm too young. I'm only just twenty-one, so it's years until I'll be allowed out. But I'd probably just have fainted and been a terrible nuisance.'

'No, you wouldn't,' said Hester firmly. 'They'd have kept an eye on you and made sure you ate and drank enough to keep you going. It's only because this was so unexpected today and no one's properly organised yet.'

Phyllida sighed. 'I didn't realise what it was like. My brother's out there. I dread to think what he's facing. Every man I saw, I was afraid it was him under the dirt, and I couldn't bear it. That's why I feel so horribly ashamed. When the war first started, I went with my aunt giving white feathers to men we thought should have signed up. There were several who told me they were only seventeen, but I thought they were lying and gave them a white feather anyhow. Supposing I made them lie about their age and sent them to this?'

'You weren't to know, Phyllida,' said Clara. 'How were any of us to know? I've never heard of anything like this before. Even Dr Graham was shocked, and I thought he'd seen everything anyone could ever wish to see.'

'It feels like the world's ending,' said Phyllida, growing tearful again.

'Well, we're here to stop it,' said Clara firmly, the old determination gleaming in her face. 'At least as much as we can. We might not be able to save the world, but we can make a difference to every last one of those poor men up there. That's what counts.'

In the early hours of the following morning, Hester climbed yet again to the makeshift hospital wards with pails of hot water. Her legs were shaking with weariness, and she could scarcely keep her eyes open. With Miss Chesterfield having been informed the next consignment of patients was due to arrive by train that afternoon, she had sent Molly and Clara off to bed, and an exhausted Phyllida to get what rest she could.

In the old drawing room, all was quiet. The men were mostly asleep, several VADs keeping an eye on them, some dozing as they sat by the bed of the most critically injured, or moving quietly between the rows to attend to any that might be restless.

'You go and get some sleep, my dear,' whispered Miss Chesterfield, rising stiffly from her chair next to a man whose entire face was covered in bandages. 'Lord knows when this will end, we are going to need all the rest we can. I've told the VADs on night duty to make their own cups of tea for the next few hours, at least one of them must be capable of boiling a kettle and knows what a teapot looks like. You go off and get what sleep you can.'

'And you?'

'I'll wait just a little longer.'

Hester felt guilty leaving, when Miss Chesterfield most probably had every intention of staying at the man's bedside all night. But she was well aware that tomorrow she would need all her mental and physical energy to spend the day boiling water and preparing meals with what ingredients she could find, as well as finding a way of getting sustenance to those men with shattered jaws who were finding it impossible to chew.

As she turned towards the stairs, her eye was caught by Clara, sitting by the bedside of the dying man. She was holding the hand resting above the bedclothes, talking to him quietly.

'He's the same age as her young man, poor thing,' whispered Miss Chesterfield, following her gaze. 'She's determined not to leave him. Not until it's over. I hadn't the heart to forbid her. I'm hoping it will bring her some peace of mind, and the trust that there was someone there with her Ralph when he needed it.'

'Yes,' said Hester, feeling hours of unshed tears rising uncontrollably. As quickly and as quietly as she could, she shot up to her room, where she could weep in private.

Chapter Twenty-Eight

She couldn't have been looking out as carefully as usual. Hester pulled her coat tighter around her, trying to stir her brain into action.

Over the weeks since the first casualties had arrived at Afalon, they had all become so exhausted that even those VADs who could return home at night to escape the horrors for a few hours were walking around in a permanent daze. Then there were the long lists of casualties in the newspapers, and the rumours swirling around the Fisherman's Arms that the Hun were making a fight of it, after all. Wherever she went there were whispers of spies at every corner and U-boats waiting out in the bay, ready to land an invasion force. They'd all heard about what had happened to the Belgians and the villages in occupied France, not to mention the stories of unspeakable horrors brought by refugees forced to flee for their lives with barely the clothes they stood up in.

Despite most of her time being spent in the kitchen, or helping Molly and Mr Hicks in harvesting cabbages and frostbitten turnips from the walled garden, Hester had seen so much pain and fear, with death ever present on the make-shift wards, she felt dead inside.

Not even the sight of Jimmy Harkness waiting for her as she stepped out of the ferryman's cottage could completely dispel the fog overtaking her brain.

'Dad's inside,' she muttered. 'There's a new trainload of casualties expected, I need to return to Afalon.'

'Then I'll walk you back.'

That got the fog stirring. 'There's no need. I'm due to meet Miss Trewarren in front of the church. She's taken Miss Chesterfield's motor car to collect supplies from Hayle railway station, she'll be expecting me.'

'Then I'll walk you to the church.'

To that there was no answer. At least none which Hester's weary mind could conjure up on the spur of the moment. These days, every step had the sensation of walking through treacle.

'I can't keep her waiting,' she said, praying that Clara hadn't been delayed. Miss Chesterfield had a somewhat steamroller approach to sourcing desperately needed medicines, along with precious supplies of flour and meat to ensure the remaining vegetables, by now almost exclusively of the kale and turnip variety, supplemented by stored potatoes and strings of onions, could be turned into nutritious and palatable meals.

With able-bodied men in short supply, even Mrs Trewarren had not been able to object to her daughter throwing decorum to the winds and driving with no hint of a chaperone, when supplies of petrol allowed. These days, Clara never stopped, as if, like for so many of them, it was the only way to keep thoughts at bay.

'I'm glad I bumped into you.' Jimmy was still smiling at her, the sentimental expression back in his eyes. 'We've had so little time to speak.'

'At least the rain has gone,' said Hester, determined to keep any conversation to the most superficial and brief.

Jimmy was not deflected. 'Sadly none of us have much time for anything, these days.'

'No.' They had reached the end of the row of cottages, attracting, Hester couldn't help seeing from the corner of her eye, more than a few curious glances from the women beating carpets in the fragile sun, or pausing in taking peelings to the expectant pig rootling around in the sty next to the outhouse.

'Which is why I had to see you.'

'Oh?' They were now only minutes away from the church. She could see no sign of Clara, or Miss Chesterfield's motor car, but at least there was a steady criss-crossing of people, and she could take refuge in Mrs Dowrick's shop, or even in Mr Treves's grocery, if necessary.

'To speak to you properly. You know how I feel.'

'Jimmy—'

'And you know that will never change, not until my last breath. If I don't come back, my last thought will be of you.'

'Come back?'

'I've volunteered. The ferry is a reserved occupation of course, being a vital transport.' It was the first she'd heard of it, but she wasn't about to argue. 'And I couldn't let your father down. But now with Robbie taking over more of the rowing, I'm free to serve my country.'

'Good for you,' she said.

They had reached the church, with still no sign of Clara. For all she was surrounded by passers-by, Hester could feel a trap slowly closing around her, the kind that didn't need bruising or any tearing at her clothes. The kind that couldn't be so easily dispelled by a well-placed knee. The breath was heavy in her body.

'Afternoon, Jimmy.' She started as Mary-Anne Blewitt, who had taken the place of Mr Treves's assistant, one of the first to join up, emerged from the grocer's, dusting down her skirts, eyes fixed on Jimmy, ignoring Hester completely. 'Dad says to come and see us at the Fisherman's before you go. He's a pint for every man who volunteers.'

'That's very kind of you, I will.' Jimmy was all smiles. His chest had swelled and he appeared to have grown at least half an inch in height.

'And I might be persuaded to offer a kiss for a hero,' said Mary-Anne boldly. She gave a pointed stare at Hester. 'At least I can appreciate a man prepared to die for his country.'

In the distance there came the roar of a motor car being driven at speed. 'That sounds like my lift, I must go.'

'You can spare a few minutes, Hester? Just a last few.'

What could she say? Mary-Anne pouted as a customer arrived at the grocer's, prompting a roar from Mr Treves inside for Mary-Anne to stop gossiping in the street and get her idle bones back behind the counter or he'd be talking to her father, and then she'd be in for it, and no mistake.

'I can wish you good luck, Jimmy,' said Hester, doing her best to avoid the complacent look on his face at such signs of female admiration.

'Nothing more?'

'I must go.'

'You know I don't feel anything for Mary-Anne, don't you?'

'She seems very fond of you,' she countered. Did he expect her to be jealous? If he thought that was a way of getting her to fall at his feet, he had another think coming.

'But I don't love her. Not the way I love you.'

'Jimmy—'

He grabbed her hand, his grip vice-like. 'You will wait for me, Hester, won't you? I can bear any kind of pain, even death, if I know you are here waiting.' His voice wheedled, low and insistent, until it became a drumbeat in her head, pummelling her into submission. 'Is it so much to ask for a man going away, maybe never to return again? Just a few kind thoughts? You can see I could have any woman I choose, but it's only you I want. You can see I'm prepared to die for you, Hester. Don't I deserve just a little love in return?'

From the corner of her eye, she could see Clara pulling up beside her. Hester yanked herself free, jumping into the passenger seat before Jimmy could realise what was happening.

'Just drive,' she said.

Clara didn't hesitate. They raced through the streets as fast as she dared, boxes and containers banging and rattling on the back seat as they went.

'What did he want?' Clara demanded, slowing a little as they reached the open road up to Afalon. 'He looked in such a temper and as if he was about to drag you off to his lair. Vile little man.'

'He was saying goodbye,' said Hester. 'He's joined up, now Robbie is able to take over the ferry.'

'Oh.' Clara was apologetic. 'At least he's brave. He must know what he's letting himself in for. So he can't be all bad.'

'I suppose not.'

'But he's still a vile little man,' added Clara, as they swept through the gates and up towards Afalon.

Chapter Twenty-Nine

Within days, Jimmy had left for training, leaving not a bad word to be said about him. Even old Mr Timson was overheard to declare him a brave lad, who could do well for himself, if he could apply those talents of his in the service of his country. There was no mention of why exactly Jimmy had left his employment quite so abruptly. Being prepared to make the ultimate sacrifice had swept away the past.

At first, Hester couldn't quite trust her freedom. She was braced, waiting for this to be a trick to put her off guard, expecting to see him around every corner. But gradually, as spring arrived and then summer, she began to relax. By the time Mary-Anne Blewitt waved a letter under her nose, while informing her that Jimmy was about to be posted to France, having been selected for a secret and highly important mission, from which he might never return, she began to hope that he might not reappear until at least hostilities had ended.

'Secret mission, my backside,' guffawed Mrs Mitchell, returning wild-haired and pale from a successful delivery of the most uncooperative of babies in time to overhear Mary-Anne's triumph. 'A comfortable little job in charge of provisions, more like it. Always did have an eye for the main chance, did young Jimmy, and the art of spinning the daftest of yarns.'

'It's a secret,' said Mary-Anne, pursing her lips in scorn.

'Of course he can't tell silly old women who might gossip, or a ferryman's daughter like Hester.'

'Made bloody sure he told someone he knew couldn't keep it to herself, though,' returned Mrs Mitchell sharply.

Mary-Anne looked her up and down. 'And what would you know?' she snorted, striding off towards the Fisherman's Arms, nose firmly in the air.

'Never did have the sense she was born with, that one,' remarked Mrs Mitchell. 'And she came out daft in the first place, as I remember. I'll give that for Harkness, he certainly knows how to pick 'em. Not you, of course, my dear. I rather suspect he sees you as a challenge. Men like that take the greatest of pleasure in breaking a woman down. Gives them a sense of power, instead of being the feeble little runts everyone else sees. You are well shot of him.'

'Yes, Mrs Mitchell,' said Hester. This time, she allowed the group of local girls Mr Hicks had finally been persuaded to help in the walled garden to walk on ahead back to Afalon, until their voices faded into the distance. The sun was brighter than she had ever seen before, the trees a more vivid shade of green, every butterfly a miracle of vibrant colour.

'This is how I used to be,' she thought to herself. It felt as if she was reclaiming herself, the Hester who had once held on to her dreams and walked where she pleased, without fear. Even the memory of her head being flung against the wall of the alley, and the terror that he would kill her to cover up what he had done, began finally to fade.

She reached Afalon with her limbs relaxed, her mind clear, and ready to face anything.

'Afternoon,' she called cheerfully to Miss Chesterfield and Dr Villiers, who were standing at the entrance to the walled garden, deep in conversation.

'Gardening?' Dr Villiers was saying dubiously. 'You are

seriously proposing my patients should be set to work growing food?'

'I don't see why not,' returned Miss Chesterfield. 'I understand it's been tried with some success elsewhere. It's considered to be therapeutic, and to be at least as effective as embroidery for calming the mind. Besides, we have an urgent need to grow food, not only for here, but for the people round about, and the poorer families in Hayle. The shortages and the way food prices have gone up have caused real hardship.'

'I thought you had enough trouble persuading Mr Hicks to accept the young women who've volunteered to work in the garden in the first place,' returned Dr Villiers. 'What's he going to think of young men suddenly appearing to work alongside them? Come to that, it'll be the subject of every gossip for miles around.'

'Mrs Trewarren has volunteered to oversee the scheme,' said Miss Chesterfield. 'And she's not the kind to allow any impropriety to take place.'

'Hmm,' grunted Dr Villiers. 'What do you think of this, Miss Pearce?'

'I'm sure Mrs Trewarren can ensure there will be no hint of scandal,' replied Hester demurely. Terrorise the very thought of flirtation out of the flightiest of the young ladies, more like. Although she tactfully did not voice this thought aloud.

'I'm not going to risk my methods of returning men to health coming into disrepute, Miss Chesterfield.'

'We'll make sure they don't, doctor. You've done such excellent work here, I wouldn't wish to jeopardise that. But you know yourself, how things have changed. Men and women are far more accustomed to working together, as are those of different social standing. It's all part of the war effort. I'm sure things will return to normal as soon as this is over.'

'Yes, of course, these are indeed extraordinary circumstances. I'll consider it, Miss Chesterfield. Leave it with me. I'll give it serious thought.' With a brief nod in Hester's direction, Dr Villiers limped off towards the house.

'She'll agree to it,' said Miss Chesterfield. 'She knows it makes perfect sense, particularly now the main hospitals are managing to cope with the casualties coming over from France and we can finally become a place of convalescence I had intended and concentrate on the healing of both the body and the mind. Dr Villiers has developed many effective methods of rehabilitating the body, but I feel that sometimes she can forget the mind.' She turned to watch the figure limping heavily as she reached the steps up to the terrace, where the less seriously injured men were smoking in the evening sunshine. 'Or maybe that's a part she is unable to deal with for herself. For now, at least.'

As the summer heat began to settle on Afalon, Hester grew accustomed to finding recovering soldiers delivering vegetables to the kitchen door and weeding and pruning when she went to collect rosemary for a stew. All under the eagle eye of Mrs Trewarren, deputised in the morality department by Mr Hicks, who remained deeply suspicious of being overrun by hordes of females, many of them blatantly wearing trousers, leaving him quite unable to know where to look.

Between them, they satisfied themselves, and the more tolerant of the surrounding community, that the true order of things hadn't quite departed. All flirtations were strictly forbidden between patients eager to get out into the fresh air and find life growing again beneath their fingers and the young women gleefully taking the opportunity of escaping overbearing mamas, or an endless round of cooking and cleaning and looking after younger siblings, and the wonderful novelty of getting paid for their hard work, to boot.

Which meant that Hester quickly grew adept at being deaf to smothered laughter in the more secluded part of the grounds and perfectly blind to the occasional ropes of sheets, accompanied by whispers and muffled shrieks, descending from the highest rooms after dark.

'What's life, if it's not for living,' remarked Miss Chesterfield, when Mrs Trewarren burst into the office while Hester was drawing up the following week's menus, outraged at having caught several young women blatantly downing cider in the Fishermen's Arms, much to the mesmerised astonishment of the regulars.

'But Evangeline is a debutante,' she exclaimed. 'I know her mother. Only socially, of course. Evangeline's the goddaughter of an earl.'

'That doesn't change the fact that two of her brothers are dead and the third is on the front line. Or that she is not the only one and we could all be dead within the year.'

'But think of the scandal, if, well, if …'

'Don't worry, Violet. I've already read them the riot act on the subject of measures to prevent any unwanted arrivals and I've made sure Dr Graham has had a word with his patients. Between us we have hopefully done enough to prevent any consequences, should things get that far.'

'Well, I never.' Mrs Trewarren turned pale with shock.

'My dear,' said Miss Chesterfield gently. 'We can watch them all we can, but in the midst of so much death, I'm not sure we can prevent the young from living their lives to the very limit of existence. It might even prove a little cruel?'

Mrs Trewarren sat down heavily in the nearest chair. Her hands flew to cover her face.

'Excuse me,' she muttered after a few minutes. 'I've things I need to attend to.'

Miss Chesterfield watched her leave the room with concern. 'That was thoughtless of me,' she said, as Mrs Trewarren's boots rapped on the tiles of the corridor towards the main part of the house. 'I wasn't thinking about poor Clara. I didn't mean to accuse Violet of anything, or cause her pain.'

'I'm sure she knows that,' said Hester.

Miss Chesterfield's eyes gleamed with unshed tears. 'I never thought I'd live to see another war, my dear, let alone one more terrible than any of us could imagine. Now I can't help but dread where this might end.'

Chapter Thirty

By the summer of 1915, everyone who could be spared was fully employed in harvesting the glut of soft fruit before it spoilt, or the birds made too much of a feast, for Hester and Molly to bottle, and use any sugar they could get hold of to turn the fruit into jam. With things being so uncertain, being fully prepared for the winter ahead had become more important than ever.

Hester was returning with Clara to the house one afternoon, with their basket overflowing, when an ambulance of particularly ancient appearance trundled up the driveway.

'I had no notification of more patients,' said Miss Chesterfield, appearing on the front steps, one hand shading the sun from her eyes as she squinted towards the offending vehicle.

Clara put down her basket. 'It's Lance. I know it is. He's on leave for a few days. He said it would be too far. I told him Mama and I were most likely to be here, if he managed to make it.' Sure enough, as the ambulance came to a halt in front of Afalon, Lance could be seen emerging from the passenger seat. Clara raced towards him, flinging her arms around him.

'I'd better let Violet know,' said Miss Chesterfield, returning inside the house.

As Hester picked up the abandoned blackcurrants, which were already in danger of spoiling in the intense heat, the driver swung himself down to the ground.

'Richard!' Clara sounded more like her old self than she had since Ralph's death. 'Lance said you were in London. I'm so glad you came to see us, it's good to see you.'

'Clara.' His arms came around her. 'I'm so sorry. Dear, dear Clara.'

'Don't.' Clara burst into tears, hugging him as tightly as she had held her brother. 'Don't say anything, please. I can't bear it. Not yet. Not now.'

They looked so close, the three of them, drawn tightly together by grief. Hester was glad Clara at least had Ralph's friends, who, more than anyone, could understand her heartbreak and what she had lost. Hester could have hugged both of them for putting aside their own need for rest, using their precious leave to make the long journey to Cornwall by hook or by crook to offer what comfort they could.

But she could no more hug them than she could join them. This was not her world. From the day the first overwhelming flood of wounded men had arrived, Hester had felt herself simply a part of the effort to do the best for the patients at Afalon. It was the same among the VADs and the girls volunteering in the garden, the centuries of rigid social class vanishing, washed away in a common need.

It was an illusion, of course. At the back of her mind, she had known it. This was only for now, like the women taking over men's work and hurtling through the countryside on bicycles without the possibility of a chaperone. All the same, she couldn't help a faint sense of hurt. She was suddenly aware that she was back to simply cook again, below stairs, invisible, watching her social superiors who lived lives that were important.

Well, it was a salutary reminder not to assume things, even that a friendship with Clara could be real, she told herself, as she hastily vanished back into the kitchens with the baskets of fruit. She busied herself filling kettles, as Molly took a fresh carrot and caraway cake out of the oven. How could she have believed for even one minute that anything had really changed so much as to remove the distance between them? It was different when there was an emergency and there was no time to think and they all depended equally on each other. But the world would always return to the way things had been in the past.

'Don't you be a fool,' she scolded herself, as she began to prepare her next batch of potato bread, with flour still being hard to get hold of, followed by the rabbit pies she was making for both patients and fruit pickers.

'Cook?' She hadn't realised she'd spoken aloud. Molly was eyeing her uncertainly, as if her pastry making would never pass muster.

'That's all looking fine, Molly. Your shortcrust is coming on in leaps and bounds. Don't you take any notice of me.'

'Yes, miss,' said Molly, still wary.

Hester smiled at her. 'Miss Chesterfield managed to find some lemons, I've no idea how. She suggested we make lemonade for the fruit pickers, so we can get rid of the evidence, so to speak. It's hot enough already outside, how about I show you how it's done, once these pies are made?'

'Yes, please,' said Molly eagerly, returning to her pastry making with renewed confidence.

The heat built steadily through the rest of the morning. By midday, the workers in the garden were both thirsty and ravenous, settling down in the shade of the terrace, joining the less mobile of Dr Villiers's patients for an informal picnic of Molly's pies and the fresh lemonade, to excited chatter, interspersed with bursts of laughter. Mr Hicks shook his head at the lack of manners of the young people of today, not to mention Daisy, who was no more than Mrs Trewarren's maid, sitting on the grass next to the daughter of a lord, as if such things didn't matter.

Hester left Molly in charge of dividing up the cake, which always vanished within minutes, to collect fresh greens for the evening meal while the walled garden was quiet. The door was ajar, as it usually was during the day, with the constant flow of gardeners. As she reached the beds of spinach, interspersed with kale and wild rocket, she almost ran into a figure standing, oblivious to everything, deep in thought.

Her first impulse was to retreat, as fast as her legs would take her. But he must have heard the crunch of her boots on the path. He turned before she could take shelter behind the nearest shed.

'Hester. Please don't leave. I'm the one who's the intruder here.'

'I beg your pardon, Mr Elliot. I thought everyone was still up at the house.'

'So they are. I had a feeling Clara might appreciate some time alone with her brother. They were always close. I'm hoping he can find some way to ease her grief.'

'I'm sure he will,' she murmured, itching to complete her task and have the excuse to rush away.

He looked older than when she had last seen him, face browned by wind and sun. His civilian clothes hung off him, as if made for a much larger man. Not all the tea in China, she thought sadly, could give him the time to grow into them again, or to have them altered to fit before he was back in uniform and among the horrors that had marked deep lines on his face.

'I couldn't quite resist seeing the gardens one last time.'

'Miss Chesterfield will always make you welcome.'

'That wasn't quite what I meant.'

'Oh.' His tone was perfectly matter-of-fact. She bit her lip as the words sunk in. There was nothing to say.

'It's good to see the gardens in use again. It's got the sense of purpose I remember from when Isabella and I were children. Except then it was all centred on us, of course. I rather think this is much more useful.' A faint smile appeared. 'And there's no need for anyone to climb the walls by means of the apple trees.'

So he had seen her. Hester could feel herself growing scarlet from head to toe. She tilted her chin. 'I'm not a thief.'

'I didn't say you were.'

'Well, I suppose, in truth, I was,' she admitted ruefully. 'But it was all going to waste, and it made such a world of difference to Gran and me.' She bit her lip. 'I suppose you've guessed that it's because of the fruit I took from here that we were able to build our business, which gave me the luck to be offered the post here. Will you tell Miss Chesterfield?'

'Good grief, no. What do you take me for?'

'Thank you.'

'There's no need to thank me.' He cleared his throat. 'But there is one thing, though.'

'Oh?'

He cleared his throat again, louder this time. 'Hester, you do know Lance has a great deal of respect for you, don't you?'

Now what was he on about? 'Has he?'

'But anything more serious …'

Hester stared at him. 'What business is that of yours?'

'I wouldn't like to see you hurt.'

'So you took it upon yourself to warn me off, because a silly little village girl was bound to get ideas above her station.'

'No! Of course not. It was just that your fiancé happened to mention—'

277

'My *what*?'

'Your betrothed.'

'I know what a fiancé is, you blockhead.'

'I beg your pardon. It's none of my business, but he stopped me in Hayle while Lance was picking up the last of the supplies. He said he was worried that Lance had turned your head with promises ...'

Fear fell into place with a horrible clarity. 'Jimmy.'

'Yes. Jimmy Harkness, the ferryman.'

'But he's in France. He told Mary-Anne he was being posted to France. He can't be back. He can't.'

'He was in Hayle just a few hours ago, he said he'd be back to visit your father by tomorrow afternoon ... Hester? Hester, what is it?'

'I can't stay here. I can't go back to spending my life dreading bumping into him around every corner.'

'So you are not engaged.'

'Of course not! What kind of idiot do you take me for?'

'Thank goodness.' His face eased. 'I did wonder. I beg your pardon, Hester, I should have trusted your judgement.'

'What else did he say?'

'It doesn't matter.'

'It does to me. What else did he say?'

'That your, ah, preference for Lance was leading you astray and making you the subject of comment and gossip and that ...'

'Yes?'

'That I was to let you know that it was breaking your father's heart.'

'Then I can't ever escape,' she said bleakly. 'I thought I was safe at Afalon, but he won't stop. It won't just be you he tells his lies to. He'll keep on and on. I should have known. He'll keep on, again and again, turning everyone he can against me until he wins. I know he will. And if I don't give in to him, I think he'd rather kill me.'

'Hester—'

She couldn't bear his concern, the pity in his eyes. 'It doesn't matter. At least now I know. And that I can't stay here.'

His gaze had shifted. He raised his hand to gently trace the faint scar on her hairline. 'Was that him?'

She moved her head away. 'I was lucky that time. At least that showed me what he was capable of. But luck runs out.' She swallowed hard. 'It's not your problem, I'm the one to deal with it. I'd better get back to work.'

'Wait.' He reached into the pocket of his jacket, pulling out a battered notebook. 'Before she volunteered as an ambulance driver, Isabella worked with a charity in London.' His pencil moved rapidly over the page. 'This is the address.'

'What kind of charity?'

'It works with women who find themselves in need of escape and a place of refuge. For some, it's violent husbands, for others families. And others see danger and know they need to get away before it's too late. It's a place where you would be safe and couldn't be traced. They'd find you work. Not the kind of post you have here, you'd have to work your way up again, but at least you would be safe.' The pencil made a hasty list. 'This is the amount you would need for the train. And this for the cab from the station, it's only a short distance. If you need money—'

She shook her head, mortification complete. 'I have money.'

'Good.' He handed her the paper.

'Why are you doing this?'

'Do I need a reason?'

'We'll most probably never see each other again. I'd like to know.'

He hesitated. 'Maybe because you once helped me.'

'Did I?'

'Hester, my mother was never wise. It made her unthinking at times. But I loved her, and that day we met as children, I knew I was losing her.' His hands grasped hers. 'I didn't understand until afterwards, when I heard that your mother had died, that what I feared I was losing that day, you were losing too. I haven't forgotten that. And then being out in France...'

'You don't have to tell me,' she said, as he fell silent.

'Yes, I do. The worst bit of fighting in the French countryside is when we go through villages that have been occupied. The poor wretches are left with nothing, not even the most basic means of survival. When I volunteered, I thought it was combat for right to prevail, not mechanised slaughter, not the brushing aside of women and children as if they count for nothing. It made me understand more than ever what was most precious to me. What I would cherish most, should I survive.'

'But you've got to survive.' She grabbed the lapels of his jacket, shaking him in her vehemence. 'You've got to.'

'So my father can insist I restore the family fortunes by selling armaments to the highest bidder?'

'No, of course not, you idiot. So you can do things your own way. So you can make sure it never happens again. So the vile little weasel-faced men of this world like Jimmy Harkness aren't the only ones left. Don't give in, Richard. There's always a way.'

'I wish I could believe you.'

'You helped me just now, didn't you?'

'Only after roundly insulting you.'

'You meant well.'

'No, I didn't.' She was still holding on to his jacket. His hands came over hers, keeping them there. 'That was purely selfish. I couldn't bear the thought of him touching you. In any way.'

The garden was very still. Hester quietly freed her hands. He made no attempt to detain them. 'You don't know me. You don't know anything about me.'

'I'm sorry, Hester. I swore to myself I wouldn't say anything. I have no right. Especially now.' He half turned to go, then hesitated. 'But you are wrong. I do know you, just as you know me. We understood each other a long time ago. I think we always will.' He gave a wry smile. 'Even though my mother spent the time ordering yours to be part of one of her terrible paintings and didn't recognise a woman whose hold on life was as fragile as her own.'

'It wasn't her fault.'

'She should have known better. Ralph always said it was humanity that counted, rich or poor.'

'Then that's what you fight for,' she said fiercely. She grasped his jacket again, pulling him closer. 'That's what you always fight for, in any way you can.' He was so close she could feel the warmth of his body, the beat of his heart.

'Hester...' His breath was warm on her lips. She didn't care any more, about the world, about anything. Just his warmth stealing through her clothing, the gentle touch of his mouth on hers, with its question. She met his kiss, his breath mingling with hers, setting every part of her alive, wishing it would never end.

In the distance came the sound of voices as the gardeners returned.

'Hester—'

'Don't.' She put her hand over his mouth. 'Don't say anything. This is now, this minute. There's nothing else.'

He gently removed her hand, holding it tight. 'Then that's what I'll remember. Live your life, Hester, wherever that takes you. Don't you ever let anything hold you back.'

His lips brushed hers, then he was gone, vanishing into the shadow of the outbuildings until the gardeners had passed, before slipping unseen through the doorway as if he had never been there at all.

Hester bent over the spinach, the green shoots dancing in front of her eyes, as she returned the cheerful greetings of the fruit pickers, her mind in turmoil. She was still shaking from head to foot. No one had told her passion could be so overwhelming, shutting out everything but the need to be closer and never let go. Now it was gone.

Her fingers closed around the paper in her pocket, her one chance of escape from the trap closing slowly, inexorably, in on her. Her chance of a new life and, one day, however long it took, making her dream come true.

It had the terrible feeling of being a last will and testament. A final gift, freely given, from where it was least expected. A true gift of love. As she slowly made her way back to the house, her heart was breaking.

Chapter Thirty-One

Hester didn't have time to think. The next morning the talk in the kitchen at Afalon was full of Jimmy being back. Molly had seen him, bold as brass, striding through the little hamlet in the company of Mary-Anne Blewitt, telling anyone who would listen of his heroism behind the lines, with hints at being returned on some mission far too secret to divulge.

'Mum thinks he's lying,' said Molly hesitantly.

'Of course he is,' said Lottie, who had joined them for a cup of tea before Dr Villiers arrived and the non-stop rush of the day began. 'Always was bluff and bluster, that one. Anyone with half a brain could see that. If you ask me, he hasn't been anywhere near the front line. Most probably didn't even complete his training. He'll have done something. He always does.'

'Mum says she heard from her cousin who works for Mr Timson that Jimmy was so short-sighted he wouldn't let him drive a motorised van,' said Molly. 'Couldn't see a thing on the road. Mr Timson said he was a danger to man and beast.'

Lottie snorted. 'In that case he'll have failed the medical. He didn't even make it to training, the lying little toad. So much for secret missions. I don't think that boy knows what's real and what's not. Doesn't care, so long as he can think he looks big.'

'Mum says he was dismissed from Timson's for stealing,'

whispered Molly, round-eyed. 'And from one of the other places for fighting.'

'Wouldn't surprise me,' grunted Lottie. 'He never could help himself. Not quite right in the head, if you ask me.'

'I suppose not,' murmured Hester, her stomach too much of a knot to finish her tea.

She couldn't let Jimmy win. She couldn't let him drive her away from all she loved. In any case, she couldn't go yet, not while Gran was starting one of her colds, which inevitably ended up in an infection on her chest. She also had to give Miss Chesterfield some warning before her departure. Now it came to it, in the cold light of day, a life wasn't so easy to drop at a moment's notice. It wasn't so simple to just walk away. Besides, from the sound of things, maybe Jimmy would be the one to have no choice but to leave, after all.

'Well, he'll soon find he's not welcome here, not with so many boys lost and so many families knowing they might be next,' said Lottie. 'Only someone as desperate for affection as Mary-Anne will believe him now.'

'Let's hope so,' said Hester, turning her attention to the day's soup.

A few weeks later, Hester returned from the walled garden to find Robbie waiting for her at the kitchen door, cap turning nervously in his hands, shifting his weight from one foot to another.

'What is it? Is it Dad? Or has Gran got worse?'

'It's nothing like that, Hester. I just need to talk to you. It's Alice.'

'Alice? Has she been hurt?'

'No. At least, I don't think so. Hester, that day, just before you started at Afalon, when you cut your head...'

'It was nothing.'

'Was that why you left? I tried to ask Dad. He said it wasn't, but I know when he's lying. Was it because of Jimmy?'

'Why do you ask?'

'Was it?'

'We had an argument. He doesn't like it when girls argue with him, so he pushed me. I fell against a wall. I wasn't that hurt.' A new foreboding shot through her. 'Why?'

He took a deep breath. 'Since Jimmy's been back, Alice hasn't been going straight back to Gran's from school, especially since Gran's chest has meant she's been too ill to fetch her. And yesterday Alice came home with a new dress. She said you'd bought it for her. But it was new. Brand new. Not like the second-hand ones you get and alter from the market. It had lace, real fancy stuff, all down the bodice.'

'I didn't buy her a dress, and I certainly wouldn't buy her anything so impractical.' She felt sick. 'Robbie, are you telling me you think Jimmy bought it?'

He nodded. 'It had to be him. It was the way he was looking at her, as if, well as if he owned her.'

'But she's a child!'

'She thinks he's being kind.'

'I'll speak to Gran. I'll ask Miss Chesterfield if Alice can come and help me after school until Gran is properly well again. She might enjoy helping in the gardens, there are several schoolchildren coming regularly to help after school, I should have thought of that before. Don't worry. We'll sort something out.' Her heart sank. Far from relief appearing on her brother's face, he was still standing there, twirling his cap between his hands. 'What else is it, Robbie?'

He bit his lip. 'We owe rent. Hester, I'm sorry, I've put everything I can from what I earn on the ferry in the rent tin, but now it's gone. We missed last week, and there's not enough for this Friday when Mr Bolsover comes, and I don't know how we are going to pay for last week as well. It's not that we've had no passengers. We've had more than ever, now even rich people can't use their motor cars as much.' He swallowed. 'Dad's been going every night to the Fisherman's Arms with Jimmy. He says it's because he misses you, but I think that's an excuse. He's always making excuses.'

Despair flooded through her. She couldn't win. After all she had worked and all she had learnt, she still couldn't win. She had scrimped and saved since starting work at Afalon, mending her old dress rather than buying even the cheapest of second-hand ones to alter for when she was out of uniform. She had shivered all winter with no proper coat to make sure that once the food for the children was covered and Jenifry paid to cook and clean for Dad three days a week, she could put money by for her own future, once this war was over.

Despite everything, she had held on to the dream that, one day, people would once more want fine meals and afternoon tea and she could build up her cake business again, even if by then Gran had become too old and tired to help. All this time, she had been so sure she would eventually succeed in establishing a cafe in St Ives, just as Mum had dreamt all those years ago.

Even after Jimmy returned, her savings, along with the information Richard had given her, had been the safety net enabling her to escape to London at the first sign that Jimmy's irrational obsession with her was still there. In her heart of hearts, she'd hoped he'd transferred his attentions fully onto Mary-Anne. She might have known that Mary-Anne, being willing to obey his every whim, would never satisfy that need of his to break a woman down, to control her and destroy everything about her, to feel the power of making what had once been strong so completely his own.

Why, oh why, hadn't she fled to London, that first day after Richard warned her of Jimmy's return? Because, deep down, she'd known what he would do? That he would guess she'd never abandon her family completely and, wherever she was, however securely hidden, she'd hear how he had reasserted his influence over Dad, and placed Alice next in his sights. Jimmy would always find a way of signalling to her that it was going to be her or Alice, and he knew her well enough to be certain she would never allow her little sister, or any of her family, to come to harm.

At least there was something she could do. 'Wait here. I'll just need to ask permission to leave for an hour from Miss Chesterfield, and I'll come back with you.'

Dad wasn't at home, most probably already drowning his sorrows with Jimmy in the Fisherman's Arms. Hester took down the rent tin. She could tell it was far too light, even before she opened it.

'I kept these under my mattress,' said Robbie, returning with a few more coins.

'What was Dad thinking of? That's still only just over half the rent for this week. How could he be so selfish!'

'I tried, Hester.'

'I'm not blaming you, dearest. Things would be much worse if you weren't here to keep an eye on him and to at least put some money in the tin.'

'But I can't stop him.'

'Don't worry, I couldn't either. Mum had a hiding place to keep most of her earnings so he couldn't find them. I should have shown you it before. I just never thought he'd use the money you earned, with my wages there to keep him comfortable. Unless you'd feel safer giving it to Gran or me to keep?'

'Can I give it to you?'

'Of course. You bring it up to Afalon when you can. Just tell Dad you are coming to see me, and put something in the tin to keep him happy. If the rest isn't there, he can't spend it, and he'll be too embarrassed to ask you for money. Let Jimmy buy him beer, if that's what he wants.'

They took the coins to Mr Bolsover's office, thankful to find him there rather than on his rounds. Making up this week's rent and paying last week's left Hester with very little of her precious savings. If Robbie couldn't make enough to cover the following week's payment, there would be nothing left.

Hester sent Robbie to meet Dad and Jimmy, with instructions not to let Jimmy out of his sight, and hurried to the school, catching up with Alice as she came out of class.

'Hester! I hardly ever see you these days. Did Gran send you?'

'No, I wanted it to be a surprise. I should have been to see you more. I'm sorry Gran's been so ill.'

'It's her chest, but she's getting better. Jimmy's been very kind.'

'Has he?'

'He bought her fruit, and he found me a dress because my old one was worn out.'

'Dad should do that for you. I'm sorry, Alice, I should have noticed about your dress. I'm earning money now, you know you can always come to me.'

'Jimmy says he'll buy me shoes next. Nice ones that fit.'

'Alice, Jimmy doesn't have enough to buy things for you. Besides, he isn't working with Dad any more, he isn't part of the family, like he used to be, before he went away.'

'Oh, but this is money Jimmy earns. He's nice. I know you don't like him, Hester, but he's always nice to me.'

What could she say? Hester held her little sister's hand

and listened to her chatter, her mind working fast. At least Alice was just as she had always been, with no signs of hiding anything, especially anything more sinister.

'Come on, you come back to Afalon with me,' she said, doing her best to sound cheerful. 'We'll call in and see Gran, and then you can see where I work. I'll ask Miss Chesterfield if you can sleep in my room tonight.'

'Isn't Afalon full of soldiers?'

'Not now, sweetheart. It's not like at first. Afalon now just has a few patients who are getting better and stronger. They won't hurt you. Come on, you can help me. We've been collecting the fruit in the walled garden. While I'm getting jam ready, I'm going to make a summer pudding. Wouldn't you like to help me, and bring some back for Robbie and Gran tomorrow?'

'What's summer pudding?'

'It's made with blackcurrants and redcurrants, and all the fruit we can find. Mum used to make it when she worked as head cook in a hotel in St Ives. It's her recipe I'll be using.'

Alice nodded and took her hand. 'Can we see Gran first?'

'Of course, sweetheart.'

As they turned towards Gran's cottage, Hester discovered Jimmy making his way between the schoolchildren racing home in the freedom of escaping the school gates, with Robbie on his heels. When he saw them, Jimmy stopped in his tracks.

Hester bent and said quietly, 'you tell Robbie where we are going, sweetheart, I'll ask Jimmy to explain it to Dad.'

Alice nodded, happily running past Jimmy with a casual wave. So not completely under his spell. Not yet.

'Hester! You came to meet your sister,' said Jimmy, watching her uncertainly. 'I was just about to walk her back to her grandmother's.'

'I'm taking her back to Gran's. It's only a few minutes' walk, Alice is quite safe going there on her own.'

'I'm only thinking of you, Hester. Your gran's not well, you know. I came back to find she'd been having trouble with her chest for weeks. I'm worried about her, and the children. They need someone to look after them. I am practically family, after all. They need my help, Hester. Your dad knows I'm trustworthy.' A sly look came over his face. 'Don't you know how much it hurts him that you don't trust his judgement, when he is so much older and wiser than you? Shouldn't a young girl trust her father? I haven't said anything before because I would hate to cause you pain, but I've seen the hurt he feels knowing you have left him to follow your ambition, after all he has done for you, all these years. He's not a well man, Hester.'

Just seeing him there, so close to her, hearing him cunningly pummelling her into submission with her own doubts, sucked the breath from her body. Well, she wasn't giving in that easily. Without even the option of escaping to the refuge in London, she was cornered. All she could do was turn and fight.

'Did you know Dad's not been paying the rent?' said Hester. Jimmy blinked. 'No, I thought not. So much for looking out for him. I've covered it for this time, but I can't do it again. I won't do it again. I've told Mr Bolsover that. This is Dad's last chance. If he doesn't put the rent money aside, he won't have a roof over his head. Will you pay his rent? If he's evicted, will you give him a bed and put food on his table?'

'I—' He scowled.

'I thought not.'

Jimmy recovered himself. 'Of course I would look after him. And your gran. For your sake, Hester. I'd do anything for your sake. I'd lay down my life for you.'

'Easy said,' she retorted, before she could stop herself, fear and temper shooting to her head in a rush of blood. 'Another story once you'd reeled me in. Guess who'd be doing the laying down, then?'

Jimmy was puce, mask momentarily stripped away. 'You foul-mouthed little bitch. Someone should teach you what's good for you, good and proper.' He stopped, his eyes travelling beyond her. She turned to find Robbie, who, from his expression, had heard every word of this exchange. Another fear went through her.

'Robbie—'

'It's all right, Hester.' Robbie's fists were clenched, but he was ignoring Jimmy, as if he didn't exist. 'I've told Dad I'm walking you and Alice back to Afalon. There's talk of strange people about, with the war on. Dad doesn't want to risk either of you getting hurt.'

'Thank you, Robbie. I think that is for the best.'

'As you wish.' Jimmy turned and strode between the houses, but not before Hester had seen the look he had shot in their direction.

'You will be careful, won't you, Robbie? Jimmy isn't someone to be crossed.'

'Don't worry about me. I never liked him and I hate the influence he has over Dad.'

'It's not entirely Dad's fault, Robbie. It's frustrating for us, but it's been hard for him since he lost his arm.'

'That's still no excuse. He shouldn't put someone who buys him pints in front of his family. Especially so much that he drives you away, and then still expects you to look after him if something goes wrong. I'll try and make him see sense and that he's always with me on the ferry, like he used to be with Jimmy. Even if he does tell me what to do all the time, it'll be worth it. I wish Jimmy had stayed away.'

'Just be careful.'

'I'm not afraid of Jimmy. Don't worry, Hester.' He kissed her cheek as they turned to join Alice, who was waiting uncertainly a little way ahead. 'I'll make sure the rent is paid from now on, and I'll make sure we pay you back, just as soon as we can.'

Gran was sitting in her garden dozing in the warmth of the sun when they arrived.

'I'm sorry,' she said, as Robbie followed Alice inside to make tea. 'I don't know what came over me. I was all ready to meet Alice, then I was so tired I could barely put one foot in front of the other. I must have dozed off again.'

'It's all right, Gran. You can't help being ill. I should have thought and made other arrangements for Alice until you are better. Don't worry, I'll take her back to Afalon, she can stay with me for a few nights. Miss Chesterfield will understand.'

'She's a good girl. She's been so thoughtful and taken care of me, and she's walked back on her own when I couldn't make it. It will do her good to have a few nights away.'

'Are you sure you'll be all right? Robbie has said he'll stay with you until you are back on your feet.' She smiled. 'I promised Alice we could bring you some summer pudding once it's made.'

'Summer pudding.' Gran's pale face brightened. 'I haven't had summer pudding in years.'

'I'm using Mum's recipe.'

'Then I know it will be delicious.' She was lost in thought for a while, not moving for so long Hester thought she had fallen asleep again. Finally, she stirred. 'I haven't made any jam this year. It's so much more tricky without sugar, and it doesn't last. I'm not sure if I'll ever make any again.'

'Of course you will, Gran! We'll have sugar again, one day, and you'll be back to normal in no time.'

Gran was still frowning. 'Was it Jimmy?'

'Gran?'

'The reason you're taking Alice to Afalon? There's no need to answer. I can see it from your face. I'm sorry, Hester, I should have known. I should have been more careful.'

'There's no harm done. I was the one who should have realised he wouldn't give up so easily. The first thing is to get Alice safely away from here.'

Gran sighed. 'I'm afraid I have to agree. Alice is growing up fast, for all she's still a child, and when my chest is bad, I can't be her bodyguard every hour of the day and night.'

'There has to be somewhere she can go to finish her studies. She can stay with me until I find a suitable place for her.'

'And you?'

'I'm old enough to look after myself.'

'I'm sure you are, *cariad*. But you might find it better to find a post in St Ives yourself, my dear, if Jimmy's still determined to trouble you. No one would blame you. Or if you decided to move away completely.'

'I'll think it over,' she murmured, as Alice returned, teapot in her hands.

Chapter Thirty-Two

As September 1915 drew to an end, Hester left Molly in charge of preparing the stew for the evening meal and waited with Alice in the driveway at Afalon.

'This is such a good opportunity for you,' she said cheerfully. 'It was kind of Mrs Trewarren to recommend you to the headmistress of the girls' school in St Ives. It will give you a much better chance of being able to train as a doctor.'

'I'd rather be here with you, or with Gran.'

'I know, sweetheart. But Gran still isn't fully recovered, and my time is taken up with my job. It's been lovely having you here over these past weeks, but you need to continue your education.'

'I could live at home and cook for Dad.'

'And end up doing that all your life? Is that what you want?'

Alice shook her head. 'No.'

'That's why the school is the best idea. None of us want to see you leave, but we want the best for you.'

'Yes,' said Alice, sounding unconvinced.

Hester cursed Jimmy with all her might. Alice clearly felt she was being punished. She hadn't done anything wrong, but she was the one being sent away.

Miss Chesterfield had been the one to suggest consulting Mrs Trewarren, who, as chairwoman of the local school board, knew everyone there was to know, and had influence. Mrs Trewarren had rapidly taken matters in hand, sweeping Alice off to see the headmistress of a school on the outskirts of St Ives with an excellent reputation for teaching its girls the sciences. Alice had clearly made a good impression, being immediately offered a place at the school, along with the opportunity to board with the family of one of the teachers.

'You still want to be a doctor, don't you?'

Alice nodded. 'Especially now.'

Hester kissed her. 'There, you see. Dr Villiers thinks you have the makings of a doctor, and she's nobody's fool.'

'I could never be like Dr Villiers,' sighed Alice, eyes bright with hero worship. After much muttering about Alice being far too young and impressionable, Dr Villiers had relented and allowed Alice to observe her on her rounds. On the first occasion, Alice had returned deathly white and deep in thought, but she'd insisted on going back the next day, and had accompanied Dr Villiers ever since. In a VAD uniform, she didn't look conspicuously younger at a casual glance, and had obeyed instructions to stay in the background and not draw attention to herself.

It would be the making or the breaking of her as a doctor, Dr Villiers had remarked. So she might as well find out now. It sounded brutal, but Hester could see her point. With still no sign of any end to the war in sight, and many of the injuries suffered by the men who made it to Afalon to recuperate being the kind to trouble them for the rest of their lives, who knew what Alice might face, when she eventually began to train in earnest?

Mrs Trewarren's Ford appeared, trundling up the driveway.

'Ready?' said Clara, pulling up next to them.

'Yes,' said Alice, sounding more confident.

'Good. Get in then.'

While Alice clambered in next to Clara, Hester placed her sister's small bag safely next to her on the back seat. She had spent the last evenings cutting down two dresses given to her by Clara, in order to give Alice some kind of respectable wardrobe. The lacy bribe from Jimmy had been quietly removed.

Clara drove them between the high hedges of the lanes until they reached St Ives. There, she headed off to collect supplies for Afalon from the railway station, while Hester provided Alice with new underwear and a pair of boots, the best she could afford. Yet more of her savings gone. But it was worth it to see her sister safe, at least for now. There was nothing else to be done, and at least she had employment, and, so long as Dad didn't find Robbie's money before he could hide it carefully away, no need to pay Dad's rent from her earnings. Robbie was only just managing as it was, she couldn't expect him to try and repay the money she had used to keep the roof over Dad's head. She was just going to have to try to save again.

By the time they arrived at her lodgings, Alice was walking proudly in her new boots, looking much happier now none of her clothes could humiliate her, chatting cheerfully away as they made their way to the row of Victorian villas set safely back from the harbour.

'Are you sure it's this one?'

'Oh, yes. This is Mrs Evelyn's.' By now Alice was bubbling up with excitement. 'Isn't it wonderful?' She lowered her voice to a whisper. 'I've a room all to myself. With a desk so I can study when I want to. They have books. Rows and rows and rows of books, and they've promised I can read as many of them as I like.'

'That's wonderful, sweetheart.' Hester brushed down her coat, feeling shabby and insignificant. This was the kind of house where cooks went through the side entrance, rather than the front door.

The maid who greeted them was courteous enough, but Hester couldn't help seeing herself as out of place, in a way she never felt at Afalon. That was because of Miss Chesterfield, who, having fought her own way up, had scant regard for the differences between the classes. This, on the other hand, was the household of a professional man, where she would always feel out of place. Alice, however, already seemed at home among the expensive wallpaper and fine furniture.

Hester could feel her sister beginning to move away from her. No wonder the wife of the teacher of biology had refused to take payment for Alice's board. Like the headmistress, they were forward-looking, passionate about women entering the professions and had spotted a girl with potential, worthy of being encouraged.

One who would inevitably become more like them, thought Hester, a little sadly. She was glad for Alice, but, try as she might, she couldn't be the self-sacrificing sort who could live her life contentedly watching her sister follow her dreams, and rise in social standing until they barely had anything in common. In her future life, Alice would most likely hire a cook. Hester winced. She couldn't help but wonder if, one day, Alice might even be a little ashamed of her.

It was a clear, bright day, with the sea so calm it barely appeared to move, even in the wilder part of the bay, with the curve of sand on the opposite side from the harbour.

Clara had already returned. Hester could make out the Ford parked by the roadway while Clara walked along the edge of the waves.

'Successful?' asked Clara, as Hester joined her.

'Mrs Evelyn was friendly, and has a daughter the same age as Alice. I think Alice will be very happy there.'

'I know it wasn't exactly what you wanted, Hester, but I feel sure it has worked out for the best.'

'I expect you're right. Clara, do you mind if we don't go back just yet? There's somewhere I'd like to see. It's not far from here.'

'Of course. There's nothing that's needed urgently and to be honest, I'll be glad of the distraction.'

Hester led the way to Porthgwidden beach. 'There's a cafe, with a view of Godrevy lighthouse. My mother brought me here once, when I was a little girl. I'd like to see it again.'

'Excellent. In that case we can have afternoon tea. My treat,' she added to the quickly suppressed dismay on Hester's face.

They followed the path onto the beach. The green water moved gently against the pebbles, while a pleasure boat made its sedate way towards the lighthouse, sails golden in the sinking light.

'Oh.' Hester came to a halt in front of the cafe. 'It's boarded up.'

'What a pity. It's such a quirky little place. You'd have thought people would have loved it, especially with such a view. It looks as if it's falling to bits. Papa says lots of places have been forced to close because of the war, and prices going up so much and things being short, and people not able to come to Cornwall on holiday.'

'It looks so sad.'

'That's odd.' Clara peered at the wind-bleached terrace. 'I've been here, too. Mama brought me once. We didn't go in, we just stood on the beach and looked. What a strange coincidence.'

'Yes,' said Hester. 'I suppose it is.'

'It is lovely.' Clara gazed at it wistfully. 'It seems such a pity to let it rot. Let's hope visitors come back in their droves once this war is over, and the owners are able to open it up again.'

'Let's hope so.'

The fire was back. This was the cafe Mum had dreamt of, the one that would have meant she would never be forced to rely on Dad's willingness to hand over his earnings. Hester took a deep breath. She wasn't going to give up. By hook or by crook, and whatever it took, she was going to find a way of renting the cafe, or at least running it for the Carltons until she could afford to take it over. She had no idea how, but was more certain than ever that Mum's dream was one worth fighting for.

She wasn't going to lose this. She wasn't going to let Jimmy drive her away. Now she knew Alice was safe, she was going to stay and fight and she wasn't going to let Jimmy win.

It was dusk when they arrived back. Clara parked by the church while they went to reassure Gran that Alice was settled and happy. As they returned to take the road up to Afalon, Hester found Jimmy walking up from the direction of the Fisherman's Arms.

'Good evening, Miss Trewarren. I'm glad you've found the time to visit your father, Hester. He will be happy to see you. His bad arm has been aching for days, I'm just going to check if he needs any help. I'm afraid he may need to visit the hospital. But it will do him good to see you.'

'Hester's expected back at Afalon,' said Clara sharply. She pulled herself to her full height, shoulders back, every inch her mother's daughter. 'She has been on an errand for Miss Chesterfield to ensure the men who have sacrificed so much for their country have the correct nutrition to help them heal. It was unfortunate that we have already been delayed by the suppliers. Hester has no time to visit her father tonight.'

'Tell Dad I'll see him soon,' put in Hester, as Jimmy took on the look of a man about to explode at being put in his place by a slip of a girl.

'As you wish,' he snapped as they clambered into the Ford.

'Thank you,' Hester said, as they sailed with dignity past Jimmy.

'Obnoxious little man. Trying to make you feel guilty so you'd go running to your dad. You don't think your father could be really so very ill, do you?'

'Robbie would have left a message for me at Gran's if he was.'

'Of course he would. I like your brother, Hester. He has sense.'

'So he does,' she replied. In the mirror, she caught a glimpse of Jimmy, standing in the middle of the road, watching them. Much as she wanted to, she couldn't tear her eyes away. He remained stock-still, ignoring the frantic ringing of bicycle bells as a collection of VADs, making the most of the sun, swept past, heading towards Afalon before Miss Chesterfield called out the constabulary to round them up, and keep them corralled within the walls for the rest of the war. He didn't even look round at the shouts of warning from the stragglers, who only just swerved in time to miss crashing into him.

Jimmy remained like a statue, unaware of any of them, his gaze focused on the motor car, until Clara turned into the lane and he vanished from sight.

Chapter Thirty-Three

Winter had come again to Afalon. Even this close to the sea, the air had been bitingly cold for days on end.

Frost lay heavy on the grass as Clara pulled up outside Afalon's kitchen door and swung herself wearily to the ground. She stamped her feet, rubbing her chilled hands, her every breath surrounding her with a chill mist. After nearly two years of war, there was no sign of the conflict ending, and finding supplies was as haphazard a business as ever.

'I managed to get flour,' she called, as Hester came out to meet her, wiping her hands on her apron. 'And a little sugar. There's very little meat to be had, but I've got as much as I can.'

'Clara, what is it? You look terrible. Is it Lance?'

Clara shook her head in silent misery. 'Lance is well. I had a letter from Isabella Elliot this morning. Richard's been wounded.'

Hester turned to reach for the bag of flour, face hidden. 'Is it very bad?'

'Isabella said he was trying to save one of his men when a mortar got them. One of his legs is so smashed he might lose it and she's not even sure if he'll be strong enough to make the journey back for treatment. He might die out there and I'll never see him again.'

'There's still hope, Clara. Some of the men here have

recovered from terrible wounds, and many of them were not expected to survive. We have to hope.'

Clara burst into tears. 'I can't bear it. So many of Ralph's friends are dead, I can't bear to think of losing another one. It's like losing a little bit of Ralph all over again, as if there's a little piece of his memory, gone forever.'

'It'll be all right.' Hester held her. 'He's strong and he's a fighter. I'm sure he'll come through this.'

'He's got to,' Clara wept into her shoulder. 'I can't lose him too. He's got to, he's just got to.'

They unloaded the rest of the goods in silence. Clara shook her head at the prospect of tea, busying herself instead in taking the much-needed medical supplies to Dr Villiers. As Clara vanished inside the house, Hester set Molly to prepare the vegetables for the day's stew. Pulling on her coat and winding a long woollen scarf around her head, she slipped into the walled garden on the pretence of inspecting whether their remaining stock of fresh herbs in the greenhouses had survived last night's freezing.

For once, the garden was deserted. Even as the sun rose in the palest of blue skies, a deep chill lingered inside the walls. Ice gleamed on the branches of the apple trees and among the dark green veins of kale. In the stillness, there was not a bird to be heard, not even shouts from old men and boys in the surrounding fields as they started the day. A hint of smoke from wood fires from the cottages below hung in the stillness, catching the back of her throat.

Hester made a cursory inspection of the pots of parsley, barely noticing if they were alive or dead. All she could feel was a great silent vastness, devoid of life. Somewhere out there, in a field hospital on the edges of the battlefield, Richard was lying, his life in the balance, perhaps already dead and cold in the ground. She had so willed him to survive, to come back, if not to her, simply for her to know he was alive, somewhere in the world.

The emptiness had crept inside every part of her, leaving her numb. Perhaps it was as well her plans had come to nothing. What was the point of her dream of a cafe? She no longer had the energy to even feel. Nothing mattered any more.

'You all right, miss?' She hadn't heard the approach of Corporal McDonald, a fair-haired young man in his early twenties, one sleeve hanging empty at his side, the remaining hand holding a pruning saw.

'Yes, yes thank you.' She pushed away her despair. Amidst all the grief and unbearable loss, somehow life carried on. The corporal didn't press her any further. No one did any more, these days. It was better to focus on the practical. Sometimes it was the only way to survive. 'More clearing of the new vegetable beds, is it?'

'Seems a pity to waste the fine weather, miss. We'll have a blaze in here in no time, to keep us warm. And looks like we'll be needing the vegetables, if this war carries on.'

'They will be very welcome,' she replied mechanically, as with much coughing and breath spiralling upwards, more of the men arrived, collecting saws and wheelbarrows from the sheds, ready for the day ahead.

Slowly, Hester made her way back to the kitchens. Everyone she knew had to somehow find the strength to continue, no matter what the obstacles they faced or the grief they were holding inside. None of them might have much hope for the future any more, it had become simply a matter of survival.

Christmas 1915 came and went, with no one much in the mood for the usual celebrations.

At least regular letters came from Isabella. By February

1916 she was able to reassure Clara that Richard had survived the worst. By April, she announced he was strong enough to be transferred to a London hospital.

'Isabella's trying to get him sent to Afalon for his recuperation once the surgeons have finished doing what they can,' said Clara. 'Oh, I do hope she manages to, it would be so good to have him here.'

'Yes,' said Hester. He was alive. He was going to live. The emptiness inside began to ease a little. She would see him again.

'I know it must be unbearable for him to be crippled,' exclaimed Clara miserably. 'But I can't help being glad that at least they can't ever send him back to fight. At least I'll be able to keep him safe. Is that so very wicked of me?'

'How could it be?' replied Hester gently, as Clara's face collapsed into tears of relief.

Later that afternoon, Clara took several jars of pickles and preserved blackcurrants from Afalon, accompanied by one of Hester's cakes, sweetened with honey and carefully stored apples to replace the missing sugar, to the church hall.

She found the Women's Institute ladies were already there in force, tying on aprons and rolling up their sleeves, as they prepared bread and a vast pan of soup with much noise and chatter. In one corner, a group were rolling bandages, in another the women were knitting socks and mufflers for the troops with all the wool that could be found, with a motley collection of children carefully rolling up balls of wool from old jumpers, much to the delight of the church cat.

So many of the women were wearing black armbands, but the atmosphere was industrious and quietly cheerful. Mrs Teague, who before the war had worn her distant relation to a duke like a tiara everywhere she went, was chopping onions with Mrs Mitchell, deep in discussion over the lack of footwear for some of the poorest of the families, as if dukes were two a penny.

'Aha, that's a welcome sight,' said Mrs Mitchell. 'Thank you, my lovely. This is just what we needed.'

'Apart from a good side of beef,' called one of the rollers of bandages with a grin, setting the hall echoing with rueful laughter.

'And a pig or two,' added another. 'I never thought I'd dream of bacon and eggs.'

'I'm afraid I can only offer cake,' Clara replied in the same tone. 'But it is Hester's and it is apple cake.'

'Oh well, in that case ...'

Clara stayed for a while, joining in the chopping of last year's frostbitten turnips. The atmosphere in the hall was always infectious. However dark her mood, however terrible the news from the front or the agony at finding a name she knew among the lists of the dead, this always had the power to bring back her determination to get through. It always reminded her that she was no different from any of the other women who had lost sons, husbands or sweethearts, many with elderly parents to support and children to keep healthy on their own, as well as their work for the war effort.

Today, she was careful to keep to herself her glee that Richard was recovering and might soon even be back at Afalon. You never knew who might have received bad news that morning, or was waiting in dread to hear of a loved one reported missing, or lying wounded in a field hospital far from home and any possibility of comforting. It was best to keep hands and mind occupied on the small things, the ones that could make an immediate difference and kept them all going.

Chopping finished, and with a supply of medicines ready to collect from the London train at Hayle station in an hour or so, Clara walked slowly back to the Ford, hands in the pockets of her walking skirt, deep in thought.

'Afternoon, Miss Trewarren.'

Startled, she only just avoided bumping into the man placing himself squarely in front of her. She recovered herself quickly. 'Good afternoon, Mr Harkness.'

'You remembered.'

'I beg your pardon?'

'You'd be surprised, Miss Trewarren. Not everyone notices a poor working man. Some think they are above me. Not that I resent it, of course. That wouldn't be in my nature. Not in the least.'

'I'm sure it wouldn't, Mr Harkness.' Everything about the man made her skin crawl. Her strongest urge was to get away as fast as possible. 'If you'll excuse me, I've medicines to collect for Dr Villiers.'

'In St Ives, would that be?'

'St Ives?' So that's what this was about. She opened her eyes wide in feigned astonishment. 'Good grief, no, Mr Harkness. What on earth would I want in St Ives?'

'I thought you were seen there.'

'Me? You must be mistaken.' She smiled blandly. 'Unless I was passing through on the way to Penzance. I generally go to Truro to collect supplies for Miss Chesterfield, unless the train can bring them to Hayle, but I've collected some from Penzance once or twice. I mustn't keep you, Mr Harkness. Good afternoon.' She pulled herself into the Ford, setting off as fast as she could, heading past the church and onto the roadway following the estuary towards Hayle.

As soon as she was certain she was out of sight, she slowed to a halt. St Ives. Was that just a shot in the dark, or had he guessed that was where Alice had been taken to escape his influence? Either way, he had hit too close to the truth for comfort. She set off again on her mission, this time at a slightly more sedate pace, unable to shake off a sense of deep unease and a need to talk to Hester as soon as she was able.

'That means I'll have to move Alice again,' exclaimed Hester in dismay, when Clara dragged her out of the kitchen to give her the news.

'He might just be guessing. He could have gone on to mention other places, if I'd let him.'

'But why start with St Ives? I should have known that would be too close. He knows she's the best chance he has of getting at me. This is my fault, I should have left for London when I had the chance.'

They stood on the driveway, ignoring the curious glances of the patients taking the air on the terrace of the house, some dozing or reading, while others were deep in a game of chess.

'You weren't to know he'd be so persistent,' said Clara. 'The man's clearly not right in the head. Besides, even if he guesses that's where Alice might be, he can hardly go there every evening to meet her from school, or to meet her at all. I find it hard enough to get enough petrol, and I'm on official business for Miss Chesterfield, who has contacts, and money. I can't imagine Jimmy to have either.'

Hester pulled her coat closer around her against the gusts of wind blowing in from the estuary. 'Robbie told me only yesterday that Jimmy is trying Timson's again, now they are so desperate for drivers. Timson's might not want him back, but some other delivery firm might take him and if they do, he's bound to make sure he has at least one route that takes him into St Ives. I can warn the school, but Alice won't have any of her family to look out for her. Maybe it would have been better if she'd never left here at all.'

'Don't worry, Hester. We'll work something out. I'll have a word with Mama. She knows everyone, I'm sure she'll have some ideas.'

'I just know she can't stay anywhere near here.' Poor Alice. On the few occasions Hester had managed to see her, Alice had sounded so happy with her school, but she couldn't hide how much she desperately missed the ferryman's cottage and not being able to spend time with Dad and Robbie and chat away for hours on end with Gran. For all the comfort of her new life, it wasn't the same as having your family around you.

If Alice was to be moved again, Hester knew deep in her heart she couldn't abandon her to yet another new school and new lodgings. Dad was a grown man who had to make his own choices, while Robbie was now old enough to look after himself. It was Alice who needed her. Jimmy had shown that if they stayed anywhere close, war or no war, he wouldn't stop until he found them. The only way was to get as far from here as possible. Maybe even to the extent of changing their names and making sure Dad could never guess where they were living.

It broke her heart to think of not being able to see Robbie and Gran for months, maybe years, and of leaving everything she knew behind. But if that was the only way of keeping Alice safe … She would talk to Miss Chesterfield and start applying for new posts in the morning. At least she was now an experienced cook and cooks of any sort were in short supply. She thought briefly of the cafe on Porthgwidden beach and pushed the thought aside. That had only ever been a dream. She couldn't afford to dream, not now. She had to be practical. She couldn't abandon Alice.

'Looks like more patients arriving,' said Clara, nodding to where an ambulance was turning into the driveway. As it reached the house, Phyllida and one of the older VADs appeared at the door, followed by Dr Villiers, limping down the steps, ready to supervise.

'They told us they wouldn't be arriving from London until tomorrow morning,' Dr Villiers exclaimed in exasperation. 'I've no idea about any of them, and no instructions. They could all be comatose for all I know.'

'I'll give you a hand,' called Clara. Hester followed her. They helped down several men, who hobbled painfully inside, many with limbs missing or leaning heavily on crutches. As the last man was helped away, one of the drivers pushed a wheelchair to the door of the ambulance.

'It's all right, captain, we'll get you down,' he said to the final occupant, who was shuffling painfully towards the door.

'I can manage,' he muttered.

'Oh my lord,' said Clara. 'It's Richard.' She reached the ambulance as the patient was carefully lifted down and placed in the wheelchair.

'Wouldn't go on a stretcher,' said the nearest ambulance man. 'Stubborn as they come. He needs to be, mind. The journey from London knocked him sideways, good and proper. Shouldn't have been let out of the hospital, if you ask me.'

'It's all right, I'll take him,' said Clara.

'You sure, miss? Them steps look steep and these are heavy old things.'

'There are plenty of helpers.'

The ambulance man nodded. 'We'll be off then. There's supposed to be another lot on their way from London, expected any minute. Them hospitals must be eager to get rid of them. Usually means they are expecting a whole lot more new ones in from France, poor sods.'

Hester watched, unable to move, as Clara began to push Richard towards the front door. If it hadn't been for his voice, she would have barely recognised him. He was white-faced and gaunt, barely anything of him left but the framework of his bones. His face was contorted with pain, eyes closed as he leant back, breathing heavily with the effort of any movement. He didn't seem to know where he was, or as if all places were the same to him.

As they passed, his eyes flew open. His gaze rested on her face, the crease between his brows deepening as if attempting to recognise something through the densest of fogs. The effort was clearly too much. He collapsed in on himself, eyes lost in a world of horrors from which there was no escape.

Dr Villiers met the wheelchair at the foot of the steps, beckoning for several VADs to help lift him up into the house. Hester could see her face was tight with the anger she showed when a man had been sent from hospital too soon, or with little chance of any long-term improvement.

The men on the terrace had stopped their occupations and were watching the scene with close attention. Hester could practically feel the memories of their own arrivals stirring up to haunt them.

'You're all right, doctor,' called Corporal McDonald, abandoning his chess pieces and striding towards them, empty sleeve flapping. 'I've manoeuvred many of these in my time. Cumbersome things, there's a trick to it, you'll find.'

'Thank you, corporal. I'm worried about hurting him even further.'

'No fear about that, miss. Now then, sir, you just hang on and we'll have you up and safe before you know it.'

Hester watched as the wheelchair, with its silent, unmoving occupant, was lifted up and into the house.

'I'll send up tea and hot water,' she muttered to no one in particular, fleeing towards the kitchens before tears overwhelmed her.

Chapter Thirty-Four

'Ah, Hester,' said Dr Graham, appearing a few hours later, meeting her in the corridor leading to the little side room that had been set aside for Richard Elliot, who had been too weakened by the journey to join the men in the main part of the house. 'I hear my patient has finally arrived.'

'Yes, Dr Graham. I came to see if he wished for anything in particular. Phyllida says he hasn't touched a thing.'

'And did he?'

'He was asleep. I left a cup of tea, but I didn't like to wake him.'

Dr Graham clicked his tongue. 'I'm afraid I still can't get used to treating young men I've known all their lives. I was there when Richard was born. I dragged him through measles and the whooping cough, both of which were touch and go at times. He had such a fighting spirit, even as a lad. He was so full of curiosity about the natural world and so many ideas about changing the human one for the better. He doesn't deserve this. But then nor does anyone. At least here we've more of a chance to get him back to some form of himself, body and soul.'

'Yes, Dr Graham.'

He patted her hand. 'There, my dear, no need to look so downhearted. You are playing your part in all this magnificently, you know. You are doing sterling work, creating the nutrition these poor lads need, and a bit of comfort a hearty meal brings. I feel sure your mother would have been proud.'

'I need to get back to my work,' murmured Hester, retreating as fast as she could.

For the first weeks, Richard was barely conscious. Infection had set in on his shattered leg once again, sending Dr Graham muttering that he might have to lose it, after all. But for the moment he was too weak to be moved, let alone withstand an operation.

It was a relief when one morning Clara declared him to be showing signs of being over the worst. When a little later Hester helped the VADs take dishes of soup up to the long dining table set up in the conservatory, which had been pressed into a makeshift dining room for those mobile enough to use it, she made her way back past the little room. The door was slightly ajar.

'Can I get you anything, Captain Elliot?'

'Who's that?'

She took a few steps inside the room. He still looked drawn and exhausted and as bloodless as the freshly laundered sheets. A deep furrow remained between his brows, as if pain held him permanently in its grip, his eyes closed.

'It's Hester, Captain Elliot. Hester Pearce. You're at Afalon.'

'Hester.' The furrow of his brow deepened. 'No. Nothing. I don't want to trouble you.'

'It's no trouble.' She took a step closer. 'It's good to see you recovering.'

'It's all right, Hester.' Clara pushed through the door with a tray containing two bowls of soup and slices of fresh bread. 'Don't take it personally. Richard's not speaking to anyone.'

The furrow deepened even further. 'Don't be ridiculous.'

'Well, it's true. I asked the VADs. You can't accuse them

all of being liars. You can't get out of it this time, my dear. Dr Graham has given me permission to bully you into eating something, or he won't ever let you out of bed, and Dr Villiers will come and lecture you until you do. She's perfectly fearsome. Now, you don't want that, do you?'

The faintest of smiles appeared. 'You sound just like your mother.'

Clara put the tray down on the bedside table. 'Good. Mama always gets things done and even the mayor is scared of her. I'll get us some tea while you decide whether you are going to feed yourself or I'm going to do it for you.'

'Certainly not!' His eyes shot open. 'Clara, don't you dare.'

'Male pride. It always does the trick,' said Clara, in the tones of a woman twice her age. She firmly blinked away the glisten of tears, maintaining her determined tone of cheerfulness. 'Ralph always said you were the best friend a man could have, Richard, so I'm making it my mission to send you out of here on your own two feet. And don't you have any thoughts of fading away, because I won't let you.'

'Do you ever give up?' he muttered irritably, raising himself a little, slowly and painfully, until he was propped against the pillows. Even that small movement had clearly exhausted him, his lips tightening again with pain.

'Never,' retorted Clara, steadfastly ignoring any signs of physical weakness. 'Ralph and I always beat you at tennis, remember?'

'Only because you cheated.'

'Rubbish. In that case, you'll have to prove it, and you can only do that if you get well again.'

'I'll fetch the tea,' said Hester. They barely heard her. Bless Clara for being so determined to make him improve, as if she could will him back to life. But at the same time, she could not help a faint twinge of pain at their easy familiarity, of shared memories from a childhood mixing in the same circles.

She wouldn't know how to begin to play tennis, she acknowledged gloomily, even if she had the time to learn, let alone own the correct costume and racket. In the rush and anxiety of war, there had been no distance between any of them. In just this small space of quiet the normal order of things had already returned. To Richard and Clara it did not matter, but she could see they were worlds apart.

When she returned, the two were deep in conversation, both soups forgotten. Hester quietly placed the teapot and cups and saucers on the table, along with a small jug of milk, and returned to the preparation of the evening meal.

She tried not to mind that neither noticed her presence. Richard clearly had no memory of the kiss they had shared in the gardens, or was choosing to forget it out of embarrassment and a wish to spare both their feelings. She was a fool for that moment to have stayed so vividly in her memory, like a silly schoolgirl, dreaming of a prince who would never even notice her existence. She should have known that moment had been an instinctive reaction to war, a fleeting sharing of warmth as he was returning to horrors beyond comprehension, convinced he was facing his own death within days, hours, even.

That was her punishment, she told herself as she made her way downstairs, for thinking only of herself and her own emotions, while desperate battles were taking place only a few hours away, the survivors facing a daily struggle to heal both body and mind.

Perhaps it was as well that she wouldn't be staying much longer at Afalon. That morning, there had been several advertisements for cooks in the papers. One in Birmingham and several more in London. The one in Birmingham she had seen advertised several weeks running. They had increased the pay and added an additional afternoon off. Which meant they must be getting desperate. There was bound to be a good school in Birmingham, and if the family were that anxious about securing a cook, they might agree to Alice staying with her until she could find permanent lodgings.

All she needed was to ask for a letter for recommendation and to give Miss Chesterfield as much notice as she could, and pray that she understood. She had been putting off speaking to her employer since breakfast. It seemed so horribly final.

As she reached the office, Hester came to a halt. She could hear Miss Chesterfield inside, pen squeaking as it flew over paper. She took a deep breath. There was no time like the present. At least then she would know that things were moving forward towards her new life with Alice and there would be no going back. Smoothing down her hair and apron, she knocked firmly on the door.

As Hester waited for a reply to her letter of application to the family in Birmingham, Richard began recover. She saw him at a distance, first in a wheelchair in the main room when he was well enough to join the other men and later on the terrace, wheeled out for reviving fresh air. Dr Villiers, who was a great believer in the benefits of keeping her patients moving, with the aim of keeping the blood flowing and the heart and lungs strong, had firm strictures about too much reliance on wheelchairs.

By the time she heard she had been accepted, and was spending as much time as she could instructing Molly in everything she would need to take her place, he was starting to make slow and painful attempts at walking. Each time she passed the terrace on the way to the walled garden he seemed to be there, come rain or shine, his mangled leg making each step an almost impossible task, even with Clara's encouragement.

'Poor Richard,' sighed Clara. 'It must have been hours before he was found. He's lucky he didn't bleed to death. I'm glad Isabella made sure he came here to recuperate. At least it's somewhere familiar. The trouble is, he's so horribly aware he'll never be the same. I sometimes think he just wants to go away, far from all of this, and never have to see any of us, ever again.'

A few days before she was due to leave for Birmingham, Hester made her way back from the ferryman's cottage in the company of several VADs, who were wheeling their bicycles along the path to keep her company. It was her afternoon off, allowing her to spend a few last hours with Dad, who, with Robbie on the ferry and Jimmy now fully occupied, had grumbled even more than usual at her imminent desertion.

'It's only for a short while, Dad,' she told him. 'I wouldn't miss such a good opportunity to work for a family. It's better paid than a convalescence home, and it will give me the experience to find a post with the richest families in Cornwall. I'll be back in a few months, just you see.'

She had taken care to make her new position sound as if it was a temporary arrangement, and to gloss over the things he didn't need to know. His interest perked up at the information that she would be sending back money for him, and she would write every week to let them know how she and Alice were getting on.

'But I'll make sure I send the letters to you,' she told Gran, as she arrived at the little cottage to say her goodbyes. 'Robbie has promised to collect them. The less Dad knows of my address, the less chance of Jimmy managing to prise it out of him.'

'You shouldn't have to be the one to leave, *cariad*,' sighed Gran. 'But I can see there is no other way. You take care of yourself, and Alice. One granddaughter is not so easy to find, let alone two.'

'Dear Gran.' Hester hugged her tight, fighting back tears. 'I will come back, I promise. I'm sure Jimmy won't stay around forever. We know he's never stuck at any job for long, we can hope he doesn't with this one. Something is bound to happen, sooner or later. I'll send money back to Robbie, so he can make sure Dad doesn't have more than the price of a single pint at the Fisherman's Arms. I just hope Jimmy soon tires of paying for Dad when there's no advantage in it. I hate the thought of him moving on to some other young woman, but I've a horrible feeling that's the only way I'll ever be free.'

'Whatever the case, the less your dad's seen with that Jimmy the better. The more of his stories he tells, the more people are beginning to see through his lies. There's plenty starting to avoid him. Mr Blewitt told Mary-Anne to have nothing to do with him, or she'll be out on her ear. And that girl isn't so besotted she doesn't know which side her bread is buttered. When he went up to get a pint yesterday, there was a whole handful of white feathers appeared from nowhere on his seat. They said you should have seen the look on Jimmy's face. That stopped his stories, right in their tracks.'

'Then maybe he will leave,' said Hester.

'Let's hope he will, my dearest.'

Hester kissed her. They both knew that even if the war ended soon, which seemed ever more unlikely, travel to and from Cornwall to Birmingham was so long and costly, she might as well have secured a post in darkest Africa. Like many who left to find work, the chances were that she would never return.

*

As they reached the safety of Afalon's grounds, Hester fell behind the VADs, who raced their bicycles along the drive, shouting loud encouragement to each other.

Evening was falling, the last rays of sun silhouetting the house against a luminous sky. All was calm and still, with the wide estuary stretching down to the sea. A few days more and she would be in the noise and smokiness of a large city, where it was said no one stopped, day or night, and the noise of factories and vehicles was deafening. She might never know such evenings again.

'Damn and blast it.' From one of the large shrubs at one side of the pathway came a muffled curse, followed by the crashing of branches.

Hester hurried towards the signs of disaster. 'Are you all right?'

'Yes,' came the answer, by the sounds of it through gritted teeth and unmistakably a lie. She would know that voice anywhere.

'If you take my hand, Captain Elliot, I'll help you up.'

'I can manage.'

'Well, I can help you back to your feet, or you are going to have to take your chances with whoever comes along to find you. It'll be one of the men if you're lucky, Dr Villiers if you're not.'

That worked.

'Bloody woman,' muttered Richard, reaching up for Hester to pull him upright.

'Is that me or Dr Villiers?'

'Dr Villiers. She's not a doctor, she's a sadist.'

'But an effective one.' Hester reached for the fallen crutches, waiting while he adjusted them under his arms and regained his balance.

'That's true,' he admitted. 'She's very good at getting us back on our feet. Those of us who have feet, that is.'

'And also the ones who don't.'

He grunted absently in reply, concentrating on balancing himself so he could set off again towards the house. She could see his face was deathly pale, and despite the cool breeze coming up from the river, beads of sweat stood out on his forehead.

She hesitated. She had watched him so many times over the past days, taking his place on the flat section of grass in front of the terrace, stubbornly placing one foot in front of the other, a few more steps each time, before collapsing back into his chair, completely drained. She had never yet seen him stray so far down the driveway. From his laboured breathing, it had proved far too ambitious.

The sensible thing would be to leave him to his own devices and send one of the VADs with the wheelchair to meet him. Hester winced. She'd seen him crumple to the ground before and his utter mortification at being scooped up by Phyllida, whom he most probably felt he should be protecting with an imaginary sword and shield, rather than lying sprawled, helpless, in the manner of an upturned turtle, at her feet. She couldn't bear to see him humiliated, but she couldn't leave him to collapse again, to hurt far more than his pride.

'I'll walk back with you, it isn't far.'

'There's no need.'

'Very well, you can escort me.'

'You don't need escorting.'

'Because I'm not a lady, you mean,' she snapped, hurt despite herself.

'No, of course not. You know me better than that, Hester.

I meant because you are strong and capable and take your own way.'

'That doesn't mean I have to avoid company, if I choose.'

'I don't want to hold you back.'

'If you were holding me back I'd tell you.'

He came to a halt, breathing ragged with effort, head lifted towards the men on the terrace enjoying the last of the sun. 'Poor devils. You'd think you'd grow numb out there, with so many dying around you. In one way you do. It's the only way to survive. Being back here is like coming back to life. It's not possible to shut off the usual emotions any longer. You can hear it in men's dreams.'

'I've heard Dr Villiers say that dreams can be eased over time.'

'Maybe.'

'And that you are getting stronger every day.'

'As much as I can.' His face was turned away. 'I know I'm one of the lucky ones, but that won't stop me from being a crock for the rest of my days.'

'At least you are alive.'

'Yes.' He turned slightly towards her, as if he couldn't bear to meet her gaze full on. 'But I'm also a liability.'

'A liability? You have a life ahead of you.'

'Exactly,' he replied. 'Don't look at me like that, Hester. Believe me, I'm grateful for my life, and I will be for every hour of my existence. But I have to face it that, from now on, I'll always be in need of some kind of care.'

'So is everybody I've ever met, if you ask me.'

'I mean I will require the kind of care that would hold any ambitious woman back. As far as I can see, you've spent your life being responsible for your family and those around you. The last thing a woman like you needs is yet another stumbling block to following her dreams.' He turned his head away. 'Perhaps it's as well you are leaving tomorrow.'

'It's not my choice.'

'But it still may be for the best, and not just because of the man you fear so much.'

'I've every intention of trying to return, if I can.'

'I'm sure you will. But that doesn't change anything. You told me when we were children that you were going to have a cafe of your own. From what Clara has been telling me, you are still fighting for that dream.'

'That's not the entirety of my life, Richard.'

'But it is the core that gives your life its meaning.'

She couldn't hide behind a lie. 'Yes.'

'Good for you. I've seen enough of senselessness out there in France. I thought I'd never find meaning again. Dr Graham is right. You bring health to the men here with your cooking as much as he does with his medicine. I've seen the way you can conjure memories of childhood and of home from so little and how much that means to all the men here. I know a passion when I see it and I hope I would never be so selfish as to take that away, especially for my own ends. You've enough of that as it is.' He was silent for a moment. 'Dear Hester. It wasn't supposed to be this way. I was so sure I would end my life with the rest of them, among the mud. I never thought of a life afterwards. And now all I can offer any woman is the opportunity to be a personal nurse for the rest of her life, with no idea of how I am ever going to be able to financially support her.'

'You could be like Dr Villiers. She uses her own experience of pain to help others who have been injured.'

'I'm not doctor material.'

'There could be other ways. You wanted to be a scientist, observing the natural world, didn't you? If that's no longer possible, maybe you could transfer your passion to finding ways of easing men's dreams?'

'Or the Hun might invade, then we're all finished.'

'Well, I don't know about you, Richard, but I intend to survive, whatever happens. There has to be someone left to build the future, or what's the point?'

'Are you always the optimist?'

'I try to be.'

'Hmm.' He was about to say something further, but they had reached the terrace, where the men were sitting, their cigarette smoke filling the quiet dusk air.

Richard cleared his throat. It hadn't escaped either of them that all conversation had fallen silent and, to a man, the patients were closely following their every word.

Richard coughed, the pallor of his face briefly tinged with colour. 'Good evening, Miss Pearce,' he said loudly. 'Thank you for your assistance. I shall take care to be rather more circumspect in practising my walking from now on, so hopefully I shall not require rescuing again.'

'Not at all, captain,' she replied, in the same carefully formal tone, 'I'm glad you are unharmed.'

She turned to leave, pride attempting to push even the memory of him to one side. As she did so, she caught his eye. His look made her heart stop. She couldn't help but slowly return his smile.

Chapter Thirty-Five

The day of her departure from Afalon had approached so quickly, Hester could scarcely believe these were her last hours as Cook at Afalon.

After the final meal had been served and everything put ready for the morning's breakfast, she couldn't resist stepping inside the walled garden for one last time. In the softening light, it was free from its usual bustle of workers. She stood for a few minutes drinking in the peace. Birds were still chirping and bees humming busily among the sun-warmed flowers.

There might be a touch of excitement at the thought of a new life in a city, but she was going to miss this more than she could say. She hated leaving the beds in full swing, with rows of beans climbing up networks of twigs, and potatoes and leeks neatly set between the tall stems of beetroot and the feathered tops of carrots, flanked by the green of cabbages and kale.

Saying goodbye to Afalon, she realised more strongly than ever, was letting go of the only life she had ever known. It was letting go of Dad and Gran, and even the cafe in St Ives. But so long as Jimmy was here, she would have to make her life elsewhere, if she was to have any kind of life at all.

The trouble was, she had a horrible feeling that she had just set her life along the path of being a cook in a large house for the rest of her days, working all hours fulfilling the demands of the rich, or even not so rich. Her dreams of her own cafe felt even further away than ever.

'Hester.' She nearly jumped out of her skin.

'Jimmy.' She hadn't heard the garden door, but he was so close behind her he could reach out and grasp her in an instant. 'How did you know I was here?'

'The men on the terrace were helpful. They told me they'd seen you come in here. They understood.'

'Understood?'

'That, rules or no rules, you'd want to say a final goodbye to your fiancé before you left.'

Dad must have told him. She'd tried to be vague about which day she was leaving, but just hearing of her departure would have been enough for Jimmy. How could she have been so careless as to come in here alone, to a place that was so secluded? She should have guessed she would not be safe, even at Afalon, once he knew she was planning to put such a distance between them. He would never allow her to escape.

He was between her and the door. Keep calm. Keep him talking. It wouldn't be so easy this time. He knew she was quick and strong and he knew she fought back.

'I'm expected in the house,' she said, stepping away from him deeper into the garden. 'Miss Chesterfield is waiting for me.' Jimmy followed, keeping close. She didn't dare look, but from the corner of her eye she could see the windows of Afalon above the wall. If she could see them, anyone looking out could see her, like Isabella had done that day, and hopefully see Jimmy, too. It was a long shot. But she was already late for her meeting with Miss Chesterfield and this was the only chance she could take to signal she as being kept against her will without alerting him to the fact that she was determined to escape.

'They'll wait. They'll understand. You might never see me

again. Or maybe that would make you glad, if you heard that I was dead.'

'Of course not.'

'Then you do care for me.'

She could say yes. Agree to anything, just so he would let her go. 'We're friends, Jimmy. I don't like to see any of my friends harmed.'

'Especially not Mr hoity-toity Trewarren, you mean.'

'Of course not! Lance Trewarren wouldn't think twice about a girl like me.'

'Making up to his sister won't do you any good.'

'Then it's as well I'm not.'

'No good at all.' His mind was set on the subject and there was no deflecting him. Thank goodness Lance was still in France, and even Jimmy's cunning hadn't helped him to get wind of her exchanging so much as a word with Richard Elliot. At least she could keep Richard safe.

Without moving her head, she tried to make out anything from the corners of her eyes she could use to defend herself. To one side, there were planks of wood that had been stacked up over the past days to mend the rotting beams of the greenhouse while the weather was fine. She had no idea how heavy they were, or if she would have time to reach them before he caught her, but they were her only chance.

'Clara is doing her best for the war effort. Just like all of us. We're not friends, Jimmy. I wouldn't expect it.'

'We can be better than her. Better than all the Trewarrens put together. You and me. When this war is over, I'll take over Timson's and get Mr Trewarren and his rich friends to invest in expanding. Then I'll buy one of the large houses in Hayle and employ a cook and you'll never have to work again.'

He believed it. That was the frightening thing. He believed

the stories he spun, as if just telling her would make them real. That's why he wanted her, so that every day of his life, every moment of her existence, she could be the distorted mirror he needed to make his grandiose vision of himself real.

She had to play for time. She thought she had seen a shadow cross one of the first-floor windows, but she couldn't be sure. She couldn't wait for Miss Chesterfield to raise the alarm. If she was going to survive this, she was going to have to rescue herself.

'I enjoy my work,' she said, hoping to at least keep him in conversation for a few minutes, to turn his mind back to some kind of reality where she stood a chance, however small, of convincing him he could safely let her back to the house.

He didn't hear. 'Then we can be rich, you and me, Hester. We can look after your dad and give him the kind of life he deserves. The banns can go up tomorrow.' He moved a little closer. 'We can be married within weeks.'

He was never going to give up, whatever she did, whatever she promised. It would only feed into his fantasy. He was never going to let her go.

She stepped back, praying that someone outside the walls would hear her and that she was within reach of the wooden planks. 'I'm not going to marry you, Jimmy,' she said, as loudly as she dared. 'Whatever you do, I won't ever marry you. Not now, not ever.'

As he reached for her, she jumped out of range. The top plank was heavy, solid. She swung it with all her strength. He grunted, stumbling as the weight caught him. She sped as fast as she could towards the garden door.

It was locked.

She should have known. Already his footsteps were behind

her. She shot between the glasshouses. He might be faster and stronger, but he didn't know the garden and she knew it like the back of her hand. The only other way out was to reach the other side and climb the apple trees. At least dusk was now turning rapidly towards darkness. That gave her a chance.

She set off, trying to make as little noise as she could, staying near to the greenhouses. As she reached the vegetable beds, she saw his shadow on the path. Waiting. The door to the little office was next to her. It opened. As carefully as she could, she slipped inside, feeling for the bolts, pushing them to behind her.

'Hester?' His shadow passed the window next to the central path. She crawled between the desk and the chair, curling herself up against the wall as small as she could, hidden in shadow. 'Bitch! I know you're here somewhere.' Something jangled. 'I've got the key, see. Didn't think of that, did you? There's no way out.'

His footsteps went further away. Hester held her breath, fearing to betray her presence. She heard Jimmy curse as he stumbled over what sounded like the metal of a watering can.

She waited motionless for what seemed like hours as darkness slowly gathered around her. After a while, she no longer heard the sound of stumbling around. Then, in the distance, there came the sound of a key turning in a lock and the familiar creak of the garden door opening. She remained motionless. He wouldn't give up that easily, surely? He could still be waiting for her outside the garden door. But she couldn't stay here. The smell of chemicals was overpowering, and she was horribly aware of being trapped inside a small space.

Slowly, experimentally, she crawled towards the door. Nothing. No sound outside. Just an owl calling from the woods. She undid the bottom bolt as quietly as she could. Still nothing. She took a deep breath and reached for the top bolt. As she touched it, instinct stopped her. There was something ominous about the deathly quiet outside. She snatched her hand away, just as a body landed violently against the planks.

'So you are in there. It had to be. You can't outsmart me, you see.'

She shoved the bottom bolt home again and sank down, back against the door.

'All right, you little bitch.' Jimmy's whisper came through the cracks in the wood. 'Have it your way. If I can't have you, nobody will.'

There was a smell of paraffin, overwhelming in the small space. Then smoke. Thick, choking smoke, followed by the flicker of flames that lit up the office around her, rapidly turning the bone-dry wood into a crazy, white-hot light. Hester grabbed the chair. It wasn't much against a madman, but it was better than nothing. The fire was rapidly taking hold, sucking the air from around her, sending smoke to fill her lungs. As she pulled the first bolt, she could have sworn she could hear the sound of voices. She pulled the second and leapt into darkness, illuminated by the fierce glow.

She was hit from behind. The pole caught her hard between the shoulder blades. She swung the chair wildly around, losing her grip as the pole came down again. She stumbled with the force, raising her arms instinctively as blows rained down on her body. A blow landed by her ear. He was aiming for her head. The next would smash her skull. She threw her arm over as best she could, braced for the end.

But it never came. The light streaking across her face was not fire but the beam of a flashlight. Many flashlights.

'She's here.' It was Richard's voice, through the pain and the darkness. 'She's alive.'

'He went this way,' called another voice. 'Corporal McDonald is guarding the door. Don't you worry, sir, we'll get him.'

'Stay still, Hester,' came Richard's voice. 'Some of the men are fetching Dr Villiers and a stretcher from the house. The rest will find him, don't you worry. You're safe now.'

'I'm all right.' Hester coughed and retched, then pulled herself into a sitting position.

'He tried to burn you alive.'

'But he didn't.'

'Thank heaven.' He shrugged off his jacket, wrapping it around her. 'I'm afraid I can't carry you, Hester. I can't even chase the bastard.'

'It doesn't matter,' she whispered. 'Please hold me. Just this once, please hold me.'

His arms came around her, encircling her gently, holding her uncontrollable shaking against him. She held on, as tight as she dared without hurting him, his warmth keeping her safe.

Voices echoed urgently around the walls. In the light from the remaining flames, Hester saw shadows hurrying towards them, directed by Corporal McDonald. She could not have moved if she tried.

'My dear.' Miss Chesterfield was the first to reach them.

'I'm all right,' said Hester, gently freeing herself from Richard's embrace.

'Thank goodness you're alive. I thought I saw someone in here. When you didn't turn up for our meeting and the men told me your young man had come to say goodbye, I remembered those bruises from the day you accepted the post at

Afalon and I had the most dreadful feeling. I'd never have forgiven myself if we hadn't found you in time.'

'You're safe now,' said Richard, as Hester was wrapped in a blanket and lifted up into strong arms. He struggled to his feet. 'At least you are safe now.'

'Yes,' whispered Hester. She couldn't find the energy to say she would never be safe. Not ever. However far away she went, however carefully she hid herself. She would never be safe, and nor would anyone who loved her. Not ever again.

There was no question of Hester leaving to take up the post in Birmingham. By the next morning, her head was pounding sickeningly and she could barely move.

'Well, at least the major damage is no worse than two cracked ribs and a broken wrist,' pronounced Dr Graham. 'And that black eye is going to be spectacular before it fades.' He busied himself with his medical bag. 'I'm afraid, my dear, you are going to have to allow yourself to be the patient for a while.'

'But my work...'

'Don't worry about that. Miss Chesterfield is telephoning your new employers in Birmingham to tell them you've suffered a fall. Don't worry about that for now. My dear girl, you are lucky to be alive.'

There was no sign of Jimmy. For all the hours searching for him, with his description circulated to every port and fishing cove along the coast, his whereabouts could not be traced. But he was bound to turn up again once the furore had died down, ready to spin a tale he felt would explain it all away. She could feel it in her bones.

He'd appear, as if nothing had happened. As if it had all been a mistake. He could swear he hadn't seen her in the garden and left before she arrived. That it must have been someone else. A secret assignation. Women were like that, he'd reason, everyone knew they'd say anything to preserve their reputation when caught out in their uncontrollable passions.

No one had seen him set fire to the shed. Everyone at Afalon might know it was him, but in the end it would be her word against his, and officialdom was still all too willing to see a woman as hysterical. After all, on the face of it, what reason had Jimmy for harming her? He was a friend of the family. He had known her for years. It did not make rational sense. He might have been suspected of misdemeanours by his former employers, but there had never been enough evidence to bring him to trial. Jimmy had been so very careful about that. It would always be her word against his, which meant she would always lose.

'That means I can't stay here,' sighed Hester, a few weeks later, when she was finally able to hobble outside to sit in the sun. 'And I still have to get Alice away.'

'Don't worry about that now,' replied Clara, fussing over cushions and the softest rug she could find. 'We're all making sure Alice is never let out of anyone's sight for now. You just get yourself better. Then we can plan for what happens next. And anyhow, Jimmy might have been found and arrested by then. Someone has to know where he is. We'll make sure you are safe here.'

Hester leant back in the sun, watching Clara return to helping Richard with his walking. She could see how he had grown stronger since she'd been confined to bed, still leaning heavily on two sticks and pausing every now and again, bent over as if in agony. But he was walking further each day. Clara walked alongside him, talking to distract him from the pain. She watched them, deep in discussion, as if the rest of the world did not exist. They came to a halt, clearly disputing some point. Clara's laughter floated towards her, as they set on their way again, heads close together.

Richard had been kind, asking after her recovery, but even when she had emerged from her room she had barely seen him, exchanging only a few words. She couldn't help feeling he was avoiding her. Besides, now he was so much recovered, he would soon be leaving. Isabella was returning from France in a few weeks to help him settle in the Elliots' house in London. Clara had told her Richard had written to volunteer at the Maudsley hospital to learn more about men suffering in their minds from their experiences and had asked Isabella to finalise the arrangements. She was glad he at last had a purpose to look forward to, and a way of dealing with his own changed future. But he felt further away than ever.

She was still too bruised to think of returning to work, for all that the family in Birmingham were still eager for her to start there once she had recovered, while Molly wasn't hiding her feeling of being overwhelmed by her new responsibilities and was more than willing to return to being Afalon's under-cook. All the same, she couldn't put it off for much longer. She would have to make a decision soon.

A shadow crossed her face. It was Corporal McDonald, bringing her a cup of tea, balanced carefully in his remaining hand.

'Good to see you looking better, miss,' he remarked, as he sat down, placing the cup beside her. 'We're all glad to see you recovered.'

'Thank you, corporal.'

'Good place this, glad I was sent here. I'll be sad to leave.' He grunted. 'But time I got home, see how things are. See how things work out.'

'Your family will be glad to have you back.'

'Aye, that's true. Mum always did want an excuse to spoil

me.' He coughed. 'I hear you are still thinking of leaving yourself.'

'When I'm well enough.'

'Beautiful place, this. If this was my home, I'm not sure I'd want to leave.'

'Sometimes it can't be helped.'

'That's true.' He was silent for few minutes. 'Never did hold with rats,' he observed at last, in a casual manner.

'Rats?' Hester blinked.

'Aye.' He was gazing out into the far distance. 'None of us can. Seen too many of them. Of all kinds. We're good lads, you know, miss. Sick of war and killing. But sometimes, there's no other choice, see. That's the thing with rats. Me dad allus taught us to root them out from the farm, before they took hold, like. Can do a powerful lot of damage, can rats, unless they're hit over the head and put six foot under. Sometimes, when they're not the kind to give up, it's the only way, see.' He stood up. 'Of course, it's none of my business, miss, but I'm leaving tomorrow and it seemed to me a pity you feeling you couldn't stay. Unless you have a powerful wish to go, that is, and I couldn't see that, somehow.'

'Thank you. And good luck, Corporal McDonald.'

'And to you, miss. Made a world of difference, you have. To me and all of us. Your cooking has been the best medicine.' He grinned. 'I'll be dreaming of your rabbit pie and your seed cake. Although I'd better not be telling Mum, she's a proud cook, she is. She might never forgive me.'

Hester watched him go to join the others, a strange buzzing in her head. For a moment, she felt violently sick. Then it was gone, the tension in her body easing.

'Are you all right?' asked Clara, joining her. 'You look very pale. You're not too tired, are you?'

'Not at all.'

335

'What was it Corporal McDonald was talking to you about so earnestly?'

'Oh nothing. Nothing of importance. He was telling me about his mother's cooking, that's all.'

'I hope he wasn't saying it was tastier than yours.'

'No. Not in the least. He was thanking me.'

'There you are, you see. You are a genius of a cook, Hester. Everyone says so. You have a way of making people happy.'

Hester smiled. 'It seems I do.'

Clara kissed her. 'So you see, you've got to open a cafe. When this war's over, people are going to need things like that, to make them feel human again.'

'I suppose they will.'

As Clara returned to join Richard, Hester sat in the sun, feeling its warmth flooding through her. She could feel her broken wrist healing, and her ribs were a little less painful when she breathed. She shut her eyes. The cafe on Porthgwidden beach was as clear in front of her as it had ever been. She could see the terrace filled with laughter and the contented peace of people enjoying the luxury of a good meal together, with the view over the sea, and Godrevy lighthouse shining in the distance.

Calm flooded through her. Whatever happened, whatever it took, whatever the future might hold, her dream was back and this time she would not let it go.

Chapter Thirty-Six

1920

She still could not quite believe the war was over. After all those long, hard years of loss and grief, followed by the cruelty of the influenza that had struck down so many of the survivors, just as they seemed safe, she could not fully trust that life was returning to some kind of normality again.

Hester stood on the beach in St Ives that spring day and looked up at the crumbling cafe, determination as strong as ever.

'It's not impossible,' said Clara, sounding dubious.

'It *has* to be possible.'

It was the only rent she could afford. It might have been where she wanted to set up her own cafe, but the state it had fallen into was daunting. It had stayed empty for the last years of the war and, after the ravages of influenza and the weariness of both those at home and the returning soldiers, it was no wonder the Carltons had not had the enthusiasm to open it again themselves, and none of their family had been willing to take it on.

Hester smoothed down her skirt to hide her nerves. All the years of war, all they had gone through, this had remained her dream. Now it was within her grasp. The rent might be cheap, but the repairs looked terrifying from the outside, and heaven knows what she would find on the inside. Besides, who was she to think that her cooking could compete with that to be found in the cafes and restaurants already established in St Ives? Even if she did get it up and running, all her hard-earned savings might be gone within the year. If so, she could hardly ask Miss Chesterfield for her job back for a second time. Molly had been far more confident this time about stepping into her shoes, when Hester had announced she was finally leaving to set up her own cafe, and she couldn't in all conscience take that away from her.

Terror shot through her. It was impossible. She was a fool to risk everything for a dream, to give up a good post with an excellent employer, one that was, as far as anything in life could be secure, hers for life.

'Well?' said Clara.

Hester took a deep breath. She had worked so hard for this. It had been easier to save after Jimmy had disappeared. Gone, it was generally presumed, on some business to do with the war effort. Or lining his pockets peddling goods on the black market, more like. So many young men were lost, so many, like poor Tom the gardener, whose bodies were never to be found, that one more did not raise a question. Besides, even Ben, the only one of the gardeners to survive, had not returned home, making a life in Liverpool. And Jimmy had been a strange one, with no close friends or family who cared to claim him. His absence had soon closed over, like a wound, finally healed.

With Jimmy no longer there, it had been simpler for Robbie to make sure Dad didn't spend his time at the Fishermen's Arms, or take more than a small amount from the rent tin. Robbie had paid back some of her savings, although she had refused the rest, telling him to keep it hidden away at Gran's in case of emergencies, or if Dad should ever exchange all their cooking pots for the promise of an extra pint.

She couldn't go back. Even Dad had accepted that she

wouldn't return to the ferryman's cottage and, with so many young men lost, she was likely to be one of those who remained unmarried. She was one of the new breed of women, who, out of necessity, would always need to find ways of supporting themselves.

Hester took one last inspection of the crumbling facade of the cafe. 'Come on,' she said. 'I'm going to have a closer look.'

The inside was no less daunting. A window had been broken and roughly boarded up, leaving the effects of salt wind peeling the paint. Hester followed the bent figure of Mr Carlton, thankful that she had asked Clara to accompany her on this inspection. If she'd braved it on her own, she might have run away.

'It will only take a lick of paint on the walls and polish on the tables,' said Clara.

'I've the services of a good carpenter who can do the repairs on the terrace,' added Mr Carlton. 'I can get that done for you before you move in, Miss Pearce, if you decide to take it on.'

'Thank you,' said Hester, trying not to look too closely at the peeling wallpaper and the newspapers stuffed into the rotting corners of window frames. 'Perhaps if I could see the kitchens?'

'Yes, of course.' He took them to the back of the building to a plain kitchen with a range and an array of pots and pans. 'A bit old-fashioned, I'm afraid. My wife likes to do things the old way. But she managed well enough to cook all the meals we offered. Nothing fancy, just good plain cooking. She said there was no point in offering more. Couldn't compete with the likes of them London-type restaurants, see. But we had a good trade in visitors before the war, the kind who liked a bit of peace and quiet, this being tucked away, like.

And then there was those artist types, never much money, most used to a good meal, but with little taste for cooking their own. Now those, we got summer and winter. Not as much profit as the visitors, but kept us going. And they're back now. More of them than ever.'

'You could always make it a place for artists,' said Clara. 'Not all of them are poor. Papa was always scornful of the rich ladies who come to St Ives to play at being painters. He called them twittering fools, with more money than sense. I'm sure he still knows some of them. That's what made Richard's mother take up painting. Isabella said coming here in the carriage to paint the seascapes made her mother happy. When we're in London, Papa is always taking us to restaurants just because they have a good reputation. Some of them are hideous, but they give off such an air they make a fortune.'

'I'm not sure I want to give off an air,' said Hester, finding Clara's enthusiasm creeping inside her all the same. 'But I like the idea of providing good simple food that's tasty and cheap. I've had enough practice at that.'

The kitchen was basic and old-fashioned and she suspected most wishing to start up a restaurant or tearooms would rip out the old-fashioned range and put in all new equipment. But for her, it was familiar, both from home and at Afalon. She was already mentally going through Mum's recipes, selecting ones that were tasty and filling and, if done to perfection, might have artists emerging from their garrets, or retreating from the windblown cliffs, not to mention the parties of lady walkers and cyclists that were also beginning to return to Cornwall following the end of hostilities.

'There's accommodation up above,' said Mr Carlton, indicating a steep flight of stairs. 'Only small, mind. Mrs Carlton and me lived there when we first started, then it was where a couple of the staff were accommodated. It's enough to save you renting a house, at least at first.'

Hester clambered up the short flight of stairs, followed by Clara. There was a landing at the top, with two tiny bedrooms, each just wide enough to accommodate a single bed and a chest of drawers. The landing was small, but there was space for an armchair facing the window overlooking the sea. Hester brushed the dust from the seat and sat down. Despite the grubbiness of the panes, the view over the beach towards Godrevy lighthouse was clear, with the coast a shadow in the distance. She could hear the soft pull on sand as small waves collapsed, one after the other in a rhythmic fashion, accompanied by the cries of seagulls. From the beach, a child called to a companion. A sense of peace settled.

Hester shut her eyes, trying to imagine the rush of the kitchen, of taking orders and keeping control over young waitresses who, from the sophistication of a town like St Ives, might look with contempt on the ferrywoman deluding herself she could match Rosa Lewis and the greatest chefs alive.

But she wasn't deluding herself, or planning to offer peaches in Chartreuse jelly and twelve courses at each meal. M. Alphonse had been right, when she had finally plucked up courage to visit him once it was clear the war was ending. The world had changed. The fine dining might return, but its previous opulence would never be quite the same again.

'You have the skills, my dear,' he had said. 'You should take the cafe. Go for it now, establish yourself before anyone else gets the same idea. There is an opening in St Ives for a cafe as well as the restaurants. I will teach you anything you wish to know and I will most certainly recommend you. But I think there is little I can teach you now. You have learnt from your mother and you have acquired skills at Afalon I do not know. You are ready in your own way.'

She took a deep breath. There was no reason why anyone from St Ives would know anything about her, or even be interested. She had been cook for a large house, that was all anyone needed to know. No one wanted to hear about wounded men any more, or anything about the war. They wanted cheerfulness and comfort and to be able to enjoy life, in a way that reminded them of the past, and they thought they would never be able to enjoy again.

Besides, with the men back to take over their old jobs, there were plenty of young women who would be grateful to find work. And, even more than in the kitchens at Afalon, she would be in charge. If they wanted to keep their jobs, or at least be given a good reference, they would need to obey her and be polite, at least to her face. What they said in their free time she didn't care.

'I'll take it,' she said, as they rejoined Mr Carlton and before she had a chance to change her mind. 'I'll need to work my notice before I can start.'

'That will give the carpenters the chance to mend the balcony and repair the worst of the window frames. I'm sure we can work out something that suits us both.' His face brightened. 'To be honest, Miss Pearce, me and Mrs Carlton will just be glad to see the place used. As I told you, we may be looking to sell at some point, but it will be good to see it thriving again.'

'Yes, it will,' said Hester, squashing any second thoughts. Hopefully by then she would have gained a reputation and be able to afford the rent on bigger premises. Or even have enough saved to buy the cafe herself. She pushed that one out of her thoughts. For now. One dream at a time.

'You did it!' exclaimed Clara, as they made their way back to the centre of St Ives.

'I'm not sure how I'm going to manage.'

'I'll help you. If you'll let me. Oh, I don't want to be paid. I've got my allowance and Miss Chesterfield no longer needs me for fetching her deliveries and helping in the garden now the war is over. Richard and Isabella have suggested I join them in London, if Papa won't take me, and find an occupation there. But they're both so busy, and I'm not sure I want to help men who are still recovering from the war. I know it's terrible of me, and I'll never stop missing Ralph or loving him, but I don't want to live with that any more. I'd far rather be here in St Ives and help you.'

Chapter Thirty-Seven

Over the next weeks, Hester and Clara used every spare minute to scrub away years of grime and filth. They put fresh whitewash on the walls and cleaned the windows until they shone, cleaning and polishing the tables and chairs and the balcony along the terrace. They still looked old and weather-beaten, as if the ghost of the fisherman's cottage that had been expanded to create the cafe was still there.

'I like its old-fashioned look,' said Clara, as she and Hester altered the curtains Hester had found in Hayle market, which had once belonged to a great house, fallen into ruin after being requisitioned by the army during the war, and was now being transformed into a hotel. The curtains were slightly faded, and had not come from the grandest apart-ments, but after being washed and cut down to remove the worst of the sun-bleach, they were bright and fresh and had the appearance of a slightly downtrodden drawing room.

'So do I,' said Hester. Tomorrow was her last day at Afalon. From tomorrow this would be her only source of income. The thought still terrified her if she dwelled on it too much. Miss Chesterfield had made no attempt to prevent her, instead offering her every encouragement and a promise to be one of her first clients, and to inform her London friends that, if visiting St Ives, there was a hidden gem of a cafe that just had to be visited.

The first night she spent in the cafe, Hester sat on the

armchair in the landing, looking out to sea. She wished Mum was here, so she could show her. She felt the peace and quiet settle around her, and even through the exhaustion of the last week, her energy and determination was not diminished in the least. She was going to make Mum proud, and she was going to make the cafe work.

Over the next year, Hester worked day and night to make her cafe a success. She was glad of Clara's enthusiasm that kept her fighting even when she wasn't sure she could pay the next month's rent, and the first days when only a handful of visitors found the cafe. At least she was used to surviving such uncertainty and making the most of few and cheap ingredients.

But gradually things began to improve. Miss Chesterfield was as good as her word, arriving in state at the end of the first week, remarking loudly to anyone who could hear that she had missed Hester's cooking and having a first-class cook was not to be sniffed at. She clearly made the most of the occasion to round up support, with a slightly hesitant trickle of families appearing over the following week. This was followed by a lady artist who automatically ordered a cup of tea and a teacake, as the cheapest items on any menu, but as soon as her eyes fell on the prices of the main meal of thatched pie, followed by apple cheesecake, ordered that instead.

'I couldn't make that more cheaply at home,' she announced. 'Besides, pigeon is so fiddly and I never have the patience for puff pastry, and you've placed the vermicelli so charmingly into the appearance of a thatched roof, I couldn't possibly compete. Particularly as the cooking facilities in my rooms are dire, to say the least.'

Hester hid a grin. Her years of being trained by necessity

to make a delicious meal from the cheapest, most nutritious ingredients she could lay her hands on, were paying off. The next day the lady artist was back for the day's dish of stuffed herrings, bringing with her a lady potter and a sculptor. The three women remained in the corner for most of the afternoon, deep in tea and cake and discussions that mainly revolved around their irritation with how the men took their own work so very seriously and theirs not at all.

'It's so refreshing to find a place to be able to talk without the men interrupting and telling us how much more important they are,' said the potter as they left.

'Good,' replied Hester, smiling at the woman's large hands and broad northern accent. 'It was a woman who gave me my chance when I was fighting against the odds.'

The potter was back within days, bringing even more friends. Hester soon found the cafe becoming a place for artists, particularly women. Respectable surroundings with excellent dinners and an afternoon tea any woman of the house would be proud to put on the table.

Finally, things were going her way. She could even begin to replenish her savings again, this time for the far more ambitious task of one day, in the years to come, managing to buy the cafe, just as she had always dreamt.

It was the following spring that Mr Carlton died.

'I'm so sorry, my dear,' said Mrs Carlton, when she came to tell Hester that she was selling the building. 'If I had my way, I would keep it on, but I'm moving to Ireland to be with my grandchildren, and my sons are insisting I have it settled before I go. You know I will always give you first refusal.'

'I understand,' said Hester. She felt for her, but at the same time frustrated that it was too soon. She was far from raising even a fraction of the money required.

At least she hadn't yet brought Gran to St Ives. They'd planned that she'd make the move that summer, once it became busy again. As well as helping with the cooking for the cafe, Gran liked Hester's suggestion of using the kitchens when it was quiet to make pickles and preserves to be offered as accompaniments to their dishes, with the most popular being properly bottled up, labelled and offered for sale. It could be a valuable sideline if it took off. Clara had suggested trying the big emporiums in London, such as Selfridges and Fortnum and Mason. They had even discussed the possibility of opening branches of the cafe in different towns around Cornwall, in the manner of Lyons' corner houses.

The new owners might wish to continue renting out the cafe, but Hester wasn't betting on it. They were more likely to want to build on its existing success for themselves, or to change it entirely. Now, instead of plans to expand, she was going to have to find new premises fast, go back to the beginning and start all over again.

Chapter Thirty-Eight

The cafe was sold within the week.

'No one has heard who the buyer is,' said Hester gloomily, as she sat in Gran's garden a few days later.

'It may well be someone who wants to keep it just as it is.'

'I do hope so. I hate this uncertainty. I hate the thought of having to start from scratch, just as we were building a successful name for ourselves and I was hoping you'd come and join me.'

'*Duw*, child, don't worry about me. Robbie pops in to see me as much as he can. That young woman he's courting seems to have her head screwed on, too. I suspect your dad is going to have to toe the line with that one.'

'I thought he seemed subdued this afternoon.'

'Well now, between you and me, I have a feeling he tried to get round young Lizzie and came up against a brick wall. It'll do him the world of good, my dear.'

There was a knock at the open front door of the cottage.

'That'll be Clara,' said Hester, gathering up her coat. 'She's teaching me how to drive a motor car, Gran. Although I don't expect I'll be able to afford to buy one now, not even one that's very old, not for a while at least.'

'Oh, my lord,' said Gran, scrambling to her feet.

'I hope you don't mind, Mrs Evans. The door was open.'

'Not at all,' said Gran, with more than a little frost to her voice. 'Do come in, Mrs Trewarren. What can I do for you?'

'I wish to speak to Hester. In private, if you don't mind.'

Gran had the look of a woman who did mind, and was about to throw a pillar of the community out onto the street, feathered hat and all, and hang the consequences.

'Yes of course, Mrs Trewarren,' said Hester, before her grandmother could build up a head of steam.

'As you wish, Hester.' Gran sniffed loudly. 'I've jam to attend to. I'll be just inside if you need me. Pinch of salt,' she remarked, in a pointed manner, as she gathered up the cups and saucers.

Mrs Trewarren flushed scarlet. 'I'm afraid your grand-mother is of the view that you should not trust me.'

'And should I?'

Mrs Trewarren traced circles with the end of her umbrella on the flagstones at her feet. 'Possibly not.'

'You mean, because of Mum?'

'So you do remember. I had a feeling you might. You always were a sharp little thing. How much did you overhear, that day on Porthgwidden beach?'

'Only that you were trying to persuade Mum to join you in something to do with a cafe, and she refused.'

Mrs Trewarren winced. 'Well, if I'm honest, I can't say I blame her.'

'To be frank, Mrs Trewarren, I had a feeling you had per-suaded Mum to do a similar thing once before. My mother would have given anything to have a cafe of her own. She would have never let such an opportunity pass her by if she didn't feel, in her heart, that you would let her down.'

'You mean, because I had failed her once before?'

'Yes.'

There was a moment's silence. 'I knew Sadie from Afalon,' said Mrs Trewarren, at last. 'Before you were born. She used to visit your grandmother there, when I was friends with

Richard and Isabella's mother. I admired Sadie for everything she had achieved, working her way up from nothing to becoming such a respected head cook. She had such a passion for her work, and in those days it was even more difficult for a woman to follow a profession than it is now. I wanted her to be able to fulfil her dream of running her own cafe.' The umbrella came to a halt. 'But I'm afraid, in the end, I was the one who ensured it was destroyed.'

'You?' Hester stared at her.

Mrs Trewarren grimaced. 'I had a dream too, of being a businesswoman and making my own way in life, rather than being married off to secure my family wealth and connections. In your mother I saw an opportunity to use my allowance to secure my independence. I persuaded your mother to join me in my venture. I would provide the money to rent the cafe and set it up and Sadie would cook. We had such plans. Between us, we could have been as successful as Rosa Lewis. We could have made our own futures, chosen carefully who we married and how we lived our lives.'

'But I thought the cafe never opened.'

'I was the one who lost courage. We were all ready. I'd informed my family and Sadie had given up her work at the hotel. But, when it came to it, I couldn't. I didn't have the courage to defy my family. I didn't dare take the risk of failure and being seen as unwomanly and a laughing stock among my friends. To my shame, I took the easy way, bowed to my mother's wishes, and married Mr Trewarren.' She jabbed at the paving stone. 'I've never forgiven myself.'

'I'm sure Mum understood.'

'But I did her a terrible wrong, building up her dreams and then killing them. I'm afraid she lost confidence in her dream. I made her doubt that anyone would ever take her seriously as a fine cook, because she was a woman and her father had been a fisherman. I will regret that all my life.'

'Mum was happy in her way, Mrs Trewarren.'

'I hope so. I know she loved her children more than anything. It made me realise what a remarkable woman she was, and how much more she could have been, if it hadn't been for my selfishness. I'd tried to put all that behind me when you appeared, that night you saved Clara's life, looking so like her you could have been an accusing ghost. Then you did far more for my child than I could have done when Ralph was killed. I dread to think what might have happened otherwise. At least now Clara seems to be finding some kind of solace with Richard...' She shook her head.

'I need to go,' muttered Hester. 'I've an appointment to see new premises, near Smeaton's Pier.'

'Yes, yes of course.' Mrs Trewarren pulled out an envelope from her pocket. 'I want to help you to set up a new cafe.'

'I don't want your money.'

'Hester, I can't ever make things right for your mother, but I can for you.'

'No.' Hester shook her head vehemently, biting back tears. Mum had been right, all those years ago, when she had warned her not to get too close to the Elliots or the Trewarrens. It would always lead to heartbreak, just as it had for Mum. 'You owe me nothing, Mrs Trewarren. Nothing at all. Now excuse me, I have to go.'

A few days later, Hester was alone in the cafe, replacing the tablecloths all ready for the morning, when the clanging of the doorbell announced a new arrival.

'I'm afraid we're just closing,' she said, adjusting the final cloth to her satisfaction.

'That's a pity. I was looking forward to a pot of your most excellent tea.'

'Miss Chesterfield!' Hester smiled with pleasure. 'Do come in. We're never closed for guests.'

'Then I hope you'll join me on your terrace. It's such a beautiful evening, it seems a pity to waste it.'

'Of course, please take a seat.' Hester made the tea, adding the remainder of a fruitcake, taking it out into the sunshine and the shelter of the terrace. 'This is all that's left from today's bake, I'm afraid.'

'Then I shall have to come back to taste your scones,' said Miss Chesterfield. 'I've been hearing such good things about them, and I still miss your cooking. You've got a way of turning the simplest of ingredients into something that is a perfect delight.'

'Thank you,' said Hester, a little warily, cutting slices of cake.

'Oh, don't worry, my dear. I haven't come to persuade you to return to Afalon. I can see you are happy here. Being in charge clearly suits you.' She savoured a mouthful of cake. 'That is just as delicious as I remember. Don't get me wrong, you've trained Molly up to be an excellent cook, but there's something about your way with flavours that is quite unique.'

'I'm glad you think so.'

'Sadie's Tearooms. That's such a lovely name you've chosen. After your mother, I take it?'

'She once had a dream of running a cafe here. I hope she would be proud of what I've done.'

'I'm quite certain she would. I know that since the war it's a little more acceptable for women to be seen running a business, but there can still be plenty of obstacles. I'm sure your mother would know how hard you've struggled and how much you've had to overcome.'

'I hope so,' said Hester, gazing over the sands of the little beach. The remains of the afternoon's storm lingered on the horizon, dark clouds parting to send great shafts of golden light, like gigantic fingers, across Godrevy lighthouse, illuminating its column of white against the shadows of the wild north Cornish coastline behind.

She loved this bay, peaceful and secluded, yet only minutes away from the bustle of St Ives. She had arrived here still fearful, as if, even after so many years, Jimmy hadn't quite let her go. The first nights, she had jumped at every creak of the boards, her dreams filled with darkness smothering her and the smell of burning. But gradually, her days running the cafe and her quiet evenings sitting on her own on the terrace, watching the seals squabbling over prime position on the rocks as the tide ebbed, and the leap of dolphins out to sea, had banished the memories. She would be sad to leave, but she knew now she could face anything.

'That's my one regret,' remarked Miss Chesterfield, finishing her cake. 'Not having a daughter of my own, that is. When I was nursing, I had planned, I had hoped...' Her eyes gazed into the far distance. 'But like so many of the young men in this last war, he was also not to be spared.'

'I'm sorry.'

'Don't be, my dear. I've had a rich life and a happy one. Fulfilled in ways I hadn't considered when I was a romantic young girl, but fulfilled all the same.' She sipped her tea, a glint in her eye. 'And I'm intending to continue for many years more. Running Afalon is my passion, it makes me feel more alive each day. Much like running this place must do for you, my dear.'

'I can't compare it to helping those injured in accidents or still recovering from their wounds. But I know what you mean.'

'I think providing a convivial meeting place and good food is not so very different from my work at Afalon. The years of the war have left more than soldiers in need of healing.' Miss Chesterfield sent her a sharp glance. 'Clara told me this place had been sold. I'm sure the new owner will wish you to carry on as you do now.'

'I hope so. But I'll be ready if they choose not to.'

'So I believe. Clara said you'd started looking at new premises. As it happens, I'm acquainted with the new owner. I thought you might like to know where you stand before you make any decision.'

'But shouldn't that be for my new landlord?'

Miss Chesterfield chuckled, deep in her chest. 'You're right. I've no wish to interfere. I think I can safely leave you to sort it out between you. This might help.'

Hester stared at the document placed in front of her, its edges lifting slightly in the breeze from the sea.

'It's in my name. The cafe's in my name.'

'Yes, my dear. The cafe is yours. Legally yours. No one will ever be able to take it away from you.'

'I can't accept.'

'Why ever not?'

'It's too much. Miss Chesterfield, I can't accept this.'

'My dear, if your mother had succeeded in her dream and passed the cafe to you to carry on, would you have refused her?'

'Of course not!'

'Well then. Accept it. It's a free gift, my dear. I know how hard it is for a woman to make her own way in life. I have no daughter and my nephews and nieces are well provided for. This is the least I can do. I've watched you making your own way against the odds, always being dragged back down again by circumstances, and your family's needs, always battling on.'

'I'm not afraid of hard work.'

'And I don't doubt that wherever you went you would succeed. But that doesn't mean you can't accept assistance. If you were a rich man's daughter like Clara, you'd have taken your allowance or your inheritance without a thought. No one, however skilled or determined, can make their way without help, not even Rosa Lewis. And only the rich, who've never had to try, believe otherwise. This is a gift freely given. Take it as that, my dear. The gift your mother would have left you, if she had been able. I'm well aware that Afalon would not have so easily survived the war, or gained its reputation, without you. If you want to repay me, then it's by succeeding. Showing to the world what a woman can do, when given the chance. And by leading a long and happy life, in the way that you choose.'

Chapter Thirty-Nine

Hester was setting up the tables on the terrace one morning, before the rush of the day began, when she became aware of familiar figures making their way towards her across Porthgwidden beach.

'Are we too early?' called Clara.

'We don't want to put you to any trouble,' added Lance, following close behind.

'Of course not. Sadie's Tearooms will never be closed for my friends.'

'Excellent,' said Lance, smiling at her. 'I know it's rather early in the day, but Miss Chesterfield instructed us to come and taste your scones and your strawberry jam.'

'She's told us they are better than ever,' added Clara.

'That's because Gran is helping me now,' said Hester, laughing. 'Her jams always were the best.'

'Excellent.' Lance had lost much of the haunted look that had hung around him when she'd seen him last, just after he had returned from France. Working with his father in the city clearly suited him. He was looking younger, more like the man she had first seen that day Clara had set out so desperately to cross the river. The admiration, she noted with faint embarrassment, was still there.

Her eyes followed Clara, who had run back to the shoreline to join the man walking slowly behind them, leaning heavily on his stick. Hester's heart beat fast. But it was too

356

late to back out now and claim she was closed. Besides, she would have to face him some time. Clara might have been helping her less since Gran arrived, but she still enjoyed helping waiting on tables, chatting to their customers while extolling the unmissable deliciousness of Hester's pies. Even if she'd wanted to, Hester knew she couldn't avoid either of them for the rest of her life.

'Take a seat, Mr Trewarren,' she said, hurrying back to the safety of her kitchen. 'It won't be long.'

Hester was proud of herself. The tea and scones had gone smoothly, with Gran visibly gratified at the praise lavished on her strawberry jam, before setting out to secure the freshest of the morning's catch in St Ives.

Hester had taken out the food herself, smiling cheerfully at them all in her best professional manner, but without stopping to engage in conversation, using the excuse of needing to finish the pies to go into the oven, ready for luncheon, telling them it wouldn't take long.

Only long enough to make sure they were on the point of leaving, she promised herself as she returned to her pastry. Richard had been settled in a corner by the time she had taken out the tea, contemplating the carved handle of his walking cane, as if determined not to meet her eye.

'I've brought the tray.' It was Clara, pushing in through the door, teacups and plates neatly stacked up, placing them next to the sink with a practised air.

'Thank you.'

'That was so good, Hester. I'm glad Richard could come too. He's been wanting to come and see what you've been doing with your cafe when he could get to visit us in Hayle. Then he nearly didn't once he was here, until Lance dragged

357

him along. He's thinking of coming back to Cornwall to live, you know.'

'Lance?'

'No, you goose. Richard. Lance is quite the city gent nowadays. I expect he'll become fearfully rich and buy up a stately home in Hertfordshire abandoned during the war and make all sorts of modern improvements and be utterly wonderful to his tenants.'

'I'm sure he will.'

'It's Richard who's coming back to Afalon, to work with Miss Chesterfield. They are looking at developing the new methods of dealing with the effect on the mind of physical injuries and accidents, the things you can't see. Besides, Richard never did quite settle in London, anyone can see his heart is really in Cornwall. I can't imagine him anywhere else. Of course, Mama is convinced he's come back to marry me.'

'I see.'

Clara took a deep breath. 'Except, I can't. I can't, Hester. Not when I know he's in love with someone else, and always was, all the time.'

There was a moment's silence.

'Clara—'

'Don't you dare deny it,' said Clara fiercely. 'I only wormed it out of him last evening, once he started saying he wasn't going to take up the post at Afalon, when it was obvious his heart was really here. I had to practically bribe Lance to drag him along today.'

'I would never wish to hurt you, Clara.'

'Hurt me?' Clara laughed. 'Of course you wouldn't hurt me, silly. I'm very fond of Richard, I have been all my life. Apart from Ralph, he's by far the best man I've ever known. But that's not the same as love.'

Hester stared at her. 'But I thought...'

'Mama wants me to be safely taken care of. That's the trouble. She thinks I can't manage on my own and I need a husband, any husband, to guide me. The thing is, I'm certain in my heart that most people only meet one soulmate in their lives. Some never meet them at all. I loved Ralph with all my heart and soul. I always will. I've got my allowance. Papa won't leave me destitute, Lance won't let him. I don't need to marry. I can be like Miss Chesterfield, only not so public-spirited. I'll open a hotel for walkers, like I planned to do with Ralph. Or I'll be an adventuress and travel the world. I'll find some way. Heaven knows, there are hundreds of thousands of women like me and I see plenty of them already making a success of their lives. I'll find a way of being happy, just you see.'

Hester put her arms around her and held her tight. 'I hope we will always be friends.'

Clara returned her embrace. 'Of course we will. If you ask me, friendship is the most precious thing of all. I'm not throwing that over, not for anything.' She stepped back, blowing her nose loudly. 'Richard's a good man, Hester. One of the best. He deserves happiness, just as much as you do. The trouble is, you're just as proud and stubborn as each other. And if either of you lets that get in your way, I shall come back and knock your heads together, just you see if I don't.'

Stuffing her handkerchief in her pocket, she disappeared. Hester could hear her calling for Lance to take a photograph of the lighthouse with his new Kodak Brownie camera, so that he could show her how it worked.

By the time Hester made her way out onto the terrace, the two were already at the water's edge, engaged in squabbling over which was the best view.

'It seems you've been abandoned,' she said.

'So I see.' Richard cleared his throat. 'I shouldn't have come today. I should have gone straight back to London. Seeing you again ...' He pulled himself to his feet, supporting himself with the railings, face turned half away from her.

'But you did.'

'I couldn't stay away. Not knowing you were here. I couldn't bear not to see you again, to see this place you've fought for, for so long. I could never take this away from you.'

'You don't have to go away, Richard. I know your heart is in Afalon and I'm perfectly capable of knowing my own mind. You don't have to protect me.'

'But I'm a terrible bet, Hester. I'll never fully recover. They've told me that. You've spent most of your life looking after your father. I can't ask you to spend the rest of your life looking after me.'

'I've no intention of looking after you. Although Dad will most probably spend the rest of his life trying to cadge a pint off you in the Fisherman's Arms. And I'll nag you mercilessly if you do.'

That started the beginnings of a smile, which quickly faded. 'I've no right to ask any woman to share my life. The path I've chosen means I'll barely ever have the means to support a wife. I'll certainly never be rich.'

'Good,' said Hester firmly. 'Because I will. Which means you will never be able to tell me what to do.'

He turned to face her. 'Hester, dearest Hester, I'm perfectly serious.'

'So am I,' she returned. 'I love you, you fool. That's what counts. And you can tell me why I shouldn't love you until you're blue in the face, but no one is ever going to stand in the way of my happiness again. Not even you.'

'You have everything before you, Hester. Clara has told

me of your plans, your ambitions. I couldn't bear to think of being the one who might prevent you.'

'You could never do that,' she replied, pulling his arms around her. 'It's not in your nature. Why else do you think I love you?' She leant in to meet his kiss. 'And the one thing I am certain of in this uncertain world is that I'll carry on loving you until I draw my very last breath. So, you see, my dearest, you really have no choice but to love me back.'

'That's one thing I can safely promise to do,' he replied, smiling at last. 'I love you, dearest Hester, with all my heart, now and for the rest of my days.'

'Then the rest we can work out as we go along,' said Hester, holding him close.

Down at the seashore, Clara had taken charge of the camera, directing it towards Godrevy lighthouse as the sun burst through the cloud, illuminating the crash of waves flung high against the cliffs. Hester smiled in the morning warmth. The smell of cooking filled the air. Gran was back, knives clattering as she prepared her fish in the little kitchen. Sadie's Tearooms was filling up as the lunchtime rush approached, customers already spilling out onto the terrace to secure the best view.

'Time to get to work,' said Hester, tucking her arm through Richard's as they made their way inside the little cafe, within the shelter of the bay.

Read on for some delicious recipes inspired by

The Ferryman's Daughter

1. Jan's Scrumptious Apple Cake
(The inspiration for Sadie's Best Apple Cake)

250 g butter
225 g caster sugar
3 eggs
Half cup milk
1 teaspoon vanilla extract
260 g sifted self-raising flour
2 lemons

For decoration:
Two or three eating apples (coxes or russet are best) unpeeled
One lemon
Sugar and water for lemon syrup

Preheat oven to 180c/ 350f/gas mark 4. Grease and line a 23cm/ 9inch springform tin.

Combine butter and sugar until pale and creamy. Slowly add the eggs, milk and vanilla extract. Fold in the flour and the grated rind of two lemons. Spoon batter into the tin. Slice the apples and arrange until the top of the cake is completely covered. Bake in the middle of the oven for one hour (or until a skewer comes out clean).

Meanwhile, cut thin strips of lemon rind and boil in water and sugar until crystallised. Roll into curls. As the cake cools, make holes with a skewer and pour in the sugar syrup. Decorate the cake with the crystallised lemon peel.

Serve warm or cold, with a generous dollop of clotted cream.

2. *Watercress and potato soup*

Salt and pepper
30 g butter
1 medium onion
1 stick celery
Approximately 250 g potatoes
Approximately 250 g watercress
Approximately 300 ml water

Salt, pepper and cream to taste.

Melt butter in pan. Chop onion and cook until soft. Add chopped stick of celery. Peel and chop potatoes into small pieces. Add to pan and stir. Add enough water to cover and simmer until potatoes are soft. Chop watercress, add to soup and warm through. Blend until smooth. The original recipe says to add milk, but I like to keep the tang of watercress and thin slightly with water (or stock) to the preferred consistency. Add salt and pepper to taste and stir with a swirl of cream. Serve with slices of crusty bread.

Watercress can be easily grown in pots – no need for running water! You can buy seed commercially, or sprout watercress from supermarkets.

3. Mick's Sourdough Saffron Loaf

This is a delicious sourdough twist on a Cornish favourite. A sourdough starter is simply flour and water and easy to make – there are plenty of instructions out there on the internet (be warned, it can become a bit of an obsession!).

270 g	strong bread flour
70 g	milk
135 g	starter
70 g	butter
1	egg
4 g	salt

Large pinch of saffron filaments (not powdered)

Heat the milk and steep the saffron. Leave to cool and strain. Melt the butter and add to the milk, along with the starter and egg.

Mix in the flour and salt to form a dough and knead. Form into a rough ball, place in a lightly oiled bowl, cover. Allow to ferment for about four hours (if you stretch the dough once an hour for the first three hours this will improve the dough structure), or ferment overnight in the fridge.

Prepare a proving basket. Shape the dough and place it in the basket seam side up. Cover and leave for 3½–4 hours until risen.

Preheat the oven to about 210c/ 400f/ gas mark 6

Gently turn out the dough onto a baking sheet dusted with flour (preferably wholemeal rye). Mix an egg wash (an egg + a splash of milk) and brush the dough generously. Slashing is optional according to the loaf shape and the effect you wish to create.

Bake for 15 minutes then reduce the temperature to 180c/ 350c/gas mark 4 and bake for a further 35 minutes brushing with egg wash again halfway through.

Cool on a wire rack.

Slice and serve with lashings of butter.

4. Ginger Fairings

115 g butter
115 g sugar
230 g flour
60 g grated lemon rind
4 tablespoons golden syrup
Half-teaspoon salt
2 teaspoons baking powder
2 teaspoons bicarbonate of soda
2 teaspoons mixed spice
3 teaspoons ground ginger
1 teaspoon cinnamon

Rub in butter and flour until like breadcrumbs, then add dry
ingredients. Warm syrup and stir in. Roll into small balls and
place on greased baking tray. Bake at 200c/400f/ gas mark 6
for about 10 minutes, then turn down to 180c/ 350f/gas mark 4
for approximately a further 5 minutes.

5. Rosehip Syrup

Rosehip syrup was used in both world wars as a source of vitamin C and a soothing home remedy for coughs and colds. The recipe is not exact and (especially the sugar!) can be adjusted to taste. It is based on traditional versions that would have been passed down generations of women to keep their families safe and healthy in a world where a visit to the doctor cost money that poorer families simply could not spare.

900g   rosehips
500g   sugar
1.5 litres boiling water

A fine jelly bag or muslin for straining pulp
Glass bottles

Crush the rosehips using a food processor or potato masher. Add to the water, bring back to the boil and leave for approximately twenty minutes.

Strain, hanging up the jelly bag or muslin and leaving to drip. If you want to get the last bit of goodness out, you can put the rosehips back in a pan and add a further 850 ml of boiling water and do the whole thing again.

Boil the liquid until it thickens, then add the sugar and boil for approximately five minutes. Then it's ready to bottle.

Dilute with hot water to make a soothing drink – and it's also delicious used as a syrup on ice cream.

Acknowledgements

First of all, I would like to thank everyone at Orion, especially my inspirational editor Victoria Oundjian (face-to-face edits are definitely the best!), along with Olivia Barber and Kate Shearman. It's been great working with you all. Thanks also to my tireless agent, Judith Murdoch, for the endless support and advice, without which *The Ferryman's Daughter* would never have seen the light of day.

Thank you to Janet Bark-Connell for the recipe for the best apple cake I've ever tasted, and Mick Hartley of *The Partisan Baker* for the recipe for the delicious sourdough saffron loaves.

I'm blessed to have so many wonderfully supportive fellow authors, in particular fellow Wyrd Sisters, Trisha Ashley and Louise Marley, and the NW Novelistas, the best of writing friends for celebrations as well as letting off steam. Along with Carol Lovekin and Eliza Jane Tulley, for nitty gritty discussions, supportiveness – and fun! Thanks also to my reading group for cheering me on, and my fellow dog walkers for keeping me sane and propelling me back towards the computer each morning.

I couldn't have done this without the support of friends and family, as well as the best of neighbours, Dave and Nerys, Delyth and Catrin and their help with the menagerie. Finally, a big thank you to Rhys Griffith – the inspirational English teacher every aspiring teenager writer needs!

Credits

Juliet Greenwood and Orion Fiction would like to thank everyone at Orion who worked on the publication of *The Ferryman's Daughter* in the UK.

Editorial
Victoria Oundjian
Olivia Barber

Copy editor
Kate Shearman

Proof reader
Jane Howard

Audio
Paul Stark
Amber Bates

Contracts
Anne Goddard
Paul Bulos
Jake Alderson

Design
Debbie Holmes

Rachael Lancaster
Joanna Ridley
Nick May

Editorial Management
Charlie Panayiotou
Jane Hughes
Alice Davis

Finance
Jasdip Nandra
Afeera Ahmed
Elizabeth Beaumont
Sue Baker

Production
Ruth Sharvell

Marketing
Tanjiah Islam

Publicity
Patricia Deveer

Frances Doyle
Georgina Cutler

Sales
Jen Wilson
Esther Waters
Victoria Laws
Rachael Hum
Ellie Kyrke-Smith

Operations
Jo Jacobs
Sharon Willis
Lisa Pryde
Lucy Brem